Allison O'Brian
❖ on Her Own ❖

Volume 2

Books by Melody Carlson

WORDS FROM THE ROCK SERIES

True

Life

Always

Just Another Girl

Anything but Normal

Never Been Kissed

Allison O'Brian
on Her Own

Volume 2

MELODY CARLSON

Revell

a division of Baker Publishing Group
Grand Rapids, Michigan

© 1998, 1999 by Melody Carlson

Published by Revell
a division of Baker Publishing Group
P.O. Box 6287, Grand Rapids, MI 49516-6287
www.revellbooks.com

Combined edition published 2011

ISBN 978-0-8007-2012-4

Previously published in two separate volumes:
Autumn Secrets © 1998
Dreams of Promise © 1999

Printed in the United States of America

Library of Congress Cataloging-in-Publication Data is on file at the Library of Congress, Washington, DC.

11 12 13 14 15 16 17   7 6 5 4 3 2 1

THE
❧ SECRET ❧

To Frank and Patsy Carlson
with love—me

1

Allison couldn't believe she'd done it. Whatever had pos-sessed her to slip that poem under her mother's door? She frantically tried to recall exactly what the poem had said, but any memory of the rhyming verse, like the misty dusk gathered on the estate lawn outside her window, was foggy and obscure now.

She paced the floor of her room, feeling once again like a prisoner. Was Marsha reading it right now? Would she under-stand that all Allison wanted was to be a part of a real family? She stared at her reflection in the mirror. Her auburn curls were wild and tangled from the ocean mist. Her pale skin looked almost ghostly, with dark shadows circling her green eyes like a sad raccoon. She shook her head and sighed. Just a poor little rich girl.

She sat down on the bed and stared blankly at the well-furnished room. The richly polished hand-carved furniture had probably been in the Madison family for generations, but for all she cared it could be firewood. She didn't want any of this. The Madison family fortune meant nothing to her. All she wanted was a life. *A real life.* A family that really loved her. If only Marsha could understand that. Allison whispered a quick prayer that the poem she wrote would open Marsha's eyes.

The dinner hour came and passed, but Allison couldn't bring herself to go down to eat. Instead, she wrote a letter to her friend Heather in Tamaqua Point, Oregon, telling her about her eminent return to the Oakmont Academy for Girls. Allison wrote lightly about it, hoping to conceal her honest feelings. No need to trouble poor Heather with her ongoing problems. Besides, she knew that Grace would probably be the one to read her letter to Heather since Allison didn't own a Braille typewriter, and she didn't want Grace to know how miserable she was. Allison assured them all that everything would be perfectly fine—that it was really for the best. If only she could believe her own words.

Someone tapped on her door, and Allison jumped in fright. Tucking the letter safely under a pillow, she quickly stood and smoothed the wrinkles out of her skirt. Willing her heart to quit racing like a freight train, she cautiously made her way to the door and opened it.

There stood Marsha, dressed in an evening gown the color of rubies. She was obviously going out tonight, and she appeared every bit like the famous movie star she was. But her face looked serious, and her normally smooth brow was creased with a line shaped like a *V*.

"May I come in for a minute, Allison?" Marsha asked stiffly.

Allison held the door open and nodded mutely.

Marsha sat down on a straight-backed chair, carefully arranging her shiny taffeta skirt in front of her. Allison perched on the edge of her bed, almost afraid to breathe. She studied Marsha's made-up face, trying to read the expression on it. Was she angry at Allison for writing the poem? Did she want to talk?

Marsha crossed her silk-stockinged legs, lightly folded her bare arms, and stared at Allison with a puzzled expression—as if she were thinking about speaking—but still she said nothing. The silence was making Allison very uncomfortable.

"Are you and Stanley going out tonight?" Allison blurted, realizing that this was a fairly obvious question. Still, anything would be better than silence.

Marsha nodded, still surveying Allison with a curious frown. "Allison . . . you know about the estate, don't you?"

"You mean about my inheritance of the Madison fortune?" Allison tried to sound nonchalant. "Yes, I heard you and Grandmother Madison talking. . . ."

Marsha looked down and took a deep breath. "I'm sorry you had to hear that."

Allison wondered if Marsha was sorry for the pain their words had inflicted or just sorry that their plan to keep her inheritance for themselves was no longer a secret.

Marsha cleared her throat and continued. "I read your poem, Allison. I didn't know my daughter was a poetess, but then, I suppose there are a lot of things I don't know about you. . . ." She looked directly at Allison, and it almost seemed as if her eyes were misty. But Allison was well aware of how Marsha, the actress, could turn tears on and off faster than her gold-plated bathroom faucet. Marsha stood and began to pace across the room.

"I'm really not much of a mother, am I?" Marsha continued to speak, not waiting for an answer. "No, I never wanted to be a mother, Allison, but you've probably figured that out by now. Not that you're not a nice kid. I really do like you."

Allison stared up in surprise. Any sign of affection from her mother was rare, and she sat quietly, waiting to see where it would go.

"Allison, I have been thinking about your little poem—and

about your request to live with James. . . ." Marsha paused and stared at the tranquil painting hanging over the bed. "You know, it's funny. . . . I really don't have anything against your father. He's a very decent man." She sat down in the chair again and gazed across the room as if she were looking over the years. "I really did love him at one time. At least I think I did. The truth is, I've never felt the same way about anyone since him. But, well, he was—I suppose we were—just mismatched. . . . He wanted the three of us to settle down and be a nice little family. You know, the white picket fence with a rose-covered cottage, but I didn't want that then. Can you understand, Allison?"

Allison swallowed the lump in her throat and nodded. She tried to understand how Marsha might have felt, but it didn't make much sense. The little house and fence sounded like everything Allison had ever wanted.

"It just wasn't meant to be, Allison. I'm sorry you got caught in the middle of all our unhappiness. And I'm sorry for what I did to James. It probably doesn't mean anything now, but I truly am."

Allison noticed how Marsha's black eye makeup was beginning to stream down her rouged cheeks in dark, ugly streaks, her carefully made-up party face now melting. She looked over at the dressing table to where a lace-trimmed linen handkerchief lay. Her grandmother Mercury had made it and left it for her at Grandpa O'Brian's house at Tamaqua Point. She picked up the pretty handkerchief and handed it to Marsha, who naturally had no idea of its significance. Allison watched as Marsha daubed her face, and the white linen quickly became smeared with ugly blotches of tear-stained makeup.

Marsha sniffed, then held her head high. "I have come to a decision, Allison. I am turning over a new leaf. I'm only human, but somehow I am going to try to make this whole mess up to you."

Allison stared speechlessly at Marsha, wondering if she had heard her right. Was this a dream?

"For starters, Allison, you may choose where you wish to live. After fourteen years of being shoved from pillar to post, it's high time you had a say in things. Your poem showed me that." Marsha dabbed her nose again.

"You mean it, Marsha?" Allison stood in disbelief. She wanted to rush forward and hug her, but she hesitated. Marsha always held physical affection at bay. "Oh, Marsha, thank you! *Thank you!* I can't believe it—I really get to go to Oregon, to go to school with Heather and Andrew. It's just too good to be true! This isn't a trick, is it? Do you really, honestly mean it, Marsha?"

Marsha nodded and smiled faintly. "Yes. Mother will have an absolute fit, but I do mean it. And it's my decision to make, not hers." She rose and walked over to the cherry-framed mirror above the vanity table. "Oh, my goodness, I do look a fright!"

"Marsha," Allison began in a trembling voice, "I just want you to know, in spite of everything that's happened—I do forgive you. And—" She paused and wondered if it could really hurt anything to hug her own mother. "I love you, Marsha," she whispered as she timidly stepped forward and reached out her arms. Marsha felt stiff and awkward at first, but before Allison let go, she thought Marsha softened, just a little.

Marsha's face became streaked with fresh tears, and she wiped them with the handkerchief again before handing it back. "Thanks, Allison. Tomorrow morning I'll arrange your flight. Who knows, you may even beat James home. Weren't they traveling by train with some aunt of Grace's? Now, wouldn't that be a surprise if you were already there waiting for them when they got home?"

"Thanks, Marsha." Allison smiled brightly. "Since I'll be living in Oregon now, I'll actually be closer to you down in California. I could come—I mean, if you didn't mind—I could come and visit sometimes. . . ."

Marsha's face brightened. "Now, that would be nice, Allison. I think I'd like that, and I'm sure Stanley would, too. I'll discuss it later with James."

Allison didn't know what more to say, but then she remembered the whole issue of the Madison estate and her inheritance. "Marsha, I really meant what I said. I don't want this estate. I will be happy to sign anything over to you right now, if you'd like. I'd gladly give it all back—"

Marsha laughed. "Silly, silly girl, no one takes a juvenile's signature seriously. Don't worry about the estate. It's mostly Mother's concern. We'll cross that bridge when we get there."

Apparently having said all she wanted to say, Marsha glanced at the clock on the bedside table. "Good grief! I better go fix my face. It's already after eight—although I do enjoy being late. It's always more fun to make a big entrance that way."

Marsha whisked through the door with the soft rustle of taffeta following her. Her perfume lingered in the air, and for once it didn't make Allison nauseated. She looked down at the soiled handkerchief in her hand. It was smeared with smudges of black and red, but Muriel had told her to use the handkerchief, explaining how Irish linen always laundered nicely. Allison studied the stains and decided that it would never be washed. She smiled to herself as she neatly folded the handkerchief and tucked it into a corner of her letter box, where she kept other mementos and treasures. And then she laughed out loud and thanked God. At long last, she was really, truly going home!

2

At Allison's request, the taxi driver stopped just where the driveway began. She wanted to catch everyone by surprise when she knocked on the door. She remembered the first time she'd walked down this drive. It was a similar day, foggy and damp, and she'd been more than a little frightened by the large stone house draped in the ocean mist. She remembered meeting the old man she had supposed to be a rude gardener.

A lump grew in her throat as she recalled his sharp inquisition, with shovel in hand and skeptical frown. Then how he almost fell over with a heart attack when he realized she was his very own granddaughter. Of course, she'd been just as surprised to discover he was not the gardener, and that he actually owned the big, dark house looming behind him. The bittersweet memories brought tears to her eyes, and Allison blinked them away. The tears seemed to automatically come whenever she thought of her dear grandpa.

But it was time to put away unhappiness, for this was a day to rejoice! And her grandpa was probably smiling down from heaven right now. No one could be happier than he to see that Allison Mercury O'Brian had finally come home to Tamaqua Point to stay!

Allison had deliberately not called ahead to warn them of her arrival. It had taken several days to get everything together and to get flight connections out west, but Marsha had come through with flying colors, even agreeing to Allison's plan not to telegram ahead to Oregon.

Allison swallowed a nervous sigh as she approached the house. What fun it would be to surprise them all! She couldn't wait to see the look on her dad's face. She rang the bell and tried to suppress the enormous grin that was spreading across her face like a floodlight. Her heart pounded with excitement. The last time she'd seen her father, he had seemed so forlorn, so hopeless—as if the sun had permanently disappeared from his world.

"Allison Mercury O'Brian!" screeched Muriel with delight as she jerked the door fully open. She pulled Allison inside the foyer and hugged her tightly. "Land o' mercy! It's really you! George, come here—you're never going to believe this!"

Allison looked around. "Is Dad—"

"Allison, Allison!" bubbled George as he took her bag and slapped her on the back. "Well, I'll be!"

Allison turned to Muriel. "Where's Dad?"

Muriel threw back her head and laughed. "By golly, I don't know how you did it, but you beat him here, Allison! He and Grace and Grace's aunt Mildred are due in Portland tonight at six. But I don't understand. He telegramed before they left saying that Marsha had won the custody suit, and that you would not be coming back." Muriel tilted her head and cocked one eyebrow. "Allison O'Brian, you haven't run away again, have you, darling?"

Allison detected a sly smile lurking behind Muriel's suspicious question. She laughed. "Not this time, Muriel. This time I'm home for good! And with Marsha's blessing!"

"Oh my! Oh my!" was all Muriel could exclaim, and Allison had to giggle—it wasn't often that Muriel was caught speechless like this.

"I'll take your things to your room," George offered with a big grin. "And welcome home!"

"Well, let's get your coat hung up and get you into the kitchen." Muriel had regained her speech, and as usual seemed focused on eating. "I better get some food into you before it's time to go to Portland. Andrew's picking them all up at the train station since George has misplaced his eyeglasses again. And I suspect you'll want to go along, too. Andrew's stopping by here to pick up a basket of food. In the meantime, you have less than forty minutes to tell me the whole story!"

The minutes flew as Allison recapped the story about Marsha changing her mind and arranging for the trip. Then Allison heard the familiar sound of Andrew's voice calling from the back porch. She felt certain that her heart skipped a beat, but she determined to remain composed.

"I'm here, Muriel," he called. "What is it you want me to pick—" He stopped in midsentence and stared at Allison as if she were a ghost.

"Hi, Andrew," her voice came out in a half whisper. "I guess I'm kinda like a bad penny—I just keep coming back."

"Welcome back, Penny!" he whooped. He dashed over and hugged her and swung her around. "Are you here to stay?"

She felt her cheeks redden with delight. "Yep, like it or not! I'm here to stay!"

He grinned. "Well, I guess we can put up with it. At least until you start getting bossy again."

She socked him gently in the arm and laughed. "Are Heather and Winston out in the car?"

"No, it's a school night, and we thought they better not."

Muriel frowned. "I don't even like sending you on a school

night, Andrew, but until George finds his glasses, there's no point in sending him, either. He'd end up in a ditch for sure."

Andrew looked at his watch. "I better get rolling if I want to make it by six." He turned to Allison and shook his head. "I still can't believe you're here."

Muriel handed Andrew a basket of food. "This is what I called you to pick up. James and Grace might be hungry for some real food after a week's worth of train cooking. And of course, Grace is bringing back her aunt with them, so I packed plenty of food. Also, I thought Allison should ride with you. It'll be a great surprise for Jamie, and you might enjoy the company."

"Sure would!" Andrew took the basket, and Allison grabbed her jacket.

"Muriel," Allison said, "don't tell Heather and Winston yet. I want to surprise them when we get back, okay?"

"Whatever you say, dear. Now, you two better scoot! Andrew, you drive carefully, you hear? It'll be daylight going, and then Jamie can drive back home."

Andrew promised to be careful as he waved good-bye. Then he opened the door to Grandpa's green Buick for Allison. "Muriel said to take the car instead of the jalopy," he explained. "I guess that makes sense, but I'd rather drive the jalopy."

Allison slid in. It felt strange for Andrew to open the door for her and for them to be going someplace together—just the two of them—almost like a date. Then she told herself to stop thinking such silly thoughts. After all, she and Andrew were just very good friends. Anything else was ridiculous.

"So tell me, Al, what happened? Last thing I heard was that Marsha was taking you back to Beverly Hills."

Allison once again began to explain the amazing story, this time with more details than she had shared with Muriel. The driving time seemed to whiz by as she poured out what had transpired in the last several weeks.

"Unbelievable!" Andrew exclaimed. "So your grandmother

was actually trying to cheat you out of your own inheritance? And your mother was in cahoots?"

The city lights of Portland were getting closer now as Allison hurried to tell her story. "Sadly enough, I guess that about sums it up. But you haven't heard the best part yet. I guess I went a little crazy when I found out about the inheritance business. It was bad enough thinking I was being shipped off to boarding school again, but to learn about *that* was just too much. I felt tricked and betrayed."

"I'll say! I can't imagine what I'd do in your case. I know I would've been furious!"

"I was. I was even mad at God. But it was weird, Andrew. I was out on the rocks by the ocean, and I was so confused and angry I felt like giving up. . . ." Her voice drifted away. She hesitated, not knowing if she should share something so personal. Her faith, small as it was, had always been a private thing to her.

"Yeah, then what happened?" Andrew prodded.

"You may not believe me. I almost didn't believe it myself at the time. . . ." Allison wondered if Andrew would understand. He quickly glanced her way and nodded encouragingly.

"Well, it was strange, because it was stormy and noisy with the waves beating onto the rocks and everything. But I'm certain I heard God tell me to forgive her."

"You mean forgive your mother?"

"Yes, it was as clear as you and me talking, Andrew. I asked God to help me, and He did—just like that," she snapped her fingers. "I forgave Marsha. He even showed me that I need to pray for her. It became so clear to me that even though she has all the money and fame she could ever want, she's not happy. Not really."

"But how did that change her mind? I mean, about letting you come back?"

Allison just finished the part about the poem and her talk with Marsha as they pulled up to the train station.

"Wow, Allison. That's amazing. All I can say is that God sure is looking out for you."

Allison grinned. "He sure is! Now I can't wait to see the look on Dad's face!" She was so excited she practically skipped into the terminal. They could see the train had already arrived, and Allison searched through the crowd for her father's face. Just then someone grabbed her from behind and spun her around.

"Am I dreaming or is this really my little girl?" James O'Brian squeezed Allison's arms, and his face broke into a wide grin. It looked as if someone had turned a light on inside him.

"Dad," she cried. "I'm home! I'm really home! To stay! For good!"

They hugged for a long time, and when James finally pulled away, Allison saw tears glistening on his cheeks.

"Just tell me this, Allison," James began with a frown that was threatening to cloud his sunny face. "Tell me you didn't run away again. Tell me that this is all legal and above board and that no one will come steal you away again."

Allison laughed and held up her right hand as if under oath. "I came with Marsha's blessing. She put me on the plane herself."

In that same moment a loud whoop filled the train terminal, and it seemed that everyone was staring at them. But Allison didn't care. She was home!

More hugs were exchanged, and Allison met Grace's aunt Mildred from the East. She had traveled with them and would be visiting with Grace's mother in Port View for a couple of weeks. Soon they had gathered their bags and were happily walking out to the parking lot with James' arm securely around her shoulders.

"But, Allison," Grace began, "I thought you wanted to stay with Marsha—"

"I know that's what I told you at the time, and I'm sorry

that I had to lie to you and Dad at Grandmother Madison's. I just didn't know what else to do. It seemed so hopeless, and I didn't want Dad wasting his time trying to get me back with more court battles. I hoped everyone could get on with their lives, and I believed that Marsha wanted me to live with her in Beverly Hills. Even though it wasn't my first choice, I thought perhaps I could make the best—"

Allison's words were cut off by another bear hug from her dad. "Oh, Allison Mercury O'Brian, I'm so thankful that you're back with me." And then she heard him whisper, "Thank you, God. I thank you, God."

Allison briefly explained Marsha's change of heart, promising more details later. As they reached the car, a cool autumn breeze rustled through the trees, and it felt like it was about to rain. To Allison, it felt perfectly delicious.

"Someone pinch me," James said gruffly when they were all settled into the car. He was behind the wheel now, but he hadn't started the engine yet. Grace had slipped into the backseat with Andrew and Aunt Mildred. Allison was seated in the front next to James.

"I just can't believe this is actually happening," he continued. "I had completely given up." He turned around to see Grace. "Poor Grace. She and Aunt Mildred probably wanted to drop-kick me from the back end of the train."

Grace only smiled, then shook her head. James turned back to Allison. "It's true, I was horrible! In fact, for the first two days of the trip I was downright rude. I was so angry. Finally I had to give it all up to God." He shook his head slowly, but no one else spoke, then he went on in a quiet voice. "It was a moment I'll always remember. We were going over the Great Plains, and the sun was almost down, and there seemed to be nothing but emptiness every which way you looked. It was almost symbolic of how I felt. It was there in the middle of that vast nothingness that I asked God to help me through all this and to somehow bring about justice—His justice."

Allison squeezed his hand. "And He did."

James laughed. "He certainly did!"

Large drops of rain began pelting the car, and Andrew started unpacking Muriel's picnic basket. They all dug in to fried chicken and homemade biscuits, and soon everyone was chattering at once. The car's windows became too foggy to see through, but it gave the car such a cozy feeling Allison felt she could've lived like that forever.

"Your Muriel is quite a cook," Aunt Mildred exclaimed. "These biscuits are lighter than air."

"Well, that's the best rainy-day picnic I've ever had," Grace said as she repacked the basket.

"Me too!" James chimed in. "But I think we better head for home now. I know one young man who has school tomorrow." Then he glanced at Allison. "And you and I will have a lot to do, as well. We'll need to get you properly registered at school. I only took care of the preliminaries last summer when I thought you'd be starting the school year here."

"I can't wait. You know, this will be my first time in a real school—a public school. What's it like, Andrew? How do you like it? Are the kids—"

"Whoa, too many questions," Andrew interrupted. "It's a nice school, Allison. I'm sure you'll like it."

"Of course she will," James agreed. "And guess what, Allison? Hal and Marge Jenson just moved here from Southern California. I think you met their daughter last summer—"

"You mean Shirley Jenson?" Allison asked with surprise. Andrew snickered slightly from the backseat.

"Yes, do you remember her?" James asked.

"I guess you could say that." Allison groaned. So much for

thinking that her little world would be perfect. "Why did they decide to move back to Oregon?"

"Hal decided to come up here in order to keep a closer eye on things with the shipping company. You may remember that his mother was your grandpa's partner. But Bea is getting older, and Hal wants to get more involved. You see, when your grandfather died, I inherited his portion of the business, and that makes Hal and me partners of sorts."

Allison wondered if Shirley's dad was anything like his daughter. She hoped not. One troublemaker in that family was enough!

"So, Allison," Grace said, "do you have everything you'll need for school?" As usual, Grace was a genius at changing subjects to happier things.

"I'm not sure yet," Allison said. "Marsha is sending me a box of clothing she thought I might be able to use, but knowing Marsha's taste, they could be covered with sequins and feathers!"

"Well, you and Heather could always have fun playing dress-up," Aunt Mildred offered.

"Actually, I think it's Marsha's way of saying she's sorry. . . ." Allison's voice faltered.

"Of course it is," agreed Grace. "I'll bet the box is full of great things. And you know clothing shopping around Tamaqua Point is almost nonexistent other than a few yard goods at the general store. If you like, I'd love to help you get a school wardrobe together. I sew a lot for Heather. . . ."

"Really? I knew that you did some alterations for Heather, but would you actually *sew* clothes for me, too? Are you sure they would look okay?" Allison clapped her hand over her mouth the minute she let the thought escape.

Grace laughed. "Well, keep in mind Heather is blind, but she rarely complains about how my sewing looks."

"Nonsense," James said. "Don't let Grace fool you. Heather's clothes look like they could've come from Paris. She does an amazing job."

"Grace is a fine seamstress," injected Aunt Mildred. "She always has been."

"I'm sorry, Grace," Allison said. "I didn't mean to insult you. It's just that I've never had any homemade clothing. I mean, Nanny Jane used to knit me things, but that was different."

"You're used to shopping on the East Coast, but things are a little different here. In fact, if you need to be stylish in a hurry, sometimes it's better to sew."

"Well, I'd be glad to have your help, Grace. I sure don't want to have to go to school in Marsha's clothes."

Andrew chuckled. "If you did, you'd probably fit right in with Shirley Jenson!" Both he and Allison broke into silly laughter.

"Now, I hope you kids will be nice to Shirley," James said. "It's not easy being new in school. And from what I hear, Andrew, Shirley really looks up to you."

"I know, sir," Andrew said, turning serious. "I *try* to be nice to her, but sometimes—well . . . she, uh—"

Allison finished for him. "Sometimes she just comes on a little too strong."

"Exactly," said Andrew. And this time Grace and Aunt Mildred both laughed.

"I see," James said. "Well, as they say, the fruit doesn't fall far from the tree."

"Meaning she's like her parents?" Allison asked.

"She's definitely her mother's daughter," James confirmed.

Allison wanted to question her father further, but she stopped herself. This was meant to be a happy day. She would just have to think about Shirley and Mrs. Jenson another time.

3

"I know it's late, Grace," Allison said as James pulled the Buick up to Grace's little ocean-side cabin. "But may I please go in and say hi to Heather? I won't wake up Winston."

"Of course, Allison. Heather would skin us alive if we let you get away without saying hello. And don't worry about Winston."

Allison tiptoed into the house behind Grace while Andrew and James carried in Grace's bags. Only one light was burning, and Allison smiled as she looked around the familiar living room. It was as cozy and sweet as ever, with her father's oil painting still hanging above the fireplace. She slipped into Heather's room and heard Heather stir.

"Grace, is that you?" Heather muttered sleepily.

"No, but Grace is—"

"Allison!" screamed Heather, leaping from the bed and easily finding Allison in the darkness. She hugged her and continued to cry, "I can't believe it! It's really you! It's really you! You're here. You're really here!"

Allison started to giggle as she whispered, "Shh, you're going to wake up Winston." But it was too late; he was already bounding into Heather's room.

"Allison, Allison!" he yelped. "You came back!"

"What on earth are you doing here?" Heather asked.

"Well, I just popped in to say hi, silly!"

"No, really, Al, what are you doing? Are you just passing through or what?"

"I'm home, Heather. I get to live with Dad."

"No kidding? Really, are you serious?" Heather started to cry, but Allison knew they were happy tears. The two hugged again, then Allison tousled Winston's hair.

"Winston, you better get back into bed," Allison warned. "I promised Grace I wouldn't wake you." Winston grinned and streaked back to his room.

"I better go, Heather," Allison said. "It's late and you have school in the morning. You should get back to sleep."

"As if I can!" Heather exclaimed with delight.

"I guess I shouldn't have disturbed you." She pulled one of Heather's blond curls. "I'm sure you were wanting to get in your beauty rest."

"Oh, I can see you're still your same old sweet self, Al. I sure have missed you. There's so much to tell you. High school is pretty neat. I made it into advanced band with my flute, and I'm also taking up piano. Oh, we have so much to talk about—"

"Yes, you do," interrupted Grace with a smile. "As much as I hate to break up this reunion, I think you should save it for tomorrow, girls. I just got Winston back to bed, and it's almost midnight."

"I know, Grace. Dad's waiting, and I'm sure you are both exhausted from your trip. We'll all talk tomorrow. Why don't you all come over for dinner?"

"Are you cooking?" teased Heather.

"No, but I'm sure Muriel is already planning a feast."

"We'll be there with bells on, Allison," Grace said with a hug. "I am so happy you're home, dear."

Allison made her way back outside, inhaling deeply the salt air from the Pacific Ocean. As she rode home with her father, her happiness encircled her like a warm hug, and she knew everything she had gone through to get to this point had been worth it. Utterly content, Allison let the gentle rocking of the car soothe her weary body.

Muriel had left a light on in the kitchen, and a pot of hot cocoa was still sitting on a corner of the old wood stove. A pair of cups and saucers and a plate of cookies were close by. James and Allison sat and quietly sipped and munched at the kitchen table. James kept his eyes on Allison the whole time.

"I can still hardly believe it," he said. "You just cannot imagine how glad I am that you are here."

"I think I can, Dad." She smiled.

"Maybe so. Maybe so. Promise me you'll still be here in the morning, and I'll let us go to bed. I'm sure you must be as tired as I am after flying cross-country."

"I'll be here, Dad."

She kissed his rough cheek good-night and scampered up the stairs. A little fire was burning in the ceramic-tiled fireplace, and the scent of lavender told her that Muriel must've put fresh sheets on. She kneeled before her bed—not because she thought God could only hear her if she kneeled, but because she wanted to—and she thanked Him for all He'd done. Here she was, back with her friends and family in Tamaqua Point, about to go to sleep in *her* very own room. She was truly thankful.

※

Not wanting to waste a minute of her first morning back home, Allison got up with the sun, dressed quickly, and hurried downstairs. She could hear her dad's voice in the den, and it sounded troubled. She didn't want to eavesdrop, but she couldn't help but catch a snatch of the conversation.

"I think we should discuss this further, Hal. It sounds like a risky venture. Are you sure your mother has agreed? No, I'm not disputing your word—"

She hurried past the open door. Already, good smells were enticing her toward the kitchen, and Allison wanted to get away from the disagreeable conversation. She was slightly relieved, though, to learn he was only talking to Hal. Her first response was to think that perhaps Marsha had changed her mind and was demanding that Allison return to Oakmont. That would be too horrible.

"Morning, Allison," greeted Muriel as she poured an even, round circle of pancake batter onto the sizzling griddle.

"Hi, Muriel, that looks yummy."

"I heard Jamie get up, and I thought I'd get a jump start on breakfast. But I didn't expect you to be up so soon. Is your dad still on the phone?" Muriel frowned as if she knew something was not right.

"Yeah, he didn't sound too happy. Is anything wrong?"

"I probably shouldn't say, but when it comes to family I don't keep secrets. Now, as far as the rest of the world goes—that's another story."

Allison nodded and knew it was true. If anyone could be trusted, it was Muriel.

"It's this whole shipping business. Hal has got it into his noggin that they need to expand. He wants to purchase another company that's not doing too well. Your dad is taking it cautiously, and Hal keeps acting like Jamie is going to blow the whole deal and sink the business to boot!"

"I see. . . . It must be hard for him."

"It is." Muriel continued in a quieter voice, watching for the door as she spoke. "Here Jamie is barely back to civilization after living such an isolated life, and the poor boy gets thrust right back into this whole shipping business again. In fact, it was this very business that drove him and your grandfather apart in the first place."

Allison nodded. "I remember. Do you suppose he feels like it's even more important now? Like he needs to do a really good job since Grandpa is gone?"

"I think you're a pretty smart gal for your age, Allison."

"Poor Dad."

"What do you mean 'poor dad'?" James asked from the doorway.

Allison spun around in surprise but was relieved to see him smiling. "Oh, I just mean having to talk to that disagreeable Mr. Jenson first thing in the morning," she laughed, hoping to make light of it.

"Well, then, I must agree with you—poor dad!" He reached out and touched her arm. "But having you here makes Mr. Jenson seem like much less of a problem." He turned to Muriel. "And this breakfast looks good enough to make all my problems disappear!"

❧

Later that morning, James drove Allison to Port View to register for school. Allison had changed her mind three times about what to wear. She knew they'd only be there for a short while, but she didn't want to wear the wrong thing. She had heard Marsha go on about the importance of first impressions, but after all those years of wearing uniforms in a girls' school, she didn't have a clue what was the proper public school attire.

She sat in the front seat of the Buick and fingered the cream-colored pencil skirt she'd chosen to wear. She wasn't overly fond of the straight, narrow type of skirt, but according to Marsha pencil skirts were quite stylish. This one happened to be one of Marsha's hand-me-downs from Allison's summer trip. Marsha had told her to keep the clothes, that she hadn't even missed them. Allison had chosen not to wear the matching cream jacket since she thought that might be too dressy. Instead, she'd picked a coral batwing sweater of cashmere, another castoff from Marsha. She hoped it might look more like a high school girl's outfit, but she still wasn't sure.

"You look very nice, Allison," James said as if he sensed her apprehension. "In fact, I'm the one who should be feeling nervous. Any other dad sending a pretty girl like you off to school would probably be packing a shotgun to keep the boys away."

"Oh, Dad!" she scolded him with a playful smile.

"Hopefully it won't take too long to fill out the paper work to get your records transferred and all."

"Dad," Allison began, "is there any way you could fill out the forms so that it wouldn't be too obvious who my mother is?"

"You mean you don't want me to write that she is the famous movie star Marsha Madison, queen of the silver screen?"

"Right. I'd prefer a little anonymity for starters. It would be so nice to just be known for myself. When people find out about Marsha, everything changes. I've been imagining life in a normal school with normal kids—just being one of the gang. You know what I mean?"

He nodded. "Sure do. I'll do everything I can, Allison. To tell you the truth, I've never been that comfortable with her fame myself."

"Thanks, Dad. People like Shirley Jenson would really have a heyday with that sort of information."

"Don't worry, she shouldn't give you any trouble. I've never mentioned it to Hal, and I know that your grandpa always kept that part of my life very, very quiet. Oh, by the way, I forgot to mention that Hal invited us to a dinner party on Saturday night. I figured by then you'd have had plenty of time to spend with Heather. I know it's probably not your idea of a great time, but I hope you don't mind."

"Of course not, Dad. After all, he's your business partner. Is his mother, Mrs. Jenson, going to be there? I get along pretty well with her. She's fun."

"I happen to like her a lot, too, but I doubt that she'll be there. As much as she loves her son, she barely tolerates her daughter-in-law."

James pulled up to the front of the school, and suddenly Allison felt her stomach grow queasy. This was it! This was her new school. She tried to convince herself that a new school was nothing compared to some of the things she'd already been through, but somehow she was not able to keep her legs from shaking.

"Grace and I both went to high school here, Allison. Of course, there are probably very few teachers left from my day. As I mentioned, I preregistered you by phone last summer, so I haven't actually been here in ages. Today you can have a look around while I sign some papers, and maybe you can meet some teachers."

They entered the big double doors and proceeded down an almost empty hall. Apparently the students were in class.

"James O'Brian?" called a voice. They turned to see a man about James' age approaching them. "James O'Brian?" he repeated. "I'd know you anywhere!"

"Bob Jackson!" James exclaimed. "Well, I'll be! What are you doing here?"

"I teach science, if you can believe that." He grinned mischievously and added in a quiet voice, "Remember when I hid all the dissected frog parts in the girls' locker room?" He glanced over at Allison. "And who is this?"

"This is my daughter, Allison. We're here to enroll her in school."

Bob Jackson's eyebrows lifted. "Well, then, Allison, I'll have to swear you to secrecy about that frog bit. Understand?" He grinned, but Allison sensed he was partly serious.

"Sure, uh, Mr. Jackson. Wild horses couldn't drag that one out of me."

He slapped her on the back. "I can tell you and I are going to get along fine, Allison." He turned back to James. "As well as teaching science, I'm also the vice-principal—I have a reputation to maintain."

"Hi there, Coach Jackson," said a boy coming around the corner. "Great game last week!"

Mr. Jackson thanked him and waved.

"Coach?"

"Yep, I wear several hats around here. You know how these small schools are, everyone gets into the act. I coach football, and we have a great little team this year."

"So I've heard," James said. "In fact, a good friend of ours is on your team—Andrew Amberwell."

"You bet! That Andrew is something! My star quarterback. In fact, it wouldn't surprise me if that kid got a college scholarship."

James grinned. "Glad to hear it! I've been out East since the season began. Can't wait to make the next game!"

"That would be this Friday. Home game, too." Suddenly, Mr. Jackson grew more serious. "Say, James, I heard you were the one living in the lighthouse all these years. To think that all this time we thought you'd died in the war. Sure glad it wasn't true!"

"Me too!"

Mr. Jackson laughed and slapped James on the back. "Well, it's great to see you. Don't let me keep you from getting Allison all set up." He turned to Allison. "And welcome to Port View High, home of the Port View Pirates. I think you'll like it here, Allison." He turned to make his way down the hall, then paused as if remembering something. "Say, are you still doing your art, James?"

"I'm afraid so." He smiled sheepishly.

"You remember my older brother, Clyde, don't you? He runs an art gallery in Portland. Do you have anything you'd like to be shown?"

"Actually, I have quite a collection, and I've started placing them in some small shops."

"Then I'll give Clyde a call for you."

"I'd appreciate that, Bob. Thanks."

The two men shook hands, and James began to move toward what Allison assumed was the office. She was beginning to feel a little more comfortable. It was nice to know that the vice-principal was a friend of her dad's. Just then a bell rang and kids began pouring from classes, and everyone seemed to be going a different direction. She quickly tried to study the girls to see how they were dressed, but it was just a kaleidoscope of color moving in a fast blur.

"Allison!" exclaimed a female voice with a familiar shrill. Allison didn't even need to look.

"Hi, Shirley," she said, determined to be nice, if only for her dad's benefit.

"Oh, it's so good to see you," Shirley gushed. "And you look so adorable! Are those your new school clothes?"

In that split second Allison was painfully aware that she was dressed completely wrong and totally out of place. She did a fast inventory of Shirley's outfit, not that she wanted to follow Shirley's fashion lead, but it seemed that even Shirley fit in better than she did. In fact, Shirley didn't look half bad in her navy blue sweater and matching wool pencil skirt. The skirt was cut like Allison's but more schoolish-looking. Shirley's sweater was trimmed in smart-looking bands of red, and she had a matching scarf tied jauntily around her neck. Then Allison glanced down at Shirley's feet to spy penny loafers and bobby socks turned down neatly.

"I already heard the good news, Allison!" Shirley didn't seem to be worried about being tardy for her next class as she continued. "I think it's so great that you're going to live here. I just know we're going to be best friends. And Daddy said you are coming for dinner on Saturday. I just can't wait—" Another bell rang, and the halls grew quiet again. "Oops," she exclaimed with a giggle, her eyes wide. "I guess I'm late again. See you later, Allison—Mr. O'Brian."

"Bye, Shirley," James said with a crooked smile and lifted brows. He turned to Allison and repeated, "Best friends?"

Allison laughed. "I'll try to be nice to her, Dad, but best friends is definitely out of the question."

"Well, I'm sure Heather will be relieved to hear that."

It took nearly an hour to fill out the forms and meet several more faculty members. By the time they finished, another bell had rung and Allison stood in the doorway of the office, looking on again as students passed through the hallway to their next class. She saw Heather walk by with a chunky blond girl whom Allison had never seen before, but she decided not to interrupt them. No need to make them late. Besides, she would see Heather later.

As Allison watched the students, she noticed that most of the girls wore simple tweed or plaid skirts, usually pleated or A-line, but very few pencil skirts. On top they wore blouses or sweaters, but she saw no one dressed quite as formally as she was. She didn't even see anyone dressed like Shirley. Most of the female feet that hurried down the hallway wore brown-and-white saddle oxfords with turned-down anklets. Maybe this wouldn't be so difficult after all.

"Are you ready to go?" James interrupted her thoughts.

"They said you can start classes tomorrow, but I thought you might need a couple days to recover from your long trip yesterday."

Allison linked her arm into her dad's and smiled. "Sounds good. And now that I have an idea of what girls wear to high school, I think I'm ready to do a little school wardrobe shopping. Do you think you can handle that, or should I talk to Grace?"

James grinned. "I wouldn't mind giving it a try myself, Allison. It couldn't be any worse than fighting the war in Europe."

"Don't bet on it, Dad."

4

After they got home, Allison took a quick inventory of what she already had to wear to school. Surprisingly, there were a couple of things that seemed suitable, but there were still quite a few holes to fill, and a pair of saddle shoes was a must. She made out a short list, then ran downstairs to tell her father. She knew this would mean another trip to Port View since Tamaqua Point had little to offer other than the general store, post office, gas station, and café.

"Allison." James was sitting at Grandpa's desk, and he looked up with a big smile. "I just had a phone call from Mr. Jackson's brother in Portland, remember the one with the art gallery?"

"You mean Mr. Jackson already called him?"

James nodded. "It turns out that Clyde Jackson is having an exhibit of Oregon coastal paintings this weekend. He has invited me to bring some of mine over."

"Dad, that's great! When do we leave?"

James laughed and looked at his watch. "Well, when can you be ready?"

"You mean like right this minute?"

"Sure, why not? Didn't you say you needed some things for school? Why not kill two birds with one stone?"

"That sounds like something Grandpa would say," Allison said with a grin.

"Why, thank you."

"What's this I hear?" Muriel asked. "Are you two getting ready to run out on me again? Don't you know I have a roast cooking? I thought we were having the Amberwells for dinner."

James slapped his palm to his forehead. "I completely forgot. Of course, Muriel, you're right." He looked at Allison. "First thing in the morning, then?"

"Sounds perfect. And I wouldn't want to miss the chance to see Heather and everyone. Muriel, can I help you in the kitchen?"

"How about a nice bouquet for the table, Allison. I think there are still some flowers in your grandmother's garden. And then perhaps you could set the table."

"And I'll go begin wrapping my paintings," James told them.

Just as Allison finished arranging the flowers, the phone rang.

"Hi, Allison, this is Shirley. You'll never believe what happened today."

"What happened?" Allison asked, trying to sound cheerful.

Shirley giggled. "Well, I went into the office right after you left and explained to Miss Sharp, she's the secretary, that since you and I were such good friends and all, it would probably be nice if she could arrange our schedules so we could have some classes together."

Allison frowned. "So, uh, what did Miss Sharp do?"

"She gave you the exact same schedule as mine!" More giggling. "Isn't that fab?"

Allison closed her eyes and leaned against the wall. She didn't know what to say. She felt sick.

"Allison? Allison, are you still there?"

"Yes, Shirley. I'm here."

"Isn't it great news? I knew when I saw you today that we were going to be best friends. I know we didn't exactly hit it off last summer, but that was before I knew I was going to be living here. Now everything will be just swell!"

Allison sighed. "I sure hope so, Shirley."

"You don't sound very excited."

"I guess I'm just tired."

"Of course, with all your traveling you probably are. Will you be in school tomorrow?"

"Actually, Dad and I are going to Portland tomorrow to take some paintings and do some shopping. I'll probably start school on Friday."

"A trip to Portland sounds like fun. Well, I guess I'll see you on Friday, then. Good-bye!"

Allison hung up the phone wondering if she was being unfair. Perhaps she had misjudged Shirley. But somewhere deep inside she didn't think so.

"What's the matter, Allison?" James asked as he came around the corner with several paintings in his hand. "You look like you just lost your best friend."

"No, I think I've just acquired a new best friend. Not that I was looking."

"Shirley Jenson?"

Allison nodded. "She has seen to it that we have the same classes scheduled."

James smiled. "Well, that was thoughtful of her. She probably just wants to help you adjust to school."

Allison sighed. "I hope that's all it is." Then she remembered something. "Hey, I thought Shirley was almost a year older than me, Dad. Shouldn't she be a sophomore?"

"Hal told me that Shirley had a serious illness when she was young and missed a lot of school, so they held her back a year. I'm sure that was hard on her. She could probably use a good friend, being new and all."

"I'll try to be nice to her, Dad, but I can't promise anything."

Before long, Allison finished setting the table and stepped back to admire the pretty room. This room, like so many others, reminded Allison of Grandmother Mercury. It was decorated in pale yellow and cream. Allison was fairly certain that yellow was her grandmother's favorite color.

"It looks lovely," Muriel said from the doorway. "And now you can do something else for me, dear."

"Sure, anything, Muriel."

"I want you to go take a little nap."

"A *nap*?"

"Yes, dear. You may not feel like it, but you look very tired to me. You did a lot of traveling, and I know there's a time difference between here and the East Coast." Muriel touched Allison's cheek. "And you have these wee little black shadows beneath your eyes. So I'm not asking you, I'm telling you—go have a little rest."

Allison smiled. "You're probably right, Muriel. Thanks."

Allison hardly remembered closing her eyes, but when she opened them it was getting dusky in her room and her clock said it was almost six. By the time she got downstairs, the Amberwells were coming through the front door. Allison met Heather with a big hug.

"I still can't believe you're here, Allison," said Heather. "I kept thinking that I dreamed the whole thing."

"I told her this morning that it was real," Winston said importantly.

"Muriel says dinner won't be ready for about half an hour," James said. "I've got a nice fire going in the library."

"How about a quick game of chess?" Andrew challenged.

James laughed. "I was wondering when you would ask. Just can't wait to whip me again, can you?"

Allison took Heather's arm and led her toward the parlor. "You'll never believe what happened today, Heather," she said quietly.

Grace smiled. "You two! If I didn't know better, I'd think you were sisters separated at birth—it's great to see you together again."

Allison grinned and continued to the parlor, launching into the story of Shirley and the class schedule.

"You're kidding?" Heather groaned.

"Nope. I couldn't believe it, either."

Heather was quiet for a long moment. "Shirley was quite friendly to me, too, at first. . . ."

"Then what happened?"

"Not much. I've always treated her nicely, but I think it bothers her that I can't see."

"Well, that's probably lucky for you, Heather. I hope she gives up on me, too. Hey, I saw you at school today. You were walking with a blond girl—"

"That's Caroline. She's very sweet. She was my friend in school last year, too. She volunteered to be my guide in high school, and she has every class with me."

"Sort of like Shirley and me."

Heather laughed. "The good news is now I know that I will have two classes with you because I already have them with Shirley. We'll have home economics right before lunch and then algebra at the end of the day. That will be swell having you in algebra. I could use some help in that class."

"Then you better not count on me."

"Math's not your specialty, either? Maybe we can both have Andrew do some tutoring."

Allison wondered how Heather managed to keep up with all her classes. It couldn't be easy, and Allison knew there weren't Braille books for everything. But Heather was smart, and Grace probably helped a lot, too.

"Is this a private conversation?" asked Grace as she poked her head through the doorway.

"Of course not," said Allison. "Come into the ladies' parlor and join us."

"I think Muriel is about ready to call us to dinner. Allison, James said you were going shopping for some new clothes tomorrow, and I wondered if you'd like me to have a look at any of your other clothes. We might be able to alter some things so they work for school. I got pretty handy doing alterations with all the deprivations during the war."

"That would be super, Grace. Actually, there are a couple of things that might work, but right now they look too old, or too citified, or something. Why don't you both come up to my room after dinner and I'll show you."

True to Grace's word, Muriel quickly called them to dinner. When they were all seated around the table, James said a blessing, then they all began chattering away like one big, happy family. It was hard for Allison to believe that they hadn't always been like this. She looked across the table to where Andrew was seated next to Grace. She remembered what Mr. Jackson had said about Andrew's football-playing skills. She didn't really know a thing about football, but the fact that the vice-principal was impressed made her feel a deeper respect for Andrew. He suddenly seemed taller and older in her eyes, and she found that she was unable to think of anything to say.

"How long will you and Allison stay in Portland?" Grace asked as she passed the potatoes.

"By the time I meet with Clyde and deliver the paintings,

it'll probably be lunchtime. After that I imagine we'll shop for hours and hours." James grinned at Allison.

"Dad," she said in a reprimanding tone. "My list wasn't that long!"

He chuckled. "I thought if we had time we could have a nice dinner and maybe go to a film. I heard that *Key Largo* is playing."

"Oh, I'd love to see that!" Allison said. "Did you know that I saw Lauren Bacall in Hollywood?"

"Really?" said Grace with interest. "Is she as gorgeous in person as she is on the screen?"

"Very, very classy," Allison explained as she cut into a slice of roast.

"Wow," said Andrew. "Who else did you see?"

Allison thought hard. "I saw Liz Taylor with a mud masque on her face in this fancy Beverly Hills salon. And I also saw Doris Day in a dress store where all the dresses were blue."

"All the dresses were blue?" asked Heather in amazement.

Allison laughed. "Yes, it reminded me of when Dorothy went into the Emerald City in *The Wizard of Oz*, only everything was blue."

Before long, dinner was over and Allison and Heather were helping Muriel clear the table. Once they were finished and Muriel had hustled them away from the kitchen, Allison took Grace and Heather up to her room to examine her closet.

"I think there might be hope for a lot of these things," Grace said as she looked over the clothes in Allison's closet. "Maybe not this year, but just keep them and wait. The clothes you have here are so stylish that they haven't even made their way to the wilds of Oregon yet."

"I still have a whole trunk of things coming from Beverly Hills, and Marsha said she was going to add some things to it."

"It's so amazing how Marsha changed her mind, Allison,"

said Heather. "Andrew told me the whole story. I think God did a miracle."

"I agree," said Grace. "Now, I hate to interrupt all this girl talk, but remember, Heather, tonight's a school night, so we need to get Winston home and to bed."

"We'll catch up later," Allison said as she walked them downstairs. "I have so much to tell you, Heather."

"Have fun in Portland," Heather called from the front step.

"Yeah, don't buy the stores out, Allison," Andrew warned.

"Oh, you!" Allison said in mock irritation.

"Will you be in school on Friday?" asked Heather.

"I hope so," said Allison. "We're coming back on Thursday, right, Dad?"

"That's right. And we don't want to miss Andrew's game on Friday."

"Great," said Andrew, looking down at her with a big smile. "See you on Friday, then."

That night when Allison went to bed, she could still see Andrew's face smiling at her, saying "see you on Friday." It had warmed her insides and made her heart beat a little faster. She only hoped he hadn't noticed her reaction.

❀

The next morning was foggy and gray, but it didn't dampen Allison's spirits as they drove along in the big green Buick. James had the radio on, and they sang along with Perry Como and Bing Crosby until they got into the Coastal Range and lost the radio frequency.

The first stop in Portland was The Blue Heron Art Gallery. The shop was small in front but got bigger as they were led toward the back. Clyde Jackson didn't look anything like his brother at Port View High School. Clyde's black hair was smoothed back and hung long over his turtleneck collar. He had a little black goatee that reminded Allison of some of Marsha's strange beatnik friends in New York. But Clyde was warm and friendly and didn't put on any pretenses. He even spoke to Allison as if she were an adult.

He gave them a complete tour of his gallery, pointing out names of artists that he thought James might be interested in knowing. Best of all, Clyde seemed genuinely pleased with James' work. Allison felt proud, and she could see that her father was happy, too. As they had anticipated, it was nearly noon by the time they told Clyde thank you and good-bye.

"I don't know about you, but I am feeling extremely hungry," James said as soon as they stepped out on the street.

"Famished," Allison agreed. "And I think we should celebrate. It sounds like Clyde thinks your work is quite good."

They finally settled for hamburgers and milk shakes, which suited Allison just fine. Then they set off to find some school clothes.

"I'll bet this is lots different from shopping in New York or Beverly Hills," James said somewhat apologetically as they walked into Portland's biggest department store.

"Yes, but already I like it much better."

"Really? Why?"

"It's smaller—less busy. People seem more real here."

"You'll have to lead the way, Allison. I'm sure you know much more about shopping than I do."

"We'll see about that. Until last summer, the only thing I ever wore was my school uniform or things that Lola bought for me. But I have seen Marsha shop." Allison stepped up to the cosmetics counter and inquired where the ladies' department was located.

"Second floor," said the woman with a smile. "The escalator is right over there."

"Thanks."

Allison stepped confidently from the escalator with James right behind her. In no time she had gathered several skirts and sweaters and blouses.

"You look like you know what you're doing," James commented with a grin as she handed him a small pile.

"I learned from the best." Suddenly, Allison's brow creased into a frown as she realized that she was used to seeing Marsha shop without any sort of budget. She hadn't even stopped to consider what her father's financial situation might be. It was a good thing she still had money of her own that Marsha had given her before her trip.

"You look troubled, Allison. What's wrong?"

"I—uh, I don't want you to think that you have to buy all these things for me, Dad. I have my own money—"

"Not on your life, Allison Mercury O'Brian!" James interrupted, and he lifted a hand to stop her. "This is the first time in ages that I have been able to buy something for my little girl. You're not going to take that away from me, are you?"

Allison looked into his eyes and realized that he wasn't joking. "No, not if you want to, Dad. I just didn't want to assume that—"

"Well, you better assume, young lady. I'm your dad, and I want to enjoy some of the things I've missed out on."

Allison smiled, but she could feel tears in her eyes. "I've missed them, too, Dad. Believe me, I've missed them."

He wrapped his free arm around her shoulders. "Well, let's be thankful that it's all just a memory now. And let's keep shopping. This is fun!"

"May I start a dressing room for the young lady?" asked a salesclerk with a smile.

"Certainly," James said as he handed the stack to her.

After Allison modeled several outfits, they decided on three. First there was the A-line glen-plaid skirt with a short-sleeved sweater in a soft shade of brown. The next was a pleated skirt of moss green tweed with a matching cardigan that her father said brought out the green in her eyes. And finally, Allison's favorite outfit, a circle skirt in a russet, pumpkin, and gold plaid. It fit her tiny waist perfectly, then swirled out at the bottom so that if she gave a spin it shot out at the sides. It was lined in satin and felt wonderful against her bare legs. James had actually found the perfect sweater for it: a long-sleeved mock turtleneck in the rich russet shade. Allison was pretty certain it was cashmere, although she hadn't checked the tag.

When she stepped out of the dressing room in that outfit, James whistled low and said, "I'm not sure why I'm being so helpful in getting my little girl all dolled up. The boys are going to be busting down my door before long."

"Oh, Dad," she said. The clerk just grinned and happily rang them up.

James did some shopping of his own while she selected socks and underthings. Then they carried the packages out to the car and headed for the shoe store down the street.

᭦

"This was such fun, Dad," Allison said later that day. "I've never had this much fun shopping before. Usually I'm with people who are making me get things I don't really want or even like, but I adore everything you've bought me today. And I can still hardly believe that I'll get to go to a real high school on Friday. It's like a wonderful dream!"

"It is for me, too, Allison. Hey, look over there at the theater marquee—*Key Largo* is playing tonight at six. Do you want to see it?"

"You bet!"

They piled the packages into the car, then set out to find a restaurant that James remembered from before he'd gone to New York in the early thirties.

"It's not far," James told her. "Shall we walk?"

"I'd love to." Allison put on the new coat that her father had insisted she get. It was a dark brown tweed with a brown velvet collar and velvet-covered buttons. It was very long, almost to her ankles, and the lining swished when she moved.

While they walked, she thought about the clothes they'd purchased today. They were so different from the things she had borrowed from Marsha several months back. These new school clothes seemed to suit her personality. They felt like Allison clothes. She no longer needed to masquerade as a grown-up, and she no longer needed a school girl's uniform. It felt like she was actually becoming her own person, and it felt nice.

James took them down a couple of wrong streets and through a back alley until he finally found the restaurant called Figaro's. It was a sweet little Italian restaurant run by the same family that had owned it back before James had gone off to New York.

"It looks exactly the same," James said as they were seated at a wobbly round table covered in red-checked cloth. A candle burned brightly in a wax-covered wine bottle, and Italian music played on a phonograph by the cash register. Every once in a while it would skip, but that only seemed to add to the charm.

"Did you come here a lot?" asked Allison after they both ordered the spaghetti with meatballs.

"Only once," James said as if looking back over the years. "It was with Grace."

"Oh." Allison laid the linen napkin in her lap and studied the flickering flame of the candle.

"I'd like to bring her again sometime."

"I'm sure she'd like that."

"And now, Allison," James said, shaking his head as if coming out of a dream, "I want you to tell me all about you."

"About me?"

"Yes. I know a lot about who you are now, but I really don't know much about your life up until now. Just bits and pieces."

"There's not much to tell. Eight years in a drafty old boarding school with a bunch of other poor little rich girls. Holidays either in New York with Marsha or at the estate, which was always preferable—at least until Nanny Jane passed away."

"Nanny Jane was a good woman."

"Yes, I still miss her. After she died it wasn't the same going back to the estate. And besides, it never seemed like Grandmother Madison really wanted me around. You know what she's like."

"Only too well," James nodded in sympathy. "It's really quite sad if you think about it. What does that lonely old lady have, anyway?"

"Nothing but a bunch of stinking money."

James laughed. "At least you're learning what's important and what's not early on in your life."

Allison continued on, trying to fill her father in on any major details or events that he had missed. But as she looked back, she realized her life up until last June seemed unimportant. Now the life before her looked colorful and exciting. She couldn't wait for her first day at school and her future to begin.

5

Allison awoke early and looked around to see where she was, then stretched contentedly. She was back in her sweet blue-and-yellow bedroom. Home. And today would be her first day of high school. It had been fun going to Portland with Dad, but she was glad to be home. She didn't care if she ever went on another trip. She hopped out of bed and looked over to where she'd carefully laid out her clothes last night, just in case she accidentally slept in late and had to hurry. That used to happen a lot back at boarding school, but not today. Allison pulled the window shades up to see a blanket of gray fog outside. She smiled. It looked like a perfect day for a wool sweater and skirt.

She carefully dressed, pulling the russet sweater over her head, then slipping the fall-colored plaid skirt on. She tucked the sweater into her waistband and buckled the narrow brown leather belt that was the perfect accessory to her skirts. She cuffed her socks and slid her feet into the new saddle shoes, tying neat little bows. At boarding school she had been required to wear loafers with her uniform, and while she still liked loafers, it was nice to try something new for a change. And this was quite a change to wear something other than a uniform to school. It felt a little strange to think that her own identity might actually be visible in the form of her clothing now. There had always been an anonymous security in looking just like everyone else.

She stood before the mirror and examined her reflection. It did help that she was now wearing her own clothes instead of the castoffs from Marsha. That should help her to fit in with the kids she'd observed at school the other day. She combed and styled her hair. It had grown out some and was curling past her shoulders now, and the russet sweater seemed to bring out more of the red highlights.

"Hello, in there," called Muriel's voice. "Are you up, Allison?"

"Come in, Muriel," said Allison.

"Oh my!" Muriel exclaimed, clapping her hands together. "Don't you look as pretty as a picture! What a beautiful outfit, Allison. It suits you to a tee."

"Thanks, Muriel. It's my favorite of the things we bought yesterday. I thought I might as well wear it for my first day."

"It's perfect. And when you're ready, I've got breakfast for you downstairs."

"Thanks, Muriel. I guess Dad will be taking me to school today. . . ."

"Actually, Andrew called yesterday afternoon before you and James got home. I forgot to mention that he and Heather wanted to give you a ride. I don't think your dad will mind." Muriel winked.

"That sounds great, Muriel. I'll be down in a few minutes."

Allison latched her gold locket around her neck and checked the mirror one more time to make sure everything was in place. Then she went to her closet and took out the brown corduroy car coat that Marsha had given her in New York. It was one that Marsha had gotten for a trip to the mountains last winter but had never worn since. She had thought Allison might get some use out of it, and it looked just right with this outfit.

"Okay," said Allison out loud. "Here goes nothing." Then she whispered a prayer in her heart, asking God to help her not make a complete fool of herself today.

"Good morning," James said, looking up from his coffee when Allison entered the kitchen. He set the morning paper aside, then slowly shook his head. "You look fantastic, Allison. You ready to knock them all dead?"

"Dad," she said in a dramatic tone. "I should be going to school to get an education, not to impress people." Then she laughed. "Still, just between you and me, I'm dying to know what they will think of me."

"Don't worry about that, Allison. I'm sure you'll fit in perfectly. Say, I hear that you already have a ride to school today. I guess that's preferable to being driven by the old man?"

Allison felt bad. "No, not really," she stammered. "I don't mind who drives me—if you want to—"

"Nonsense. I think it's great that you can ride with Heather and Andrew. Actually, I'm anxious to start a new painting today."

"Really? What are you going to paint?"

James smiled mysteriously. "I don't like to reveal my work till it's finished."

"Sounds interesting." Allison sat down and looked at the loaded plate that Muriel was placing before her. "Goodness, I'm getting so nervous I don't know if I'll be able to eat all that."

"Well, you don't have to clean the plate, dear, but eat something," Muriel ordered like a concerned mother hen.

Allison slowly managed to make a piece of toast and a glass of orange juice disappear before she heard Andrew's horn tooting in the driveway. "Good-bye," she said as she grabbed up her coat.

"Good luck, Allison," James called as she ran out the door.

Andrew was waiting by the old jalopy. He wore a black-and-gold letterman jacket and opened the passenger door for her as if she were a queen. "You look like you're all ready for school, Allison."

"I guess I am," she replied, wondering if that was supposed to be a compliment. She slid in next to Heather and said, "I'm so nervous I feel like I could lose my breakfast."

Heather and Andrew both laughed. "Don't worry," said Heather. "If I can do it, so can you."

Allison squeezed Heather's hand and glanced down at her friend's outfit: a blue plaid skirt with a white blouse topped by a blue vest. "Heather, you look smashing!"

"Thanks to Grace," said Heather with a bright smile.

Allison took a deep breath, dreading bringing up the next subject. "I need you two to promise me something," she began.

"What is it?" Andrew asked as he steered the jalopy onto the main road.

"I know you both know all about my mom, but I really don't want anyone else to know. It always makes things more difficult, if you know what I mean."

Heather nodded. "Like at camp?"

"Right. I want people to get to know me for who I am, not for the fact that Marsha Madison is my mother."

"Not a problem for me," said Andrew. "Mum's the word as far as I'm concerned."

"Thanks, Andrew."

"And your secret is safe with me," said Heather. "Although, I think once people get to know you they won't care a wit about who your mother is or isn't."

"I hope so, Heather. But for now, I appreciate your help."

By the time they walked into the school, Allison's palms were cold and sweaty. She hoped she wouldn't need to shake hands with anyone. Her first class was English. That was good since it was one of her better subjects. She saw Heather's friend Caroline approach, and after a quick introduction Allison and Andrew bade Heather good-bye. Andrew lingered a moment more to point Allison in the right direction.

"Relax, Allison," he said reassuringly. "You're going to do just fine. Besides, you look like a million bucks!" Then he winked and strolled off down the hall.

Allison took a deep breath, then smiled to herself. Everything was going to be okay.

"Hi there, Allison," called a familiar voice.

"Hi, Shirley," Allison answered almost without looking. "This must be our English class."

"Yep." Shirley peered over Allison's shoulder. "Was that Andrew Amberwell? Did he actually walk you to class?"

Allison felt her cheeks grow warm. "No, he was just showing me where it was."

"Oh good," said Shirley. She sounded relieved.

Allison liked the English teacher. Her name was Mrs. Jones, and she seemed to enjoy her work. She reminded Allison of the sweet woman she had met on the train last summer, the one who had introduced her to Emily Dickinson. Maybe she would show Mrs. Jones the signed book about Emily Dickinson's life later in the year.

After Mrs. Jones explained the class's writing assignment, she gave them twenty minutes to prepare an outline. Allison launched right into it. Writing was her strong suit. It didn't seem to matter that she had missed the first two weeks of school. This assignment was something she could do.

"Allison," Shirley whispered, poking Allison with a pencil and completely disrupting her train of thought.

"What?" she asked, looking up from her paper in irritation.

"You're not actually doing the assignment, are you?"

"Of course I am. Why not?"

"Well, it's your first day. No one expects you to."

"But I want to do it. I like to write."

Shirley looked at Allison as if she had two heads, then changed the subject. "Are you going to the football game tonight?"

Mrs. Jones was walking toward them now, clearing her throat. Allison immediately turned back around and focused on her paper. Mrs. Jones paused briefly by Allison's desk. She felt her cheeks grow hot. How awful to be caught whispering on her very first day, and all thanks to Shirley Jenson!

"Allison," said Mrs. Jones quietly. "Stop by my desk when class is over."

Allison looked up with wide eyes and nodded without speaking. She turned her attention back to her paper and tried to continue writing, but it was too late. She couldn't even remember what it was she had been trying to write. And to think she had every class with Shirley!

At last the bell rang, and the classroom emptied quickly. Allison walked up to Mrs. Jones' desk. She squared her shoulders and swallowed hard. "You wanted to see me?" she asked in a tiny voice.

Mrs. Jones smiled. "Yes, I just wanted to welcome you and to see if there is anything I can do for you."

Allison blinked in surprise. "No, I don't think so. You see, English is my favorite subject. I'm sorry I was talking, actually I was listening—"

"I know, Allison. But I should warn you, I don't put up with chitchat in the classroom. It's one of my little peeves. You may want to try to sit in another seat tomorrow."

Allison nodded. "Sure, Mrs. Jones. That's a very good idea."

Now Mrs. Jones' eyes twinkled as if they understood each

other. "Good. Now, you better hurry or you'll be late for second period."

"Thank you, Mrs. Jones."

Allison found her way to her next class just as the tardy bell rang. It was biology. She slipped into an empty seat in the back. Thankfully, it was not near Shirley.

The biology teacher looked to be about a hundred years old, and he spoke in a slow lecture mode the entire time. Allison tried to concentrate and take notes, but she found herself more interested in observing her classmates. It was nice sitting in the back because it allowed her to freely stare at everyone in front of her. Judging by the way some of them slumped in their chairs, she suspected they were less interested than she in the slow-moving lecture. The bell rang after what felt like several years, and Allison slipped quickly from the class before Shirley could catch her.

Somehow Allison managed to get through her third-period class without actually speaking with Shirley. The history teacher had assigned seating, and Allison was given a desk near the door, making another quick getaway opportunity. Finally it was fourth period. Now, if only she could find Heather—

"Allison!" Shirley's high-pitched voice echoed through the hallway. She ran up from behind and hooked her arm into Allison's. "It almost looked like you were trying to get away from me. You weren't, were you?"

"Uh . . ." Allison paused, thinking of a way to answer Shirley without lying. "I was just looking for Heather."

"You'll see her soon enough. We have the next class with her. Now, just let me show you the way. And did I mention how cute you look today, Allison? Just like a real school-girl."

Allison didn't like Shirley's tone, but she refused to let it get to her. She glanced at Shirley's outfit as they navigated their way down the busy hallway. Another straight pencil skirt, this time in black wool. It was topped with a gold sweater that actually made Shirley's face look a bit sallow. Naturally, Allison didn't mention to fashion-minded Shirley that gold might not be her best color. Something about the black and gold seemed familiar. Then she remembered Andrew's jacket, as well as several banners she had noticed in the hallway.

"Shirley, are black and gold the school's colors?" she asked.

Shirley nodded. "Yes, I like to wear these colors on game days to show my support for the football team."

"That's nice. Sort of like a cheerleader?"

"Sort of." Shirley's voice sounded slightly bitter. She threw her head back. "They had cheerleader tryouts during the first week of school. Of course, I didn't have a chance—being the new girl and all. But I'm sure I'll be a cheerleader next year."

Allison's brow lifted. "How can you be so certain?"

"I usually get what I put my mind to," Shirley said with a laugh. "Here we are. Home economics, where we learn how to become proper little homemakers. Just wait until you see this teacher, Allison."

Allison looked across the room. The tables were arranged in a U, and in the far corner sat Heather and Caroline. An empty seat was next to Heather, and Allison started to make her way toward it.

"Wait for me," called Shirley.

"I want to sit with Heather," Allison said. "I've barely seen her today. But there's a seat next to Caroline if you want to take it."

"Ugh, I wouldn't sit by that pig if you paid me," Shirley whispered harshly.

Allison quickly glanced at Caroline to see if she had overheard, but Caroline's face appeared blank. Allison turned and frowned at Shirley, but Shirley just giggled.

"Meet me after class," Shirley commanded with a smile as she took a seat on the other side of the room. "We'll have lunch together."

The bell rang before Allison could answer, and she slipped into the seat next to Heather, whispering a quick hello.

"Good morning, ladies," said a woman at the front of the class. She wore a dress that resembled a giant calico flour sack, cinched around her thick waist with a wide orange belt. It was obviously homemade, but not in the neatly tailored way that Grace made clothing. How could this woman possibly teach anyone home economics?

"We have a new student joining our class," chirped the teacher as she glanced at a card in her hand. "Miss Allison O'Brian? Will you please stand up?"

This was the first time today a teacher had made her stand up. Allison felt her cheeks grow warm, but she scooted back her chair and stood. "Yes, ma'am."

"Welcome, Allison. I'm Miss Wrigley, and I hope you'll be happy here at Port View High."

"Thank you," said Allison quietly. She sat back down, and Miss Wrigley moved on to a colored flip chart to review the food groups and the basics of menu planning.

"Remember, ladies, all of your menu plans are due next Tuesday. Then we will all go on our grocery shopping trip on Thursday." She said it as if shopping for groceries was more exciting than skydiving.

Allison glanced at Heather, but it was hard to read her expression. Caroline, on the other hand, seemed to be quite interested. Across the room Shirley yawned dramatically.

This time when the bell rang it was time for lunch, which

was good since Allison was ravenous. It seemed like ages since she had consumed that tiny breakfast.

"Do you want to eat lunch with Caroline and me?" Heather asked.

Before Allison could open her mouth, Shirley began to speak. "Allison is going to eat lunch with me, aren't you, Allison?"

"Actually, I was hoping to join Heather."

Shirley's face grew cloudy. "But I already asked you—"

"Maybe we can all eat together," Heather offered sweetly.

Shirley studied Heather and Caroline with a look of disdain, then rolled her eyes. "Maybe some other time."

Allison wanted to cheer as Shirley walked away. "Which way to the cafeteria?" she asked. "I'm starved."

"I'll show you," offered Caroline with a shy smile.

When they were settled at a table with their trays of food, Allison looked around her contentedly. This was much better than eating in the stuffy dining hall at Oakmont. Just as she took a big bite of macaroni salad, Andrew walked up and asked to join them. She grinned up at him with a full mouth.

"Sure, have a seat," Heather said. "If you're sure you want to be seen with lowly freshmen."

"Thanks, sis. I don't think it'll hurt just this once." He sat down across from Allison. "So how's it going, Allison?"

"All right, I guess. Everyone is pretty nice, and I think I'm starting to know my way around." She glanced over at Caroline, who was staring at Andrew with buggy eyes.

"That's great. See . . . I told you it would be fine." Andrew took a bite of his sandwich.

"As usual, you were right—well, mostly . . . Allison noticed that Shirley was quickly heading toward their table. She had another girl with her—a pretty blonde who was also dressed in school colors.

"Mostly?" Andrew repeated.

Allison pressed her lips together and nodded.

"Hi, Allison," Shirley crooned sweetly. "I want you to meet someone." She stopped and looked at Andrew as if she hadn't noticed him sitting there. "Well, hello, Andrew! What are you doing sitting with a bunch of freshmen?"

"Hi, Shirley," Andrew said politely. "As you may remember, one of these freshmen happens to be my sister. And, of course, Allison is my good buddy."

Allison beamed proudly.

"Speaking of freshman, that applies to you, too, doesn't it, Shirley?"

"Oh, I know, Andrew," gushed Shirley, slapping him on the back. "You know me, I just like to give you a hard time. So are you all ready for the big game tonight?"

"I guess so." Andrew glanced over at the girl behind Shirley. "I thought you had someone to introduce to Allison."

"Oh, silly me," said Shirley, pulling the girl forward yet still ignoring Allison completely. "You already know Karen Brown, don't you, Andrew?"

"Sure, I see her with the other cheerleaders at every game. How's it going, Karen?"

"Just fine, Andrew. Shirley wanted me to meet her new friend." Karen looked down at Allison and smiled as if she really did want to meet her.

"Yes, this is Allison O'Brian," said Shirley quickly. "And I suppose you've already met Heather Amberwell—she's Andrew's sister, of course."

Heather smiled politely up toward them. "Actually, we haven't, but it's nice to meet you, Karen."

"Hi, Heather. I sure love the way you and Andrew talk—the English accent and all." Karen turned her gaze back to Allison and smiled. "How do you like Port View High?"

"So far I like it just fine, thanks," Allison replied honestly, then suddenly realized that poor Caroline was being completely ignored. "And perhaps you've also met Caroline," she said. "Being new and all, I wouldn't know."

Karen nodded toward Caroline, who was looking up hopefully. "Yes, I think I've seen you around, Caroline." Then Karen looked to Shirley as if she were ready to move on now.

But Shirley didn't budge. "Karen is a freshman, too, Allison. She's the only freshman to make it on the cheerleading squad."

"Yes," said Karen. "I was pretty lucky."

"So are you all going to the game tonight?" asked Shirley.

"You bet," said Allison. "I've never seen Andrew play before." She grinned over at him. "I wouldn't miss it for anything."

"We're playing a pretty tough team tonight," Andrew said grimly. "So far, they're undefeated. I hope you won't be disappointed."

"Of course she won't be disappointed," Karen injected. "Anyone who's seen you play wouldn't be disappointed, Andrew."

Andrew looked up at Karen. "Thanks."

Karen laid a hand on his shoulder. "And in case I forget," she said in a low voice, "good luck tonight, Andrew. I'll be cheering especially for you."

Allison stared up at Karen, seeing her with new eyes. Karen was very pretty. In fact, she almost seemed to sparkle with prettiness. She reminded Allison of the Blue Fairy in *Pinnocchio*. Her blond hair glistened like spun gold, and her eyes were a bright, shining blue. Even her teeth seemed to shine, white and straight, as she smiled down on Andrew. And he smiled back.

"See you all later," said Karen. Then she turned and walked away, her pleated cheerleader skirt swinging jauntily from side to side. Allison saw Andrew's eyes follow Karen across the cafeteria where she joined her other cheerleader friends. Suddenly, Allison's world seemed to grow dark and cloudy.

Shirley remained by their table with a slightly puzzled expression, also watching Karen as if she didn't quite know what to think. Allison wondered if Shirley had been working on some little plan that had somehow backfired.

"Allison, are you ready to go to gym class?" Shirley asked bluntly.

Allison glanced at her empty plate, then at her watch. "Is it time?"

"Yep," said Andrew, standing. "See you girls later."

Allison dumped her tray with the others, then allowed Shirley to lead her toward the gymnasium and dressing rooms. She stopped by her locker to pick up her gym clothes, and for a pleasant change, Shirley remained quiet. When they reached the dressing room, Shirley finally spoke.

"I think Karen likes Andrew."

Allison nodded glumly. "It seemed that way."

Shirley looked at Allison with renewed interest. "Does that bother you?"

Allison studied Shirley, not liking the curious gleam in her eye. "Of course not. Karen seems like a very nice girl. And she sure is pretty."

"She is, isn't she?" Shirley's voice cheered up. "I want to get to know her. I thought it might not hurt my chances for being a cheerleader next year. She wanted to meet you guys, and I told her I knew you. I guess she mostly wanted to meet Andrew." Shirley frowned for a moment. "But that's okay. I can still be her friend."

Allison bit her lip. Better to keep her mouth shut. If Shirley wanted to buddy up to Karen in order to gain prestige, that was Shirley's problem. Allison had known girls like that in boarding school—girls who thought it wasn't *what* you knew but *who* you knew. Some would stoop pretty low just to get in with the "right" crowd, but in the end they usually paid for it in one way or another. She had also seen Marsha play this way, and it was a game Allison refused to participate in. Friends were not something you used. Friends were for keeps.

Allison liked P.E., and the teacher was young and energetic. While they played soccer, Allison tried to keep a distance between herself and Shirley. It seemed that all Shirley wanted to do was complain, and Allison wanted to play, and play hard. It was a good way to keep from thinking about Andrew.

Unfortunately, Karen was also in P.E. with them, and she was playing on the opposite team. Like Allison, she played competitively. Several times she and Allison went head to head, scrambling for the ball. Under different circumstances Allison would have admired Karen, maybe even sought her out as a friend. But not today. Today Karen was the enemy, and Allison played as if her life depended on it, kicking the ball with every ounce of strength. Finally the teacher blew her whistle and told the girls it was time to shower and get dressed.

"Gosh, Allison," said Karen breathlessly. "You're quite a little fireball!"

Allison pretended to laugh. "Sometimes it's fun to play rough."

"Well, just don't get carried away," Karen warned.

"Same to you," Allison muttered under her breath as she jogged back to the locker room.

She quickly showered and dressed, managing to ignore Shirley the whole time and leave for the next class without her. At least the next class was art, something she liked. After that she could join up with Heather again. And then, at last, they could all go home.

❀

Allison sighed in relief as the last bell of the day finally rang. She and Heather gathered what they needed from their lockers, then trudged out to the parking lot. The fog had lifted, and now the sun was shining brightly.

"Hi, girls," said Andrew as Heather and Allison waited by the jalopy. He opened the door for them. "Game days are the only days I can give you girls a ride home, Allison," he explained as he climbed into the driver's seat. "The rest of the time I have practice after school, but Grace picks up Heather on those days and you can ride with her. Or if you want, there's always the bus—but it does take forever."

Allison just nodded.

"Are you okay, Allison?" Andrew asked.

"Just tired" was all she said.

"Sure, I bet it was a drain. Your first day and everything."

Allison nodded again, trying not to remember how Andrew had looked at Karen.

"How was it having every class with Shirley?" Heather asked.

Allison just groaned.

"When I was a little boy, my father used to say that what doesn't kill you will make you stronger." Andrew looked at her knowingly.

"Then I should be able to sprint a hundred miles and lift a ton," Allison replied with a sad sigh.

"That bad, eh?" Andrew said with a note of sympathy.

Allison swallowed the lump in her throat. If only he knew. Her troubles with Shirley Jenson seemed like nothing. Shirley was a piece of cake compared to the gorgeous Karen Brown. But how could she explain to Andrew, or even Heather, that it was Karen who was making her life perfectly miserable right now?

6

"Are you just about ready?" James called up the stairs. "We should be on our way pretty soon."

Allison stared at herself in the mirror again. Maybe she should have changed her clothes. But then again, she liked this outfit, even though it was the same thing she had worn to school today. Why should it matter when her jacket would just cover it up anyway? Besides, Andrew wouldn't be able to see her sitting up in the stands. Why was she so worried about all of this in the first place?

"Allison?" James called again.

"Coming." She told herself to quit fretting as she ran down the stairs.

"We don't want to miss the kick off."

"What's that?" asked Allison as they got into the car.

James began a long-winded explanation about football as he backed out of the driveway. It sounded a little like soccer, but Allison was unable to follow everything—first down, interception—what difference did it really make?

They picked up Grace, Heather, and Winston. Allison was relieved to end the football lecture and hop in the backseat next to Heather and Winston, but Winston and James began the subject again.

"Heather, do you understand football?" Allison asked.

"A bit. Andrew has tried to explain it to me, and I've gotten so I can imagine all the guys moving up and down the yard lines. But there are a lot of rules, and I must admit it seems just a little silly sometimes."

Allison laughed. "But everyone seems to be very excited about it. I guess I'll have to learn to appreciate it."

Heather smiled. "Perhaps for Andrew's sake . . ."

Allison stared at Heather, trying to understand if there was more to what she was saying. "For Andrew's sake?"

"Yes, he was very excited that you were finally going to see him play, Allison."

"Really?" she asked, her hopes soaring.

"Of course, you silly. You know how much Andrew thinks of you." Heather reached over and squeezed Allison's arm.

Allison wanted to hug Heather and thank her over and over, but instead she just said, "That's nice to know." Heather giggled.

They arrived in plenty of time for the kick off. Grace, James, and Winston sat in the general admission area in the center of the grandstand, while Heather and Allison sat off to one side on the perimeter of the student section. Allison wasn't sure she wanted to sit right in the middle of a bunch of kids she didn't really know yet, and Heather seemed more comfortable along the edge of the boisterous crowd.

"Does Caroline come to the games?" Allison asked as they waited for the game to begin.

"She doesn't care much for football," said Heather. "I've invited her before, but she usually says no. I think she doesn't like to be away from home very much."

"Why is that?"

"Her brother was taken as a prisoner of war in Germany. He never returned with the other soldiers."

"Oh dear," said Allison with a sigh. "I didn't realize that any of our boys were still there."

"You don't hear much about it. But Caroline's parents learned that some U.S. prisoners are still in Siberia."

"Do you think her brother is still alive?"

"Caroline is good at keeping a positive outlook, but I'm not sure what I think. I hope he's okay. Anyway, that's why she worries about her parents."

"So that's why she stays home."

War never seemed to completely go away. Even today she had been warned that the high school still performed regular bomb drills and not to be surprised if they had to duck under their desks at a moment's notice.

Allison looked down to where the bright lights glared on the big green field below them. With its neatly marked white lines, it didn't look all that different from a well-kept soccer field. In the stands kids were calling out to one another, laughing and shouting with anticipation. It was strange to think she might actually get to know them all by name someday.

Everyone seemed happy and excited; even the night air felt as if it were charged with electricity. Allison watched with amusement as the school mascot, dressed as a pirate, leaped around the field in crazy antics. Just behind Allison and Heather the pep band played zippy show tunes. Both football teams were in uniform and down on the field doing warm-up exercises.

"Heather, do you know what Andrew's uniform number is?" Allison asked.

"It's thirty-two. Can you see him?"

"Yes, he's right in the middle. They're doing jumping jacks. They look sort of silly in their knickers and padded shoulders, not to mention their yellow helmets. They remind me of some science-fiction film about creatures from outer space."

Heather laughed. "I suppose so. It's funny hearing you de-

64

scribe it. Grace has gotten so she understands football pretty well, so she usually just tells me what they're doing, the plays they're making, field goals, and stuff like that."

"Maybe we should go sit with Grace and Dad," offered Allison.

"No, this is more fun," Heather said. "Do you see anyone you know?"

"I see some faces that look a teeny bit familiar, and—oh no, there's Shirley. I hope she doesn't come sit with us." Allison looked the other way, hoping to avoid Shirley's eye as well as Heather's frown. She knew that Heather was still trying to be nice to Shirley. "And now I see Karen Brown down on the field with the other cheerleaders."

"Karen seemed nice," said Heather.

Allison bit her lip. "I suppose so. She sure is pretty. . . ."

"Is she a friend of Shirley's?"

"Shirley is hoping she will be." Allison wanted to change the subject. "I'm surprised you're not in the pep band, Heather. Or don't they use flutes?"

"I suppose they do," said Heather. "But I don't think I'd care much for it. They have to march at half time."

"I'll bet you'd do just fine," Allison said.

Heather began to laugh. "I could just imagine me turning left when everyone else turned right and never being able to get back into step. Besides, I prefer orchestra. Hey, I got a letter from John today. You know he's been writing ever since camp, but Grace always had to read his letters to me. Now he's gotten his hands on a Braille typewriter at his college, and I can read them myself."

"That's super, Heather. Was it a romantic letter?"

Heather smiled. "It depends on what you think is romantic."

Just then the announcer began to speak, introducing the

starting lineup of the visiting team. Then when he started to introduce the home team, the Port View fans began to clap and cheer. Allison found herself joining in and liking it. When Andrew's name was announced, she actually put her two fingers in her mouth and let out a loud whistle. It was a trick that her friend Patricia had taught her back at Oakmont Academy and something that Miss Snyder, the boarding school's headmistress, always frowned upon as unladylike.

"Wow, Allison!" said Heather with admiration. "I didn't know you could whistle like that. You'll have to teach me how."

The coin was tossed high in the air, and it was determined that the Port View Pirates would kick off to the visitors.

"Why isn't Andrew playing?" asked Allison with concern as she watched the ball sail through the air toward the visiting team.

"Because he's the quarterback," Heather explained as she listened intently to the announcer. "He plays on the offense team. Since we're kicking off, you see our defense team. When we get the ball, Andrew will go out."

Allison nodded, impressed with how well Heather seemed to understand what was going on only by using her ears. Allison tried to follow what was happening down on the field. It didn't resemble soccer at all. There were several more rules and a lot more stopping and waiting and reorganizing of themselves. She wished they could just get on with it.

"When does Andrew get to play?" she asked after several of these starts and stops.

Just then the students in front of her began to cheer wildly, and the band behind them made lots of noise. Allison looked down at the field but only saw a pile of bodies. The ball was nowhere in sight.

"Right now, I think," Heather said. "I'm guessing that we just got the ball."

Allison watched with wide eyes as both teams switched players. "There he is!" she shrieked. "Andrew is on the field. They're all lining up again. Now that guy in the middle is putting the ball between his legs and throwing it backward. Andrew has it, Heather! He's walking backward, and all of his guys are running all over the place. He's throwing the ball, Heather! He threw it really far down the field—and another one of our guys caught it and he's running, but the other team has almost got him."

Allison stood up and screamed. "Run! Run!" Everyone else was yelling, too. The player made it to the goal posts. "He did it, Heather!" yelled Allison. "He scored! Andrew threw him the ball and then he scored!"

"I know, Allison!" Heather screamed above the rest of the noise. "Isn't it swell?"

Allison whistled loudly, then turned and hugged Heather. "This is the greatest!" she shouted. "I never realized how much I like football."

Heather laughed. "And if you keep it up, you might be able to get a job as a sports commentator!"

Allison laughed, too. "Now they're lining up again. What do they do now?"

"Hopefully they'll kick the ball over the goal post and make an extra point." Even as Heather said the words, the little brown pigskin ball sailed over the goal posts, and the crowd cheered again.

Allison watched Andrew and the others running to the sidelines. It almost seemed as if Andrew was looking for them up in the stands. She was still standing and waved down at him. He didn't wave back, but she thought she saw his eyes light up—or maybe she imagined it—and it made her feel warm in the cool night air. She remembered what Heather had said in the car. Allison glanced down at Karen as the cheerleaders led another victory yell. Sure, Karen was pretty, but perhaps Allison had overreacted today. Andrew wasn't the kind of guy to fall for a pretty face. What Allison and Andrew had was much more than that. At least she hoped so.

By half time the Pirates were leading, twenty to thirteen, most of the points a direct result of Andrew's fine throws. Now Allison knew beyond a shadow of a doubt that she was definitely a football fan!

"Do you want to get any cocoa or anything for half time?" Allison asked. "I'm starting to get a sore throat from yelling so much. I'll have to try to whistle more during the second half."

"I don't think I want to fight the crowd down there, but if you don't mind I'd love something to warm up on," said Heather. "I can save our seats."

"Sure, if you don't mind me leaving you alone," Allison said. "I'd like to stretch my legs a little. I'll hurry back." She trotted down the stairs and toward the concession stand.

"Hi there, Allison!" called Shirley, waving from where the cheerleaders stood. "Come here and meet some of my friends!"

Allison smiled and waved, wishing there were some gracious way to avoid this. But then again, it made no sense to be unfriendly, and she didn't want people to think she was stuck-up.

"Hi, Allison," said Karen. "So what do you think of our little team?"

"I think they're great," Allison said honestly. "And Andrew seems to be having a pretty good night!"

"I'll say," said Karen. "Isn't he something?"

"You know Andrew?" said a tall brunette cheerleader with interest. "I'm Beverly Howard. I don't think I've met you. . . ."

"This is Allison O'Brian," said Karen before Shirley had a

chance to jump in. "Beverly is a sophomore." Karen turned to Beverly. "Today was Allison's first day at Port View. She's good friends with Andrew and Heather—"

"Allison's *my* best friend," interrupted Shirley importantly. She stepped right next to Allison. "We have every class together, don't we, Allison?"

Karen and Beverly both looked from Shirley to Allison. Allison didn't know what to say. "I'm here with Heather," she said lamely. "I just came down for some cocoa. But it was nice to meet you, Beverly." She turned to Karen and smiled. "And nice to see you again." To Shirley she said nothing. "I better get those cocoas. Hope we win!"

The girls told her good-bye, and Allison got in the concession line. *That Shirley Jenson—best friend indeed!* she thought. She knew she had to work on her attitude toward Shirley, but at the moment she was just too steamed. She would have to think about that later.

She carried the hot paper cups of cocoa back into the stands. Now she was almost beginning to see the humorous side of Shirley's little act. It would make a good story to tell Heather, and they could laugh about it together. As she started up the steps, she was actually chuckling to herself, but her laugh disappeared when she saw Shirley waving at her, sitting right next to Heather. Allison took a deep breath. *Forgive and forget*, she told herself as she handed Heather her cocoa.

"I hope it's still hot," Allison said. She glanced at Shirley. "Did you change seats?"

"Yes, I thought you two looked lonely up here."

"No, we're fine," Allison said coolly.

"But you're certainly welcome to join us," said Heather warmly.

"It looks like they're ready to kick off again," said Allison. She sipped her cocoa and looked down at the field, determined that Shirley not ruin this for her. "The other team is kicking to us this time, Heather. Do you think Andrew will catch it?"

"Probably not," Heather said. "But you never know."

By the last part of the fourth quarter the other team had made quite a comeback, and now the Pirates were down by a few points.

"Oh dear," Shirley moaned. "I think we're going to lose."

"Don't say that!" Allison said. "We still have two minutes to make a goal."

"That's right," Heather added. "We won't give up hope!"

"Well, it doesn't look very hopeful to me," Shirley muttered.

Allison blocked Shirley's negative words out and focused down on the team. "Come on, you guys, you can do it!" she yelled along with the rest of the crowd as they started another play. But Andrew only threw a short pass, and they didn't move very far down the field.

The clock steadily ticked away, and it was looking less hopeful all the time. Both Allison and Heather were standing now, along with everyone else in the student section. Allison quickly glanced at Shirley, then noticed with irritation that Shirley was actually sitting and nonchalantly filing her nails. It figured!

Allison looked down on the field again. The team was lined up and ready to give it another shot. "Come on, Andrew," she whispered. "You can do this." Her teeth were clenched, and every muscle in her body felt tense, as if it might somehow help their team.

The fans were yelling now—encouraging them to make a goal. The guy in the middle, whom Allison now knew was called the center, hiked the ball to Andrew. As usual, Andrew stepped back, getting ready to pass. Even though Andrew's teammates were spreading out all over the field, the other team's defense seemed to be all over them. No one was open!

Suddenly, Andrew acted like he'd thrown the ball and began

to run, but Allison could see that he had only tucked it under his arm. The crowd went wild! Andrew ran toward the left where the field was open. Soon there were several players from the opposite team chasing him, but Andrew kept running. He was fast—his knees flying high in the air as players dove after him. Finally, just when Allison was sure she could stand the tension no longer, Andrew crossed the goal line, and the crowd went absolutely bananas! Allison too. She leaped into the air and hugged Heather.

"He did it! Andrew did it!" she cried. "He ran it all the way, Heather! It was amazing!" The buzzer sounded and the scoreboard changed. "We won!" Allison screamed.

"I know!" said Heather. "Isn't it great?"

"Come on," Allison said. "Let's go down there." She grabbed Heather's hand and led her down the steps, careful not to go too fast. They joined the rest of the students down on the field. Everyone was laughing and cheering and recounting Andrew's amazing run.

"Hi, Allison!" Karen called. "Wasn't that super? Hey, do you and Heather want to join us at Wally's to celebrate? It's a burger joint in town."

"I don't know," said Allison, turning to Heather. "What do you think, Heather?"

"It sounds like fun. Maybe we could get Andrew to take us."

"Of course," Beverly said as she stepped up. "By all means, bring Andrew. We'll all want to congratulate him! Come on, you two, it'll be fun!"

"Of course we'll come," Shirley said, stepping up beside Heather. "Right, Heather?"

"Sure," said Heather. She was still holding Allison's sleeve. She turned and said quietly, "Allison, do you think Grace and your dad will mind?"

"I don't think so. After all, we'll be with Andrew. The question is, will Andrew mind?" whispered Allison. She led Heather to Grace and James where they stood by the fence. Winston was walking shyly over to where Andrew was being mobbed by fans.

"Hey, you guys," Andrew yelled as he broke away from the crowd and ran to join them, swooping up Winston on his way. "Wasn't that something!"

"I'll say!" James exclaimed. "No wonder everyone in town is talking about Port View's star quarterback!"

Andrew looked slightly embarrassed. "I just happened to be in the right place at the right time." He turned to Allison with bright eyes and ruddy cheeks. "So, Al, how do you like football?"

"I love it!"

He grinned. "Bully for you."

Allison warmed at the odd-sounding British praise. She knew Andrew reserved such compliments for a very select few.

"Andrew, some girls invited us to join them at Wally's," said Heather. "We thought it might be fun, but of course we'd need someone to drive. . . ." She smiled sweetly in her brother's direction.

"I wouldn't mind chomping down on a Wally burger myself," said Andrew. "Is that all right with you two?" He looked at James and Grace.

"It's fine with me, Andrew," Grace said. "Just don't stay out too late."

"You don't expect me to tell the star quarterback no, do you?" James teased.

"I wanna go, too," Winston declared.

"I think not," said Grace. She wrapped an arm around his shoulder. "I need you to go home with me." Winston made a twisted face, and Allison could tell he was feeling left out.

"Hi there!" Shirley called, waving frantically at their group. "Hi, Mr. O'Brian. Hi, Grace." She waved up to the stands. "There's Mommy and Daddy, Mr. O'Brian. They're waving at you."

James turned and waved at a couple standing up in the grandstand. Allison stared up at Shirley's parents. Mrs. Jenson wore a fur coat and was tugging on Mr. Jenson's arm as if she was ready to go.

"I told them that I would get a ride home with you guys," said Shirley brightly. "That is if we're all still going to Wally's to celebrate." She turned to Andrew. "You were brilliant tonight, Andrew. I just knew that if anyone could save the day, it would be you!"

Allison tried not to groan as she recalled Shirley's dismal predictions. But Andrew, almost as gracious as Heather, simply smiled. "It'll take me about twenty minutes to shower and change. Do you girls mind waiting?"

"Not at all," Shirley gushed.

"Well, Andrew," James said. "Looks like you've got your hands full tonight with three beautiful young women." He put his hand on Allison's shoulder. "Keep in mind, one of them is mighty important to me, and you take special care, now."

"You can count on that, sir."

Andrew didn't keep them waiting for long. It was a tight squeeze with four in the jalopy, but Heather made sure that Shirley didn't get to sit next to Andrew. Allison was trying to get Heather to slip in first, but at the last minute Heather gently pushed Allison ahead of her. Allison didn't mind sitting so close to Andrew, but she had a hard time thinking of anything to say. They ended up singing the team fight song over and over until Allison knew all the words, and soon they were laughing and walking down the sidewalk toward a well-lit restaurant on Main Street where a neon light flashed the diner's name.

The diner was crowded, and all the tables appeared to be taken. As they waited at the door, Andrew pointed out that Wally's had been recently remodeled by Wally McGillicudy with all the latest in restaurant equipment. Wally had saved every penny he'd earned while serving in the Pacific as a Navy cook during the war. He had come back and revamped the family business, pumping new life into it. Now this was the favorite spot of all the students at Port View High, and Wally treated all the kids like family.

Allison admired the shiny black-and-white-checkerboard tile floor. The round barstools and comfy-looking booths were covered in deep red vinyl and trimmed in stainless steel. The plastic-covered tabletops had a swirly pattern with red and black and white, and the whole place felt bright and new and modern to her. Suddenly, it seemed very glamorous and fun to be going out with friends after the big football game—and with the star quarterback!

A colorfully lit jukebox was playing a Sammy Kaye swing number, and several couples were dancing in a space hardly big enough to turn in.

"Hey, it's Andrew Amberwell," cried Beverly as she dashed over to them. "Come on, Andrew, we can squeeze one more into our table!" She pulled him by the arm, and he looked helplessly back to the three girls.

"Go ahead, Andrew," Allison said to her own amazement. "You're probably starving. We'll get a table as soon as there's room."

"Are there any tables?" Heather asked quietly.

"Not right now."

"This is just great," Shirley said sarcastically.

"Maybe you can join someone else," said Allison hopefully.

Shirley looked around. "Maybe I can," she huffed. She began

wandering from table to table, looking to squeeze in and reminding Allison of a beggar.

"Hey, there are two people leaving the counter," said Allison. "Do you mind sitting on a stool?"

"Not at all," said Heather. "What about Shirley?"

"I think she can take care of herself," Allison said as she led Heather to the stools.

"Hi, ladies," said a round man with a smooth bald head and a tattoo of a naval ship on his arm. "I'm Wally. What can I get for you?"

"I'd like a chocolate shake and some French fries, please," Allison said. She had barely glanced at the menu but didn't want to miss out on a chance to order when the place was so busy.

"I'd like the same, please," said Heather as she fingered the menu without even looking.

Wally studied Heather's eyes for a long moment, as if he suspected that something was amiss. Then he nodded and smiled. "Coming right up, ladies."

Allison decided that she liked Wally's, and she liked Wally. She glanced over to see how Andrew was faring. He was grinning and talking, surrounded by pretty cheerleaders who seemed to hang upon his every word. It figured. Well, it was probably her own fault. She had told Andrew to join them, and she had wanted to come here tonight.

"Here you go, ladies," said Wally with a smile. "I don't think I've seen you two around, but I thought I noticed you come in with Andrew Amberwell, the local football hero." Wally grinned.

"Yes," explained Heather. "Andrew's my brother. My name is Heather Amberwell, and this is Allison O'Brian. She's sort of new in town."

"Hey, are you James O'Brian's little gal?" asked Wally.

Allison smiled. "Yes, that's my dad."

"I went to school with him. I was so pleased to hear about him being okay and being back in town, and to think he has a daughter to boot. You two ladies will have to excuse me. I've got lots to do tonight, but it was real nice meeting you both. Hope you'll make my place your place."

"We will," said Heather with a smile, and Allison nodded as she sipped her shake.

After a while Allison and Heather were nearly finished, but it seemed that Andrew was still the life of the party at the crowded corner table. To Allison's dismay, Shirley had managed to squeeze in with them. Allison suspected that Karen's earlier invitation to join them at Wally's tonight was just a cover-up to get Andrew here. Allison should have known better, but it still hurt a little. What looked worse, though, was seeing Karen at the same table with Andrew. As much as Allison hated to admit, she admired Karen and thought she seemed like a fun person. Unfortunately, Andrew seemed to think so, too.

"So," Heather said as if reading Allison's mind. "Do you wish we hadn't come?"

"No," Allison said slowly. "Not exactly. But it didn't turn out like I thought it would. I guess I still have a lot to learn about public school and friends, and guys and girls, and everything."

Heather chuckled. "Well, you can't expect to figure it all out on your first day."

Allison laughed. "That's right. I almost forgot. This is still my first day, isn't it? I don't know whether to be relieved or terrified."

"Do you think Andrew will be ready to go soon?" Heather asked in a tired voice.

Now Allison allowed herself to turn around and look directly at the corner booth. Andrew was wedged between Beverly and Karen, and Karen was talking quietly to him with sparkling blue eyes. Allison couldn't see Andrew's face, but he seemed to be listening intently. "I . . . I don't think Andrew's quite ready to go yet," said Allison in a faltering voice.

"Is something wrong, Allison? Are you okay?"

Allison's stomach twisted. "Maybe it wasn't smart to eat French fries and a milk shake this late at night." She turned away and sighed. No, things had definitely not turned out the way she had thought they would.

7

As tired as she was, Allison had a hard time falling asleep. She kept envisioning Andrew and Karen sitting so cozily in the booth. Try as she might, she couldn't stop the waves of jealousy as they washed over her like the surf pounding the beach. Even after she finally drifted into a fitful slumber, she was haunted by a crazy dream where Karen, Beverly, and Shirley, all dressed in strange-looking cheerleader outfits, had chased Andrew down the football field. Meanwhile, Allison stood in the stands watching helplessly. She awoke in frustration and promised herself *never* to eat French fries and milk shakes late at night again. But in the morning light, as much as she hated to admit it, Allison knew it had more to do with her feelings toward Andrew than it had to do with French fries.

After breakfast James invited Allison to take a ride. They drove silently for a while. Allison just looked out the window, enjoying the reds and golds of the fall foliage set against the clear blue sky. It felt relaxed and comforting to be with her dad. She sighed and told herself to forget her silly worries about Andrew and to simply enjoy this time with her father instead.

"You're awful quiet this morning," James said. "Did everything go okay last night?"

"I guess so." Allison forced a smile to her lips.

"It's probably not easy being the new kid on the block. I'm sure it will take you some time to adjust, to make new friends and all." He paused, frowning slightly as he glanced at her. "You're not sorry you came out here to live, are you, Allison?"

"No!" she exclaimed in surprise. "No, of course not, Dad. I wouldn't change that for anything."

James sighed in relief. "Thank goodness. I don't know what I'd do if you decided you didn't like it here."

"Don't worry, Dad. I love it here. This feels more like home to me than anything I've ever known. Please, don't ever think that I'm not happy here. It's just kind of hard trying to figure everything out with friends and school."

"That's perfectly understandable, Allison. And I'm sure in no time you'll be as happy as a clam at Port View."

Allison nodded, not quite as sure as her father but not wanting to let on otherwise. At that moment her attention was turned to her surroundings as James pulled into what looked like an airport. "Where are we, Dad?"

James laughed. "Don't worry. I'm not shipping you off anywhere. I just want to show you something and have you meet a good friend of mine."

He parked the car, and they got out and walked over to a small office situated by a long hangar.

"Hi there, Jamie," called a weathered old man who reminded Allison a little of Grandpa. In fact, just seeing him made a lump grow in her throat as she remembered the feel of Grandpa's callused hand holding hers.

"Morning, Mac," James said, extending his hand in greeting.

"And who's this young lady you've with you today?"

"This is my Allison, the one I've been telling you about. And, Allison, this is my friend Orvil MacPhearson."

The old man's blue eyes twinkled. "I figured as much, Jamie. She looks a wee bit like you, only a lot prettier. Reminds me of her grandmother."

Allison blushed and shook his hand. "Nice to meet you, Mr. MacPhearson."

"You better call me Mac, Allison. All my friends do." He squinted up at the sky. "Perfect day, Jamie. You ready to go up?"

"Up?" asked Allison.

"I forgot to mention that I've been taking flying lessons from Mac." James cleared his throat. "I've . . . uh . . . been wanting to get my pilot's license, Allison."

"And not too far away from it, either," added Mac.

Allison looked at her dad with complete astonishment. "Your pilot's license? That's swell, but when did all this start?"

Mac chuckled. "I think it started when he was about your age, Allison."

James rubbed his chin. "I suppose so, but I've gotten a lot more serious about it in the last few months. It's something I had always wanted to do but never got the opportunity to really go after it. The thing is," he looked at Allison with a creased brow, "I haven't been able to bring myself to tell Grace about it. And so, for now, you'll have to help keep my secret."

Allison shook her head. "I don't know, Dad. I'm not very good at keeping my mouth shut."

James frowned. "Maybe I shouldn't have brought you out here. . . ."

Allison looked up at him with a sly grin. "I'll promise to keep your secret, but only if you take me up with you."

Mac hooted. "A girl after my own heart! Well, what are we waiting for?" Mac looked over his shoulder to where a man in greasy overalls was leaning against the hangar with a push broom in one hand and a cigarette in the other. "Mind the office for me while we're up there, Larry," called Mac. "And don't you wear yourself out working too hard." Mac shook his head and spoke quietly. "That Larry Burns—he worked here during the war when the pickin's was slim, but he's lazier than all get-out."

Within moments Allison had climbed into the cramped backseat of the tiny Piper airplane and buckled up. James, with Mac's supervision, inspected wheels, fuel tanks, flaps, propeller blades, and everything on the outside of the plane. Then they both climbed in, and he began to check the controls and dials. Soon they were slowly taxiing out to the single airstrip that dominated the airfield.

Allison kept quiet, watching as her father prepared to take off. He looked completely at ease behind the stick, and so far Mac hadn't said a word, but Allison suspected he would jump right in if anything wasn't right. James poised the plane at the end of the runway, then turned to look at Allison.

"You all buckled up and absolutely sure that you still want to go—with me at the stick?" he asked with lifted brows.

"You bet! And if we crash, we crash together."

Mac laughed, but James just groaned. "What a thing to say, Allison Mercury."

"Sorry, Dad, I was just joking. You know, like how you tell an actor to break a leg. Go ahead and take off. I'm fine."

James turned back around and focused his attention on the controls in the cockpit. Soon they were speeding down the runway, and Allison watched as James confidently pulled the stick firmly back and they began to lift up, then soar quickly into the sky. Allison loved the feeling of being pulled back in her seat and flying straight up into the sky at the same time. She could feel an enormous grin spreading across her face.

Mac turned back to check on her. "Looks like you're enjoying yourself, little lady."

Allison nodded. "I absolutely love it! The first time I ever flew was in a little plane a lot like this. It was just last summer, right after camp. I was with Marsha, and I must admit I was a little scared at first, but then I loved it. Oh, Dad, I wish I could learn to fly, too!"

James smiled as he banked the plane to the right and began heading toward the ocean. "Maybe it's something in our blood. With my father it was boats, with us it's planes."

"I like boats, too," said Allison. "But if I had to choose, I'm sure I'd go with airplanes."

"Good for you, lassie," said Mac. "I'd rather be a bird than a fish any day."

"Mac's been flying since World War I," James explained. "He used to live in Canada. He even trained RAF pilots for the last war. You probably know that RAF stands for Royal Air Force—the British flying arm. Grace's husband was an RAF pilot. If I'd had more time to think before I enlisted, I'm sure I would have tried to figure out a way to get up in the air. Instead, I found myself hoofing it around in Europe."

"Probably just as well, Jamie," said Mac sadly. "We lost a lot of good boys in the air over there. You were safer on the ground."

James banked another right-hand turn, and now they were flying directly over the ocean. "See those fishing boats down there, Allison?"

"Yes, they look so tiny. Hey, can we see our house from up here?"

"Of course. We'll fly over it in just a couple minutes."

Allison watched the shoreline where the blue of the ocean

met a thin strip of sand, and then rocks jutted out, cutting into the surf. It looked vaguely familiar. "I see the lighthouse!" she yelled, pointing. "So that must be our house right there. The roof blends so well with the rocks, it's hard to spot it at first. And there's Grace's house. I almost didn't recognize it."

They flew a wide circle over the area where they lived, and Allison spotted the red jalopy in Grace's driveway. She wondered if Andrew was home, then silently scolded herself for even thinking about him. After last night she had been trying to convince herself that she was only a friend to Andrew. Nothing more. He was probably nice to her simply because she was Heather's best friend, and everyone knew how deep Andrew's loyalty was with his sister. Besides, Andrew could have his pick of all the girls in school, and with beauties like Karen and Beverly around, Allison didn't have a chance. No, she was determined not to think about him anymore.

James took off and landed four times for practice before they finally called it quits. Each time went perfectly, without a single hitch. Finally, he taxied the plane back to the hangar, where they all climbed out. James pulled out a small brown flight log and began to write in his time, then Mac signed his name by it.

"You did great, Dad. How long will it be until you have your license?"

James did a little figuring. "Not long. It looks like I only need about eight more hours, then I can solo. Right, Mac?"

"That's right. And you're ready for it, Jamie. If you get those eight hours in this week, you could be soloing by next Saturday."

"Really?" exclaimed Allison. "That's swell. Then you could probably take me up, and *I* could sit in the copilot's seat, and—"

"Wait, wait," said James, holding up his hands but grinning just the same. "I think I know where this is going."

"Well, you do want me to keep your secret, don't you?"

"This smells like blackmail, Allison."

Mac laughed and slapped Allison on the back. "Not blackmail, Jamie. Just a smart little lassie. And she's right, once you have your license you can take her up with you, just the two of you."

"No excuses, Dad."

"I think I've created a monster," he said dramatically.

"That's right. A flying monster," Allison teased. "And right now this monster is getting hungry."

"Well, Mac, I guess I better go feed the lady. I'll call to schedule those eight hours with you later. Thanks for everything."

"Yeah, thanks, Mac," said Allison. "It was a pleasure meeting you."

"And you, too, Allison," Mac said with a grin. "I expect I'll be seeing a lot more of you."

"You can count on it." Allison winked at him.

"Well, I can see that I've really left myself wide open with this flying thing," James said as he drove away from the airport.

Allison smiled smugly. "I guess so, but I kind of like this arrangement. Where are we heading now?"

"I needed to run some errands in Port View. Maybe we can eat lunch at Wally's, unless you're tired of it after last night."

"No, of course not. I liked it a lot, and Wally is real nice. He even remembered you from school."

"He did? I haven't seen Wally in years. I don't think he ever married, but then he was always real devoted to his family's business. Apparently, he still is."

"Yes, Andrew told us how he's turned the place around with money he saved up while he was in the service during the war."

"I'm sure he's made his parents real proud."

Something about James' face troubled Allison, then she remembered the problems that he had had with Grandpa all those years. It must still be hard on him, especially with Grandpa gone.

"I think Grandpa would be proud of you right now," Allison said quietly.

James glanced at her quickly. "You think so?"

"Yep. The way you flew that plane today, and the way you stuck with your art and are selling your paintings now. Not to mention working with Mr. Jenson in the shipping business."

James shook his head. "I sure wish he were still around to tell me what to do about this shipping business. The Jensons have some different ideas about things, and I'm just not sure what your grandpa would think about all their plans."

"It must be hard being partnered with the Jensons," Allison said with true sympathy.

"Probably not any harder than having Shirley acting like she's your best friend."

Allison groaned. "And I just remembered we have to go to dinner at their house tonight."

"Yes, the official welcome for you. Sorry to put you through this."

"I can handle it, Dad. I can do it for you."

"Thanks, Allison. I appreciate it." James smiled warmly as he reached over to squeeze Allison's hand.

"Do the Jensons know all about me?"

"What do you mean?"

"I mean, do they know about Marsha?" Allison asked hesitantly.

"Well, your grandfather was never very pleased about my marriage to Marsha. For so many years he acted like I was dead, so I doubt if he ever told anyone about it. But it's possible that Mother might have mentioned it to Bea. I'm really not sure, Allison. But remember, my lips are sealed."

Allison sighed. "Good."

Wally greeted them warmly and seated them in a booth by the window. The place wasn't nearly so crowded today, but it still seemed busy enough. From the jukebox Dean Martin crooned a love song that had been popular during the war.

"I really like Mac," Allison said as she absently perused the menu.

"I'd say the feeling was mutual," James said with a grin. "I think I'm going to have to keep my eye on you, Allison Mercury. You seem to have a way about you that charms the fellows."

Allison rolled her eyes at him. "Just the old men, you mean."

"If only it were so. Well, I don't know about you, but I think I'll have the blue plate special."

A waitress who looked a lot like Wally, minus the tattoo, came and took their order. She smiled brightly at James as if she knew him from somewhere. He smiled politely back and thanked her.

"Looks like I'm not the only one who can turn a head," Allison teased.

"That's Wally's sister, Vera," he whispered. "She was a year or two behind me in school. And like Wally, I don't think she ever married."

"I see," Allison said. "She has probably heard that you're a somewhat-eligible bachelor since you and Grace haven't made any sort of official engagement announcement."

James looked down at his hands. "That's right, we haven't."

"Are you going to?" Allison asked.

"I suppose so. I mean, of course, eventually. I'm just not sure when."

86

"You mean like *before* or *after* you tell her about the pilot's license?"

James looked up with a creased brow. He reminded Allison of a little boy who had just gotten caught with his hand in the cookie jar. "I know it was probably stupid and selfish of me—"

"No, Dad," Allison interrupted. "Not at all. I'm sorry, I didn't mean to suggest anything like that. Actually, I think it's really great what you're doing."

His eyes lit up. "Really?" He sighed and looked out the window. "You know, Allison, I used to watch planes flying overhead while I was staying out at the lighthouse. And they seemed so—so free. As you can imagine, I felt trapped there, imprisoned on my little island. I didn't know what else to do, but I promised myself that if things ever got straightened out, I would learn to fly."

Allison reached over and laid her hand on his. "The thing I don't really understand is why does it need to be a secret?"

"Here you go," said Vera as she set their plates down, taking special care to arrange James' just right. "Now, can I get you anything else?"

"This looks fine, Vera," he replied. "Thanks."

Her already ruddy cheeks blushed an even darker red. "No problem, James. You just holler if you need anything else."

He waited until Vera was out of earshot before continuing quietly. "I don't know how Grace would react to my desire to fly. Since her first husband was a pilot—"

"Oh," Allison said as realization dawned on her. "Now I get it. She would probably worry about you. I guess that makes sense, but have you talked to her about it?"

"I told her last summer that I had always dreamed of being a pilot. She let me know in no uncertain terms how much that idea didn't appeal to her."

"That doesn't sound like Grace." Allison frowned.

"That's what I thought, too, but this happens to be one area that Grace feels very strongly about. All I know is that when I do tell her, I will have to break it very gently, and even then I better be ready for some fallout."

"Serious fallout?"

James shrugged his shoulders. "I don't know how serious." He glanced over at Vera, who was vigorously scrubbing the counter and watching them from the corner of her eye. "But it wouldn't surprise me if someone like Vera threw a celebration party."

"Oh, Dad," said Allison. "It couldn't be that bad. Grace is a reasonable woman."

"I hope so, Allison. In the meantime, please don't breathe a word of this to her."

"Loose lips sink ships," Allison said, remembering how this little saying used to pop up in all sorts of places during the war as a reminder not to let any national security information leak out. Not that she had ever known anything worth repeating.

After James had completed the rest of his errands, they went home. Allison decided to make the most of this warm fall day by taking a walk on the beach. Perhaps it would be wise to clear her head a bit before they went to the Jensons' for dinner.

She walked for a while, finally settling on a big piece of driftwood away from the surf. She sat and looked out across the ocean. It was bluer than blue today, and the breeze barely ruffled the air. The sky was still cloudless, and it was hard to determine where the line on the horizon met the sea. Allison breathed deeply of the fresh air. She shook her head as she recalled how her father had asked her this morning if she was still happy that she'd come here. Just because she was moping about Andrew, he'd actually thought it had something to do with living here. Well, she would just have to watch herself on that account. For truly, there was no place on earth that she would rather be!

She closed her eyes and thanked God once again for bringing her here. She also asked God to help her not to pine away over Andrew. Then she took off her shoes and socks, rolled up her pants, and went wading in the ice-cold ocean until her toes were numb and slightly blue.

"Hey there!" called a familiar voice.

Allison looked up to see Andrew walking toward her. Her first response was to rejoice, then she reminded herself of her earlier resolve to expect nothing more than casual friendship.

"Hi, Andrew," she called as she scooped up her shoes and socks and walked over to meet him. "What are you up to?"

"Just out enjoying the weather. Isn't it great?"

She nodded. "Not too many days left like this, I'd imagine."

"You might be surprised. We get a nice balmy day every once in a while."

"Really? I guess it's a little milder here than on the East Coast."

"I was about to take a walk," said Andrew. "Want to come along?"

Part of Allison, the sensible part, wanted to say, "No, I've already taken a walk, thank you very much," but before she could even form the words, she said, "Sure, why not?"

"I felt sort of bad last night," Andrew began. "I didn't realize that I wouldn't be sitting with you and Heather at Wally's. I felt like I abandoned you."

Allison looked up at him in surprise. So he *had* cared. "Oh, that's okay, Andrew. It was so crowded, and we knew you were hungry—"

"I know, but I felt like a bit of a heel."

Allison suppressed a smile. "Well, I guess that's because you're such a gentleman."

Andrew laughed. "I don't know about that." He picked up

a rock and chucked it into the sea. "So you really liked the game last night?"

"I suppose it was okay," she replied flatly, deciding to play coy.

"I thought you *really* liked it." Andrew said, peering down at her with piercing green eyes and a furrowed brow.

She laughed. "Of course I liked it, you big ninny. I just figured you were fishing for more compliments, and it seemed like you were getting plenty last night."

He cocked his head slightly. "So that *did* bother you?"

"I didn't say it bothered me. Why should it bother me if a bunch of silly cheerleaders want to get all gaga over you. That's *their* problem, not mine."

Andrew threw back his head and laughed, and soon Allison was laughing, too. The next thing she knew, they were having a rock throwing contest, which, of course, he won.

"You do throw pretty well for a girl."

"And you throw pretty well for a boy," she teased. "Now let's see how fast you can run to the big rock up there. Ready, set—" Then Allison took off without even saying go.

"Hey, no fair," Andrew yelled, but he caught up and passed her just before they reached the rock.

"You run pretty well for a boy," Allison said breathlessly.

Andrew smiled, barely out of breath. "Thanks."

They walked slowly back, pausing now and then to throw rocks out into the ocean. Allison watched as a sea gull swept down low in front of them, then expertly swooped high into the air. It reminded her of an expert aviator.

"You'll never believe what I did today," she said without thinking.

"What?" asked Andrew with obvious curiosity.

Suddenly, she remembered the secret. "Oh, uh, nothing much really."

"What was it?" Andrew had stopped walking now. "Tell me."

"Oh, it was really nothing." Allison looked away, trying to think of something else to say that might distract him.

"Come on, Allison," he pleaded. "You can't start something and not finish it."

She pressed her lips together and thought. She had promised her dad that she wouldn't tell Grace—not Andrew. "Well, if I tell you, I'll have to swear you to secrecy."

"This is sounding pretty interesting."

"I mean it, Andrew. I won't tell you unless you can promise to keep this a secret. You can't even tell Heather, and most of all, not Grace."

He held up his hand as if taking an oath. "I promise to keep the secret. Now, tell me what this is all about."

"I went flying today."

"Flying?"

"Yes, in an airplane. Four times, up and down. And it was fantastic, Andrew."

Andrew's face was clearly confused. "You went flying today? In an airplane? How?"

"Okay, but remember your promise." She looked at him sternly then continued. "My dad is getting his pilot's license. It's something he's always wanted to do, and he's doing it. Isn't that swell?"

"Yeah, it's great. But why the secrecy?"

"Well, he's worried about what Grace will think."

Andrew nodded as if seeing the light. "Of course. Grace hates planes and flying. She would have an absolute fit."

"Exactly. So poor Dad has to think of some way to gently break the news to her."

"That'll be tough. But tell me more. You went up four times?"

"Yes, and by next weekend, Dad will have enough hours to go up solo. After he gets licensed he can take me up, and I can copilot."

"That's great, Allison." Andrew smiled dreamily. "I've always wanted to fly. I wish I could go up, too."

"Well, maybe we can work something out, but only if you keep your promise. Understand?"

Andrew nodded. "You bet. Wild horses won't be able to drag it from me."

Allison noticed the sun was sinking lower in the sky. "Do you have on a watch, Andrew?"

"Yeah, it's almost five—"

"Yikes, I better skedaddle. We have to go to the Jensons' for dinner tonight."

"That should be fun," Andrew teased with a smirk. "Shirley seems to think you are her new best friend."

"Ugh, don't remind me. I promised Dad to be on my best behavior tonight. It'll be a challenge." She looked Andrew straight in the eye. "Now, remember your promise, Andrew. Please don't tell. I'm trusting you."

Andrew smiled reassuringly. "My promise is good, Allison. You can trust me."

"Thanks. I'll see you." Allison began to run toward the steps that led up to the house.

"See you!" Andrew called.

Suddenly, Allison felt as if she were flying again, but this time without the aid of an airplane. What she and Andrew had *was* special. She just knew it! As she climbed the steps, she felt a little guilty about spilling the beans to him about her dad's flying lessons, but then she knew she could trust Andrew. She was certain of it. Besides, it was so delicious to share a secret with him. Surely Dad would understand that.

8

"Come in, come in," said Hal Jenson as he met James and Allison at the front door. "Let me take your coats. Marge is in the kitchen, and Shirley is still in her room." He led them to a small living room, where they all sat down.

Allison tried not to stare at the strangely furnished room as James and Mr. Jenson made small talk. The decor reminded Allison of Marsha's taste, but somehow this was even more garish. Everything in the room seemed to be either black or red or white. Allison felt slightly out of place in her mossy green tweed skirt and sweater; in fact, a jester's costume would have been more appropriate. She was seated in a glossy black high-backed chair, but the rest of the furniture looked equally uncomfortable. It was all very modern and stiff and nothing like the comforting furnishings in Grandpa's house. Allison wondered if Mrs. Jenson had picked it all out, or if they had actually hired an interior decorator.

"Good evening," said Shirley in a formal voice. Allison looked up to see Shirley wearing a black-and-white-spotted party dress. No surprises there, Shirley fit in perfectly with the bold decor.

"Hi, Shirley," said Allison politely. "How are you?"

"Fine, I guess." Shirley yawned, not even bothering to cover her mouth, then flopped down on the shiny red sofa.

"Does Mrs. Jenson need any help in the kitchen?" Allison aimed this more at Mr. Jenson than Shirley.

"No, I don't think so," said Mr. Jenson with a small smile.

Shirley laughed. "No, we definitely do not want to go in there right now. Mother doesn't especially enjoy being in the kitchen, and she can get a little edgy. Do you want to see my room, Allison?"

"Sure." Allison was curious about what Shirley's room would look like. It couldn't be any worse than this one.

"I didn't realize we needed to dress up tonight," said Allison as she followed Shirley to her room.

"Oh, this old thing," said Shirley, looking down at her dress. "This isn't anything special." She opened a door, and Allison walked into a room that was very pink.

Allison swallowed and smiled. "This is nice, Shirley." It wasn't exactly the truth, but she couldn't think of anything else to say. Maybe it was just a little pink lie.

"Thanks," said Shirley as she flopped down on the canopy bed. "Have a seat."

Allison sat down on a pink slip-covered chair and looked around. The bedspread and canopy were pink, the rug was pink, even the walls were pink. "You must like pink," Allison said weakly.

"It's okay. All this stuff is from my room in California. I've been thinking about changing it, but my mom said not this year. So what did you do today?"

Allison thought for a moment. Because of her promise, she didn't want to mention flying and certainly not her wonderful walk on the beach with Andrew. "Not much, I guess," she finally answered. "I had lunch in Port View with my dad, then I took a walk on the beach."

"Pretty boring stuff," Shirley said. "There's not much to do around here."

"I think there is," said Allison. "I really like it here."

Shirley sniffed. "I guess if you're not used to much action, it's okay."

Allison nodded, unable to think of anything to say. Shirley wasn't much fun to talk with. "Do you like music?" she asked as she spied a phonograph and stack of records.

"Yeah, it's okay." But Shirley made no move to put on any records.

"So what do you do for fun?" asked Allison.

"Not much. At least not around here." Shirley flopped back against the bed dramatically and sighed. "I used to go shopping a lot when we lived in California."

Allison nodded again as she began to absently tap her toe, wondering if every second spent with Shirley really equaled an hour. What would Heather do if she were here? Of course, Heather would think of something cheerful to talk about, something that would interest someone like Shirley.

"Wasn't that a fun football game last night?" Allison tried.

Shirley sat up. "Yeah, it was pretty good. Andrew is so great. Everyone at Wally's was talking about him last night. Karen thinks he's really something."

"I noticed that you finally got to sit at the table with them," Allison said, trying not to sound as jealous as she had felt last night.

"Yeah, I really like Karen and the others. I think in time I'll get to be good friends with them. It will be a lot more fun to live here once I get some *good* friends."

Allison wondered what that made her but didn't really care. She'd just as soon not be classified as one of Shirley's "good friends." "It is hard moving to a new place, but I think everyone seems pretty friendly."

Shirley didn't say anything. After a long, painful silence, they heard Mr. Jenson calling them for dinner. Allison popped up, relieved to escape moody Shirley and her painfully pink room.

The dining room was very much like the living room, except the red was absent. Everything was black or white, very formal and cold.

"Marge," James said to a woman who looked like an older version of Shirley, only harsher and with deep frown lines creased into her forehead. "This is my daughter, Allison. I don't think you've actually met."

"Nice to meet you, Allison," Mrs. Jenson said with what Allison supposed was a smile. "Please be seated, everyone."

They were quickly seated and Allison waited for the blessing, but Mr. Jenson immediately began carving what looked like a very well-done roast. Shirley passed her the potatoes, and Allison spooned out a very stiff dollop that landed on her plate with a loud *whack*. She felt her cheeks grow warm and sensed Mrs. Jenson's eyes upon her.

"This looks very good, Marge," James said. Allison knew he was trying hard to be friendly.

"I've been telling Hal that we really need to get a cook," she said curtly. "Especially considering there're no good restaurants around here. Seven days a week is a lot of cooking, and I don't much care for it." This comment seemed directed like a bullet at Mr. Jenson. Allison felt badly for him as he looked down at his plate.

"I'm sure it shouldn't be too hard to find someone," James said. "Maybe even for just a few days a week. Perhaps I could ask Muriel to recommend someone."

"That would be nice," murmured Mr. Jenson.

Allison thought it would probably be very nice for *everyone* as she took a bite of the tasteless, overcooked peas that were the color of old seaweed.

"Yes, that would be very nice," agreed Mrs. Jenson in an acidic tone. "In fact, I may just try to lure Muriel away from you."

James smiled. "That wouldn't be easily done."

"That's right," Hal said. "Besides, James needs a cook. Being a single man and all."

Mrs. Jenson frowned at her husband. "And are you suggesting that since I'm a woman I shouldn't need a cook?"

"No, dear," Mr. Jenson said soothingly. "I only meant that James and Allison must appreciate having Muriel."

"A lot of people have cooks," Allison offered, hoping to make peace. She was remembering Marsha's cook in Beverly Hills, but she didn't want to mention anything to do with Marsha. Instead she said, "Even my grandmother has a cook."

Mrs. Jenson looked at Allison with interest. "Really? I guess I do remember hearing that your mother's family was fairly well to do."

Allison quickly looked down at her plate, longing for someone else to pick up the conversation.

"Say," James said. "I remember Muriel mentioning a friend of hers who—"

"You know," interrupted Mrs. Jenson, "I just received a note from my friend Gladys down in California this morning. She had a most interesting bit of gossip. She mentioned that she had heard about some daughter of an actress who had recently moved up here to Tamaqua Point." Mrs. Jenson's gaze narrowed onto Allison. She reminded Allison of a lioness about to devour her victim. "And Gladys said that the girl was about the same age as our Shirley."

"How interesting," James said nonchalantly. "Please pass the butter, Hal."

"Really, Mother?" Shirley sat up with interest. "Tell us more about it."

Mrs. Jenson turned to her husband, pointing with her fork. "Hal, didn't you tell me once that James had been married to some actress in New York City?"

Hal swallowed a bite and nodded, looking at Allison's father as if for confirmation. "Wasn't your wife an actress or singer or some sort of entertainer, James?"

"I don't really like to talk about the past very much." James smiled stiffly and attempted to change the subject. "But say, how about that football game last night? Wasn't Andrew something else?"

"What exactly was your wife's name?" Mrs. Jenson demanded. Allison stared at her with wide eyes. This woman's blunt rudeness almost made Marsha seem angelic in comparison.

"Mrs. O'Brian," James retorted with a sly grin.

"Oh, come now," Mrs. Jenson said with exasperation. "Don't be so tiresome. Tell me your ex-wife's name. What can you possibly have to hide? You must realize that all I need to do is pick up the phone and call Bea to find out. In fact, if I'd had any idea that you were married to someone halfway interesting, I would have looked into it ages ago."

"Marge," James began with a sincere tone, "the past is the past. Can't we just let it go now?"

Mrs. Jenson ignored his plea and turned her attention back to Allison. "I can see I'm getting nowhere with your dad. Why don't you tell me, dear." She smiled a pathetic little smile. "Just *who* is your mother, Allison?"

Allison looked from Mrs. Jenson to her dad. She knew it was useless; this relentless woman would soon uncover the truth. Perhaps it would be best to just tell them. At least she could plead with them to keep quiet.

"These rolls are quite good," James said. "Did you bake them yourself, Marge?"

Allison smiled at his last-ditch effort to change the subject.

"No," she snapped without even looking at him. "They're from the bakery."

Now Shirley joined in pleading childishly, "Please, Allison, just tell us—who is your mother? Is she really an actress? Come on, tell us."

"Yes, it can't be such a big deal," said Mrs. Jenson. "It's not like she could be anyone *really* famous."

Allison felt slightly indignant. Marsha Madison was *really* famous. What right did Mrs. Jenson have to act like she wasn't? Allison looked at her father, and he simply raised his brows as if to signal it was up to her whether she wanted to spill the beans or not.

"Come on, Allison. It's not as if your mother is some big *movie star*." Shirley laughed. That same sarcastic laugh, as if nothing in the world could ever impress her.

"As a matter of fact, she is," Allison said. If they had to know, they might as well hear it from her.

"You've gotta be kidding," Shirley said. "A *real* movie star? I don't believe it. Who is she, then? Anyone we've ever heard of, or just some little no-name?"

Allison took a deep breath and continued in a serious voice. "I really hadn't meant for people at school to know about this, Shirley." She looked pleadingly at Mr. and Mrs. Jenson. "If I tell you who my mother is, can you keep it a secret?" Even as Allison spoke the words, she knew it was probably unrealistic. How could she trust Shirley, not to mention her mother, with something like this? But then again, if she didn't tell, it was certain that Mrs. Jenson would just call Bea, Shirley's grandmother, and drag it out of her.

James immediately jumped in to help. "I'm sure you can all understand how this might be something that Allison wants to keep quiet, being new at school and all. Sometimes it's nice to get to know people without bringing *all* your history with you." This he directed to Shirley, as if he knew something that she might not be comfortable having announced to all of Port View High.

"Shirley won't tell her friends," said Mrs. Jenson persuasively. "And I can certainly keep a secret. Come on, James, tell us. This is just too good."

"It's up to Allison."

"Please, Allison," Mrs. Jenson said with a suspicious smile. "We won't tell a soul. Will we, Shirley?"

"Of course not," Shirley answered. "Probably no one would care anyway."

"Have you ever heard of Marsha Madison?" Allison asked abruptly.

"Well, of course, but—" Mrs. Jenson stopped. She looked from Allison to James, and he nodded slightly as if to confirm it.

"You're kidding!" Shirley exclaimed. "Marsha Madison is *not* your mother!"

"I can't believe it!" cried Mrs. Jenson. "Why didn't Bea ever tell me this?"

"I guess Mom just knows how to keep her mouth shut," Mr. Jenson said, and his wife threw him a dark look.

Shirley put down her fork with a bang. "This is too much! Marsha Madison's daughter is sitting right here, at our table." Shirley and her mom both stared at Allison as if she were a specimen under a microscope.

"Remember your promise," James warned.

"You don't look a thing like your mother," said Mrs. Jenson.

James laughed. "She can't help that her good looks come from my side of the family. She looks just like my mother."

Suddenly, Shirley and Mrs. Jenson began to ask dozens of questions until Allison finally held up her hands. "Stop, stop. I can't even begin to answer all those. For your information,

I make it a rule not to discuss any of Marsha's personal life. If you want to learn all that stuff, you might as well read a movie star magazine."

James smiled at Allison, then turned to Mrs. Jenson. "Now, how about another slice of that roast?"

Allison looked over at the dried-up roast and thought he was being an awfully good sport. Mrs. Jenson was distracted for a moment, and Allison launched into a sneak preview of what Marsha's next movie was all about. She managed to keep the movie star questions at bay until dessert was served, then James began to discuss business with Mr. Jenson, steering them away from Marsha completely.

After dinner the men went to the den, and Allison offered to help clean up in the kitchen.

"Thank you, but no," Mrs. Jenson said. "You and Shirley can go and visit. I wouldn't want Marsha Madison's daughter cleaning up my dinner dishes." The way she said it made Allison want to scream. It was exactly what she had been afraid of.

Back upstairs, Shirley dug out a pile of movie star magazines and began spotting Marsha in many of them. "I can't believe it, Allison. This is just great. My best friend's mother is a movie star."

Allison gulped. She wasn't sure which was worse—the best friend part or the movie star mother. "The thing about good friends is that they know how to keep secrets," Allison said in a conspiratory tone. "Right, Shirley?"

"Sure. Hey, look at this shot of her in *Desert Rose*. I just loved that movie. Gee, Allison, I don't understand why you didn't want to live with your mom. That would be so glamorous and exciting. I can't believe you gave all that up to come here to the end of the earth."

"I just wanted to live a normal life, Shirley. I've always been in boarding schools. I've never lived in a real home and gone to a public school."

"But don't you miss her?"

"I've never been close to her. I actually spent more time with her this summer than my entire life put together. It was really nice getting to know her, but she's so busy she doesn't have time to be a mom. This is the best way. I'll go to Hollywood to visit and everything—"

"Hollywood?"

"Well, actually, she lives in Beverly Hills."

"Beverly Hills," Shirley breathed as if it were heaven.

An idea began to form in Allison's mind that perhaps it would be in her best interest to wow Shirley with all this movie star talk. Perhaps it would prove a useful tool in getting Shirley to keep her mouth shut. She told Shirley about her summer visit in Beverly Hills and other tidbits that she felt would suitably impress the star-struck girl. Her plan seemed to be working because when it was time for her to go home, Shirley's jaw was literally hanging open in amazement.

"Now, remember our secret, Shirley," Allison said as if they had a little conspiracy going. "I'm counting on you."

"You bet," said Shirley.

Allison could only hope.

❀

Allison and James sat with George and Muriel right behind Grace and the kids at church the next morning. Andrew sat directly in front of Allison, and she smiled to herself as she remembered her time with him on the beach yesterday. Then she remembered *their* secret, but she knew she could trust Andrew.

The Jensons weren't at church, but Shirley's grandmother, Bea, was there. Allison didn't get the impression that Mr. and

Mrs. Jenson were regular attendees, and while she knew she shouldn't be glad about that, she was, nonetheless, relieved not to see Shirley today. Monday would be soon enough.

After church James suggested they all go crabbing. They agreed to go home and get changed, then meet at the dock. Allison quickly pulled on jeans and a sweater and went downstairs to help Muriel pack a picnic lunch.

"George is already down there making a big fire to cook the crabs in," said Muriel as she wrapped a loaf of freshly baked bread. "How was your dinner last night?"

"Don't ask," said Allison.

Muriel chuckled. "I'll bet you're extra hungry today."

Allison grinned. "Mrs. Jenson said she was going to try to lure you away from Dad to be her cook."

"Fat chance," laughed Muriel. "Grab a jar of those strawberry preserves there, Allison. And don't forget the butter. We'll need enough for the corn on the cob, too."

"Muriel, you're making me hungry. I hope it won't take too long to get enough crab to make a decent meal."

"George says they are plentiful right now. He and your dad went down to the dock already to drop down a couple of pots to get us started, and I'll bet Andrew is there with them." She closed the lid of the basket. "No reason you can't go ahead and haul this basket down while I finish up the next. Don't forget to take a blanket to sit on."

"Thanks, Muriel. See you down there." Allison scooped up the basket and blanket and headed to the dock.

It was getting misty and cool outside with the fog rolling in, but it was perfect weather for a bonfire. George had the big iron kettle full of water hanging over the flames. It was already starting to steam as Allison set the picnic basket beside it.

"Hey, Allison!" Winston yelled. "Come and see these." He

was leaning over to watch as Andrew pulled a crab pot out of the water and set it on the dock.

"Those look pretty good, Andrew," James said.

Winston stood by with a basket ready to hold the strange-looking creatures. Allison watched with curious interest as Andrew carefully picked up the crabs, holding them on the back end of their shells, and placed them in Winston's basket. Crabs were such odd things with their big pincher claws, looking as if they were very angry. Andrew held one close to Allison's face, and she drew back and shuddered in mock fear.

"Ugh! They look so mean and crabby. But you can't really blame them." Allison frowned slightly as she peered into the basket. "After all, they are about to become our Sunday dinner."

"They don't even know that," said Andrew as he chucked another into the basket. "We've already got four—it won't be long until we can start cooking them up."

Allison helped Winston wire some nasty-looking fish bait back into one of the empty crab pots. "This is disgusting," said Allison, rinsing her hands in the salt water, then wiping them on the back of her jeans. "And just a few minutes ago I thought I was actually hungry."

"Well, that's what crabs like to eat," said Winston with a grin. "And just think, Allison, you'll soon be eating them. *Yummy!*"

She playfully punched him in the arm. "You get so much delight in the grotesque!"

Soon Grace and Heather arrived, and finally Muriel came lugging down a basket. Winston ran up the road to help her.

"It's about time," said George as he began plopping crabs into the bubbling kettle of water. "We're starving down here."

Heather and Allison took charge of one of the pots, and

when Allison pulled it up, there was actually a good-sized crab inside. "We got one, Heather!" she shouted as she set the dripping pot on the dock. Then she pushed up her sleeve and reached in, just as she had seen Andrew do, and gingerly picked up the crab with one hand. With the other hand she reached for Heather's. "I'll help you to touch it, Heather. He's a mean, ugly cuss with beady little eyes. His claws look like they could break your finger." Heather pulled back slightly. "Don't worry, Heather. I won't let him hurt you." Allison gently laid Heather's fingers on the back of the crab, careful to stay away from the big claws.

"That feels weird," said Heather. "I've felt crab shells before, but they were always dry. This feels all cold and wet." Allison watched as Heather's fingers gently traced the embossed design on the crab's back. The crab's legs wiggled, and Heather pulled her hand back. "Thanks, Allison. It felt kind of creepy . . . but interesting."

Soon Muriel was calling them over to eat. James said a short blessing, and everyone began filling their plates. Allison and Heather sat down together and began to eat, laughing about how it was as much work to get the crab out of the shell as it was to catch them. But the reward was worth it because the crab meat was delicious. When Allison couldn't eat another bite, she set her plate down and leaned back.

Grace and James were sitting on the end of the dock eating together and visiting quietly. Suddenly, Allison remembered Dad's secret and wondered if he might be telling Grace about his plan to get his pilot's license. Allison glanced over at Andrew, who was also watching. She could tell by the look in his eyes that he was probably thinking the same thing. To her surprise she almost hoped that Dad *wasn't* telling Grace just yet. It had been kind of fun to have this special secret to share with him, and she didn't want Grace to know about it. Besides, she wondered what would happen if Grace disapproved. If he gave up flying, she wouldn't have a chance to go up again. She wondered if Andrew was worried about the same thing.

Allison considered all the disappointments that life had given her father over the last ten years. If only he could stick to his dream and see this thing through. She decided then and there that she would do everything possible to help him. His secret was safe with her. And as dearly as Allison loved Grace, she was beginning to resent, just a little bit, that Grace could possibly become an obstacle in Dad's plan. If Grace really loved Dad, wouldn't she want him to follow his dream?

Please don't tell Grace, Dad, Allison thought. *Not yet*. If only they could keep this their special secret for a while longer.

Andrew looked at Allison and winked. He understood. She sent him a half smile and winked back. At least she could trust Andrew to keep this secret. If only Dad could keep it, too.

9

Allison's first full week at school went a lot better than her first day had gone. By the end of the week she actually felt hopeful that she was starting to fit in. Already she had made several casual friends, and of course there was always Heather. Even Karen Brown had continued to be friendly with Allison, which only seemed to aggravate Shirley Jenson. Still, Shirley stuck to Allison like glue. Allison worried that her patience with Shirley might one day give out and that she would do something deeply regretful. But at least Shirley had kept her secret about Marsha—that was something to be thankful for and another reason to try to stay within Shirley's good graces. So far, Allison's secrets were intact. Her father had still not revealed any of his piloting activities to Grace, and Andrew's lips were sealed. Tomorrow, if the weather permitted, Dad would be ready to fly solo. Allison couldn't wait!

"Too bad the football game is away tonight," said Shirley as they joined Heather and Caroline in the cafeteria. "I'll miss seeing Andrew's great playing ability."

Allison looked down at her plate as she sat down, hoping against hope that Heather wouldn't go and invite Shirley to ride with them to the game. But she knew it was useless to drop a hint because sometimes Heather was just too nice.

Allison quickly tried to change the subject. "This lunch looks pretty good today. In fact, it looks downright appetizing after what we put together in home ec."

"Ugh," Shirley said. "Don't remind me."

Heather laughed. "Well, judging by the way it smelled, I'm thankful Miss Wrigley didn't make us sample it."

"It's a good thing, I think she might have gotten in trouble for poisoning us," Allison said as she took a bite of meatloaf.

"Are you going to the Harvest Ball, Allison?" Shirley asked, nodding at a bright poster nearby that promoted the dance. "It looks like it could be fun."

It bugged Allison that Shirley so often ignored Heather as if she were not only blind, but also deaf, and she rarely acknowledged Caroline at all. "Not that I know of," she answered curtly. "Don't you have to be asked first?"

"Well, of course," said Shirley as if Allison were the village idiot.

"Maybe Andrew will ask you, Allison," Heather said quietly.

"Really?" Shirley exclaimed. "Do you really think Andrew would ask Allison?"

Heather smiled a little knowing smile. "I don't know why not."

Allison felt her cheeks growing warm. "Oh, I don't think so, Shirley—"

"Wouldn't you like to go with him, though?" demanded Shirley loudly. "Imagine going to the Harvest Ball with Andrew Amberwell."

Allison glanced around nervously, hoping that Andrew wasn't anywhere close by. "I don't know. I've never even been to a dance before."

"Nor have I," said Heather. "But remember when you taught me how to jitterbug and we had that little dance at our house?"

Allison started to giggle. "Yes, that was fun." She could feel Shirley's attention on her again. Whenever anything about Andrew came up, it seemed Shirley was all ears. It worried Allison, but there seemed little way to avoid mentioning his name. After all, Andrew was Heather's brother and Allison's good friend.

"Well, I know I'd certainly like to go to the Harvest Ball," Shirley said.

Allison glanced around the crowded room. "Do you know who you'd like to go with? Maybe you'd better start dropping some hints since it's only a week away," Allison said in a friendly, teasing tone, but Shirley didn't seem to take notice.

"Sure, I can think of several fellows that I wouldn't mind going with." Shirley looked right at Allison. "And maybe you're right, Allison. Maybe I should start dropping some subtle hints. Boys can be so thick, you know."

Allison stared at Shirley in surprise. "You're kidding! You mean you would actually hint to a boy about taking you to the Harvest Ball?"

Shirley nodded. "Why not? Like I've always said, if you want something, go out and get it."

Allison shook her head. "In some things, maybe, but I don't think I'd like to get a reputation for going after the boys."

Shirley threw back her head and laughed. "Believe me, some boys like girls who go after them!"

Allison didn't think that Andrew would. And that was a relief because Allison had no intention of ever chasing after a boy—not even someone she liked as much as Andrew.

The bell rang, and Allison told Heather and Caroline good-bye and headed for the gym with Shirley at her heels. Shirley had been like Allison's shadow all week, making little comments about movie stars and winking and such. Allison wasn't sure how much of this she could take, and at this rate she might never be able to shake her. It was a pity that they wouldn't get new class schedules until after Christmas. In her heart she knew that God wanted her to love Shirley—Sunday's sermon had been about loving your enemies—which seemed to describe Shirley in a way. But Allison figured loving them was one thing—being best friends was something else!

"Hi, Allison," Karen said as they approached the locker room. "Let's try to get on the same soccer team today for a change. Then the other team won't have a chance. Hey, are you going to the game tonight?"

Allison tossed Karen a sideways glance that she hoped said, "Don't ask me right now," then she said, "I . . .uh . . . I'm not sure. Say, Karen, I really like what you've done with your hair today. How do you get it to turn under like that?"

Thankfully, Karen seemed to catch the hint and immediately launched into a step-by-step hair-styling lesson. "That's all there is to it," Karen finished, giving her pretty golden locks a shake.

"Thanks," Allison said. "I think I'll give it a try." She watched as Karen went over to her locker on the other side of the room. Allison longed to follow her, but Karen's cheerleader friends were already there. As friendly as Karen was, Allison still didn't quite feel like she fit in; and as hard as Shirley tried, she seemed to fit in even less. So for now Allison seemed stuck with Shirley. Perhaps even more so since she had disclosed her mother's identity. She was afraid that Shirley could hold that over her head.

Although Allison tried to convince herself that it might not really matter, she couldn't forget the time a couple of years ago at Oakmont when she had tried to use her mother's fame to buy prestige with a group of snooty girls who weren't really interested in her. It had actually worked at first, but in the end it had backfired and been a painful lesson. Since then, Allison always tried to keep her mother's unusual career anonymous. She wanted people to like her for who she was.

When the school day finally ended, Allison and Heather were picked up by James. Andrew had left with the football team to travel to the game that was two hours away. Allison suspected by the smile on her father's face that he had been at the airport with Mac getting in his final flying hours before the big solo flight tomorrow. She knew she could not say a word and winked at him instead. When he winked back, she knew she was right.

"Are you girls all ready for the big game tonight?" James asked as he opened the door for them.

"You bet," Allison said. "When are we leaving?"

"Grace suggested about five. She's putting together a picnic dinner for us to eat along the way."

"Sounds good," Heather said. "I smelled a chocolate cake baking last night."

James smacked his lips. "Can't wait. Better take along some warm things, girls. I felt a little nip in the air this afternoon."

❦

It was very cold that night, but the Port View Pirates played heartily and Andrew was in peak form.

"That was a great game," Allison said after everyone got to the car. "Andrew must be feeling pretty good right now."

"I'll bet he's flying high," Grace agreed, pulling out a Thermos of hot chocolate to warm them up. "But thank goodness he's one young man who never seems to get a big head about all this hoopla."

"That's because he's sensible," James said. "I heard Coach Jackson saying that Andrew might be able to get a college scholarship if he keeps playing like this."

"Wouldn't that be wonderful!" Heather said. "Andrew would be so pleased."

"That would be nice," Grace agreed. "He has really worked hard at football. Sometimes I worry about him, though. He works so hard I don't know if he takes time to stop and smell the roses. I wish he didn't always take life so seriously. I'd like to see him have more fun."

"Maybe he'll go to the Harvest Ball next week," Heather suggested. Allison swallowed a gulp of cocoa.

"When is it?" asked Grace.

"Next Saturday, but I don't think he's made any plans yet."

"Well, maybe I should encourage him to go," Grace said thoughtfully.

"He shouldn't have any difficulty getting a date," James said. "From what I've seen, every girl in the school is crazy about him. Right, Allison?"

"Oh, Dad!"

"I don't know why you all think Andrew would want to go to any silly old dance," injected Winston with ten-year-old wisdom. "If I was him, I sure wouldn't want to have to dance with any dumb old girls!"

"Oh, Winston," said Heather, "just wait a few years." And everyone laughed. Everyone except Winston.

⚘

The next morning, James and Allison drove out to the airport. Allison could sense her father's anticipation. This really was a big event, and she wished she had gotten him a little gift. Perhaps she could pick up something later. This week he had completed all his required hours and was now ready to go up for his first solo flight, then Mac would present him with his pilot's license. But just as they got out of the car and greeted Mac, Allison noticed a familiar truck driving up.

"Dad," she whispered, nudging him with her elbow. "Isn't that Grace's jalopy coming this way?"

James turned and looked with wide eyes, then nodded his head. But as the old red pickup drew closer, they saw it was Andrew in the driver's seat, and he was alone.

"What's going on?" James asked with a puzzled expression as Andrew parked nearby.

Allison was afraid to answer but knew that an explanation was in order. "I . . . uh . . . I'm not sure what he's doing, but I did sort of let it slip out to Andrew—"

"What?"

"I'm sorry, Dad. But as soon as it was out, I made Andrew promise to keep the secret. He swore he wouldn't tell a soul. You can trust Andrew."

"I hope you're right, Allison."

Andrew was climbing out of the jalopy with a sheepish grin. "I don't want to intrude, Mr. O'Brian. I was just so excited about what you're doing that I thought it would be okay if I stopped in to watch—from the ground, of course. And I won't breathe a word of it to anyone. I promise."

James' shoulders relaxed and he laughed. "Okay, okay. I know I can trust you. Besides, it's only a matter of time until I have to break the news to Grace, and it can't hurt to have some supporters when I do. I know how much Grace respects you, Andrew. Maybe you can pull for me on this."

"You bet, Mr. O'Brian," said Andrew. "I'll be glad to."

James turned to Mac. "Mac, this is Andrew Amberwell, Port View's local star quarterback."

"Pleasure to meet you, sir," Andrew said politely. "I have often wondered about this airport. I would give anything to go up in one of those." He nodded toward the planes in the hangar.

"Nice to meet you, too, Andrew," said Mac as they shook

hands. He turned back to James with a twinkle in his eye. "Looks like we've got another potential aviator on our hands."

James frowned slightly. "Grace is going to want to boil me like a crab dinner."

"I promise your secret is safe with me, Mr. O'Brian," Andrew said. "I understand completely. I know how Grace is about flying. You won't have an easy battle ahead, but I'll stand by you, sir."

James patted Andrew on the back. "Thanks, son. And believe me, I'll remember that when the time comes."

"All right, now," Mac said. "The big moment is upon us. Are you ready, James?"

"You better believe I am! I've been waiting for this moment for years." He turned to Andrew and Allison. "Any final words of wisdom for the old man?"

"You'll be fine, Dad." Then Allison thought about it for a moment. "Won't you?"

"Of course."

"Have fun," Andrew said. "And God bless."

"Yes," Allison agreed. "God bless you!"

"Thanks, you two. That's just what I needed." James grinned at them, then marched ceremoniously toward the little two-seater plane. He went through all the proper checks and was soon taxiing toward the runway. Allison held her breath as the little yellow Piper Cub began quickly picking up speed and finally lifted off. Then she let out a big sigh as the plane climbed easily into the sky.

"Simple as pie," said Mac. "Your dad's a natural, Allison."

"Yes, sir. That's what I thought."

"That looks so fun," Andrew said. "How long will he stay up?"

"Oh, we agreed on an hour," Mac said, pulling out a gold pocket watch. "There's nothing quite like your first solo flight.

No sense in cutting it too short. I'll be in the office if you need me."

Allison and Andrew stood out on the field, watching the yellow plane flying south until it became a tiny speck.

"That is so great," Andrew said. "I would love to be able to do that."

"Me too," Allison agreed. "I think I may get the chance." Then she looked at Andrew. "You could probably go up, too, but you'd need to ask Grace first."

Andrew scuffed his toe in the dirt. "I suppose I should."

"Don't worry about it, Andrew. I'm sure you will get to go up sooner or later."

"I just hope it's sooner!"

Allison decided to change the subject. "That was a great game last night, Andrew. As usual, you played really well."

"Thanks, it was fun. The whole team seemed to be right on the money last night."

"I heard Dad saying that you might be considered for some kind of football scholarships for college."

"Yeah, that's what Coach was telling me. I wouldn't want to count my chickens before they hatch, but that would sure be swell. I really want to go to college, and a scholarship would take some pressure off Grace. Of course, I plan to work, too. I can pay my own way."

Allison thought about what Grace said about Andrew being too serious. "It's still a long way off, Andrew. I'm sure it will all work out just great. Besides, I hate to think of you going off to college anytime soon."

Andrew grinned. "Don't worry. It's nearly a year away. Say, Grace was hinting that I should think about going to the Harvest Ball. I hadn't really given it much thought. I haven't been one to go for those kinds of things."

Allison felt her cheeks glowing and knew it was silly to get her hopes up. Andrew could ask any girl he pleased to the dance. "I think Grace is right, Andrew," she said seriously. "You know what they say about all work and no play. Besides, I happen to know there are many girls who would love to go to the dance with you—"

"Oh, go on—" Andrew waved his hand in the air as if to brush her words away.

"You can't mean to act like you don't know, Andrew. All the cheerleaders are just crazy over you. Like Karen Brown, for instance, or Beverly Howard, or Janet Bartley. Not to mention people like Shirley Jenson who practically worship the ground you walk on."

Andrew rolled his eyes at her. "Stop, please. You're embarrassing me. I already decided who I'd like to take to the Harvest Ball. I'm just not sure if it's an acceptable idea or not. I'd like to hear your opinion."

Allison waited for him to continue. He looked up in the sky for a long moment while trying to spot a plane. "Hey, there he is, Allison." Andrew pointed to the south where she could just barely make out a tiny speck that seemed to be moving closer.

"I think you're right, Andrew. He's just turning back this way. Wow, I wonder how he's feeling right now."

"Probably having the time of his life." Andrew sighed and slowly shook his head.

"Anyway," Allison prodded hopefully. "You were saying . . ."

"Right. About the dance. Last night when I got home, Grace and Heather were sitting up waiting for me. Had a fire going and everything. They had been talking about the dance, and it seems that Heather was wishing she could go, but of course, she doesn't think anyone will ask her. She was saying how it was too bad that girls couldn't go together, then you and she could get all dressed up and go."

116

Allison laughed. "Now, that *would* be funny!"

"I know. But then I got to wondering why I couldn't take Heather. I mean, not as my date but just as my sister. I'm not worried about anyone making fun of me. I can take whatever they can give—"

"I'm sure no one would bother you a bit, Andrew. I think that's a very sweet idea."

"Well, that's not all. I thought since Heather is my sister and all, maybe it wouldn't seem too weird if I took another girl—"

"Two girls?"

Andrew laughed. "When you say it like that, it does sound strange, but I thought perhaps I could take her best friend, too."

Allison thought for a moment, not wanting to assume anything. "You mean Caroline?"

Andrew threw back his head and laughed. "Caroline is nice and all, but I didn't think that Caroline was Heather's *best* friend. I've never heard Heather say that before."

Allison smiled. "Well, I know who Heather's best friend is, and Heather knows who her best friend is. I just wanted to make sure we were talking about the same person."

"So what do you think, Allison? I know it sounds a bit silly, but how would you like to go with Heather and me to the Harvest Ball? We could probably have a lot of fun, the three of us. It wouldn't be like a date or anything, since I'm pretty sure that your dad doesn't want you to date yet. I know that's what Grace has said about Heather, but we could all just go and have a good time."

"I think it sounds like a swell plan. Are you sure you really want to take us? I mean, like I said, you could take any girl you want."

Andrew smiled. "I want to take you two. It would mean a lot to me. Would you like to go?"

"How can I refuse? Of course I'd love to!"

When the hour was up, the little yellow plane appeared flying overhead. The wings tipped from side to side, and Andrew and Allison jumped up and down and waved their arms. Before long the plane smoothly touched down and landed on the runway, then taxied over to them. James hopped out and they ran over to congratulate him, but Mac was already there with a certificate and a fat cigar in hand.

"Well done, Jamie," Mac said as he slapped James heartily on the back. "Wish I had a good bottle of champagne."

"That's okay," James said. "I feel pretty lightheaded already just from the excitement of actually soloing. It was great! That little Cub handles so nicely. I wouldn't mind having a plane like that myself."

"You did great, Dad," Allison said. "How exciting! I bet this is a day you'll remember for a long, long time."

"I feel like a kid. I just can't believe how wonderful that was to go up and down all on my own."

"Congratulations, Pilot O'Brian," Andrew said as he shook his hand. "That's quite an achievement. I hope someday I can do the same."

"I hope so, too, Andrew. I'll tell you, there's nothing quite like it."

When Allison and James arrived home, a delivery truck was making its way out of the driveway.

"You're just in time," huffed George as he paused from pulling a large trunk into the house. "This just came for Miss Allison, and it weighs a ton."

"Let me help you," James offered. "What is it?"

"It's from Miss Madison," George grunted as they carried it into the foyer.

"Oh, that must be the clothes Marsha promised to send me," Allison said. "It arrived so fast . . . how nice of her."

"You will want to write her a thank-you," James said as they set the trunk at the foot of the stairs.

"I've been keeping lunch for you," Muriel called. "What in the world is this?"

"Marsha sent me some things," Allison explained.

"How nice, but I have clam chowder and fresh bread waiting. You all go wash up."

"Can we eat in the kitchen?" James asked with a boyish grin.

"I was hoping you'd want to," Muriel said. "Now, come along."

After a cozy and delicious lunch, Allison coaxed her father and George to carry the trunk to her room so she could open it.

"Need any more help?" George asked after they set it in the middle of her floor.

"Not unless you like looking at girl clothes and things," Allison teased, but she could tell by his expression that it wasn't his cup of tea.

"I'll leave you to it, then."

"Well, *I* wouldn't mind looking at some girl things," announced Muriel from the hallway.

"Come on in, Muriel," Allison called. "I could use some help."

Muriel made all sorts of appropriate sounds as she helped Allison unload the trunk. "Oh my, Allison," she said. "Just look at this . . . isn't that lovely . . . my, this must have cost a pretty penny. . . ."

Allison held up a formal gown that Marsha had encouraged her to buy in Beverly Hills but had never worn. It was a buttery-colored satin with a tiny waist and sweet little puffs at the sleeves.

"Oh my." Muriel clucked her tongue. "That looks just like a princess gown."

"I could wear this to the Harvest Ball," Allison said.

"The Harvest Ball?" Muriel's brows raised slightly.

"Yes, Muriel. Andrew wants to escort Heather and me to the Harvest Ball next Saturday. Doesn't that sound wonderful?"

Muriel nodded. "That sounds very nice. I don't think your daddy will mind a bit. Andrew is such a good boy—and taking both you and Heather." Muriel chuckled. "He'll be the envy of the ball."

"Oh, Muriel," said Allison. "Say, there might be something in here that Heather could wear. Let's keep looking."

Soon the trunk was empty. Three more evening gowns were found. One dark green, one pale blue, and the awful orange gown that Allison had worn to the Beverly Hills party with Marsha. Allison held it up and began laughing uncontrollably.

"What is it?" asked Muriel.

"It just reminds me of a horrible trick I played on Marsha," Allison gasped. Then she told Muriel the whole story until poor Muriel was laughing so hard she had tears running down both cheeks.

"Allison Mercury O'Brian, you have more nerve than a fox in a hen house!" Muriel sank into the rocking chair. "Sometimes you remind me of your dear sweet grandmother, God bless her soul."

Allison sat down on the footstool and smiled up at Muriel. "I still have so much to learn about her, Muriel. I want you to tell me as much as you can remember about her."

"Certainly not all at once." Muriel dabbed her eyes with a handkerchief. "But right now I am remembering a certain time when Mercury—she always had me call her Mercury unless there were guests in the house—anyway, I remember the time she and your grandfather were invited to a Christmas party back when your daddy was a boy. Mercury was always a fine-looking woman, and she had a good sense of style when it came to clothes. Well, your grandpa was off to the city, and Mercury asked him to buy her a new party dress like she'd seen in a magazine. She tore out the picture and wrote down a detailed description along with her measurements.

"That was back in the twenties when skirts were getting shorter, and the flapper style was all the rage with the kids. Would you believe some crazy salesgirl talked your grandpa into paying a fortune for this flimsy scarlet red dress with dangly beads on it instead of the one that Mercury wanted. Well, your grandmother was just appalled when she saw it—besides, with her auburn hair, she never wore red. He kept begging her and begging her just to wear it to the Christmas party, but poor Mercury felt it wasn't respectable for a mother to dress in such a fashion. They went round and round for days.

"Finally, the night of the party came, and I went upstairs to help her get ready, and lo and behold if she didn't have on that little red flapper dress. At first I was shocked, but then I realized she looked pretty good. In fact, it made her look a lot younger—like a college girl. We did up her hair, then she put on her big fur coat and off they went to the party." Now Muriel began to chuckle. "They came home early that night, and your grandpa was angry something fierce. He was sputtering and fuming and fit to be tied."

"What went wrong?" Allison asked.

"Seems every man at the party couldn't take their eyes off of Mercury. She was the life of the party, dancing up a storm, and your grandpa was sitting in the corner in a fit of jealous rage!"

Allison was laughing now. "Served him right, didn't it!"

"Yes, and that was the last time he ever told Mercury O'Brian what to wear!"

"Thanks for telling me. That was a wonderful story."

Muriel picked up a pale blue gown and glanced at her watch. "I need to get some things going for supper, Allison. But if I were you, I'd tell Heather about this blue dress. Grace could probably rework it for her, and it would be beautiful with her blond hair and blue eyes."

"It would. Say, would it be okay if I invited Heather over? Maybe she could spend the night."

"I don't know why not," said Muriel. "Of course, you'll need to check with your dad."

It was quickly settled. Allison called and arranged for Grace to drop Heather by around four, and before Grace left she would take a look at the blue gown to see if it needed to be altered. In the meantime, Allison put everything away. It was nice having all of her own things now. It made it seem like this was truly her room. Allison didn't think she would ever take having a home of her own for granted.

"Hello, up there," called Heather from the bottom of the stairs a little while later.

"Hi, Heather," Allison yelled. "Hi, Grace. Come on up."

"Isn't this exciting," said Heather. "We are going to the ball just like Cinderella."

"I can't wait to see these dresses, Allison," said Grace. "This is almost as good as going shopping in New York."

"Okay," Allison said. "You two sit down on the bed, and I will show them to you." After a brief description for Heather's sake, Allison pulled her own dress out and held it up.

"Allison," Grace breathed. "That is gorgeous. You will look like an angel in it."

"Thanks, Grace." Allison laid it in Heather's lap.

"It feels as smooth as swimming in a summer lake in the

evening," Heather said as she caressed the satiny fabric. "I'm sure you will look stunning in it."

"Okay, now for the one Muriel and I think might work for Heather. First let me describe it. It is the same color as the sky on a clear day and matches Heather's eyes. It has a fitted bodice with a sophisticated roll-down neckline and three-quarter-length sleeves. The fabric is moiré satin. Maybe you can feel the grain, Heather, but when I look at it, it reminds me of when you drop a pebble in the water and it makes lots of little circles. It's really beautiful." She held up the dress for Grace to see.

"Oh, Allison. I think it would look lovely on Heather. The color is amazing, and the fabric is perfect in that style. So classic and stylish. Heather, you will look like a movie starlet in this."

Allison laid it on Heather's lap, and Heather gently fingered the fabric. Suddenly, tears began to fill Heather's eyes.

"Heather, what's wrong?" asked Allison with concern. She had rarely seen Heather cry.

"It's nothing," Heather said. "I'm sure it is a beautiful dress."

"Oh, Heather, it is," Grace assured. "We never could have found anything like this in Oregon. Both you girls are going to look like princesses."

"I know," Heather said. "I'm sorry I'm crying."

"What is it?" Allison asked. "What's the matter? Did I say something wrong?"

"No, no," Heather said as Grace handed her a handkerchief. "It's just sometimes . . . sometimes I so badly want to see. I know it's silly. Most of the time I'm fine, but sometimes it's so hard to imagine what things look like to the rest of you."

Allison sat down and put her arm around Heather's shoulders. "I kind of understand, Heather."

"You do?"

"Maybe." Allison leaned over to look at Grace, hoping for direction, but Grace just smiled sadly and nodded at her to go ahead. "All the time I was a little girl and growing up, it felt like I never belonged anywhere. I was shipped back and forth like a piece of luggage, from Grandmother Madison's house to boarding school. I never really had a place of my own—a real home or family who loved me, and I used to imagine that I was the only one in the world who felt like that. So all alone. Almost as if everyone else was able to see and I was blind. I know that it's not really the same. . . ."

"Oh, Allison, it is similar. Only I think what you went through was much, much worse. I shouldn't feel sorry for myself—"

"Nonsense, Heather," Grace said. "What you feel is perfectly natural. The way you keep your sunny disposition is a challenge for many, and if you need to feel blue now and then, it's perfectly fine, isn't it, Allison?"

"Of course!" Allison exclaimed. "You should be you, Heather. That's all anyone expects. We don't want you to be anyone but Heather."

"That's right, and if you want to pout or feel sad, that's perfectly fine," Grace said. "We will never stop loving you."

"Thanks, but I really don't like to feel blue." Heather touched the dress again. "It does feel very pretty. Do you think it will look nice on me?"

"Why not try it right now," Grace suggested. "Then I could mark where it needs adjusting and take it home. If that's really okay with you, Allison."

"Of course. That's just what I wanted you to do."

Soon Heather was standing in the middle of the room draped in sky-blue moiré.

"Heather," Allison said, "you are truly a vision. Very chic. And I have an excellent idea."

"What's that?" asked Heather.

"On the night of the ball, we will have Dad take photos, and when we get the pictures we can send one to John."

A big smile spread across Heather's face. "Do you really think he'd want one?"

"Of course he would," Grace said. She reached over and gave Allison's arm a little thank-you squeeze, then began pulling and tucking here and there on the gown. "There's really not too much to alter, Heather," she said. "It's a little long—"

"Oh, I almost forgot," Allison said as she dove back into her closet. "There are shoes to go with all the dresses. This one has some pretty little blue satin pumps. I know that Heather and I wear the same size, and Marsha's feet are just a half-size bigger." She guided Heather's feet into the high-heeled shoes.

"Now I do feel like Cinderella," giggled Heather. "These are pretty tall high heels. I hope I can walk all right in them."

"Well, you can hold on to Andrew's arm," said Grace. "And with that extra height I will only have to take the dress up about an inch. I might even be able to take it up in the bodice instead of the hem." Grace stepped back and looked at Heather for a long moment. Then she let out a sob and threw her arms around her. "Oh, sweetheart, you look so glamorous! It makes me think you're all grown-up and that you won't need me anymore."

"Don't worry, Grace. I'll always need you."

After a while Grace lifted the gown off of Heather and gently hung it back on the hanger. "Allison, it's very sweet of you to let Heather use this gown."

"I'm so glad that there were things in the trunk that will work." Allison almost mentioned Marsha's generosity but quickly checked herself for Grace's sake. It was easy to forget that they had once been rivals. "Anyway, I can't wait for next Saturday night. I think it will be the greatest."

"You have a lot of high school dances to look forward to." Grace held up her hands. "But that's enough about that. I'm going to go say hello to James, then head for home. I'll see you in church tomorrow, girls. Have fun."

And that's exactly what they did. All night long they talked and giggled until it was long past midnight, and James tapped gently on their door and reminded them they had church in the morning.

"Sure, Dad," Allison whispered. "We're just about to fall asleep, right this very minute." This was followed by uncontrollable giggles.

"I just don't want to see any snoozing in the pew tomorrow," he warned good-naturedly. "Good night, ladies."

"Good night," they called in unison.

10

The upcoming Harvest Ball was the talk of the school for the entire week, but Allison and Heather made a special pact not to tell anyone they would be going. They knew it wouldn't be easy to explain why Andrew was taking *two* girls to the dance, even if one was his sister. Shirley was now gloating over Allison since she had somehow convinced poor Mark Spencer to take her to the dance. Allison heard that Shirley had actually paid for the tickets herself! A small part of Allison wished that Andrew was only taking her, but mostly she was glad that Heather was coming, too. It would be such fun!

On Friday, the day before the dance, Andrew stopped Allison in the hallway on her way to lunch. Shirley, as usual, was only a few steps away.

"Allison," Andrew said with urgency, "I need to talk to you about the dance—"

"Sure, but let's go over there," Allison quickly interrupted, nodding toward an empty stairwell. She could tell by Shirley's overly interested face that her curiosity was already aroused, and she could just imagine the inquisition that would follow.

"Shirley," Allison said with a nervous smile, "why don't you save me a seat in the cafeteria?" Allison waited a long moment for Shirley to reluctantly leave, then turned back to Andrew.

"It's like this," Andrew began. "You know Curt Boyd, the redheaded guy who plays left tackle on the football team? Anyway, Curt was telling me that he didn't have anyone to take to the Harvest Ball, then I opened up my big mouth and told him that I had *two* dates. I was just joking with him, but when I saw the look on his face, I felt so bad that I explained why I was taking two girls. Then I went ahead and asked if he would like to join us." Andrew smiled sheepishly.

Allison blinked in surprise. She didn't know what to say. She wondered if this meant that Curt would be her date. What would her father say?

"He's a real nice guy, Allison. He's just never been comfortable talking with girls, but he thinks Heather is swell. Do you think that would be okay? I know it will probably seem more like a date now, but it doesn't have to be like that. And I promise that I'll explain everything to your dad—"

"Oh, I don't think it should be a problem," Allison said, trying to keep the nervous excitement out of her voice. "But why don't I call him at home before this goes any further, just to make sure. Then you can call him later."

Andrew smiled. "You're super, Allison."

She blushed. "I was about to say the same about you. I think it was very kind of you to invite Curt. He seems like a nice fellow, but have you mentioned this to Heather yet?"

"No, I wanted to run it by you first. I was hoping to catch her at lunch."

"Then you better get to it. I'll call Dad right now."

When Allison called her dad, he seemed surprised and asked several fatherly questions. Then he agreed, saying that he trusted Andrew's judgment on this. Finally he suggested that they might need to borrow a car since it would be a tight fit with four in the jalopy.

Allison hurried to the lunchroom, anxious to tell Andrew the good news, but she couldn't see either him or Heather anywhere.

"Well, it's about time," said Shirley with exasperation. She was sitting at a table with Caroline and a deserted tray that Allison assumed must belong to Heather.

"Where's Heather?" Allison asked.

"Andrew just swept her away," Shirley said with raised brows. "What's going on with you guys and the Harvest Ball? Why did Andrew need to talk to *you* about the dance?"

Allison didn't want to lie to Shirley, nor did she want to divulge any information yet. "I'm not really sure. . . . I need to talk to Heather."

"Is *Heather* going to the Harvest Ball?" asked Caroline, giving her glasses a shove up the bridge of her nose.

"I . . . uh . . . I'm not sure. . . ." Allison wished those two would return.

"Don't tell me that Andrew has set his sister up with a date!" Shirley exclaimed.

"Oh, there they are," said Allison in relief as Andrew and Heather walked over. Allison tried to send Andrew a look that said his plan was A-OK as far as her dad went, and Andrew nodded as if he understood.

Andrew escorted Heather back to her seat and looked down at Allison. "Allison, we better hurry if we want to get any food today." He glanced at the cafeteria counter. The cafeteria workers were just starting to put things away.

As they hurried over, Allison told him her dad had agreed with the new plan. "And he suggested you might want to use his car," she added as she picked up a tray.

"Swell. And Heather, as usual, was very sweet about everything. It looks like we're all set for Saturday. Sorry to spring this on you at the last minute like this. I hadn't meant for it to turn out this way—"

"It's perfectly fine, Andrew. And don't worry, I don't think this means we're out on a date or anything. I know you are just helping out a friend." Allison wanted to be sure he knew that she didn't think any more of this than before.

Andrew winked down at her. "Well, don't be so sure about that."

Allison felt her eyes open wide, then she checked herself. Surely he was just teasing her.

"I think we'll all have a lot of fun," Andrew said more seriously, more like the Andrew she was used to. "And you know what they say, the more the merrier, right?"

"Right." Her tray was full now, and she looked up at him questioningly. Normally he ate with his football buddies. "Did you—uh . . ."

He smiled. "I guess we don't want to give them too much to talk about yet."

"That's right." She grinned.

Back at the table, Allison could tell that Heather was being grilled by Shirley. She wondered how Heather had handled it. Maybe it didn't matter anymore, but she still thought it would be fun to surprise everyone on the night of the dance.

"Tell us all about your dress, Shirley," Allison said, hoping to change the subject with the detailed description of what sounded like a rather strange dress.

"I've already told you," Shirley said in exasperation.

"Caroline and Heather might like to hear—"

"Well, I think I've had just about enough of visiting with them," said Shirley. She stood and glared down at Allison. "And I'm tired of waiting for you." She turned and stormed away.

Allison couldn't help but giggle. "Goodness, whatever did you two say to her?"

Caroline's cheeks were bright red. "Well, I told her to quit pestering Heather about the Harvest Ball, and that if Heather wanted Shirley to know, she would tell her. But I don't think Shirley liked that very much."

Heather giggled. "Thank you, Caroline. You are a dear friend. Now that Shirley's gone, I want to fill you in on what all the secrecy is about." Heather paused for a moment. "Is anyone else within earshot?"

"No," said Allison. "Go for it. I'll nudge you if anyone comes."

She quickly ate as Heather filled Caroline in on the story of how their threesome had just turned into a double date. Allison thought Caroline's eyes were going to pop right out.

"That's nice, Heather," Caroline said. "I sure wish I could see you all. . . ."

"Oh, Caroline, I wish you were going, too," Heather said sadly.

"My dad's going to take photographs," Allison added brightly. "We'll bring them to school for you to see."

Caroline sighed. "That'd be nice."

Suddenly, Allison felt sorry for Caroline. It must be hard for her to hear all this talk of dances and dresses and know that she would not be going. Allison remembered how it felt to be on the outside looking in; that's how she had felt when she had longed for a home. It had seemed everyone else had a family to love them—everyone except her. And only two weeks ago she had felt left out, the new girl, the stranger. That was probably how Caroline felt right now. Like an outsider.

"You know, there will be lots more dances, Caroline," said Allison reassuringly. "I bet you'll be going to some before long."

Caroline shook her head. "I don't think so, Allison. Boys don't ever talk to me. I know I don't look right, and I sure don't dress right. I can't hardly even talk right."

"Well, maybe we could help you," offered Heather.

"Really?" Caroline asked with a spark of hope in her eyes.

Allison studied Caroline for a moment, wondering what they could possibly do to help her. Naturally, Heather couldn't know what Caroline *really* looked like. Helping Caroline seemed like a pretty big challenge, but then Allison had always liked a challenge.

"Sure," Allison said finally. "That is, if you want."

Caroline was beaming now. "That'd be great."

"I probably won't be much assistance," said Heather. "Grace is the one who helps me with my appearance—well, I assume I look okay. That's what Allison always says. And from what I hear, Allison must know what she's talking about. It seems she's the most stylish girl in school."

"You're joking. Where did you hear that?" Allison asked in wonder.

"Lots of places," Heather said with a knowing grin. "I may be blind, but I'm certainly not deaf."

Allison just shook her head. She'd never heard anything like that, but it was nice to think that perhaps someone had said such a thing.

"It's true," said Caroline as if to defend Heather. "Everyone says it's because you're from New York. I also know that lots of the girls are jealous of you, Allison. I hear them talk."

"Well, that might explain why some girls don't seem very friendly," Allison said thoughtfully.

Just then the bell rang, and it was time to get back to class. For the rest of the day, Shirley completely ignored Allison, but it was nice for a change. During gym Allison and Karen walked outside together, chatting freely as they went. Perhaps now she would have a better chance of making more new friends. Allison almost hoped Shirley's snit might last awhile, but at the same time she wasn't eager to make Shirley her enemy. She had to keep in mind that their dads were business partners, and Shirley was holding her deepest secret. It wouldn't do to be on bad terms. Perhaps at tonight's football game Allison would casually mention the Harvest Ball to Shirley. That might smooth things over once more. Shirley would enjoy hearing this little tidbit of information before everyone else. Shirley was like that.

Allison dressed warmly for the football game that evening, wrapping a woolen scarf around her neck. It had been a damp, foggy week, and it promised to get colder by nightfall. When they reached the stadium, Allison and Heather found seats in the upper rows again. Heather said she felt more comfortable back there, and Allison didn't mind a bit. They wrapped up together in a big woolly blanket, and she surveyed the students below them. She noticed Shirley once again wearing her black-and-gold outfit and flitting around from group to group. At first Allison thought she was imagining things, but every time she saw Shirley, it seemed she was looking up at Allison, almost as if she were actually talking about her.

Finally she could stand it no longer. Allison turned to Heather and said quietly, "I know this sounds crazy, but I think Shirley is down there talking about me."

"Talking about *you*?"

"You know what I mean, Heather. It's like she's saying bad things or something."

"What in the world makes you think that?" Heather asked incredulously.

"She keeps looking at me."

Heather laughed. "Oh, Allison, sometimes you are so suspicious of people. She's probably just irked that her *best friend* might be keeping something from her."

"Perhaps . . . But I don't want her to be irked. Don't forget, Shirley has a mean side to her."

"People can change." Heather smiled. "Don't worry about it, Allison."

At half time Allison went down to get them some hot cocoa. By now she had decided to avoid Shirley altogether. She slipped quietly into the back of a line, hoping that she wouldn't bump into her.

"Did you hear about Allison O'Brian?" whispered a girl off to Allison's right loudly enough for her to hear. She vaguely knew the girl from her English class, although they had never actually had a conversation. The girl obviously hadn't noticed Allison standing there as she continued to speak, and the shocked tone of her voice sounded as if she were disclosing some horrible revelation. "Well, I just heard that her mother is a movie star!"

"You're kidding!" said the other girl. Allison froze as she listened to the first girl continue with her story.

"No, it's absolutely true. It turns out that her mother is *the* Marsha Madison!"

"Unbelievable!" said the other girl. "Well, then, that explains everything."

"What's that?" asked the first girl.

"Why she's so snobbish, of course. Haven't you noticed how she lords it over the rest of us? She's always walking around with her nose in the air. It's obvious that she thinks she's too good for us."

"Well, now that you put it that way, I can see—"

Allison moved away from the line, away from the cruel words and straight to the rest room. She went into an empty stall and closed the door. Hot, angry tears began to flow down her cheeks. *Snobbish? Too good? Nose in the air?* Since when? When had she done any of those things? She had tried to be friendly to everyone.

"Did you hear about Allison O'Brian's mother?" said an unfamiliar female voice. Allison's fist flew up to her mouth—what was going on here? Perhaps she should just step out and stand up to them, but how could she with these stupid tears running down her face? Instead, she just stood and listened again in horror.

"Yes, can you believe it? I always thought she acted sort of snooty and superior. And then, of course, she's best friends with that awful snob Shirley Jenson."

"Well, I just heard that she's even turned on Shirley Jenson now."

"Really?"

"Yes, it seems the only one she talks to anymore is Heather Amberwell, and that's just because Heather is Andrew's sister. She must think she can get to Andrew through his poor blind little sister. Isn't that just too horrible!"

"Ha! Well, Shirley Jenson already tried that trick and it didn't work. It's a good thing that Andrew is so sensible and nice. I'm sure he won't fall for that snooty Allison O'Brian. I sure wish he'd look my way, though. Speaking of Andrew, I'll bet they're starting the second half by now."

Allison flushed the toilet to cover her sobs. It was all so unfair. How could they be so awful? They didn't even know her.

After several minutes the bathroom became quiet, and Allison finally slipped out and splashed cold water on her face. Fortunately the cold night air had turned lots of cheeks pink and eyes bright. Maybe no one would notice hers. She went out and quickly got their cocoa since the lines were gone now. Then she walked back up through the stands, holding her chin out and her head high. It was all she could do to keep the tears back. Let them say what they wanted. She knew it wasn't true. She passed by Shirley and felt her eyes on her, but Allison didn't even look her way. She was much too hurt and angry to talk to Shirley right now. It took all her willpower to not throw her cocoa in Shirley's face.

"Hey, slowpoke," said Heather. "What took you so long?"

"You know how those lines can be, plus I had to use the bathroom." Allison looked longingly over to where her father was sitting. "Say, Heather, would it be okay if we sit with Grace and Dad and Winston for the rest of the game?"

"Fine with me. Let's finish our cocoa first."

Allison didn't want to explain the awful scenes to Heather just yet. Maybe she would tell her tomorrow. When they finished their cocoa and moved across the stadium to the general admission section, Allison was glad to see her father's smiling face.

"What's up?" he asked. "You two actually coming to sit with the old folks tonight?"

"Sure, Dad," Allison said with a teary smile.

"You okay?" he asked quietly.

"I guess so," she whispered. "But can we go home right after the game?"

"Sure."

She could see the concern in his eyes, but she couldn't explain it to him right now. He wrapped his arm around her shoulders. It felt strong and protective and reassuring.

True to his word, they left right after the game. Once they were all safely in the car and on the road, Allison blurted out the story. She didn't go into all the details. Some things still hurt too much to even say out loud.

"I'm so sorry, Allison," James said. "But maybe it's for the best to have it out in the open now."

"That's right, dear," Grace agreed. "Your mother's identity was bound to come out sooner or later."

"It'll be okay, Allison," Heather said. "The people who really know you like you for who you are. They don't think any of those awful things."

"In time this will all blow over," said Grace. "Just you wait and see."

Allison wanted to agree with their wisdom and advice, but she wasn't totally convinced. They hadn't heard *everything* that she had heard. They hadn't felt the sharp, cutting edge of words spoken so thoughtlessly. As they drove home, Allison promised herself that she would never say anything so cruel about anyone. She was sure that she had probably repeated rumors about others in the past, but now that she knew how it felt, she would make every effort to never do it again.

Before Allison went to bed, she asked God to help her to forgive Shirley. She knew from experience that it was better to forgive than to hold a grudge, and Allison was eager to forget the whole thing. Besides, just last week their pastor had said that unforgiveness was like poison to the soul. Allison had tasted that kind of poison before—she didn't want any part of it now.

The next morning, Allison tagged along with her father to the airport again. As expected, Andrew was there waiting. James had already told him that he could join them again today.

"Good morning," Andrew said with a bright smile. "Mac and I have just been discussing how I might be able to help out here part time and earn some flying lessons in exchange for work. I guess he's been having some problems with Larry Burns."

"So I've heard," James said.

"Mac said that he didn't even show up for work yesterday."

"That's too bad for Mac, but it sounds like a good opportunity for you, Andrew." James spoke cheerfully, but his expression said otherwise.

Poor Dad, Allison thought. She knew he was still sweating bullets over how he was going to break all this to Grace, and now he had Andrew to contend with, too. It seemed that secrets were hard to contain.

"I'm going up today, Andrew," Allison announced. "Dad said I can sit in the copilot's seat and actually control the plane for a little while."

"Just a little," James emphasized. "I'm still trying to build up my flying hours, and I'll have to be stingy until my log is nice and full."

Allison glanced at Andrew and saw the longing in his eyes as he stroked the sleek wing of a small plane. "I wish Andrew could come up, too," she said, looking up at her father with raised brows.

"No, Allison," Andrew said. "Thanks anyway, but it's not fair to pressure your dad about this."

James laid his hand on Andrew's shoulder. "Thanks for understanding, son. I'm just looking for the right moment to bring this up with Grace."

Just then Mac joined them. "The right moment, James? Well, I've got an old advertising banner that you could drag behind the plane. We could arrange the letters to say, 'Look at me, Grace, I'm flying!'"

"That's just what I don't need."

It wasn't long before Allison was securely buckled into the little yellow Piper. It was fun to sit right up in the front of the cockpit and watch the blur of the propeller until it slowly became invisible to the eye. Soon the runway was speeding in front of them, then the sky loomed before them—bright blue with a bank of clouds coming in from the sea. James flew for about thirty minutes, then finally allowed Allison to take the stick.

"Just like I told you, Allison. Back toward you for up, forward for down, and of course right and left."

Allison pulled the stick toward her, and the plane's nose lifted and rose higher into the sky. It was a great feeling of ultimate control. She leveled it out for a few seconds, then firmly pushed the stick forward and they began to dive down. After a long moment of going down, she pulled it back up again and leveled it out.

"Remember, Allison, this isn't a carnival ride," James said with a grin.

"But it's so much fun!"

"I guess I should have expected as much."

Allison maneuvered the small plane around the sky for about ten minutes before James took control once again.

"That was wonderful," Allison breathed. "Even better than I thought it would be. I love to fly, Dad. When do you think I can take lessons?"

"I've already discussed it with Mac." His brow creased slightly.

"But you're worried about Grace."

"I just know she's going to be upset with me."

"Maybe you should just tell her and get it over with. Like you guys were saying last night, just get it out into the open and deal with it."

"You're probably right, Allison. Maybe I'll arrange to take Grace to dinner and break the news to her. I'm just not very eager to do it, although it will be a relief to get it over with. The worst she can do is punch me in the nose and leave me in the dust. But I'll still have you, won't I, Allison?" He grinned at her.

"That's right," Allison said protectively. "And we would be just fine, the two of us, wouldn't we?"

"We'd be just fine."

Once again Allison realized she was starting to resent that Grace should have a say about any of this. She loved Grace dearly and knew that her dad did, too, but why should Grace have so much influence about whether or not they wanted to fly?

When they landed, Andrew was sweeping out a hangar. He waved to them as they taxied over to him and hopped out of the plane.

"Looks like Mac has already put you to work," James teased as he closed the door.

"He said I could start stocking up hours as soon as I liked. Especially since he's shorthanded around here right now. In fact, he said the airport is up for sale, and if someone doesn't buy it soon it may be shut down altogether."

"Really?" James said. "I didn't know things were that bad."

Andrew nodded. "That's what Mac said."

"What did Mac say?" Mac echoed good-naturedly as he came around the corner.

"I was telling Mr. O'Brian about the possibility of shutting down the airport. Hope that was okay."

"Sure. It's no secret. I just don't like worrying the few paying customers I do have. Don't want them to give up on us just yet. But the fact of the matter is, Hugh Anderson wants to sell this place off and move down to Arizona. Don't know why anyone would want to live in Arizona—nothing but desert and cactus there. Anyway, so far no one's been interested, and Hugh is talking about shutting it down completely. He wants to be out of here by the end of November."

Mac rubbed his chin thoughtfully and continued. "I wish I could buy the place. I've set a little savings aside, but it isn't nearly enough. I've been telling Hugh for the last several years that we could build us up a nice little air shipping business if we wanted to. You know how things have picked up since the war, and there's no one doing that sort of thing in this part of the country. Many is the time I've gotten a call to go pick up medicine or what-have-you over in Portland, then deliver it somewhere along the coast. You know how long it can take to drive those curvy roads. Flying is a lot faster. I think if Hugh had taken the time to set up a regular air shipping business, it could have been profitable." Mac sighed and stuffed his hands in his pockets. "I reckon it's too late."

"I wonder," James said.

Allison looked curiously at him. "What, Dad?"

"Oh, nothing really. Just a pipe dream. . . ." James turned to Mac. "What will you do if the airport shuts down?" he asked.

"I don't know. I like living here, but I'd have to move on . . . or else look for work in Port View. I haven't really given it a lot of thought. I keep hoping things will change."

James scratched his head. "Maybe they will, Mac."

"I sure hope so," said Andrew. "I want to learn to fly."

"Me too," Allison agreed. "Someone just has to buy this place."

Mac grinned. "Well, don't you folks worry. Things seem to work out in the end."

James and Allison told Mac and Andrew good-bye and headed for home. On the way, Allison kept pondering over the trouble with the airport. Finally she spoke.

"Dad, I know this sounds crazy. But I wonder if *we* could buy the airport."

"*We?*"

"Well . . . I don't know how these things work—it may not even be possible, but apparently I have some sort of fortune in the Madison estate—"

141

James chuckled. "Yes, I can just imagine your grandmother Madison's face if you even suggested cashing in your inheritance to purchase a rinky-dink airport. Besides, any inheritance of yours is tied up until you turn eighteen."

"Oh." Allison frowned. "I guess it was a silly idea."

"Not really, Allison. I was toying with the idea myself."

"Really? How, Dad? Can you afford to do something like that?"

"Your grandfather left me pretty well off, and with the way things have been going with the Jensons lately, a new business opportunity might be a nice change. Marge seems to want to run the shipping business right into the ground, and Hal just idly sits by twiddling his thumbs."

"And?" Allison looked at her dad with wide eyes, but he didn't continue. It was almost as if he couldn't bring himself to actually say the words. Finally Allison said them for him.

"So maybe you'd like to get out of ocean shipping and get into air shipping instead?"

He nodded slowly. "That's what I was thinking."

"Dad, that's a terrific idea. You would be doing something you really loved. It's fantastic!"

"Except for one thing . . ."

Allison thought for a moment. "Grace."

James nodded. "I can't plan my future without giving her a chance to say something."

"But why should she have the final say?" Allison asked.

"Oh, Allison, you know Grace would never be like that. But knowing what I do about how strongly she feels about flying . . . well, it's hard to ignore her opinion."

"I know, Dad. I didn't mean to sound cruel. I respect Grace's opinion, too. I just wish that she saw the fun in flying like we do. Maybe she will eventually."

"Maybe she will."

"So will you look into it, Dad? Will you consider getting out of the partnership with the Jensons and buying the airport?"

"Of course I'll consider it. In fact, it's probably all I'll be thinking about for the next few days."

Allison smiled as she thought about what a huge relief it would be not to have to be nice to Shirley anymore, but then she reminded herself that she had already forgiven Shirley. Once again, she had to let go of her bitterness. There was no point in hanging on to hurt feelings. She sighed, hoping Shirley wouldn't always be her cross to bear.

Allison tried to turn her thoughts to more exciting subjects, primarily the Harvest Ball, but her spirit sank once more. Would they still be talking about her and her mother's identity? Would people think poorly of Andrew because he was taking her to the dance? Would they think she had used Heather to get to Andrew? Oh, it was all just so ridiculous and unfair! This was a night she should have been looking forward to, and now she was dreading it so much she wasn't even sure if she wanted to go.

11

"Oh, Heather," Allison exclaimed for the third time. "You look so gorgeous! Just like a princess." Allison replaced a golden lock that had come loose from one of the glittering combs that Grace had used to sweep back Heather's hair. Allison stared at Heather in wonder. The sophisticated cut of the moiré satin gown made Heather look like she was at least twenty. The neckline seemed to frame Heather's ivory skin like an elegant picture frame. "And this necklace is perfect with the dress. The stones are the same color of pale blue."

"They're just rhinestones, of course," said Grace apologetically. "But, actually, I think you *both* look like princesses, and I don't know if we should even let you two out looking so grown-up. Please don't forget you're still just kids." She turned back to doing Allison's hair.

"Don't worry, we don't want to grow up yet." Allison watched in the mirror as Grace skillfully styled her auburn curls. "You know," said Allison thoughtfully, "Marsha picked out this gown." She ran her hands down the smooth satin skirt that flowed from the tightly fitted waistline.

"Marsha has exquisite taste," Grace said as she tucked a bobby pin into Allison's hair to discreetly pull her hair back from her face. "That soft shade of yellow makes your skin glow, Allison. And those sweet little sleeves remind me of a porcelain figurine that my mother used to have. It's too bad Marsha can't see you right now."

"I'll have to send her a photo."

"Yes," agreed Heather. "And I will send John a photo, too." Heather spun around in a pirouette. "Don't you love the rustling, swishing sound of satin and tulle? It sounds so happy—it reminds me of water rushing down a creek."

Allison smiled. "You're exactly right, Heather."

"There," proclaimed Grace, stepping back. "I think that should do it."

"Grace, you are an absolute whiz with hair." Allison couldn't believe how Grace had smoothed the curls into a perfect style. "It reminds me of Lauren Bacall's hair."

"There was a time when I thought I wanted to become a beautician instead of a nurse, but I finally decided that perhaps it was better to make people well than to make them pretty. Still, it doesn't hurt your health to look good." Grace went over to her handbag on Allison's bed. "I don't know if you want to try this or not, but I saw some ribbon at the fabric store, and I thought it might look pretty in your hair, Allison. . . ."

"It's beautiful, Grace. But what will you do with it?" Allison stared at the stream of satin ribbon. The color reminded her of the ocean on a day when it looked almost green.

"Let me show you," said Grace as she slipped the ribbon around Allison's head and tied it like a headband. "It's just a little touch, but I thought this color of green was a lot like your eyes." Grace stepped back. "There, now, doesn't that look pretty."

"Thanks, Grace," said Allison. "It's perfect."

"You girls stand still." James popped his head through the door and aimed his big camera. "I want to get some candid shots before the boys get here."

Allison's room was getting crowded as James squirmed in and out popping flashbulbs until Allison was sure that she would be seeing blue spots all night. He finally handed the camera to Grace and stepped up to Allison with a wide grin. Then he reached into his jacket pocket and pulled out a lovely strand of pearls.

"These were your grandmother O'Brian's," he said as he slipped them around her neck and clasped them in back. "You don't have to wear them if you don't want to, Allison, but I thought they might look pretty with your dress."

Allison spun around to look in the mirror, then turned back to her father. "They're absolutely perfect, Dad. But are you sure you want me to wear them? What if I lose them?"

He grinned and gave her a gentle hug, as if he were afraid of crushing her dress. "Don't worry about that. They are meant to be worn. Your grandmother would be so happy to see you wearing them, Allison. She would be so proud of you." He stepped back and looked at her with glistening eyes, then shook his head. "And to think I could have missed out on all this. I thank God every day, Allison. I really do." He got his camera again and took several more shots, finally one with all three of them together. Then he caught Muriel in the hallway and made her come join them for a photo.

"Goodness," Muriel exclaimed with a bright smile. "I'll surely spoil the photograph for everyone."

"No, you won't," declared Allison as she pulled Muriel into the room.

"Okay, now let's get some photos of the girls downstairs," James suggested after several more pictures.

A few minutes later the doorbell rang, and George formally led Andrew and Curt into the library, treating them as if they were visiting royalty. Allison studied Andrew's expression as he walked into the room and saw her. She was satisfied when his face lit up like a Christmas tree. Then she looked at Curt as he greeted Heather—it looked like his eyes were going to pop right out of his head! Allison wanted to clap her hands with joy and laugh out loud, but instead she maintained a dignified sense of decorum. More photos were taken, then coats were put on and it was finally time to leave. James slipped the keys into Andrew's hand and gave him a look that Allison knew was meant to be fatherly but looked almost threatening. Andrew nodded respectfully, as if they had some unspoken understanding, and then the four of them were off.

Allison sat in the front seat beside Andrew, with Heather and Curt in the back. There was an uncomfortable formality in the air that none of them were used to. They made polite small talk as Andrew carefully drove. At Heather's timely prompting, the boys began to rehash last night's football game, and the conversation became more natural and relaxed. Unfortunately for Allison, the talk of last night only reminded her of the mean gossip she'd overheard at half time. She tried to push those awful comments from her mind, but it was of little use.

By the time they were walking across the crowded school parking lot, Allison felt certain that everyone at Port View High thought she was the most horrible girl ever. She imagined the stares she would receive, the murmurings she would overhear. Her stomach began to tie itself into dozens of tight little knots.

As they entered the decorated gym, Andrew extended his arm like a perfect gentleman. She took his arm, trying not to reveal how nervous she felt by clutching it too tightly. Taking a deep breath, she fixed her focus on the colorful harvest decorations. She observed the pumpkins, scarecrows, and cornstalks neatly arranged by the doors, and above their heads hung an array of fall-colored crepe paper streamers crisscrossing all about the gymnasium. Finally she allowed herself to look at her fellow students, who were also dressed formally for the dance. It was a kaleidoscope of color, full of nervous energy and life. And she was not surprised to see many sets of eyes fixed on her and Andrew. She couldn't tell if they were staring with hostility or simply amazed that Andrew had brought *her* as his date. Perhaps it was better not to know.

"We should find a table," Andrew said with polite confidence. He began to head toward an empty table near the back wall.

"Hey, Andrew," Karen called. "Why don't you all join us?" She stood and waved her hand to indicate their half-filled table. "We've still got some room here."

Andrew glanced at Allison as if to ask if this was acceptable to her. "That would be nice," she murmured.

She recognized the boys as some of Andrew's teammates and knew that he would probably enjoy their company, and of course, she knew Karen and her friends Beverly and Janet. She had just learned that Janet was also a sophomore, and that these three girls usually stuck together because they were the youngest cheerleaders and were sometimes picked on by the older girls. Fortunately, these three were not among the ones that Allison had overheard talking about her last night. Just the same, she had no doubt that they'd heard the news by now.

"Great," Andrew said as he pulled out a chair for Allison. "And how about if Curt and I get you girls some punch." The other fellows immediately leaped up from the table to join Andrew and Curt. It was amusing how stiff and uncomfortable these normally confident athletes looked in their formal suits and ties. They seemed relieved to get up and move around.

"Allison and Heather!" Karen gushed. "You two look absolutely gorgeous tonight!"

"Thank you," Heather said, smiling politely.

"What beautiful gowns," Beverly added as she moved closer to examine their dresses. "You couldn't have gotten those anywhere around here. You two look just like glamorous movie stars!"

Allison tried not to grimace as she thanked Beverly for the compliment. Then she said sincerely, "You all look really fantastic, too."

The five girls stood for a while, chatting and admiring one another's dresses. After several minutes Allison began to relax a little. Perhaps these girls hadn't heard about Marsha after all. Or better yet, perhaps they simply didn't care.

"Okay," Karen said in a conspirator's tone. "We might as well ask what we're all dying to know. Allison, is it true? Is Marsha Madison *really* your mother?"

Allison felt her cheeks begin to glow, but she did appreciate Karen's frankness. It was certainly preferable to the catty comments of the girls in the bathroom. Allison nodded. "I really didn't want everyone to find out—"

"Goodness, why not?" cried Beverly. "If it were me I'd be telling everyone, then selling them autographs for five bucks a pop."

The others laughed while Allison began to giggle. "I never thought of that, Beverly."

Karen reached out and clasped Allison's hand. "Well, we've heard that some people are acting very childish about the whole thing, and we wanted you to know that we think they're ridiculous. We don't think you're a snob at all. We heard Shirley Jenson going around last night and saying all sorts of stupid things—"

"That's right," interrupted Beverly. "And we think Shirley is—well, it wouldn't be very ladylike to say exactly what we think." Everyone laughed, even Heather.

"Why don't we sit down," Janet suggested. "It looks like the guys are over there replaying last night's game."

"Now, Allison," Karen began in a serious voice. "You've got to understand that we're all desperate to know everything about your mom, but I told the girls here that we needed to respect you as our friend and not invade your privacy. So if we accidentally forget and get too nosy, you just let us know, okay?"

Allison smiled. "It's all right. You're all being so sweet about the whole thing that I really don't mind a few questions. It's not fun having a famous mom. Sometimes it's just easier to keep the whole thing a secret."

Karen nodded. "I can understand that. I'm sure I wouldn't want everyone only thinking of me as someone's daughter." The other girls agreed.

Allison filled them in about what her mother's current movie project was and what Marsha's luxurious home in Beverly Hills looked like, and the girls all listened with wide-eyed awe, asking appropriate questions here and there. For some reason they seemed very different from boarding school girls. Perhaps it was because everyone at boarding school had rich or important parents; not to mention that movie stars were not always highly regarded and sometimes were actually looked down upon among wealthy families.

"And if it wasn't for Allison's mother sending these gowns," Heather interjected, "we would have looked like Cinderella *before* the fairy godmother came."

"Really?" Janet said. "Your dresses actually came from Marsha Madison?"

Heather nodded. "She sent them to Allison along with a bunch of other things."

"Wow," said Beverly. She touched Allison's sleeve as if the fabric itself held some sort of magic.

"Well, Marsha didn't actually wear this one," Allison explained. "She and I got it while I was in Beverly Hills last summer. I was supposed to wear it to a big party, but I ended up wearing something else." Allison turned to Heather, nodding at her dress. "But I think that Marsha may have worn that one a few years ago."

All the girls turned and stared at Heather. Janet and Beverly both touched the moiré satin sleeves.

Just then the boys returned with their drinks, and to Allison's relief the talk of movie stars momentarily ceased as they sipped their punch and tossed corny jokes back and forth. Allison glanced over to where the small amateur jazz band was playing a slightly off-key Bing Crosby tune to an almost-empty dance floor. Only two couples were dancing, and they were the grown-up chaperones, probably hoping to get the ball rolling. Allison wondered if any of the students actually planned to dance, or if they would just sit and visit all night.

"Do you want to dance, Allison?" Andrew asked as if reading her mind. Everyone else stopped talking and looked at her expectantly.

"I . . . uh . . . sure, I guess so," she stammered. As much as she wanted to dance with Andrew, she wasn't certain that she wanted to be out on the dance floor when it was so bare. But, as if on cue, the other boys at their table began to ask the girls to dance, and soon their whole group was out on the floor together. Apparently they were the perfect ice-breaker, for by the next song the floor was crowded. Allison even spied Shirley with Mark clumsily dancing along. It seemed that Mark's sense of rhythm was sadly lacking, and by the sour expression on Shirley's face, he would be hearing about it soon. Poor Mark.

Andrew was surprisingly comfortable on the dance floor, but then Allison figured that might have to do with his involvement in sports. "Your dancing skills have improved since last summer," commented Allison with a sly grin.

Andrew laughed. "Actually, Grace has been giving me some lessons."

After several dances the group returned to their table and replenished their refreshments. Everyone seemed more comfortable and relaxed now. Allison looked around at the happy faces at her table and marveled at how only an hour ago she was fretful and nervous about tonight. She tried not to look around the gym. She didn't want to spot the girls who had said the mean things last night. She felt certain they couldn't possibly be having as much fun as she was. She glanced over at Heather and Curt engaged in a lively conversation. It was wonderful to see Heather having a good time. Allison sighed and smiled over at Andrew, but an odd expression creased his brow as he looked over her shoulder.

"Can we join you?" asked a familiar voice behind her.

Allison turned around to see Shirley with Mark in tow. Shirley had on the dress she had described to Allison. It was a strange orange-pink shade of taffeta and reminded Allison of a giant flamingo. Before she could answer, Beverly spoke up.

"Sorry, kids, these chairs are taken."

Shirley scowled darkly for a long moment, then finally turned and pulled on Mark's arm. Allison watched as Shirley marched off. She felt a little guilty, but then she thought of all the mean things that Shirley had said and figured it was Shirley's own fault that she had not been invited to join them.

"I can't believe the nerve," Beverly whispered. "After all the garbage she said last night—"

"She actually thought she'd be welcome at our table!" Janet exclaimed. "Doesn't that just beat all."

"I feel a little sorry for her," began Allison. "She brings these things on herself."

"Well, maybe this will teach her a lesson," Beverly said.

"Okay, okay," Bruce Williams cut in. "Enough about that. I think it's time for another dance."

Within seconds they were all out on the floor again, this time trying to do the jitterbug. Allison saw Shirley and Mark sitting alone at a table. Mark was leaning back in his chair as if exasperated, but Shirley was sitting ramrod straight with her arms folded tightly across her chest and staring coldly at Allison as if she were a mortal enemy. A shiver went down Allison's spine, and she forced her eyes to look a different direction. She was not about to let Shirley Jenson spoil *this* evening.

When the Harvest Ball finally ended, Karen invited Andrew and Curt and the girls to join them at Wally's for a late-night snack, but Andrew said that he had promised to have the girls home before midnight.

"Otherwise we might turn into pumpkins," Allison joked.

"Perhaps another time," Heather said politely.

"You bet," Karen said. "There'll be lots more times. Thanks for joining us tonight. It was fun getting to know you two better."

Allison was glad that Andrew didn't seem mind not going to Wally's. She knew that her father expected her home by midnight. Besides, the long day had made her tired. The drive home was much more relaxed than coming. The four of them chatted comfortably about the events of the evening. Andrew even mentioned Shirley.

"I hate to say this, Allison," he began, "but I think Shirley Jenson may have it out for you now."

"I'll say," agreed Curt. "If looks could kill, you'd be dead right now."

"Really?" Heather questioned. "What makes you think that?"

"Well," began Curt, "you should have seen her face. She reminded me of that old witch in *The Wizard of Oz*!"

Allison laughed. "Oh, she wasn't quite that bad, just a little unnerving. What's hard is that her dad is in partnership with my dad."

"You're kidding," said Curt. "What rotten luck."

"So somehow, I'll have to try to make things up with Miss Jenson," Allison said. "I've already forgiven her for what she pulled last night."

Curt looked confused. "You actually forgave her? How could you? I mean, if some guy did something like that to me, I think I'd want to meet him out in the back parking lot."

Andrew chuckled. "That's understandable to feel like that, Curt, but I think Allison is trying to forgive others the way the Bible says to. Right, Allison?"

Allison smiled. "That's right. And even though it's never easy, especially with people like Shirley, in the end I'm pretty sure it's worth it."

"I can't imagine how," said Curt skeptically.

"I'm still just learning about it myself," Allison explained. "But I know that when we *don't* forgive people it just builds up inside of us—all the anger and bitterness—and it ends up making us even more miserable than the people we refuse to forgive."

"I see your point," Curt agreed.

"Here we are, Allison," Andrew announced as he pulled up to her house.

The lights were glowing warmly through the foggy night. It felt good to have a dad waiting up to hear about her evening.

Andrew walked her to the door. Allison paused for a moment on the porch, thinking about how people in movies often kissed at the door and wondering if she was ready for that. Was Andrew?

"Thanks, Andrew," she said smiling brightly. "It was a wonderful night."

He took her hand in his and gave it a warm squeeze. "Thank *you*, Allison. I had a swell time. I really did. And I think Heather enjoyed it, too."

Allison nodded. "I just hope that Curt doesn't fall head over heels in love with her. It might break his heart to find out that hers belongs to another."

Andrew laughed. "I hope her heart doesn't really belong to anyone yet. She's far too young for that sort of nonsense."

A sickening sensation began to grow in the pit of her stomach, and Allison quickly pulled her hand out of his. "Of course," she said stiffly, wondering why she had even bothered getting her hopes up over Andrew. He would always see her as a young girl.

Confused at her reaction, Andrew looked slightly surprised. "Well, thanks again, Allison. I really did have a good time."

"Thank you, Andrew. I better go in now."

She went inside and leaned against the closed door, and her frustration turned to understanding. Andrew was probably right. She was only a freshman in high school—it was silly to feel this way about a boy. Why, only last year she had made fun of lovesick girls who acted all swoony, and she and Patricia had always giggled during the mushy scenes of movies.

"How did it go, Allison?" her father asked, interrupting her thoughts.

"It was wonderful, Dad," she answered honestly.

"Then why are you frowning?"

She laughed. "I guess I'm just tired. Really . . . it was an almost perfect night."

"Almost?"

Allison shook her head. "I doubt you really want to hear all about it."

"Muriel has gone to bed, but she left milk warming for cocoa, as well as some delicious molasses cookies. I guarantee you, Allison, I want to hear everything."

"I should warn you that some of it involves Shirley Jenson," Allison said as she hung up her coat.

"Ah, well, that explains a lot."

Over cookies and cocoa in the cozy kitchen, Allison told her dad all about Shirley's little scene at the dance. "The sad thing is that Shirley just seems to be digging herself into a deep hole. No one at our table seemed to have any respect for her at all. I feel sort of sorry for her. Her attempts at making friends have all backfired."

James stared at his cocoa with intensity. "I hate to say it, but people like that just seem to go for whatever it is they want, and they don't care very much about who gets hurt along the way."

Allison noticed the dark look in his eyes and wondered if he wasn't referring to his own situation, as well. "Are things getting worse in the business?"

"They're sure not getting any better. It's hard to see Marge making decisions that seem to have no regard for the people who have worked so hard for the business all these years."

Allison nodded. "That must be awful."

"Not only that, but Hal won't stand up to her. She has no respect for my opinion on anything. She acts like everyone would be better off if I just went back to the lighthouse to live." He forced a laugh.

Allison smiled. "Well, I hope you're not taking her seriously."

"No, of course not, but it's difficult being partnered with

someone you cannot agree with. I know that my dad and Hal's dad had a great business together, but it just doesn't seem like it can continue—not like this."

"Grandpa wouldn't have wanted things to be like this."

"I know, and it makes me feel bad that I can't just make it work somehow. I feel like I am failing him—"

"No, Dad," Allison interrupted. "You're not failing him."

"But I'm not making the business work—not the way he would."

Allison thought for a moment. "Tell me—do you think that I'm failing you when I can't manage to get along with Shirley Jenson?"

"Of course not, Allison. Good grief, I don't think anyone can get along with that girl."

"Then why would Grandpa judge you any differently?"

James slowly smiled. "How'd you get to be so smart?"

"I think it runs in the family." She grinned and pointed her finger at him. "Now, what about buying that airport? What about selling out the shipping business and starting something completely new?"

"It's sounding better all the time." He sighed dreamily, then looked down at his watch. "It's long past midnight, Cinderella. I think your ball gown should be turning into a nightgown about now." He stood and gently took her hand as if escorting her to the dance floor.

"I am pretty tired, and these high heels are starting to really hurt my feet."

"Off to bed with you, then, my princess." He leaned down and kissed the top of her head. "I'll clean things up in here so Muriel won't have to get up to a messy kitchen."

"She'll appreciate that. Good night." Allison paused at the kitchen door. "You know, Dad, I'm going to pray that God will show you just what to do in regard to the business and the airport possibilities."

"Thanks, Allison. I could use some divine direction. I keep finding myself wishing for Dad to tell me what to do. I missed out on so much by not being around my father. . . ."

"Well, God is our father, too. I'm sure He can tell you what to do."

James smiled. "I hope so."

12

The week following the dance went smoothly for Allison, especially since Shirley seemed to be avoiding her. At first Allison felt a little sorry for Shirley because she seemed rather lonely and isolated, but by the end of the week, a gathering of girls seemed to attach themselves to her, and Shirley basked in their attention. Not surprisingly, Allison recognized several of them as the ones who had repeated the gossip the night before the dance. It figured.

Allison and Heather had eaten lunch with Karen, Janet, and Beverly throughout the week, but it hadn't seemed as if Caroline was entirely welcome in that crowd. Allison was pretty certain that Heather sensed this, too.

"You go ahead and have lunch with Karen and her friends," said Heather on Thursday when Allison invited her to join them.

"But I want to eat with you," Allison said. "Caroline can come along, too."

"I don't think they want me at their table." Caroline looked down at her plate.

Allison sighed. It was probably true. Caroline had the uncanny ability to make people uncomfortable. Earlier in the week, just after Caroline had learned about Allison's mother being Marsha Madison, she couldn't stop staring at Allison as if she, too, were also a movie star.

"Go ahead, Allison, I really don't mind," Heather said encouragingly.

Allison looked at Karen's table. The girls were laughing loudly now, and it sounded like fun. Why did she have to choose between Heather and the others? Just then, as if on cue, Karen looked over and waved at Allison.

"Go ahead," Caroline said. "We'll be fine."

"No," Allison replied decisively. "Not unless you will both come with me. Come on, you two, let's all go and join them."

"Really?" Caroline looked skeptical.

"Yes," Allison said, pulling Heather along with her.

"Hi, there," Karen greeted. "Pull up a piece of bench."

Allison found spots for herself and Heather and nodded to Caroline to take the empty space directly across from them, right next to Janet. Allison didn't miss the sour look on Janet's face as Caroline sat next to her and hoped that Caroline hadn't seen it.

"Janet," teased Karen, "you look as if your lunch doesn't agree with you."

"Yes," Janet muttered as she rolled her eyes. "Too much spice in the meatloaf."

Allison sighed in relief.

"Are you going to the game in Trenton on Saturday, Allison?" Beverly asked.

"Yes, my dad is going to drive us. I guess it takes almost two hours to get there."

"We're going to spend the night at my aunt's house so we don't have to drive back so late," said Karen. "You could join us, but you'll probably want ride back with your dad."

"You're right," Allison said. "But thanks for thinking of us."

"Hey, Allison," Karen said between bites. "I keep forgetting to ask you something. I noticed how much you seem to enjoy those writing projects that Miss Jones keeps assigning for English. You should talk to Beverly about the *Pirate Chest.*"

"What's that?" asked Allison as she opened her milk.

"The school paper," Janet said as if Allison should know this by now. "Beverly is the assistant editor, and she's always trying to get us to join the ranks. Don't do it, Allison."

Allison laughed, then turned to Beverly with genuine interest. "Actually, I'd like to hear more about it."

Janet groaned. "You'll be sorry. . . ."

"Give it a rest, Janet," said Beverly. "Just because you're too lazy—"

"Lazy has nothing to do—"

"C'mon, you two," said Karen. "Allison might like working for the paper."

"Actually, I do like to write," she confirmed.

"Ah-ha, I suspected you were the literary type," said Beverly smugly. "Okay, meet me in the journalism room right after school, and I'll give you the whole scoop."

⚘

Allison discussed the possibility of working for the school paper with Heather as they walked to their last class of the day.

"I really think you should do it," Heather said. "You'll probably be very good at it. I remember when Grace read me your letters last summer, I always felt as if I were right there with you in Beverly Hills or wherever you were writing from. You seem to have a real gift."

"You would probably be good at it, too," Allison said. "You are always saying things that sound like they could be written in a book."

Heather laughed. "I think I'd rather focus on my music

161

right now, but I appreciate the compliment. You know, Andrew has expressed interest in working on the paper. I hear that they only started it last spring—that's why they're a little short staffed."

"It would be great to get in on the ground floor," said Allison. "Beverly seems to think it's possible. Can Caroline take you to meet my dad in the parking lot and tell him I'll be about ten minutes late?"

"Sure. Um . . . I wanted to tell you something while Caroline is in the bathroom. Remember last week when she was so glum about not going to the dance, and we told her that we'd help her to fit in better and everything?"

"Uh-huh," Allison said quickly as they neared the classroom.

"Well, I hope you don't mind, but I sort of offered to do something with her on Friday night."

"This Friday?"

"Yes, is that okay?" Heather's voice grew uncertain. "I told her I would have to check with you first."

"Sure, I guess so. What did you have in mind?"

"Well, the thing is, she was nervous about coming to my house because of Andrew, you see."

Allison laughed. "Because of Andrew?"

"Shh, she might be coming," Heather whispered.

"I don't see her."

"Well, I wondered, Allison . . . do you think we could come to your house? Grace could come over and—"

"Here comes Caroline now. Sure," Allison whispered quickly. "No problem, Heather."

"Thanks, Allison," Heather said in relief. "We'll talk later."

Allison met with Beverly after school as planned. The journalism room was off by itself in a small building separate from the school. Beverly gave her a quick tour of the facility, such as it was, including the closet, which served as a darkroom, and the mimeograph machine that was used to print the paper. Beverly introduced Allison to several students whom she had seen around school. The only name she retained was Howard Ketchum's—only because she had heard Andrew say that Howard was the smartest kid in school, maybe even a genius. Howard was tall and slim and seemed a little shy behind his horn-rimmed glasses, but he smiled and shook her hand and told her that he hoped she would want to come on board. After Howard returned to his big black typewriter, Beverly explained that although Howard was only a junior, he was the editor of the paper.

"It's not much," Beverly apologized. "But it's a start." She held up a small stack of handwritten and typed papers. "And this will be our first issue of the year. Our original goal was to have a weekly paper, but we're so short staffed that we'll start out with a monthly and hopefully speed up as the year progresses. So what do you think?"

Allison didn't have to think twice before answering, "I think I'd like to give it a try."

"Great! I work after school on Tuesdays and Thursdays. Sometimes I'm late if we have cheerleading practice, but Howard can keep you busy. He's the brains, I'm just the organizer." Beverly looked over her shoulder, and Howard smiled shyly at her.

"I'd be lost without Beverly," he admitted. "I'm not the management type."

"Well, I think this looks like fun," Allison said. "I wish I could stay and work, but my dad's waiting. I'll have to start planning on staying late on Tuesdays and Thursdays from now on."

"Excellent," said Howard. "We could use some more help around here."

Allison was so excited when she got into the car that she immediately launched into the story about working on the paper. "I'll need to stay late two days a week, Dad. Is that okay with you?"

"You could probably ride home with Andrew when he has football practice," Heather suggested.

"That's right," James said. "And we can figure the rest out later. It sounds like a fun opportunity for you, Allison. I know how you like to write."

After they dropped off Heather at home, Allison asked if she could have Heather and Caroline spend the night on Friday.

"Sure, Allison, what's up?"

"Well, I sort of promised Heather that we would try to help Caroline look more like the other girls in school. I mean, she's nice and everything, but she just doesn't fit in very well. Do you think it's hopeless?"

"Nothing is hopeless. I think it's very nice of you to care."

"We're going to ask Grace to come help, too."

James smiled. "Grace will enjoy that. I know she likes Caroline a lot. She would love to help her out."

They took the road toward the airport. "I've got some business to take care of with Mac," he said with a mysterious twinkle in his eye.

"Business?" Allison asked slyly. "Is it the kind of business I'm hoping it is?"

"Maybe. Do you want to come into the office with me? I don't mind if you listen, Allison. I'd like you to be my partner in this."

Allison grinned. "I wouldn't miss this for anything. I can't wait to see Mac's face."

It was even better than Allison imagined. Mac jumped out of his chair in excitement. "You mean it?" he shouted with glee, slapping James on the back. "You truly mean it? You're not just putting me on now?"

"Take it easy, Mac. It's not all signed and sealed yet, but it seems that Hal and Marge are ready to get me out of their hair for good. My attorney is still looking things over, and we want everything done right. Still, it looks like I could be the new owner sometime in November if all goes well."

"That's only a few more weeks," Mac exclaimed. "This is the grandest news I've heard since the war ended. This is a day to celebrate!"

"Well, let's save our celebrating until it's all done. And remember, Mac, not a word of this to anyone. I only wanted you to know because I know how much this place means to you."

"Ah-ha," said Mac knowingly. "Then I'm guessing you haven't told Grace about this new little business venture yet."

James shook his head. "Everything is happening so fast right now. I know that I should, but there just hasn't been the right time yet."

"I've still got that banner—"

"Please . . . not the banner again."

"I know you young people think differently about these things," Mac said. "But I grew up in a world where the men did what they had to do, and the women didn't have a whole lot to say about it."

"I understand," James said. "But I've learned to look at things differently. Mostly, I don't want to hurt Grace."

"You do what you think is best, James, and thanks for sharing the good news. I'll be sleeping a little easier tonight."

Allison considered Mac's words about women as they drove home. In the case of Grace and her father, she thought it sounded okay, but at the same time she knew that if she were Grace she might feel differently. Of course, Grace and her father weren't married. They weren't even officially engaged.

"You look like you're in another world, Allison Mercury. Are you thinking about that school paper?"

"No, actually, I was thinking about the airport and about what Mac said. I think that if Grace really loves you, she would be willing to stand by you—no matter what."

"You really think so?"

"I do, Dad. Maybe you can tell her tomorrow night—when she comes over to help with Caroline. Just make sure you don't spill the beans until we're all done with Caroline. I wouldn't want to blow her concentration."

James laughed. "That's my practical daughter."

※

But the next day James had to make an unexpected trip to deliver more paintings to a gallery up the coast. He left a message for Allison with Muriel saying he wouldn't be home until late. Allison knew that if they had their air shipping business he could have easily delivered the paintings and still made it back in time for dinner. One more good reason to proceed with the airport purchase.

Grace brought Heather and Caroline over as planned, and they spent their first hour flipping through the pile of recent issues of fashion magazines that Marsha had tossed into the bottom of Allison's trunk. At first Allison had a hard time looking Grace in the eye. She felt slightly guilty for the secret that she and Andrew were keeping from her. If only her father had been able to tell Grace tonight as planned. It would've been nice to have gotten everything out into the open once and for all.

Soon they were so caught up in discussing various hairstyle possibilities and wardrobe changes that Allison put thoughts of the airport business out of her head. Besides, she told herself, Grace would support them in this. She had to.

Before long it was decided that Caroline needed her hair cut. She always wore it pulled severely back with silver barrettes at the sides, then it hung straight down her back like a horse's tail. This style only served to make her rather large face look even bigger. Like Heather's hair, Caroline's was blond. But unlike Heather's thick, luxurious curls, Caroline's hair was thin and limp and barely waved.

"Some bangs will soften your face," Grace explained as she held Caroline's hair around her face, pretending it was shorter.

"Do *you* know how to cut hair?" asked Caroline.

"Well, I cut the boys' hair and my own," Grace said hesitantly.

"And you trim mine," Heather reminded her.

"Then please cut mine," Caroline said assertively.

Grace blinked in surprise but then agreed. Soon Caroline's hair was bluntly cut just above her shoulders with neat bangs that framed her face. Grace dampened and curled the hair onto rods, then wrapped a white tea towel around her head.

"You know," Allison said as she studied Caroline without her bulky, dark-framed glasses. "I don't know if you've ever considered changing your glasses, but . . ." She paused for a moment. She didn't want to say the wrong thing and hurt Caroline's feelings.

"Yes?" Caroline asked anxiously. "My mom has been telling me it's time to get some new ones. These are all sprung on the hinges. I've had them ever since the sixth grade."

"I remember a girl from boarding school who wore glasses, but the rims were so delicate and light colored that it almost didn't look like she had glasses on. She was a very pretty girl. In fact, I remember actually wishing I wore glasses because I thought I might look like her." Allison laughed.

"That's a great idea, Allison," Grace said. "You know, I've heard it said that President Truman looks like a completely different man when he takes off *his* glasses. It's amazing how such a small thing can make such a great difference."

Grace and Allison also decided that Caroline's hemlines should all go down at least three inches whenever possible, and they thought she should avoid the frilly types of blouses that she seemed to wear so often.

"They're pretty," Grace said gently. "But I don't think they quite fit your face, Caroline. I think you should go for the more classic style."

"Yes," agreed Allison quickly. "Like Katharine Hepburn. I saw her in Hollywood last summer. She's a very striking woman, and she looks terrific in trousers. I wish my legs were long like hers, then I would wear trousers all the time."

"I didn't want any new clothes for school this year," said Caroline. "My mom sure wasn't very happy about that, but I don't like shopping with her. She always wants to dress me up like I'm still her *little* girl. She doesn't understand how the other girls dress, and I'm hopeless at finding the right things myself. Besides . . ." Caroline looked down at her hands and frowned at her chewed fingernails. "It's hard to find clothes that fit just right. I know I've put on a little weight in the last year. I keep telling Mom that I'm getting fat, but she just laughs and says I look *healthy*. She's always making cookies and cakes and things—" Her voice caught, and tears glistened in her eyes.

"Grace knows a lot about nutrition and diet," said Heather. "She is a registered nurse, you know. I'll bet she could tell you what's good to eat and what you might want to avoid."

"Will you, Grace?" Caroline asked hopefully.

"Certainly, dear. We'll write up a diet for you to follow. But it will be up to you to stick with it. It takes a lot of discipline and exercise to lose weight."

"I'd really like to try," Caroline sniffed, and Allison handed her a handkerchief.

Allison remembered what Heather had told her about Caroline's only brother. He had enlisted in the army in 1944, and not long after he arrived in Europe he was reported as missing in action. Caroline rarely spoke of him, and Heather said that Caroline clung to the hope that her brother was alive. Suddenly, Allison realized that she had been so consumed by her own problems that she had hardly registered how hard all this must be on poor Caroline, not to mention her parents. No wonder Heather had been so kind and loyal to Caroline. She made a silent vow to do the same from now on.

By the time Grace left and the girls went to bed, they felt like they had made huge progress. Allison had even promised Caroline a few pieces of Marsha's cast-off clothing as incentive if she could stick to her diet and meet her weight goal. Caroline had been ecstatic, disclosing that her secret dream was to become an actress someday.

"Thank you both so much," Caroline said in the darkness. Her voice sounded stronger now, more confident. "I'm going to do everything we've said. I know it will take time and work, but I'm going to do it. When my brother, Kevin, comes home, I want him to be proud of me."

"Caroline," said Allison, "he must already be proud of you."

"Thanks, Allison. But I want him to see me happy, too."

"Good for you, Caroline," Heather cheered. "We'll do all that we can to help."

"Yes," Allison teased playfully. "I promise to smack you every time I see you biting a nail."

"And I'll ask you about your diet and exercise every day at lunch," said Heather.

"You two are the best friends I've ever had," said Caroline. "I won't let you down."

"Don't do it for us, Caroline," Allison urged. "And doing it for your brother is nice, but I think you should do it for yourself. It's your life, you know. You're the only one who can really live it."

"That's right," Caroline agreed triumphantly. "It is *my* life. And for the first time in ages, I feel like things might be getting better."

❋

The next morning, after a light breakfast and a vigorous walk on the beach, they sent Caroline home with her newly styled haircut and armed with magazine pictures of clothing styles that might flatter her bulky figure. Allison even found an advertisement for glasses that were almost identical to the ones she had described last night. All in all, it seemed like their time was well spent, and Allison was in good spirits as she joined her father for their Saturday morning flight.

Allison told him all about their time with Caroline as they flew south along the coastline. "It was so great to see Caroline happy, Dad. I guess I sort of forgot that her brother is still missing. Her parents think he's in a camp in Siberia. I know that must be dreadful. I'll never forget how awful I felt when my daddy was off in the big war. And that was when I was too young to understand just how horrible war really is."

"I hope you never understand how horrible war really is, Allison. It's something that no one should have to experience. I feel for Caroline and her family." He sadly shook his head, then turned the plane back toward the direction of the airport. He let Allison take the stick for a few minutes.

"I bet we're not too far from where Andrew's ball game is tonight," Allison said. "Isn't Trenton down there? It's too bad we couldn't fly down."

"Yes, we're almost over it now. Maybe we'll get to fly to his games sometime. But not at night—not yet, anyway. I'm still working on getting my instrument rating, and judging by that fog bank rolling in from the ocean, it wouldn't hurt if I had it now. I better take the stick back and get us safely down on the ground as quickly as possible."

"What does that mean—instrument rating?"

"See all these dials and instruments?" James motioned to the crowded dashboard panel. "If you know how to read them all, as well as maps, you can actually fly under conditions when visibility is poor or even nonexistent. I know quite a bit already, but I haven't gotten my certification yet. I'll have to study up and eventually take another test. It would be foolish for me to think I could fly commercially along the Oregon coast without it."

Allison looked out at the gray blanket of fog in the distance as James increased their air speed. It seemed like they had plenty of time, but she admired her father's healthy respect for the weather elements.

"What would you do if the fog covered the ground before you could get back to the airport, Dad?"

"I'd have to radio Mac for some other suggestions for landing places. He'd probably direct us inland to Grover or Harrison—they don't usually get this ocean fog there. Then we'd have to land and wait for it to clear up over here. That reminds me, you'll have to start learning to operate the radio, Allison."

"That'd be great. Then I might be able to help Mac in the office sometimes."

"That's right. After all, this is going to be a family operation."

"You sound fairly certain, Dad."

He nodded as he began lining the plane up to land on the strip below. "I spoke to Hal this morning. It's looking real good, Allison. Real good."

James landed the plane perfectly on the runway, but by the time he taxied to the hangar, the fog was socking them in.

"Cutting it close, James," Mac said as he helped roll the small plane alongside the hangar. "But I have to admit that fog came out of nowhere."

"Life on the coast," James said. He looked up as the sun was completely swallowed by the fog. "I've got to get my instrument rating. The sooner the better, too, if we're going to get this business off and running."

"You just say the time and the place, boss," said Mac with a grin. "Got time for a cup of coffee? It'll just take me a minute to get a pot going."

"Wish I did, Mac. But Andrew has a football game in Trenton tonight, and we need to get going in the next hour if we want to see the kick off."

"Tell Andrew to give 'em what for!" Mac hollered after them.

⚘

Once again, Muriel had a bulging picnic basket all packed and ready to take in the car. "That cocoa is very hot," she warned. "It's for you to take into the stadium, and I don't want you to burn yourselves with it."

"Sure you wouldn't like to come, too?" James teased. Muriel had already made it clear that she thought it was plum craziness to drive four hours in one evening going to and coming from a football game.

"You children go and enjoy yourselves. Just make sure you drive carefully, Jamie," she warned as if he were still in high school. "As for me, I'll watch Andrew when he plays on the home field. That's plenty of excitement for an old thing like me!"

They arrived in time for kick off, and Heather and Allison decided to sit with their family this time. It was a cold, windy night, and they all bundled up together under blankets. They shared the Thermos of Muriel's hot cocoa along with some freshly made sugar cookies as they watched the first half of the game.

Allison spotted Shirley Jenson sitting with her new group of friends. She was still relieved that Shirley was making a life of her own that didn't include her, but during half time, Shirley clumped up the bleachers toward them. Allison stared at her in surprise. Shirley hadn't spoken to her in days—what could she possibly have to say to them tonight?

"Hi, Mr. O'Brian," Shirley said, not bothering to greet the rest of them.

"Hello, Shirley," James greeted with a slightly puzzled expression.

"Did you *fly* down here tonight, Mr. O'Brian?" she asked in a sassy tone.

James forced a laugh, but Allison could see the color climbing up his neck and into his cheeks. "No, we *drove*, Shirley." His voice was tight now, and Allison could hear the warning in it.

Suddenly, Allison realized that it was entirely possible that Shirley had eavesdropped on his conversation with Mr. Jenson that morning! And if so, Shirley was fully aware that he had asked Mr. Jenson to keep his plans for the airport a secret until he had a chance to speak to Grace. Allison glanced quickly at Grace. She was pouring a cup of steaming cocoa for Winston and not paying much attention to Shirley.

"Well," Shirley announced loudly, as if she were making some sort of formal statement for the whole stadium to hear. "I just thought that since you're purchasing that old rundown airport and all, you might have flown one of those flimsy little planes down here. But I guess I was wrong."

By now she had Grace's full attention. Allison watched in horror as Grace looked with wide eyes from Shirley to James.

Shirley smiled smugly. "Well, it looks like it's almost time for the game to begin. Happy flying, Mr. O'Brian."

James' eyes dropped down, and Allison could see his knuckles turning white on his tightly clenched fists. She wanted to march right down and punch Shirley Jenson in the nose.

"Is it true?" Winston exclaimed with excitement, completely unaware of the drama that was about to unfold. "Are you really buying an airport, Mr. O'Brian?"

"Well, I . . . uh . . . I have been looking into it—" The color that had climbed into his face was now slowly draining. He was almost white now.

"Really?" said Heather. "How exciting."

James looked at Grace with a pitiful expression, and Allison felt her heart breaking for him. "I was going to tell you, Grace," he began. "I really was. . . ."

"When?" was all she said.

"I've been trying to make a time. It hasn't been easy—"

"The game is starting, James," said Grace curtly. "We can discuss this later."

Port View lost the game by six points, and the drive back home was the longest two hours that Allison could ever remember. Winston and Heather both fell asleep in the back, but Allison, sitting between them, was wide awake. She leaned back against the seat with her eyes closed, hoping that Grace and her father would think she was asleep and feel comfortable talking if they needed to. But not a single word was spoken.

Please, Grace, Allison thought. *Please forgive him—please support him in this.*

Grace was silent all the way home. When James dropped them off, Allison knew it was too late for them to discuss it. At least for tonight.

"See you at church tomorrow," he said with some uncertainty.

"Good night, James," Grace answered in a formal tone. "Thank you for taking us to Andrew's game."

James turned the car around and headed for home while Allison searched for the right words. "Dad," she began slowly as he pulled into the garage. "I think Grace is in shock tonight. She probably just needs to sleep on it, but I'm sure she'll want to talk about it in the morning."

"I hope so, Allison. I hope I haven't ruined everything."

"Dad, if Grace truly loves you, she'll stand by you. I know she will. And if she doesn't . . . well, then, you'll cross that bridge when you get there, right? Besides, you know that I'll always be here for you, Dad."

He turned and smiled at her. "Thanks, Allison, but I honestly don't know what I'd do without her."

"Everything's going to be fine, Dad. I just know it. You'll see."

13

Grace didn't speak to James for almost two weeks, and Allison felt horribly sad and guilty about it. James seemed to slink around the house like a kicked dog. At the end of the first week, he told Allison that perhaps they should put the brakes on the whole airport thing, except that he hated to disappoint Mac. But then she reminded him that this had been his dream, and how she still felt sure that Grace would eventually come around. But by the middle of the second week, Grace had not come around, and now Allison was losing her patience.

"Why can't Grace understand?" Allison said to Heather at lunch one day.

"She's terribly hurt," Heather explained for the umpteenth time.

"Well, so is Dad."

"People can act strangely when they are hurting," Caroline said quietly.

Allison turned to look at Caroline. Lately she had been seeing Caroline with new eyes. Not just because of Caroline's improved appearance, but because Caroline was starting to *act* differently, too. Her confidence was increasing, and she had become more thoughtful.

"I suppose you're right, Caroline," Allison said as she poked at her mushy green beans. "I know what it's like to be hurt."

"Maybe you can help them," Caroline suggested. "Maybe you can get them together somehow."

Allison considered this. Was it worth it? What if it turned into World War III?

"It's Andrew's birthday on Sunday," Heather announced with a spark of enthusiasm. "Maybe we could have a party for him and invite you and your dad."

"No," Allison said glumly. "That might just irritate Grace even more. Besides, if your house was full of people, there would be no place for them to be alone and to talk." Allison thought for a moment. "But . . . how about if we had a party for Andrew at *my* house? I know Muriel would love to do it. And how could Grace say no to a party for Andrew when she doesn't even have to host it? Our house has tons of room, and we could fix it up so Grace and my dad would have to be alone at some point."

"Perfect," Heather said.

"I bet it will work," Caroline added optimistically.

"And you must come, too, Caroline."

Caroline's cheeks flushed. "Oh no, not me. I couldn't. I would be too embarrassed."

"No, you wouldn't," Allison said. "We'll invite some of Andrew's other friends, too. There will be a crowd so you won't feel conspicuous."

"Are you sure, Allison?" Heather asked. "That sounds like a lot of work for Muriel—"

"Muriel will be in her element," she grinned. "Just you wait."

❋

By Sunday afternoon everything was set. As Allison had expected, Muriel had come through with flying colors. She fully understood that this was more than just a regular birthday party. She had been as worried about Grace and James as the kids were. Naturally, Allison didn't explain to her father about their mixed motive for the party, but when it came time to dress, she suggested that he wear his dark tweed jacket. She had heard Grace say how handsome he looked in it.

The party was to be a surprise for Andrew, so Heather and Winston had come home with Allison after church, supposedly to go crabbing. Allison felt a little bad when she saw Andrew's disappointment not to be invited, as well, but Grace had jumped in and said that she needed him to help her mend the porch steps.

By two o'clock all the guests were present and accounted for, and ten minutes later, Grace and Andrew stopped by, supposedly to pick up Heather and Winston. Instead, they were met by wild shouts, party poppers, and horn blowing, along with streamers and confetti. It was great! Andrew's face showed his complete surprise.

"I can't believe this!" he exclaimed. "I had absolutely no idea." He winked at Allison. "I'll bet you were behind this."

Allison threw her arm around Heather and grinned. "Just don't forget my partner in crime here."

"You two," Andrew said.

With good food, good friends, and good music, the party quickly took on a life of its own. After a while, Allison tapped Andrew on the shoulder and asked him to meet her in the kitchen for a couple minutes.

"What's up, Al?" he asked as he plucked a piece of sliced ham off a platter that Muriel was getting ready to take out.

"I need your help," she said quietly. "You see, we hoped to use this time to get my dad and Grace together to talk—alone."

Andrew nodded wisely. "I see. So this wasn't just about my birthday."

She punched him in the arm. "Of course it's about your birthday, but can you blame us for trying to kill two birds with one stone?"

"I'm teasing, Allison. I think it's a great idea. What can I do? I want them back together as much as you."

"Okay. This is the plan . . . unless you have a better one. You find Grace and tell her that you need to talk to her in the library. Act like something is wrong. Tell her you'll meet her there in a couple minutes. I'll do the same to Dad, just long enough afterward so that he'll find her already in the library."

"Are you always so devious, Allison?"

"Actually, I've been known to be, but I am trying to mend my wicked ways."

Andrew grinned. "Good girl. Now, we better synchronize our watches."

They returned to the party, and Allison watched with amusement as Andrew spoke to Grace with serious eyes while she made her way over to her dad. So far so good. After that, Allison went to meet Andrew in the hallway behind the stairs. She took his birthday present with her, since she didn't want him to open it in front of the others. The pen and pencil set had seemed like the perfect gift at the time, but now she wondered if having it engraved with his name would appear too personal. While they waited silently behind the stairs, she handed him the slim box with a meek smile. He opened it, and she kept watch on the door to the library. Just then Grace walked into the den.

"Thank you, Allison," he whispered. "This is very nice."

"You're welcome," she whispered back, then turned at the sound of more footsteps. It was James this time, and he was also heading for the library. Allison held her breath. Would their plan work, or would one of them get wise and come out? After several suspenseful minutes, Allison began to relax a little.

"Well," said Andrew quietly, "I guess it's up to them now."

Allison nodded. "If it's meant to be . . ." she began, but when she gazed into Andrew's green eyes, she forgot what she was about to say. Suddenly, her heart beat wildly, and she grew aware of how close they were standing, hunkered there behind the stairs. She felt certain that Andrew could hear her heart pounding.

"This was really great of you, Allison," Andrew said. "To set all this up, I mean. I want you to know how much I appreciate it."

"I was more than happy to do it," Allison said softly. "Even if Dad and Grace had been getting along just fine, I still would have wanted to give a party for you."

Andrew smiled down at her. "You're a great kid, Allison."

Allison felt her heart drop. When would Andrew see her as a person instead of just his kid sister's friend? "I suppose we should join the others now," she quickly said, hoping to move past the awkward moment.

"You're probably right. You never know when they might start to miss the hostess and the guest of honor."

While Allison poured herself a glass of punch, Janet came up and put an arm around her shoulders.

"This was a great idea, Allison," she said, then she winked. "And I saw you and Andrew slip out to meet each other."

Allison's cheeks grew hot. "It wasn't anything like that—"

Janet cut her off. "It's all right, Allison. We all know that you and Andrew have something going. Don't be such a baby about it."

Allison just shook her head. Forcing a laugh, she said good-naturedly, "Well, Janet, if that's what you want to think, go ahead and be my guest. Imagine away!"

Allison went over to where Heather was sitting with Curt attentively at her side. Allison put her hand on Heather's arm.

"Everything seems to be A-OK so far," she said. It was their code for the James and Grace situation.

"Perfect," Heather said with a bright smile.

James and Grace didn't reappear at the party for almost an hour, and then just in time to light the candles on the cake and sing the birthday song. Grace's eyes were red as if she'd been crying, but they were both smiling now. Allison desperately hoped that it had gone well. They could be smiling for Andrew's sake. She shot up another silent prayer on their behalf.

After a while the party died down, and finally the last of the guests said good-bye. It was already dark outside. Allison shivered as she closed the door against the cold, misty evening air.

"Why don't you throw another log on the fire in the library, Andrew," James suggested. Andrew happily obliged. Meanwhile, Grace and Heather were already in the kitchen helping to wash dishes.

"I'd like to gather everyone together, Allison," James announced. He glanced over to where Muriel was busily picking up plates and cups in the parlor. "You and George may want to join us, too, Muriel."

Muriel nodded with troubled eyes, as if she expected to hear some bad news. Allison wanted to ask him how it had gone, but she figured it would be best to get everyone together like he had asked. When they were all gathered in the library, there was a mixture of expressions on all the faces present.

Finally James cleared his throat and began. "I want to thank you kids for your efforts here today—it was very sweet of you to want to get Grace and me speaking to each other again. As you all know, this idea of purchasing the airport threw quite a wrench in the works as far as Grace was concerned, and for that I am truly sorry. I never meant to hurt Grace." He looked across the room to where Grace was sitting with Heather and Winston. Allison couldn't read Grace's face, and she wished that they would get on with it. The suspense was killing her.

"I have made my apologies to Grace, and she has graciously forgiven me." He smiled warmly. "And I have promised her never to pull a stunt like this again." James stood up and walked over to Grace. He smiled down upon her and took her hand in his. She rose from the sofa and stood by his side next to the fireplace. At last Grace was smiling.

Suddenly, Allison grew worried. What if this meant no airport? What if her father had sacrificed the airport in order to keep Grace? She bit her lip and looked at the two of them.

"And now we have an announcement to make," James said in an official voice. The room grew silent except for the crackling of the log on the fire. "Grace and I would like to announce our engagement—that is, if there are no objections."

James and Grace looked around the room at all the faces. Congratulations were shared all around, and everyone was smiling now—everyone except Allison. James looked at her for a long moment, and Allison forced a smile to her lips. After all, wasn't this what they had all been working toward? Wasn't this what everyone wanted? She tried to smile convincingly, but she couldn't seem to make the smile reach her heart.

"I've got a light supper in the works," Muriel said. "I wish it were something more festive, but I hope everyone will stay."

"We'd love to," Grace said. "Heather and I will give you a hand in there."

"I'll help, too," Allison offered.

"The boys and I can finish picking things up from the party," James said.

It was after seven by the time they finally sat down to dinner in the dining room. Everyone was laughing and chatting like one big happy family, but Allison could only play along. Grace seemed so happy, she wasn't about to rain on her parade. If the dream of the airport was over and lost, then she would just have to let it go. After all, it had been her father's dream to start with. If he was able to let it go, then so should she.

Andrew lifted up his glass of milk for a toast. "Here's to Grace and Mr. O'Brian, and to many years of happiness together." Everyone else lifted their glasses and agreed.

"Thanks," James said with glistening eyes. "A year ago, I never could have dreamed of such happiness. And now—" he paused. "I just hardly know what to say, except that I thank God every day for all of you and I pray that we will be a happy family."

"When are you going to get married?" Winston asked. "When are we all going to live together and be one family?"

"We haven't set the date yet," Grace said. "We wanted to discuss that with everyone. We want you all to have a say in the planning and participate in the wedding."

"How about next week?" Winston suggested.

James roared with laughter. "You're sounding pretty eager. I think next week might be pushing things a bit." He winked at Grace, and her cheeks grew pink.

"We'll need more time than that," Grace said. "Besides, James will be busy in the next couple weeks getting everything all set up with the airport and—"

"The airport?" Allison exclaimed. "Do we get to keep the airport?"

Grace laughed. "Well, your dad and I had a good, long talk, and I realized that it isn't fair to allow my fears to control everyone's lives. I have decided to trust God with this whole business of flying. It's silly for me to be so fearful, but you will all have to help me if I forget, okay?"

"No problem, Grace," Andrew said. "Does this mean I can start flying lessons with Mac?"

Grace looked at James with raised brows, then back to Andrew. "Yes, Andrew." She sighed deeply. "I guess you're going to give me lots of opportunities to conquer this fear thing."

Andrew laughed. "You bet, and in no time we'll have you up there, too, Grace. You'll love it!"

She smiled. "Don't count on it."

"I want to fly, too," said Winston.

James winked at him. "Let's not push Grace too hard just yet, Winston. But don't you worry, I'm sure your day will come."

After dinner Allison found Grace straightening up the parlor.

"Need any help?" Allison asked.

"This confetti seems to be everywhere," Grace said as she swept some off of a chair into her palm. "It was a nice party. Thanks for all your work, Allison."

"It was fun, and I'm glad that everything turned out okay for you and Dad."

"Are you really?" Grace sat down on the chair and looked into Allison's face. "I don't mean to pry, but you didn't look very pleased earlier this evening in the library when James announced the engagement."

Allison smiled. "I guess I was a little surprised at first. Then, to be honest, I was afraid that you were going to put your foot down on the airport deal."

Grace laughed lightly. "I wanted to, but when your dad offered to pull out of the purchase, I realized that I couldn't let him do that. I really want to support him in his dreams, even if it isn't always easy."

"I'm so glad, Grace," Allison said. "I know how much he wants to make the airport business work. He was so unhappy with the way the shipping business was going."

"I know," said Grace. "When I think of how miserable he was partnering with Hal, I am almost completely resolved about the airport. It's just that ever since the war—losing my first husband and all—flying has seemed so dangerous to me. You know I've never been up in a plane, Allison."

Allison grinned. "Oh, you will love it, Grace. I was a little scared my first time—it was last summer with Marsha. But by the time we landed, I loved it."

"Allison," said Grace, "now that we have the flying thing understood, I want to ask if you are comfortable with your dad getting married. You've only been back with him a short while, and I know you two are still getting to know each other. I don't want to come between you. . . ."

"Grace," Allison began, "I met you before I really knew my dad—I still thought he was dead then. But right from the start I remember thinking that you were the kind of person I would have picked out for a mom. Though God has taught me how to forgive Marsha and love her no matter what, she will never be a *real* mom to me. That's why I'm so happy that you're going to marry my dad. I have always wanted a family just like this."

Tears filled Grace's eyes, and the two embraced. "I have always wanted a family like this, too," Grace said. "I'm so happy everything is working out. Just last week, I had given up all hope. I knew I was being stubborn, but I just couldn't seem to get past it. If you kids hadn't gotten us together, I don't know what would have happened."

Allison laughed. "We all would have been perfectly miserable."

14

For a belated birthday present, and with Grace's approval, James took Andrew on his first airplane flight the following Saturday. Allison went along, too. It was great fun to watch Andrew's face as he sat in the copilot seat next to her dad. He was ecstatic. He couldn't wait to begin flying lessons, but at Grace's recommendation, Andrew had decided to wait until the football season ended.

After they landed, Allison smugly told Andrew that her first lesson was scheduled for the following weekend. "It's quite likely that I will have my pilot's license *before* you," she said with a sly grin. The fact that he had referred to her as a kid at the party still stung.

"I don't understand how people can learn to fly even before they know how to drive," Andrew said. "At least I won't have to worry about you driving on the roads yet."

"Don't be so sure," she warned. "I'll turn fifteen soon and get my learner's permit."

"Good grief," Andrew exclaimed in mock horror. "Neither streets nor skies shall be safe anymore!"

She socked him.

Andrew smiled sheepishly. "Actually, I think it's great that you're such an adventuresome girl. I know lots of girls who are afraid to drive, and I doubt that there are many girls or even boys your age who want to know how to fly."

"Mac said that he knew a girl in Canada who took up flying when she was only thirteen."

"Jeepers! You wouldn't think that would even be legal."

"And did you know," Allison continued informatively, "that there were quite a few women pilots in the last war—not combat, of course, but they were pretty important just the same."

"Okay, I'm impressed. And I have no doubts that you will wind up being the next Amelia Earhart. I can just see your face on the newsreels now."

Allison smiled. "I'm glad you see my point."

"Are you working here today, Andrew?" James asked as he and Allison were almost ready to leave.

"Yes, sir. And it sounds like by next week I'll be working for you."

James grinned. "That's right. We sign papers next Wednesday, which is the day before Thanksgiving. In fact, I was supposed to tell Grace that Muriel is expecting everyone for a big celebration dinner on Thursday. I'll have to tell her tonight. We have a dinner date this evening to celebrate our engagement."

"Have you set the wedding date yet?" Allison asked.

"Not yet. But I think we're going to discuss it tonight." James glanced at Andrew. "Do you have any thoughts on the subject, son? I know that this is your last year in high school. You might not like a wedding to spoil your senior year."

"No, I'm not worried about that, Mr. O'Brian—"

"You know, I think it's time you started calling me James."

Andrew grinned. "All right, *James*. And as far as the wedding date, I don't have any concerns. Whenever you and Grace think is best."

"I thought you might enjoy having my old room after the wedding," James said warmly. "It's in that turret on the very top of the house. I always liked it."

Andrew beamed. "That would be just swell, Mr.—I mean, James."

He clapped Andrew on the shoulder. "Well, we better let you get back to your work. I know Mac is relieved to have good help for a change. Tell him that I'll be by on Monday morning to sort some business things out with him."

"You bet," Andrew said as he picked up the hose and began to wash the small two-seater plane. "See you, Allison," he called.

"How about you, Allison?" James asked as they drove from the airport.

"How about what?" Allison asked.

"Any thoughts about the wedding date?"

"Not really. I don't know how long it takes to plan a wedding."

"Well, we don't really want a big wedding. We'll have the ceremony in the church with family and close friends. Grace thought it would be fun if you and Heather could be her bridesmaids. In fact, she asked me to mention that she would like to take you and Heather to Portland this Friday, the day after Thanksgiving, to look at dresses."

"That sounds great." Allison paused a moment before asking, "When do *you* want to get married, Dad?"

"I know that Grace is having a hard time making ends meet, and for her sake I was thinking perhaps sooner might be better."

"What about for your sake?"

"Sooner is fine with me, too. I'm just not so sure about you, Allison. It's been such a short time since you've come to live out here, I don't want things to move too fast for you."

"Grace seemed concerned about that, too, but I'm fine with everything, Dad. I really am. I love Grace, and I think we will make a fantastic family. We practically are one already. And just think, when Heather moves in I won't have to call her to talk to her."

James laughed. "It'll sure be nice to see that big old house finally full. I told Grace that everyone can have their own room if they want, and she seemed to think that Winston and Andrew would appreciate that. Right now those boys are packed like sardines into a room not much bigger than a closet."

"I think this is exciting, Dad, and I happen to like excitement."

"Well, then, you've come to the right place!"

On Thanksgiving morning Allison awoke to all kinds of good smells. Muriel had been busily baking pies and treats for the last two days. Allison tried to remember other Thanksgivings, but she knew that none could compare to this. Thanksgiving at the Madisons' was always cold and formal, the house crawling with strangers who seemed to walk around with their noses in the air. Today promised to be a fun and joyous celebration—her first holiday with her new family, a day to be remembered.

Allison helped Muriel get things ready for the big dinner. She carefully set the table in the dining room and then scavenged in the garden for something to make a bouquet for the foyer and the dining room table. She finally found some gold and orange chrysanthemums, which she combined with ivy and some ornamental berries to create several very striking arrangements.

"Just like your grandmother, you are, Allison," said Muriel

as she admired Allison's creativity. "She had a knack for finding beauty in anything."

"Thanks, Muriel. Say, I haven't seen Dad all morning. Do you know what he's up to?"

Muriel grinned. "He's working on something down in the basement."

"Great, I'll go down and see," Allison said.

"No, dear, I think you should stay up here and help me," said Muriel with a wink. "James said that he is working on something that's meant to be a surprise, and I'm not supposed to let you go down there."

Allison nodded. "I see. In that case, I won't bother him. But now you've got me dying of curiosity."

"Well, why don't you put your energy into some whipping cream for the pumpkin pies," suggested Muriel.

After the cream was whipped and Muriel seemed to have everything under control, Allison went upstairs to dress. She pulled out a brown velvet dress that Marsha had sent with the other things in the trunk. Allison hadn't cared much for the dress when she had first seen it. It had been adorned with a big fur collar and cuffs that actually looked like leopard skin, and it had given Allison the creeps. Grace suggested that the fur be removed, and once Muriel had performed this task and carefully steamed it, the dress looked entirely different.

Allison slipped it on and zipped up the side. It was lined with satin and had long, slender sleeves, a smooth, fitted bodice, and a long, full skirt that swished nicely just above her ankles. She decided to wear Grandmother Mercury's pearls again, since this was a special day. She looked in the mirror as she brushed her hair and thought that the dress made her look very mature. She wondered if Andrew would think so, then chided herself for even thinking such a thing. She was just a kid to him.

Suddenly, a new thought hit her like a slap in the face. Andrew would actually be living in this very house someday—under the same roof! She would have to treat him as her brother. How could she possibly do that? She couldn't think of Andrew as a brother.

She laid down her brush and stared into the mirror in horror. What did this mean? She longed for someone to discuss this with, but who was there? Not Heather. Definitely not Grace. Her own father was too involved in all this for her to approach him. She certainly couldn't tell anyone at school. For a moment she considered Marsha, but then what if Marsha thought that it was unacceptable for her to live under the same roof as a boy she cared so deeply for? Allison sat down on her bed and felt almost sick with worry.

"Ah, there you are," Muriel said as she peeked into Allison's slightly open door. "I didn't mean to disturb you."

"It's okay," Allison said glumly.

"Are you feeling all right, dear? You look pale."

Allison looked up at Muriel. "Can I talk to you?"

"Of course. I think everything in the kitchen is under control. What's troubling my girl?"

"Have a seat, Muriel." Allison closed the door and sat down on the bed again, smoothing out the velvety skirt with her hands.

"The dress looks lovely on you, dear," said Muriel kindly.

"Thanks. You did a great job with it, Muriel."

"Tell old Muriel what's bothering you."

Allison smiled weakly. "It sounds rather silly, but I don't know who else to talk to. It's sort of embarrassing. You see, I know it won't be long until Dad and Grace are married, and naturally I know they will all come here to live, which is great. We'll all be one big, happy family. I'll even have a new sister and two new brothers. But one of the brothers, well,

I've just never thought of him like a brother, and it makes me feel a little—"

"Uneasy?" Muriel suggested.

Allison nodded.

"That's quite understandable, dear. But I don't think it's anything to worry about. I think we're all aware that you are quite fond of Andrew. While some of us may think it's just puppy love, we all know that only time will tell. There's no reason that Grace and James' getting married should change anything between you and Andrew. We all know that he's not really your brother."

"Really?"

Muriel smiled. "Really. You and Andrew are both mature, responsible young people. What with the war and all, you've both had to grow up faster than most children. Besides, it won't be all that long until Andrew will have to go off to college."

Allison nodded. Somehow hearing Muriel say these things out loud made her feel as if the world were all right again. "Thanks, Muriel. I needed to hear that."

Muriel chuckled. "I'm not surprised that you did. Your life seems to be constantly changing, but I think you are holding up quite well. You're blossoming into a lovely young woman despite all the craziness that you've been through in the last six months. Now I just remembered why I came up here. Your dad is ready to show you the big surprise."

"Thank you, Muriel." She threw her arms around the dear woman. "Thank you. I'll go right now, then I'll come see if you need any more help. Our guests should be arriving in an hour."

Allison crept down the dimly lit stairs to the basement. She could smell the oils and turpentine from her father's art studio. The first time she had come down here, it had felt all damp and spidery, but James had cleaned things up since then.

He'd painted the walls white, and he kept the little wood stove burning almost constantly. It reminded her of the lighthouse, only much bigger.

"Hello, there," he called from behind a large canvas that was set upon an easel. "I was just finishing up something very special, and I wanted you to see it before I unveil it today. Now, close your eyes and I'll turn the easel around. Don't open until I say so. I want to adjust the light just right."

Allison closed her eyes. She wondered what it might be. She hoped it was a painting of the lighthouse—she had told him that she wanted one of her own. She knew just where she would hang it in her room.

"Okay, you can look!"

Allison opened her eyes and caught her breath. It was her! There on the canvas, dressed in the creamy satin gown that she had worn to the Harvest Ball, with the glowing white pearls around her pale neck. Her head was tilted slightly to the left, and the way her father had captured the light made the picture seem almost alive.

"Dad, it's amazing," she breathed.

"Do you like it?"

"I love it. I mean, I know it's supposed to be me, but it's so beautiful—"

Dad laughed. "Of course it's beautiful. If it wasn't beautiful, it wouldn't be you!"

She threw her arms around him and laughed. "Well, you know how they say parents see their children—"

"I beg your pardon. I happen to think it's the spitting image of you."

She stepped back and looked at it again, then sighed. "It's truly lovely."

"I don't usually do portraits." James stepped up and examined it closely. "But when I got the photographs developed from the Harvest Ball, I decided that I had to give it a try. It felt almost as if I was inspired. Muriel is the only one who has seen it, and she went absolutely nuts over it."

Allison couldn't remember ever feeling so loved or flattered.

"Now that you've seen it, do you mind if I show it to everyone today after dinner?"

"Of course not, Dad. And speaking of dinner, I better go give Muriel a hand."

"And I better go get cleaned up."

❋

The Thanksgiving dinner was just as delightful as Allison had anticipated it would be. She was so thankful for the little chat she'd had with Muriel. She didn't even feel uncomfortable when Andrew said she looked nice. When they couldn't eat another bite of turkey, James invited everyone to the library for a private showing of his latest achievement, and Muriel announced that dessert and coffee would be served later.

Allison suddenly felt apprehensive about Andrew looking at the portrait of her. She knew that her father had made her look far more beautiful on the canvas than she would ever be in real life. But that was a father's eye. What would Andrew think?

They funneled into the library, where James had set the painting above the mantel. Immediately Grace began to exclaim how wonderful it was. Allison tried to describe it to Heather, promising her that when it was fully dried she could trace her fingers over it while Allison described it again. But as she was speaking to Heather, her eyes were on Andrew. He stood several feet away, staring at the portrait as if transfixed. Allison felt her cheeks growing warm as if he were staring at her.

194

"It's pretty, but it doesn't have very many colors in it," Winston said before he turned to the chess set and began arranging the pieces for a game. Allison chuckled. A ten-year-old art critic.

"It's beautiful," said Andrew quietly.

"Allison didn't think it really looked like her," James said.

Allison cringed at his words. There was no need to announce the obvious.

"Of course it looks like her," Grace declared.

"Yes," Andrew agreed. "Very much so. It is amazing. I can't imagine how you do it, James. I don't have a bit of artistic talent in me, and I can't fathom how someone could take paints and a canvas and create something so lifelike and beautiful."

Allison savored those words.

"It sounds very lovely, Allison. I only wish I could see it, too." Heather said.

Allison took Heather's hand in hers and gave it a squeeze. "Many times I've wished I could perceive things the way you do, Heather. You seem to have a sense that is deeper than seeing."

Just then the phone rang, and Allison jumped, then laughed at herself as James answered it. When it sounded as if he would be on the phone for a while, they slowly trickled out of the library. Allison and Heather went to see if they could help Muriel in the kitchen.

Just as Allison was dropping big dollops of whipped cream onto wedges of pumpkin pie, James burst into the kitchen with a gigantic smile.

"Great news, everyone," he announced. "My friend Clarence Trundle just called from San Francisco. I had sent some oils down there last summer, and suddenly they have become all the rage. He sold three just last week. Now he wants everything I have."

"That's great, Dad!" Allison shouted.

"Congratulations," Heather cheered.

Grace came into the kitchen. "When does he want you to send more paintings?" she asked as she picked up a tray of desserts to carry into the dining room.

"That's the thing. He said if he had them right now, he would get a jump on the holiday traffic that starts flowing through there this time of year. And I was thinking," James paused and his brow creased. He picked up the other tray of desserts and began to move toward the dining room, too. "Well, I'll tell you all what I was thinking as soon as we get a taste of Muriel's delicious pumpkin pie."

They were quickly seated so James could continue.

"I was thinking that the fastest way to get my paintings down there would be to fly. I would want to pick up some that are still in Portland, then I could head straight down—"

"What about your instrument rating?" Grace interrupted suddenly.

"Oh, I'd take Mac along, of course. And if we needed, he would fly. It would be a good way for me to get in more hours as well as get the paintings down there."

"Can I go, too?" Allison asked, but then she remembered that she and Heather were supposed to go to Portland with Grace tomorrow. She glanced at Grace. "Oops, I forgot," she said, trying to hide her disappointment. "I'm going with you to Portland."

"Well, you don't have to—"

"No," James said. "There's no reason to change any plans."

"Maybe I could come along," Andrew suggested hopefully.

Allison looked at him with a twinge of jealousy. She would much rather fly to San Francisco than look at silly bridesmaid dresses.

"Sure, if Grace doesn't mind," James nodded in agreement. "We should be back by Sunday."

Grace frowned. "I suppose it would be all right."

"All right!" shouted Andrew.

Grace sighed and shook her head. "But to be honest, everything in me wants to say no."

"We understand, Grace." James reached across the table to cover her hand with his. "And believe me, in time your apprehension will wear off. I'm sure you'll get more and more comfortable with the whole thing."

"I sure hope so," said Grace, twisting a linen napkin with her free hand.

It was settled. James called Mac, and the three of them would leave at daybreak. Grace, Heather, and Allison would leave for Portland a little later, and Winston would stay with Muriel and George.

"Why do I get left out of everything?" Winston complained.

"You think you'd like to go look at bridesmaid dresses?" Allison teased, and Winston groaned as if that would be a fate worse than death.

"I thought maybe you and I could do us a little crabbing," George said with a twinkle in his eye.

"All right!" Winston exclaimed.

"I just hope this is the right thing," Grace said.

"Come on, Grace," James said gently. "Remember what you said about trusting God?"

"I know, I know. But it's one of those things that is easier said than done. I just have this awful feeling in the pit of my stomach."

"You probably ate too much turkey," Andrew teased.

"Perhaps" was all she said.

15

The bridesmaid dress expedition felt like a total waste of time to Allison. They didn't find anything they all liked, and Grace decided she would be better off sewing the dresses herself. Allison wished that she were flying to San Francisco with her dad, but she wisely kept these thoughts to herself.

"They're in San Francisco now," said Heather as Grace drove back home.

"Yes," agreed Grace. "They have probably been there for several hours by now. I hope it's going well."

Allison sensed the worry in her voice. "I'm sure it's going great," she said reassuringly. "I wonder if they're enjoying seeing San Francisco. I've always wanted to go there."

"I was there for a short while before I was sent overseas during the war," said Grace. "It's a very pretty city. The Golden Gate Bridge is quite spectacular. You know, if I ever get over my plane fear, it might be nice to fly down there."

Allison smiled. "That's the spirit, Grace."

When they got home, Muriel announced that James had called from San Francisco and their flight had gone flawlessly. "Not only that," said Muriel with flushed excitement, "but

198

apparently Clarence was very pleased with the paintings. He thinks Jamie is the cat's pajamas!"

Allison and Heather burst into giggles over this, and Grace seemed visibly relieved. Muriel went on to tell them that Andrew, Mac, and James would relax and enjoy the sights tomorrow, and they expected to arrive back before dark on Sunday.

❧

The house seemed very quiet on Saturday, especially after the excitement of the last few days. Muriel had gone into town to do some shopping, and George was outside working on something. It reminded Allison of when Grandpa had been ill last summer, and she had tiptoed around the house by herself. She wondered what Grandpa would think of all the developments since then. She could just imagine him chuckling with delight over everything that had transpired. And all because he so persistently kept writing to Marsha.

Although it was windy and cold outside, the sun was shining, and she decided to bundle up and head down to the beach. She took a tablet and pencil with her. She was working on a story for the school paper and thought perhaps the sound of the wind and waves would inspire her. Instead, she found herself just walking, buffeted by the wind. It was nice to brace the elements and know that when she got too cold, there was a warm house waiting for her up on top of the cliff. Her house—her home.

"Thank you, God," she prayed out loud. She was thinking about her father, the family she was going to have, and her friends. "Thanks for giving me all these wonderful people. I never, ever would have dreamed that my life could be so full and happy."

❧

Sunday afternoon Allison, Grace, Heather, and Winston decided they would surprise James and Andrew by meeting them at the airport. Allison thought that it was Grace's way of showing how she was coming around to this whole "flying thing," as she still called it. Larry was supposed to be managing the office while Mac was away, but Allison had her doubts. At least he knew how to run the radio and answer the phone. James had hinted he planned to have a serious chat with Larry and to give him the chance to become a better worker or else look for another job. When they walked up to the office, they found Larry fast asleep with his feet propped up on Mac's cluttered desk.

"Hello?" Grace said with a puzzled expression. This was the first time she had met Larry, and Allison felt embarrassed, as if somehow this reflected poorly on their decision to buy the airport.

"Hi, Larry," Allison said as he jerked awake. "This is Grace Sanders, and Heather and Winston Amberwell. We came out to meet Dad's plane. Any word from them yet?"

Larry rubbed his whiskered chin and groggily shook his head. "Nope, nothing. But they should be rolling in here any time now." He peered at the clock on the wall as if surprised by what it said. Then he stood up. "Pleasure to meet you, ma'am," he said as he nodded toward Grace. "You just excuse me for a minute." He disappeared out the back door, and Grace looked at Allison.

Allison shrugged. "He's kind of strange."

Grace nodded, then looked toward the radio. "What if James and Mac need to radio while he's not here? Do you know how to run that thing?"

"Not exactly, but I've seen Mac do it. He just pushes the button on the microphone and then talks into it."

Winston laughed. "I know how to do that."

"Do you want me to pull up some chairs to wait in here, or would you like to go outside? Dad's probably already given you the tour."

"Maybe we should stay in here. It's awfully cold out there."

"I want to go look at the planes," Winston said.

"Okay, but be careful. Don't climb into any of them, and stay away from the runway," Grace warned in a no-nonsense voice. Winston nodded soberly, then shot out the door.

Allison scrambled around finding and arranging chairs for Grace and Heather and herself. She pointed out the flight chart on the wall and offered to make some fresh coffee. She desperately wanted to make the place look good. She was certain that to Grace it looked run down and hopeless.

"There's a lot of work to be done out here," Allison began apologetically. "But I think it will be a fun challenge. Dad has all sorts of ideas. And once we get the air shipping business going . . ." Allison's voice trailed off.

Grace nodded. "Oh, I can certainly see how this place could become a bustling family business. It's obvious it needs a woman's touch, too." She wiped her finger across Mac's desk, leaving a groove in the dust.

Allison giggled. "I suppose so."

The door opened as Larry stuck his head into the room. He glanced at the radio. "Any word while I was out?"

"Nothing," said Allison. "Should you have heard from them by now?"

Larry looked at the clock again, then frowned. "Well, I would've thought so." He looked at the flight chart. "I wonder if they had any bad weather. It's been colder than usual up here. But if they weren't coming in, I'm sure they would've called by now."

Grace looked at Allison with uncertainty.

"I'm sure that everything's fine," Allison said. "And since they haven't called, we might as well assume they're on their way."

Larry looked at her as if she were a genius. "Yep, that's just what I was thinking."

"Would anyone like some coffee?" Allison asked for the second time, eyeing the encrusted little stove in back. Thankfully, no one was interested.

Winston came back, red-cheeked from the cold. They all sat and waited, trying to make small talk. Finally it was getting dusky outside, and Larry went out and turned the runway lights on.

"We didn't used to have lights," he explained. "As it is we hardly ever use them. But they are nice to have in the case of an emergency."

Allison saw Grace bristle at the word *emergency*, and Allison felt a wave of apprehension, too. What if something really had gone wrong? Why hadn't they radioed in to say where they were?

"I'm worried," Grace said, almost echoing Allison's thoughts. "I would think they would be here by now."

"Aw, planes come in late all the time," Larry said. "You don't need to worry. Maybe you should all just go on home. I'll call you as soon as I hear anything."

Grace looked at Allison. "You kids do have school in the morning," she said. "And I'm sure you're getting hungry. Maybe that would be best."

"I'd like to wait here," Allison said, not liking the idea of leaving Larry alone in the office. If he had been sleeping so soundly that he hadn't heard them come into the office, then perhaps he wouldn't hear the radio or the phone.

Grace stood up. "I don't know about that, Allison. I'm not sure what your dad would think."

"Let's walk out to the car," Allison suggested.

Once they were outside, Allison told Grace her concerns about Larry.

"But I don't like leaving you here alone," said Grace.

"Why don't you take Winston and me home," Heather suggested. "Then you can come back and wait with Allison."

"That's a good idea, Heather," said Allison. "If you want to, Grace."

"Yes, maybe I'll take Heather and Winston to stay with Muriel. I'm sure she wouldn't mind."

So it was settled. Allison went back to keep an eye on Larry and make sure that he didn't fall asleep again. This time she decided to make some coffee, and after some searching and cleaning, she finally got a pot perking just as Grace came back.

"Any news?" asked Grace hopefully.

Allison shook her head. "Nothing."

"George and Muriel haven't heard anything, either."

"Larry," Allison said, "is there a place you can call to find out if there's been any weather conditions between here and San Francisco?"

"Sure, I could do that," Larry said as if the idea had never occurred to him before. He looked up a number, then dialed. After several "uh-huhs" and "you don't says" he hung up the phone and turned to them.

"Oddest thing," he said, shaking his head. "They've had an unexpected snowstorm in the Siskiyou Mountains. Started up just before noon."

Grace's eyes grew wide, and Allison's heart began to pound. "What does that mean?" asked Grace.

"Well, I'm not sure exactly." Larry scratched his head.

"Can you find out?" Allison said in a voice that sounded overly shrill. All too quickly she understood Grace's fears about flying. Dozens of questions began bouncing through her brain.

Larry blinked at her. "I guess I could call down to San Francisco and see exactly when they left." Again he was on the phone. This time he turned away from them while he talked, but Allison could pick out a few words.

"Yep, that's their number. Ten this morning? Uh-huh . . . nope . . . nope. You think so... ? How will we know? Well, yes . . . Thanks. I'll do that." He hung up the phone but didn't turn around to face them.

"What did you find out?" Allison demanded.

He slowly turned around. His face seemed to hang, and he shook his head. "I don't know how to tell you this. . . ."

"Just tell us!" cried Grace.

"It sounds like their plane went down somewhere near Eureka, California. That's not too far from the Oregon border, but that was the last radio contact. The storm was just coming on then. The pilot said that their carburetor was freezing up, then they were lost to all contact—"

"No!" cried Grace. "No, it can't be!"

"What does that mean, Larry? What happens when a carburetor freezes up?"

Larry cleared his throat. "Well, it's just about the worst. I've heard of planes that just drop like a stone from the sky—"

"That's enough!" Grace shouted with clenched fists.

Allison felt tears streaming down her cheeks, but she couldn't form any words. This wasn't happening! It couldn't be. She had already lost Grandpa. She couldn't lose Dad, too. She ran out into the night and into the nearest hangar. She leaned against the wall and sobbed.

"Please, God," she prayed. "Please let them be all right. Please let them be okay. Please . . . please . . ." She squatted down and pulled her knees tightly to her chest as she continued to beg God not to take her father away from her. Not to take Andrew, not to take Mac. She prayed and prayed until her voice was hoarse and her throat hurt.

And then she thought of Grace. Could it be that all along

Grace had been right? Was flying too dangerous? Oh, if only they had listened to her. Why in the world had Allison ever encouraged her dad in this venture? A load of guilt like she had never known began to pile upon her until it felt like she could hardly breathe. Was this all her fault? She could hear Grace calling to her, and suddenly Allison's hopes soared. Perhaps everything was okay, perhaps they had landed someplace else. Allison leaped up and ran into the office.

"Grace," she called. "Are they okay? Did they call?"

Grace shook her head. "No. Nothing."

Fresh tears streamed down Allison's cheeks. "Where's Larry?"

"He stepped out after the last phone call and hasn't come back. I called George and Muriel. I told them not to tell Heather and Winston anything yet. I don't know what else to do."

"I've been praying."

"So have I," said Grace quietly.

As the hours dragged on, Grace looked up numbers to call in Mac's books that were scattered throughout the office. After several minutes on the phone, she turned to Allison.

"No news. Except they said that they had tried to call and radio numerous times this afternoon. No one was answering, so they just gave up."

"That explains why Larry didn't know anything. I doubt he'll ever show his face around here again. I'm sure he must feel this is partly his fault."

Allison grew so tired she felt herself slide into a place some-where between awake and asleep, but then she would jolt awake and remember with chilling clarity that the plane was still missing—that perhaps she would never see her father and Andrew and Mac again.

Just before the sun came up, the phone jangled loudly. Allison felt like she had jumped out of her skin, but she answered it quickly, hoping against hope to hear her dad's voice on the other end.

Instead, it was someone from the FAA calling to notify them that the snowstorm had abated, and an aerial search party would begin to look for the wreckage at the first break of day. *Wreckage*. The word stuck in her brain. Somehow she numbly answered their questions, giving addresses and phone numbers of the next of kin.

In the early morning dawn she and Grace prayed again. This time they prayed even more fervently than before that everyone aboard would be okay and that they would all be reunited as soon as possible.

As much as Allison wanted to believe that God would answer all their prayers, she was afraid that her faith might not be big enough. And what if it wasn't?

THE
❧ PROMISE ❧

To Kathy Gilbert,
A sweet sister in Christ.
With love,
M.C.

1

"At least the fog is lifting some," said Allison weakly. She stood and peered through the dingy window at the airport office. The dark asphalt of the airstrip was now discernible in the gray predawn morning light. Many long hours had passed since she and Grace first heard the news that the plane carrying James, Andrew, and Mac went down when an unexpected blizzard struck the northern California mountains.

"Yes, perhaps it will clear up and the rescue team will be able to land—" Grace's voice broke slightly as she spoke.

Allison swallowed hard. Worn down from lack of sleep, she didn't know how much longer she could maintain a strong front. "It's been so long, Grace!" She looked at the clock hanging on Mac's cluttered wall, wedged between posters of planes and bits of flying memorabilia, and groaned. "Shouldn't we have heard something by now? How long can it take to spot a downed plane?"

Grace shook her head. "I have no idea. Maybe I should call George and have him drive over and pick you up, Allison. You're exhausted. You need rest—"

"I couldn't possibly sleep, Grace. I'm not leaving until we hear from them."

"All right," agreed Grace. "But I'll call and have George bring us some food. I'm not hungry, but you must be starving."

"I couldn't eat a thing," muttered Allison, but Grace was already on the phone. Allison counted the seconds as Grace spoke to Muriel. Every moment blocking the phone lines was precious. Fortunately, Grace quickly hung up.

With elbows on her knees, Allison leaned over, buried her face in her hands, and allowed the tears to trickle soundlessly down her cheeks. She had no more words to pray, and guilt ebbed into her heart like a high tide edging its way up the beach. If only she hadn't encouraged Dad with his flying . . . Why hadn't she just stayed out of it? Now, if he was dead, it would feel like her fault—she would always blame herself.

"It's going to be okay, sweetheart," said Grace as she wrapped her arms around Allison.

For a long moment Allison allowed Grace to comfort her. She wanted to believe it was going to be okay, but her faith felt weaker than ever. Finally she looked up at Grace through watery eyes.

"It's all my fault," she sobbed. "If Dad, Andrew, and Mac are dead, it's all my fault—"

Grace shook her head. "Allison, we've been through that. It is *not* your fault. It's no one's fault." Grace hugged her again, her voice growing stronger as she continued. "No matter what happens, we must believe that God is in control. That's the only thing we can hang on to now. God is in control, Allison."

Allison took a shaky breath. "Okay, I'll try to remember that." She quietly repeated Grace's words. "God is in control. . . . God is in control. . . ."

Just then the shrill jangling of the telephone interrupted her. Grace picked up the receiver with wide eyes. Allison listened intently, her trembling hand resting on Grace's shoulder.

"Yes?" said Grace. "You have? Are they—are there any survivors?" She listened silently, her face blank, for what seemed like an eternity.

Allison waited, barely daring to breathe. In those moments it seemed that Allison's world had screeched to a complete halt. Yesterday was gone and tomorrow might never come. And then Grace broke into loud sobs, and suddenly Allison felt her last hope perish. She collapsed into a chair as her heart tumbled and plummeted down.

But in the next instant Grace looked up at Allison with surprise, then cried, "They're all right!"

"They're all right?" echoed Allison in a weak voice.

Grace nodded, still listening to the receiver, a huge smile spreading across her face. "You are saying that all three of them are just fine!" she nearly shouted, nodding emphatically to Allison.

Allison leaped into the air and whooped for joy, but Grace motioned to her to be quiet so she could continue to hear the other end. "So you think they'll be flying in tomorrow?" asked Grace in an even voice. "I see. . . . Yes, I'm sure they'll call as soon as you help them get safely out. Yes . . . I understand completely. Oh, thank you very much! Thank you!" Grace hung up, then turned to Allison. The two hugged for a long time, tears of relief flowing freely.

"Now, tell me everything, Grace!" cried Allison as they both wiped their noses.

"The search crew spotted a signal fire early this morning. They radioed them from the air and learned that the weather forced them to land on a snowfield. It seems their plane is in good condition, but they were nearly buried in the snow. Other than being cold and hungry, it sounds as if they're just fine. Some nearby farmers are coming over to dig out the plane, and then they'll snowplow a runway so they can take off. They'll fly to the nearest airstrip—"

"Our prayers were really answered!" cried Allison as she grabbed Grace's hands in her own and began dancing around the little office.

The two of them spun around the room, whooping so loudly they didn't even notice the front door of the office open and close.

"What's going on?" called out George. "Have you heard something?"

Allison ran over and nearly knocked him down with a big, exuberant hug. "They're safe, George. They've been found!"

"Call Muriel and tell her the good news," said George. "She's been up half the night just sick with worry." He held up the picnic basket and grinned. "And you know how Muriel gets to baking when she's worried."

As George unloaded freshly baked cinnamon rolls and blueberry muffins, Allison called Muriel and told her the good news. "It's too bad we couldn't send this basket to them," she added as she hungrily sniffed the tasty baked goods.

While they ate their breakfast, Grace told George about the rescue. "The FAA man said that the farmers expect to have them out by noon. He said it sounded like everyone was just fine. Cold and hungry, but no injuries. Just the same, they'll be checked into the local hospital to make sure everyone is A-OK. But there's probably no reason why they can't fly home tomorrow—weather permitting. Apparently, the snowstorm just dumped and blew on over the mountains."

"I hope they come home tomorrow," said Allison as she took a sip of cold milk.

Grace nodded. "And I'm sure James will want to come home as soon as possible, too."

"You two girls need to get some rest," said George. "It's been a long night."

"I don't want to leave," said Grace. "Mac's assistant, Larry, doesn't seem very responsible. I don't even know where he went off to."

"How about if I stick around here and keep an eye on things," suggested George. "I've been wanting to spend some time down here anyway. Then you can take Allison home, and you both can get some sleep. If James calls up here, I can always have him call you at home, too."

Grace looked at Allison. "I suppose that makes sense. I am tired. Thanks a lot, George."

Allison couldn't remember the drive home or Muriel tucking her into her bed. But before Allison drifted off, she remembered to thank God. Over and over.

※

When she woke up, Heather was sitting at the end of her bed. Allison sat up and yawned, then looked at her alarm clock. "Goodness," she exclaimed. "It's almost two o'clock! I've been asleep for more than five hours."

Heather laughed. "You could probably use five more. And Muriel told me not to wake you up before two. But I didn't wake you, did I?"

"Not at all," said Allison, climbing out of bed. "I guess you and Winston didn't go to school today, either."

Heather shook her head. "Muriel told us everything early this morning, and neither of us felt like we could concentrate very well at school."

Allison squeezed Heather's hand. "Well, everything worked out okay—" Allison paused, then wondered if the news of the rescue had only been a hopeful dream. "Everything is okay, isn't it, Heather?"

"Yes, everything is swell. Your dad called around noon. They're all fit as fiddles. He wanted to come home today but decided to rest up and fly in tomorrow. He left the number of the hotel if you want to call him."

"You bet I do!" Allison exclaimed as she jerked a sweater over her head. "I can't wait to hear his voice."

At Muriel's suggestion, Allison waited until four o'clock to call her dad so he could have time to rest, too. But then she listened in wonder as he replayed all the details of their near disaster.

"Other than some customary fog and a slight breeze, every-thing looked just fine when we flew out of San Francisco. But as we headed north, it seemed a system was brewing. Mac felt pretty certain we could beat it, and we were all anxious to get home, but the next thing we knew, we were smack in the middle of a blizzard. Visibility was poor, and the winds were strong—buffeting the plane up and down. I'd been flying but was glad to let Mac take the stick. The carburetor began to have some trouble, and Mac was worried about it freezing up on us. We knew we were in danger, and I'll tell you that I was praying hard, Allison."

"Oh my," breathed Allison. "It must've been scary."

"It was. Then, suddenly, the visibility improved just enough for me to spot what looked like a nice big span of land below, but it was quickly getting covered with snow. I pointed it out to Mac, and he didn't waste a second getting down and in position to land."

"How exciting!"

Dad sighed deeply. "A little too exciting, I think. Because suddenly, as Mac was going for it, I wondered if it really was such a good spot. I mean, I couldn't see that well with all the snow. What if it was rocky, or what if it was a lake?"

"Oh no," gasped Allison. "You must have felt dreadful."

"But Mac said it was our only chance. So I just prayed and held on for dear life while he put her down. And the next thing I knew, we were rolling across the smoothest field you can imagine. I told the farmer later that he did a fine job making that field perfect for our landing, not a rock or a bump on it. But after we landed, the blizzard continued to get worse until it seemed we'd be buried alive in snow.

"We suspected we had landed on a cultivated field, but there wasn't a sign of civilization in sight. And thanks to the blizzard and the nearby mountains, our radio was almost useless. We decided to save our battery for when the storm abated. We were nearly buried in drifted snow, but I think it helped to insulate the plane and keep us warm. Just the same, it got pretty cold. It was Andrew's idea to use my packing crates to light a signal fire. If not for that—" He whistled dramatically. "Who knows . . ."

"What an amazing story!" exclaimed Allison. Then she thought for a moment. "Dad, you know how I'm working for the school paper now?"

"You mean the *Pirate Chest*?"

"Yes. Well, do you think it would be okay if I wrote up this story for the school paper? I can just see the headline—'Port View Star Quarterback Survives Plane Wreck.'"

"Well, it wasn't exactly a wreck," James chuckled. "More like an emergency landing. But just the same, I think it would make an interesting story, Allison."

"I'm going to hop right to it. I might be able to get it into this week's edition."

"Good for you!"

Allison smiled. "And by the way, Dad, did I tell you how great it is to hear your voice, and how much I love you?"

"Only a dozen times, sweetheart. But I never get tired of it. Say, give Grace a hug for me, and tell her that I'll call her again this evening."

"Dad," Allison said hesitantly. "Please fly home *very* carefully."

James laughed. "Don't you worry. I'm always careful."

Allison hung up the phone and dashed upstairs. She immediately began to write out her news story. She finished it just before dinnertime and was certain it was the best thing she'd ever written. She couldn't wait to turn it in to the editor tomorrow. Wouldn't Howie be surprised. It seemed like such a long time since she'd been at school; counting the Thanksgiving holiday it had been only five days, but this last day had felt like a year.

Muriel had invited Grace and the kids to join them for dinner, and Allison hurried downstairs to see if she needed any help. But Grace and Heather were already in the kitchen, and everything seemed to be running like clockwork.

"Here, Allison," said Grace as she handed her a basket of rolls to put on the table. "Just in time."

"Maybe we should stay home from school tomorrow, too," suggested Winston with a sly look as they all sat down around the big dining table.

Grace laughed. "Nice try, but I don't think so, Winston."

"When are they flying in?" asked Heather.

"Not until late afternoon," said Grace. "I just spoke to James. He said they have to do some paper work for the FAA in the morning, so they'll probably arrive around four."

"Did you tell Dad about Larry?" asked Allison.

Grace nodded. "He wasn't too happy. But I told him that George and I would hold down the fort until they get back. I thought I might even take some cleaning things over tomorrow."

"Maybe we could have a party for them," suggested Winston. "A welcome-back party at the airport."

"What a terrific idea," said Allison.

"Sounds great," said Grace. "I'll pick you kids up at school, and we can all be there. Is that okay with you, Muriel?"

"Yes," agreed Muriel. "I'll put some things together tomorrow. We'll have an airport picnic."

"I'll make a welcome-home sign," said Allison.

"I could make some big paper flowers," offered Heather.

"I can put up party streamers," said Winston.

"What a team," said Grace with a smile. "And it will be good to get the rest of our team back tomorrow."

⚜

As Grace drove them to school the next morning, Allison couldn't wait to find Howie and show him her story. She hoped it wasn't too late to make this week's paper. If she hurried, she might find him before her first class.

"Heather, do you mind if we hurry this morning?" asked Allison as she grabbed Heather's hand. "I want to give Howie my story."

"No problem," said Heather. As they walked in the front door, they were met by Caroline. Her blue eyes seemed brighter than usual, but then Allison realized that she had new glasses.

"Good-looking glasses, Caroline," said Allison quickly.

"Are they—is everyone okay?" asked Caroline with a worried expression.

"Heather, you tell her," urged Allison. "I need to find someone—quickly."

As Allison hurried down the hallway, she wondered how Caroline knew about the plane wreck but figured that Heather must have called her yesterday. Allison looked all around but didn't see Howie anywhere, and it was almost time for class.

To Allison's surprise, Shirley walked up and actually looked as if she was about to speak. Shirley hadn't spoken directly to Allison for quite some time—not since the incident when she told everyone in school about Allison's mother being the famous Marsha Madison. And Allison wasn't eager to talk to Shirley now.

"Allison, I heard about your dad's plane," said Shirley knowingly.

Allison blinked in surprise. "How did you hear that?"

"My dad saw Larry at the gas station."

Allison sighed and shook her head. *That Larry!*

"Well, are they okay?" demanded Shirley as the first bell rang.

"Yes, of course, they're all just fine," said Allison, glancing over Shirley's shoulder in hopes of spotting Howie.

"Who are you looking for?" asked Shirley.

"Howie Ketchum."

"I haven't seen him this morning." Shirley stayed right at Allison's side as she walked. "But I did see him yesterday, after school."

Shirley reminded her of the little French poodle that Grandmother Madison used to keep; the crazy animal would dog her heels and yap as she tried to walk.

"You might be interested to know, Allison, that I am also a reporter for the *Pirate Chest*."

Allison stopped and stared at Shirley in disbelief, all at once taking in her bright red sweater, just a little too snug, and her slim black pencil skirt. "You are a reporter?" said Allison in dismay. "Exactly when did this happen? I was only gone one day."

Shirley laughed. "Yesterday. I told Howie that my dad wanted to donate a real printer to the school paper so they don't have to use that old mimeograph machine anymore and that I'd like to write for the paper, too."

Allison was stunned. It sounded almost like bribery. "I didn't know you had an interest in writing," she said lamely.

Shirley grinned. "Well, I happen to have a pretty good nose for news. Not only that, the paper sounds like it's going to become a lot more fun. I heard Beverly say that Andrew might also be joining the staff now that football season is over."

Allison blinked. Andrew had mentioned that to her, too, but she didn't think it was common knowledge. Well, maybe Shirley was right—maybe she did have a nose for news. Allison forced a smile to her lips. After all, she'd vowed not to hold Shirley's offenses against her. Shirley was just Shirley—Allison didn't have to let her get to her.

"Welcome to the *Pirate Chest* staff," said Allison, extending a cordial hand and what she hoped was a sincere smile.

"Thank you, Allison," said Shirley as she took her hand. "And by the way, I turned in my first story yesterday. It's a sensational account of Andrew's plane wreck. Now I can add a couple of lines telling how he actually survived."

As she watched Shirley hurry into class ahead of her, Allison felt as though she'd been slugged in the stomach. The final bell rang as Allison slipped into her desk. She sat and stared at the neatly typed story sitting on top of her notebook—all ready to hand in to Howie. But it was too late. Allison O'Brian had been scooped by Shirley Jenson!

2

Allison had just stepped into the lunch line with Heather and Caroline when she heard someone call out her name.

"Hey, Allison," Howie said as he got in line behind her. "I heard you were looking for me."

"Oh, hi, Howie," Allison said with a weak smile.

"So everyone's okay, then?" he asked. "I mean, with the plane wreck and all."

"Yes, although it wasn't exactly a 'wreck.' They're all fine, and they'll be home this afternoon," said Allison.

"Didn't you give Howie your story?" asked Heather as if that should explain everything.

Allison felt her cheeks grow warm. She hadn't told Heather about Shirley's story yet. "No, I . . . uh . . . I don't think he'll be interested. . . ."

"Sure, I'm interested," said Howie as he pushed his tortoise-framed glasses back into place and picked up a plate of tuna casserole. "What is it?"

"Oh, it's nothing," said Allison. She placed a dish of peaches on her tray and quickly moved down the line.

"Nothing?" repeated Heather. "It's all about Andrew's plane going down. Allison read it to me last night, and it was terrific!"

Allison smiled. Sweet, helpful Heather. But too late.

"I'd like to see it," said Howie. "Can you get it for me right away?"

"Sure," said Allison with renewed hope. "Let me put my tray on the table, and I'll get the story right now."

Allison dashed off toward her locker. Maybe it wasn't too late after all. But what about Shirley's story? Well, she'd let Howie figure that one out. That's why he was the editor. She returned breathlessly and placed the story before Howie, then waited eagerly. Howie was seated at the same table as Heather and Caroline. He laid down his fork and picked up the story.

"Nice headline, Allison," he commented as he scanned down the page. A smile played across his mouth. "This looks good. Really good. All we need now is a photo. With our new printer we can actually use photography now."

"They're flying in this afternoon," offered Heather. "You could come out and take photographs at the airport if you like."

"That would be swell," said Howie. "No doubt about it, Allison, this story's going on this week's front page."

"Really?" said Allison. "Oh, thank you, Howie."

"Don't thank me, Allison. This is a top-notch story. You've covered all the facts."

Allison wanted to ask him about Shirley's story but decided against it. No need to appear smug. "We're having a little celebration for the returning survivors," said Allison. "Maybe you'd like to join us, Howie."

"Thanks, Allison. That'd be nice—if I'm not intruding."

"Not at all," chimed in Heather. "I've invited Caroline along, too, Allison. I hope that's okay."

"Of course," said Allison. "The more the merrier."

"I better scoot, girls," said Howie as he finished his last

bite. "If I'm going to shoot pictures after school, I've got a few things to tend to right now. Thanks again for the story, Allison."

Allison turned her attention to Caroline. "Sorry I was in such a rush this morning, Caroline, but I really do like your new glasses. And you look really nice in that blue sweater. Is it new?"

Caroline nodded, blushing slightly. "And I've been exercising every single day."

"It's paying off," said Allison. "You are looking just swell, Caroline."

"Thanks." Caroline beamed.

Allison felt as though she were floating on a cloud for the rest of the day. Howie really liked her story. The only snag was, as usual, she had to see Shirley in every single class, and she felt a little guilty that her story would bump Shirley's. She would be so relieved when this semester finally ended and she could get a new class schedule, and hopefully not one identical to Shirley Jenson's!

After the final bell of the day, Heather, Caroline, and Allison hurried outside to find Grace and Winston waiting in the parking lot.

"We have less than an hour to get everything ready for the party," said Grace as she drove toward the airport. "I already dropped Muriel off. George has been working out there all day. I'm glad you could come, too, Caroline. We can use an extra set of hands to decorate."

"Yeah," said Winston. "She's tall; she can help me hang up the streamers."

"Wow," said Allison as she went into Mac's office. "Someone has been working hard in here. It looks neat as a pin."

George nodded toward Grace. "She's been at it all day long. I just hope Mac doesn't go into shock."

"Any sign of Larry?" asked Allison.

George shook his head. "I think he's embarrassed to show his face around here."

It was almost four o'clock when everything was ready for the party. Allison went outside with Winston to look at the sky, hoping to spot the plane in time to tell everyone. Instead, she noticed an old car coming down the drive.

"That must be Howie," said Allison. She quickly told Winston about the newspaper and photos.

"Swell," said Winston. "Andrew will be famous now. Uh-oh, that looks like old Shirley Jenson with him."

Allison stared in horror. Winston was right! Shirley was sitting in the passenger seat.

Howie parked the car and walked toward Allison with a stiff smile. "I hope it's okay that Shirley came along. She told me that she's a close friend of the family, and, well, since you said the more the merrier . . ."

Allison forced a smile. "That's just fine, Howie." She turned to Shirley. "Come inside, you two. Muriel has lots of good things to eat. They should be here—"

"Hey, Allison," yelled Winston, pointing to a speck in the sky that was quickly getting larger. "I see them! I see them!"

"Let's all get inside," said Allison. "We want to surprise them." Allison ushered them into the little office. She tried not to look at Shirley but couldn't help but glimpse what looked like a very sullen expression.

"They're coming, everyone!" announced Winston.

They all gathered in the cramped office until the plane landed and taxied over, then the happy crowd burst out the door with balloons and shouts, welcoming the long-lost travelers with lots of hugs and backslapping.

"Were you hungry out there?" asked Winston after things

finally settled down. "Did you get really, really cold? Did you think you'd be lost forever?"

James laughed and patted Winston on the head. "Yes, yes, and yes. When that snow just kept coming, we thought we might actually be buried alive. But it turned out to be a blessing because it kept us from freezing during the night. And the next morning, we were so glad when the searchers spotted our signal fire."

Allison introduced her dad to Howie. "Howie's the editor of the paper, Dad, and he's going to run my story on the front page. He wanted to get some photos of the survivors."

"We better get to it before it gets dark, then," said James. He and Andrew and Mac posed in front of the plane with big, heroic-looking smiles.

"Were you scared, Andrew?" asked Winston. "Where'd you get the matches to make the fire? And how come the radio didn't work?"

"You'd make a good reporter, Winston," teased Allison, trying to avoid Shirley's hostile glare. "You're just full of questions."

"I think it's time we had some food," said Muriel. "And then the heroes can regale everyone with their tales of great adventure."

Inside the crowded office, Howie pulled Allison aside. "I'm sorry about Shirley, Allison," he whispered. "She was in a real snit about your story. I tried to explain, but then it was time for me to come out here—and when she learned about it, she insisted on coming, too."

"It's okay, Howie," said Allison. She kindly patted his arm. "This is nothing new. And it's certainly not your fault." In the same instant, she looked up to catch both Andrew's and Shirley's eyes fastened on her. Shirley looked as if she had just eaten something very disagreeable, and Andrew appeared somewhat puzzled. Then Shirley turned her attention from Allison and back onto Andrew.

With an immense smile across her painted lips, Shirley began to gush loudly about what a hero Andrew would be in school and how exciting it was to know someone who had survived a plane wreck. Andrew smiled and politely endured her chatter. Everything in Allison longed to go and rescue him from Shirley, but she had already trodden on Shirley's toes once today—even if it wasn't intentional. Twice might be too much. Instead, Allison went over and linked her arm with her father's.

"I'm so glad you're safely home," she whispered.

"Me too. Don't tell Grace, but I was starting to think that she might have been right all along about this flying business."

"I know what you mean," said Allison. "But Grace was such a trooper about the whole thing. She told me how God was in control, and I believe she was right."

Allison noticed that Caroline was sitting by herself in a corner behind Mac's desk. "Come over here, Caroline," called Allison as she went over to where Howie was standing, munching on a sandwich. Suddenly, Allison had an idea.

"Caroline," said Allison. "I just got a brand-new story idea, but I'd like to know what you think first." Allison glanced at Howie, and it looked like he was all ears. "Howie, did you know that Caroline's brother served in Europe during the war, but he was taken prisoner shortly before the war ended? The thing is, he didn't come back, and now Caroline's parents have heard that he may still be in a prison camp in Siberia."

"*Siberia?* Say, I've heard rumors of secret prison camps, but I just thought it was hype. After all, the Soviet Union is supposed to be our ally."

"What if I did a story about Caroline's brother?" continued

Allison. "It would be a way for kids to hear about prisoners of war, but it would hit closer to home, since Caroline's brother was a Port View graduate. Some of the seniors might even remember him. What do *you* think, Caroline?"

"I think it would be wonderful," said Caroline. "You mean you'd really want to do a story about Kevin?"

"I know I would. I'm not sure what Howie thinks of the idea." Allison looked up at Howie expectantly.

"I think it's a tremendous idea, Allison. Run with it. See what you can do."

Caroline was beaming now. "My parents would be so proud."

"Okay, then, we'll have to get together, Caroline," said Allison in a business voice. "I'll need you to give me all the details, and I'll have to do a little research on Siberia."

"That's what I like to hear," said Howie. He glanced over at Shirley. "It's refreshing to have a writer who actually researches *before* she writes."

Allison grinned. Of course! Shirley's story must have been more fiction than fact. All Shirley could have known about the downed plane was what she'd heard secondhand from her dad—and that information had come from Larry! Poor Shirley. It was almost laughable.

After an hour, Howie offered to take Caroline and Shirley home. Allison sighed in relief as they left. She didn't think she could have withstood Shirley's dagger looks much longer.

"What I want to know," said Mac finally, "is *who cleaned up in here?*"

Grace blushed and raised her hand sheepishly. "Mac, I tried not to misplace anything. I hope it's all right—"

"All right?" he boomed. "Well, it's a wee bit better than all right, Grace. It's a sight for sore eyes!"

Grace sighed. "And I was thinking"—she glanced over at

James—"perhaps I could help out in here a few hours a day—with the office work and whatnot."

"Sounds good to me," said Mac. He looked at James, then added in a more serious voice, "I think we've seen the last of ol' Larry."

James shook his head. "Too bad. I was hoping he'd work out. But there's no doubt that Grace would be first-class help. She'll have this place running like clockwork in no time."

"But there's one more thing," said Grace in an authoritative voice. "If I'm to help out around here, I think it's only fair that James takes me up."

"Up?" repeated James with raised brows. "You mean in a plane?"

Grace laughed. "Unless you've sprouted wings lately, James."

"Sure," he answered. "When?"

"Tomorrow," she answered without batting an eyelash. "I know it may come as a shock to everyone, but while I was down here fretting over our three lost flyers, I promised myself that if they made it back safely, I would go up in a plane. And hopefully, once and for all, I will conquer my fear of flying."

James blinked in surprise. Everyone else cheered.

"And," said Grace in a more serious voice, "I think it would be only right if we took a few moments to thank God for protecting you three. You have no idea how Allison and I labored in prayer for you—"

"I prayed, too," said Winston.

"So did I," echoed Heather.

"So did we," said Muriel. "I think we all want to say thank you."

Grace led them in a prayer of thanks, followed by a moment of silence. It was one of those times that Allison felt she would remember forever.

"And now," said James, "I have an announcement. Grace and I had quite a long chat on the phone last night, and we have finally set our wedding date." He glanced at Allison, as if asking if it was okay to spring this news on her, too. She smiled as if to say yes, and James continued. "We have decided to get married on New Year's Eve."

Everyone clapped, and congratulations were shared. Then Grace turned to Andrew. "I don't mean to ruin the party, but I really think you kids should be getting on home now. After all, it's a school night, and you must be tired after all you've been through. Do you mind driving Heather and Winston home while I help Muriel clean this up, Andrew?"

"Not at all, Grace."

"I'll help, too," offered James. "Andrew, do you mind giving Allison a lift?"

"No problem."

The four of them piled into the jalopy, and Winston continued to pummel his brother with dozens of questions as they headed for home.

"I'll drop off Winston and Heather, if you don't mind," said Andrew. "Since our house is first."

"That's fine," said Allison, thinking it would be nice to have a few words with Andrew in private.

"I feel like I've been gone for a long time," said Andrew after he dropped off his siblings and drove toward her house. His voice sounded weary and not at all like him.

"I sort of know what you mean. But after all you've been through, it probably makes it seem even more that way."

Andrew cleared his throat. "I was a little surprised to see Howie Ketchum here tonight."

"Oh, he just wanted to get a photograph to go with my

story for the paper. We thought it was a good opportunity."

"Right," said Andrew. But something about his tone didn't sound *right*.

"I *was* surprised when he brought Shirley Jenson along," said Allison. "And as usual, she has it out for me."

"She says you stole her story."

"I stole her story?" Allison repeated as she stared at Andrew. He couldn't possibly believe that.

"Yep." Andrew nodded. "Shirley seems to think that you and Howie have some little romance going on, and that somehow you sweet-talked him into printing your story instead of hers."

Allison was too stunned to respond. She had expected Andrew to be happy for her, to be proud of her story—not suspicious. Since when did anyone take what Shirley Jenson said seriously anyway?

Andrew drove on in silence. He pulled up to her house but didn't shut off the engine as he usually did, nor did he hop out to open her door for her. Allison waited for a moment. She wanted to ask him if he truly believed Shirley, but it seemed like such a ridiculous question. Andrew *had* to know the truth.

"Thanks for bringing me home," she said lamely as she reached for the door handle.

"Sure." Andrew sighed, then turned to look at her. "I guess I'm pretty worn out from our recent adventure, Allison."

"Yes," said Allison. "I'm sure you are, Andrew. Get some rest."

Allison climbed down from the jalopy and went into the quiet house. For the second time that day, she felt as if someone had pulled the rug out from under her. She told herself Andrew was just tired. He probably didn't realize what he was saying. By tomorrow he'd figure it out and maybe even apologize, if he hadn't forgotten about the whole thing by then. Unfortunately, her troubles with Shirley probably wouldn't evaporate so easily. But what else was new?

It was barely eight o'clock, but Allison felt exhausted. Still, she remembered she hadn't written her weekly letter to her mother yet. She usually wrote to Marsha on Sunday evenings before bed, but with the recent events, she'd missed the last one. She sat down to her desk to write, and she told Marsha all about Dad's flying enterprise and her story for the paper. She even told her about Shirley, without mentioning Andrew, of course. Only last summer she'd compared Shirley to Marsha, but her feelings toward Marsha had changed, and she no longer cast them in the same light. Now Shirley occupied a category all her own. Still, there might be some things Allison could learn from her relationship with her mother that could also be applied to Shirley, but for tonight she was too tired to figure it all out.

The one thing she did know was that she needed to forgive Shirley Jenson—once again—and probably not for the last time. She strongly suspected that God could show her how to deal with someone like Shirley if she asked Him.

And so she did.

3

"Great story about Andrew, Allison," said Karen Brown as they walked toward the east gym for P.E. class. "I was waiting for Beverly to finish laying out the paper yesterday before cheerleading practice, so I took a few minutes to read it. I can't wait to see the photos that Howie took."

"Thanks," said Allison quietly, fully aware that Shirley lagged just a few steps behind. Allison wasn't eager for Shirley to overhear Karen's praise.

"I hear the cheerleaders are responsible for the pep assembly on Friday," said Allison in an attempt to change the subject.

"Yep," said Karen. "Time to kick off basketball season. Between you and me, it doesn't look like it's going to be much of a season, though. I sure wish Mr. Andrew Amberwell liked basketball as much as he likes football."

"Does he *play* basketball?" asked Allison.

"Nope." Karen frowned dramatically. "He says he doesn't care for the sport."

For a moment Allison considered how fun it would be to sit in the stands and cheer as Andrew shot the winning basket. "That's too bad."

"Not too bad for the paper," chirped Shirley from behind, obviously eavesdropping.

"How's that?" asked Karen in an annoyed tone.

"Well, it just so happens that Andrew Amberwell is going to start writing for the paper soon," said Shirley in her I-know-everything voice. "Beverly told me."

"That *Pirate Chest* is getting to be pretty popular these days," said Karen. "But at least having more kids to help on the paper should give Beverly time to keep up with her cheerleading responsibilities. Not that I blame her. Sometimes I wish I hadn't gone out for the squad—it makes me miss out on so many other things."

"You mean you'd give up being a cheerleader to work on the school paper?" asked Shirley, sounding shocked.

"Maybe," said Karen thoughtfully. "Being a cheerleader isn't that big of a deal, Shirley."

"Maybe not to you," snapped Shirley.

Karen just shrugged and went into the gym. *"That girl,"* she whispered to Allison as they lined up for roll call.

Thankfully, Allison managed to make it through to her last class without having an actual conversation with Shirley. But as she hurried out the door from her algebra class, she heard quick little heel clicks coming directly behind her.

"What's the big rush, Allison?" called Shirley in a taunting voice.

Allison turned and faced Shirley, unsure what to expect. "No big rush," she said casually. "I'd just like to get home, is all."

"You mean you're not off in hot pursuit of some big *news-breaking* story?"

Allison took in a slow, deep breath, praying a silent prayer for patience. "Look, Shirley, I'm really sorry that your story about the plane going down was tabled because of me, but there's nothing I can do about it. Okay?"

Shirley folded her arms across her front and knotted her brows together. No one could scowl quite like Shirley. "No, it's not okay, Allison. You *stole* my story."

Allison tried not to roll her eyes, determined to remain patient. "I did not steal your story, Shirley. I had no idea you were doing a story. I didn't even know you were on the paper then. I wrote it right after I got off the phone with my dad. He gave me all the details." Allison cocked her head slightly. "And where did you get all of your information, Shirley?"

"I have my sources."

"Shirley, no one in town knew *any* of the details besides me and my family. Sure, Larry might have shot off his mouth about the plane going down, but he didn't *really* know anything specific."

"What makes you so sure?" insinuated Shirley.

Allison frowned. "Are you trying to say that Larry knew more?"

"I don't reveal all my sources."

Allison shook her head. "Look, Shirley, I don't really care about your sources, but the fact is, *I did not steal your story*. And I would appreciate it if you wouldn't spread that sort of rumor around school."

Shirley laughed. "It's a little late now."

Allison felt her teeth clenching tightly, probably a good thing, since she was afraid the next words out of her mouth would be all wrong. She turned on her heel and marched off to her locker, grabbed her book bag, then stormed toward the exit. It was a good thing Wednesday wasn't her day to work on the paper. One more moment spent in the company of Shirley could make the hydrogen bomb look like a party popper.

Naturally, it was raining in torrents outside. Allison pulled a rain scarf over her head and dashed out to where the jalopy was parked. Fortunately, Heather and Andrew were already waiting. She climbed inside and slammed the door with a loud bang.

"Looks like someone's in a foul mood," said Andrew.

Allison exhaled noisily through her nostrils. She wasn't ready to speak. Especially to Andrew.

"What's wrong, Allison?" asked Heather kindly.

"Don't ask," muttered Allison. "It'll be fine as soon as I cool off a bit."

"Let me guess," said Heather. "Do the initials S. J. mean anything?"

Allison groaned. "She's still accusing me of *stealing* her story. I think she's probably told the whole school by now. And the paper comes out tomorrow. Everybody is going to think I'm a horrible reporter."

Heather reached over and patted Allison's arm. "Anybody with half a brain will know that you didn't steal anyone's story."

Allison looked past Heather and tossed an accusing glance at Andrew. "You really think so, Heather?"

"Of course." Heather smiled. "You shouldn't let her get to you, Allison."

Allison sighed. "I know . . ."

"Yeah," agreed Andrew. "You know that nobody takes Shirley Jenson seriously."

"You don't say?" Allison said with raised brows as she remembered his words from last night.

Andrew just grinned sheepishly, then started the engine.

"Did you know that Shirley Jenson has been saying something about you lately, Andrew?" teased Allison.

Andrew's eyes darted her way. "What's that?"

Allison laughed lightly. "Goodness, could it be that you're actually interested in something Shirley Jenson has to say?"

"I never said people weren't interested, Allison. I only said that no one really takes her too seriously."

"Oh yes. I see." Allison shut her lips tightly, enjoying this moment of power over Andrew.

"Yes," said Heather in a conspirator's tone, as if teaming up with Allison. "Shirley Jenson certainly has said some interesting things in the past, don't you think, Allison?"

Allison nodded. "Yes, she sure has. . . ."

"Come on, you two," pleaded Andrew. "Cut it out and tell me what Shirley is saying about me."

Allison laughed heartily this time. Soon Heather was giggling, too. Andrew's face puckered up, and Allison couldn't tell if it was from amusement or pure frustration. She finally felt sorry for him and stifled her giggles long enough to speak.

"Okay. Shirley told Karen and me that you are going to write for the *Pirate Chest*, too. So should we take Shirley seriously about this one or not?"

Andrew grinned. "All right, Allison. Shirley might be right about that."

Allison nodded. "I see."

"It's no big deal. I would have started with the paper this fall, but football took too much of my time. Beverly asked me about becoming the sportswriter, and I thought it would be fun, plus I'll get into all the sporting events for free." Andrew chuckled. "And I figured it wouldn't hurt for me to be around the paper to help keep tabs on you."

Allison frowned. She could feign offense but thought better of it. The truth was she sort of liked the idea of Andrew checking up on her.

"This will be perfect," said Heather. "Mrs. Foster, my orchestra teacher, asked me about staying after school a couple afternoons a week so I can practice clarinet. Now we can all ride home together."

"Clarinet?" asked Allison.

"Yes, she thinks I'd be a natural, and I'd like to give it a try."

"Well, aren't we a talented little threesome," teased Andrew. "Writers, musicians . . . who knows where we'll end up." Then he turned on the radio and they sang along.

"Hey, I forgot to mention that Grace wants you to stop by after school today, Allison," said Heather. "The fabric arrived for the bridesmaid dresses. Since the pattern is fairly simple, she's going to sew them herself, but she needs to get your measurements. Will that work?"

"Sure," said Allison. "I forgot—what color is the fabric?"

"Grace says it's powder pink."

Allison made a face. She detested pink. Marsha had always said that regardless of what they say in fashion magazines, redheads should never wear pink. Oh well, it was only for one day, and Marsha wouldn't be there.

"Grace is going to have a lot to do this month," commented Allison. "Sewing dresses, preparing for the wedding, and she wants to help out at the airport."

"I think she likes being busy," said Andrew. "She seems happier than ever right now."

Heather nodded. "Yes, it's odd. Having the plane go down seemed to help her somehow. She seems a lot more relaxed about everything."

"Sometimes a near catastrophe can do that," said Andrew wisely. "It sort of puts things back into perspective."

Allison nodded. "I know what you mean. Still, it feels like things are happening so fast. It's hard to believe they're really going to be married by the end of next month."

"Well, don't you think it's about time they got it over with," Andrew said in a matter-of-fact voice.

Allison glanced over at him. "Got it over with? Don't make it sound so terribly romantic, Andrew."

Andrew laughed. "I guess that wasn't exactly what I meant. But if you think about it, they could have gotten married a long, long time ago."

"But then where would I be?" asked Allison in a small voice. "Marsha may have her problems, but she is my mother."

"And furthermore, Andrew," scolded Heather, "where would we be if Grace hadn't been in England when we lost our parents?"

Andrew smiled as he pulled in the driveway. "I guess you ladies make a pretty good point. God must've been in control all along."

⚜

Allison was thankful when Grace took her into the privacy of her bedroom to measure her. She had no desire for Andrew to watch this humiliating process. Allison was well aware that Marsha claimed to be a perfect 36-24-36; Allison had to puff her chest out like a rooster to achieve a meager 32-22-32. Funny how only a year back she didn't give a hoot about silly measurements. How things had changed.

Allison glanced around the simply furnished bedroom while Grace got out her measuring tape. Blue chenille bedspread, chintz curtains, a wooden rocker painted white, and a pine dresser. Nice and neat, but nothing fancy. Suddenly, Allison wondered if Grace might want to change things in Grandpa's house when she moved in after the wedding. Allison felt it was absolutely perfect just the way it was. Grandmother Mercury, in Allison's opinion, had shown wonderful taste and a great sense of decor. And Allison had never felt so completely at home anywhere else. She didn't want a single thing to change.

"I think that takes care of it, Allison," said Grace as she folded the tape measure back into her sewing basket. "Do you want to see the fabric?"

"I guess so, though I'm not terribly fond of pink. . . ."

"I'm sorry. I didn't know." Grace pulled out the material, a very pale pink satin.

Allison touched the smooth fabric. "I guess for pink it's not so bad, Grace. I'm sure the dresses will be okay. And after all, it's only for one day."

Grace laughed nervously. "It might be only one day to you, but I'm hoping it will be one of the happiest days of *my* life."

Suddenly, Allison felt very selfish and immature. She threw her arms around Grace's neck. "I'm so sorry, Grace. I must sound like a spoiled brat. It will be a wonderful day for all of us."

"I know your dad announced it suddenly last night. I hope you didn't mind, Allison. We had discussed it on the phone, but I don't think he had the chance to tell you about it."

"It's okay, Grace. We all knew it was going to happen soon. I think I was just feeling grumpy because I'd had a difficult day with Shirley Jenson—again."

Grace laughed. "In that case, I won't take it personally. I think these dresses will look very pretty on you girls. I couldn't imagine having lovelier bridesmaids."

"Thanks," said Allison. "I'm sure the dresses are going to be terrific. I better get home now. I have a mountain of homework to do."

❧

At dinner, Allison told her dad about the bridesmaid dresses, and how she hoped she hadn't offended Grace by not liking pink.

"Don't worry, sweetheart," said James. "It takes quite a bit to offend Grace."

Allison smiled. "Yes, it's hard to fall from grace with Grace."

James chuckled. "And I've certainly pushed her on that one."

"Dad," began Allison carefully, "I was thinking about the way this house is . . ."

"Yes?"

"Well, I just love it so much. It feels like Grandmother Mercury's touch is everywhere. I like that."

James nodded. "I know exactly what you mean."

"But I'm worried that might all change when you get married—you know, when Grace comes to live here."

James nodded thoughtfully. "I see what you mean. How about if I talk to Grace about it and see what she thinks. I want her to feel at home, too, and it's only fair that she should have her say in things. But it would be nice if we all felt at home."

"I know. I feel guilty even mentioning it. It's probably very selfish—"

"Don't you ever feel guilty for telling me what you think, Allison Mercury. I always want to know how you feel about things. Understood?"

Allison nodded. "Understood."

"That's my girl."

Allison grinned and began to clear the table for Muriel. "I better get to my homework. The pile is starting to look like Mount Everest."

"Then why don't you let me finish this," James offered, taking the plates from her hands. "Like my mother used to say, schoolwork comes first."

When Allison got to her room, she found an unopened letter from Marsha on her desk. It was only the second one so far, and still a novelty. Like the previous one, it was quick and breezy, but the last few lines threw Allison for a loop.

I'd love to have you come down and visit for Christmas vacation. Stanley needs to stay in New York, but I'm throwing a little wingding and it would be fun to have you with me. Do you think your old man would mind?

Allison read it again. In the past, Marsha had put up with Allison during the holidays only when Grandmother Madison backed out, and then always grudgingly. This was something entirely new. Allison frowned. What would Dad say? This would be their first Christmas together, and in all honesty she'd prefer staying here. But on the other hand, if she rejected Marsha's gesture of goodwill, would she ever get a second chance?

Allison put the letter back in the envelope and sighed. Homework first. She'd have to deal with Marsha, and Dad, tomorrow.

4

Throughout the next day, Allison heard mixed reviews on her story about Andrew's perilous escape from death. The majority of the readers thought it was great, but a few girls, mainly staunch admirers of Shirley Jenson, openly criticized her. Allison tried to ignore them, but it still hurt. Fortunately for Allison, Shirley's nose seemed to be seriously out of joint for the entire day, so she wasn't speaking to anyone. Just the same, Allison had begun to dread the idea of working on the school paper with someone like Shirley. Who knew what she might pull next?

After school, Allison noticed Heather and Caroline giggling together as they walked arm in arm toward the orchestra room. Heather had explained that she was receiving clarinet lessons for free in exchange for tutoring Caroline on the flute. Allison felt a small pang of jealousy mixed with gratitude. She felt slightly possessive of Heather's friendship but at the same time was glad that Caroline was so devoted to her.

Heather continued to amaze everyone at Port View High with her ability to fit in. Many times even Allison forgot that Heather couldn't see. Occasionally, Allison said stupid things that only a sighted person would understand, like, "Did you see that?" But Heather never took offense. Allison knew that angels weren't made of real flesh and blood, but she often thought that Heather was the most angelic person she'd ever known, and she frequently wished she were more like her best friend. Especially now, as she got closer to the journalism room, Allison longed for Heather's gracious ways of smoothing things over.

"How's our star reporter?" called Andrew as he waited for her.

"All right, I guess." Allison glanced around to see if Shirley was lurking nearby.

"Howie said he's going to start with a meeting today and not to be late," he said as he held the door open. "Sounds like a good idea, if you ask me."

"Howie's a pretty smart guy," said Allison. She noticed a slight crease in Andrew's forehead as he closed the door.

Soon they were all seated around a large table, with Howie at the head. It reminded Allison of a boardroom scene from a Katharine Hepburn movie. Howie cleared his throat and stood. His cheeks were slightly flushed, and Allison noticed his hands trembled slightly as he held his notes. He cleared his throat again and began to speak.

"It's great to have you all here today. Last year, the idea for the newspaper grew out of the yearbook, but most of the yearbook staff were too busy to help out. So we had two seniors who made all the decisions and did most of the writing; I took care of the layout, mimeographing, and distribution. But this fall I was invited to become the editor of the *Pirate Chest*, and fortunately for me, Beverly decided to help out. But we've been pretty short staffed. Not long ago, Beverly brought Allison on board, and now we have Shirley and Andrew, as well. And as some of you know, Shirley's father has generously donated a special new printer so we can use real photography. Now I think it's about time to get organized and assign roles. That way we can become more efficient—"

"And not have two people covering the same story," said Shirley in a wounded voice.

"Yes." Howie looked down at his notes. "We want to avoid duplications. Now, I will continue as editor, but due to Beverly's responsibilities associated with cheerleading, she'd like to change her assistant editor position into a straight reporter—"

"So you'll be looking for a new assistant editor?" asked Shirley eagerly.

"Eventually," said Howie. "I don't think it's a decision we need to make today. Continuing with what I was saying, I'd like Allison to be our feature reporter—"

"What's that?" asked Shirley.

Allison wondered if anyone else was getting irritated by Shirley's constant interruptions.

Howie continued. "If Allison agrees, it means she'll still be a reporter but will do longer, more in-depth stories." Howie looked at Allison. "Is that okay with you?"

She smiled at him. "Sounds great."

Shirley made a noise that sounded like "humph," and Howie continued.

"Good. And you may have heard that Andrew has agreed to be our sports reporter. It seems a natural fit. Great to have you on the team, Andrew."

Andrew thanked him, and Howie looked down at his notes again.

"What about me?" asked Shirley, hardly missing a beat.

"Oh, you'll be a reporter, too," said Howie with a stiff smile.

"Well, I have another idea," said Shirley. She stood up as if to make a speech, straightening her shoulders and adjusting her short, fitted jacket. "I thought it would be nice to have a society column in our paper."

Howie looked blankly at Shirley, Beverly rolled her eyes, and Andrew groaned. It was obvious that everyone was getting a little fed up, but Shirley seemed oblivious as she continued.

"A society column could be a way of informing students about what's going on around school, who's doing what and going where. My mother still has a newspaper sent up here from Los Angeles just so she can read the society column—"

"This is not Los Angeles," said Howie wearily.

"Yeah," agreed Andrew. "No one around here wants to read that stuff."

Shirley frowned, then sank back down into her chair. "It figures," she muttered. "No one ever likes *my* ideas."

Suddenly, and unexpectedly, Allison experienced a tiny twinge of compassion for Shirley. Was it fair to dismiss her idea so quickly? And before she knew what hit her, Allison was speaking out in Shirley Jenson's defense.

"What's wrong with a society column?" she asked. "I'm sure students would enjoy hearing about what other students are up to." Allison glanced at Shirley; the shocked girl's mouth gaped slightly, and her eyes were large with surprise.

Allison continued with a slight warning edge to her voice. "As long as the column was honest and fair, included everyone, and was interesting to read—what could it hurt?"

"You know," said Beverly. "I think Allison makes a good point. And I bet a lot of the girls would like it."

"We could call it 'Jenson's Jetsam'" blurted Allison.

"Huh?" said Shirley. "What's that?"

"You know, like flotsam and jetsam," said Allison patiently, but Shirley still looked blank.

"Flotsam and jetsam are those bits and pieces of miscellaneous things that float in with the tide—all sorts of things," said Howie, suddenly gaining enthusiasm. "Allison, that's brilliant! Our paper is the *Pirate Chest*, and to have a column called 'Flotsam and Jetsam' is a stroke of genius."

Allison felt her face beam with his high praise.

"But I thought it was *my* column," said Shirley, "and she said 'Jenson's Jetsam,' not 'Flotsam and Jetsam.'"

Howie frowned. "Well, okay. I guess it can be 'Jenson's Jetsam.' Does everyone agree?"

Andrew pointed out that it was a bit of a tongue twister, but finally they all concurred. And although Allison felt like "Flotsam and Jetsam" sounded better, she was not ready to rock Shirley's boat again.

"Now let's discuss next week's paper. Beverly, you'll cover the pep assembly on Friday. Andrew will get the game. Allison, do you still want to do that story about Caroline's brother?"

"Caroline's brother?" repeated Shirley. "Who cares about him?"

Allison took a breath and looked evenly at Shirley. She would remain patient. "Caroline's brother fought for our country in Europe," said Allison. "He was a prisoner of war but never returned home. He may be imprisoned in Siberia, or he might even be dead. I thought we could do a story about prisoners of war there with a focus on him."

Shirley blinked. "Oh."

"I think it sounds like a terrific idea," said Andrew.

"The paper will continue coming out on Thursdays," said Howie. "I will handle layout, but I'm willing to train anyone who's interested." He went on to tell them about deadlines and details, finally handing out an information sheet. "Any questions?"

"Not from me, Howie," said Andrew. "I'm impressed. You seem to have everything under control."

"Thanks," said Howie. "But it doesn't make much difference unless I have a good team behind me. That's why each one of you is very important."

"It doesn't say anything in here about *my* word count," said Shirley, holding up the memo.

"No, Shirley, that's because I didn't know we were having a society column then. I'd estimate about a hundred words should do."

"But it says here that the feature editor gets about five hundred words. That means Allison gets five times as much as me."

"Good math," quipped Andrew. Shirley scowled.

"We're looking for quality, not quantity," said Howie with finality. "Okay, then, we better get to work."

Allison immediately started outlining her story, jotting down questions she wanted to ask Caroline about her brother. One question had to do with Christmas, and suddenly Allison stopped writing and stared blankly at her paper. What was she going to do about Marsha's invitation for Christmas?

"Writer's block?" asked Andrew as he leaned against her desk.

"Not really." Allison looked up at him. "I was just distracted."

"What's up?"

She thought for a moment. Andrew might have some good insight. "It's about Marsha," she began in a quiet voice, glancing around to make sure no one else was listening. "She wants me to come for Christmas."

Andrew frowned. "*This* Christmas?"

Allison nodded. "I think it's really sweet of her to want me. And I sort of want to go—"

"But this is your first Christmas with your dad . . . and the rest of us."

"I know. But in all my life, Marsha has never treated me like this—like she *really* wants me around—and I don't want to hurt her." Allison stopped in midsentence. Andrew's brows lifted and his eyes focused on something just behind her, as if giving her a cue to stop talking. She knew it must be Shirley and turned in her chair to see.

"It doesn't look like you two are getting much work done," said Shirley lightly, then flitted away.

Allison rolled her eyes. "Great. A nice little piece of jetsam for her column. 'Allison tells Marsha Madison she won't go to Beverly Hills for Christmas.'"

Andrew's eyes lit up. "Does that mean you've decided to stay here?"

Allison shrugged. "Of course that's what I'd *like* to do. But is it the right thing?"

"I see what you mean. I guess it's not an easy choice. You should discuss it with your dad. And if you decide not to go to Marsha's, you could always make up for it at Easter or in the summer."

"Yeah, I suppose it's not such a big deal. But sometimes I get tired of being caught in the middle, trying to please everyone."

"It's okay to please yourself sometimes."

Allison smiled up at Andrew. "Thanks. I'll try to remember that."

"Say, that was nice of you to speak out on Shirley's behalf."

"Thanks." Allison looked down at her paper uncomfortably. Andrew's praise meant more to her than almost anything.

"Want me to leave you alone so you can keep working?" asked Andrew.

"No, I think I'll wait until I get together with Caroline. Maybe this weekend."

"I don't really have much to do, since the game's not until

247

tomorrow." Andrew glanced at the darkroom, where Howie was working behind a closed door. "I wouldn't mind learning a little about photography, though."

"You should talk to Howie—"

"Looks like you two are hard at work," said Beverly sarcastically. She looked at Andrew. "First day and you're already slacking on the job."

"It's hard to write a story about a ball game that hasn't been played," said Andrew.

Beverly laughed. "Good point. Lucky me, I already know what we have planned for the pep assembly, so I have my outline all done."

"Very efficient," said Andrew.

"Thank you very much." Beverly flashed a smile at him, and Allison thought again how pretty Beverly was with her dark brown hair and eyes. She was nearly as tall as Andrew, and she reminded Allison of Katharine Hepburn. Beverly turned her attention to Allison. "I think we have a new rising star in our midst."

Allison looked up in surprise. "Who?"

"*You*, silly. Howie thinks you're the best thing since sliced bread. He was just going on again about that flotsam and jetsam idea of yours. He thinks you're a genius."

Allison blushed. "He's just being nice."

Beverly shook her head. "No, he's being honest. But just between us, I think he has a bit of a crush on you."

Allison felt Andrew's eyes on her, and her cheeks grew warm. She looked down at her notebook, longing for some silly, glib response to take her out of the limelight, but none came. "I better finish this," she finally mumbled without looking back up.

"Hey, Andrew, let me show you a book I found about sports writing," offered Beverly. "We'll let the little genius get back to work." The two moved away from Allison, but she could still hear their chatter and laughter float toward her from the other side of the room. Why had Beverly mentioned that nonsense about Howie? And of all people, Andrew should know better. Well, they could say what they liked; she would prove that she and Howie were nothing more than friends and business associates.

❧

When Allison got home, she told her dad about Marsha's invitation for Christmas.

"Do you want to go?" James ran his fingers through his hair. It looked as though he hadn't shaved that morning, and he still had on his splotchy painting shirt. She smiled as she remembered the first time she'd met him in the lighthouse. *The mad artist!*

"I don't really *want* to go, Dad. But I feel sort of guilty. You know, Marsha's never actually wanted me before—I mean, with no ulterior motives."

"Are you sure there are none now?" He turned toward the fireplace in the den and gave the smoldering logs a poke, sending sparks shooting up the chimney.

Allison thought about that for a moment. Was he suggesting that Marsha hadn't changed after all and might still be up to her old tricks? "I don't know for sure, Dad. It felt like she just wanted me to come. Stanley's going to be in New York, and she's all alone. . . ."

He turned and looked at her. "I'm sorry, sweetheart. I guess I've been through so much with Marsha that it's hard not to think the worst. I'm not worried about me; it's just that I don't want you to get hurt again."

"I know, but I don't want to hurt her, either. Especially after she let me come live with you. It seems only fair that I go visit occasionally."

James laughed. "Poor child, caught in the middle. I wonder what King Solomon would have suggested."

"Hopefully not cutting me in two."

"I'd never agree to that. Well, how about if I give the old girl a call and try to figure this all out."

"Would you?"

"I would for you, Allison."

"Thanks, Dad." Allison thought for a minute. "Please don't hurt her."

He chuckled. "Now, wouldn't that turn the tables. Don't worry, Allison. I have no intention of hurting her, but I still don't completely trust her."

"Okay, Dad. That seems fair enough."

"It's almost time for dinner. I better get cleaned up before Muriel comes after me with her scrub brush."

Allison told her father about the Howie situation at dinner. She was still unaccustomed to boy-girl relationships. "I just don't know what to do, Dad. Howie's a very nice person and very smart, but now I'm afraid I'll feel awkward around him."

"It's too bad that girl had to say that, Allison. It might not even be true. Why don't you try to forget the whole thing and just act as if everything is the same as always. Then if it's not true, you won't be embarrassed. And if it is true, it will probably just blow over in time."

"That makes sense."

"And how's our old friend Shirley Jenson doing these days?"

"Actually, I had a small success with her today." Allison launched into a dramatized story about Shirley's new society column until James was laughing so loud that Muriel had to come see if everything was all right.

"I'll explain the whole thing, Muriel," said Allison as she

began carrying dishes into the kitchen, and before long both George and Muriel were chuckling, too.

"It's a wonder they didn't end up calling it 'Flossie's Flotsam,'" laughed Muriel.

"I just hope this helps smooth things over between me and Shirley," said Allison as she dried a plate.

"Well, I remember what Mercury O'Brian used to say about *her* adversaries," said Muriel.

"Grandmother Mercury had adversaries?"

"Not many, mind you. But some of the best people are just born to it, Allison. Anyway, your dear grandmother used to say, 'I'll kill them with kindness, I will.' And she would."

"Kill them?"

"Not actually kill them. But she would lavish so much pure, sweet kindness on them that it would actually kill their mean spirits. It seemed that even her worst enemies eventually came around and usually turned into her most devoted friends. My, but she had lots of friends."

"Really, even her enemies came around?"

"Sometimes it took years and years. In fact, one cantankerous old woman didn't come around until after Mercury's death."

"It figures," said Allison. "I can just imagine Shirley Jenson at the ripe old age of ninety-three, standing at my funeral saying, 'Whatever shall I do? My very best friend has gone off and died on me!'"

Muriel laughed. "You never know, darling. You just never know."

5

"Would you girls like to come to the basketball game with me tonight?" asked Andrew as he drove them to school on Friday. "I've got to cover it for my news story."

"I don't think I'd care to," said Heather. "I promised to help Grace with some wedding things, and besides, I don't even like basketball."

"You don't?" said Allison in surprise. "I think it's swell. I used to play forward on the team back at Oakmont. Next to soccer, it's my favorite sport."

"Really?" said Andrew with interest. "I don't care much for it, myself."

"Why not?" asked Allison.

"The truth is they didn't play it in England, and I don't know much about it. I mean, I know how to dribble and shoot, but I don't know the actual rules. It was easier to learn to play football, since it's quite a bit like rugby, and I always loved rugby. But I've never taken the time to learn anything about basketball."

"Won't that make it a bit difficult to report on it?" asked Heather.

Andrew smiled. "Not if my good buddy Allison lends me a hand."

"Oh, I see. And what do I get out of this little arrangement?" asked Allison.

"I'll treat you to a hot dog." They all laughed as Andrew pulled into the parking lot, then he turned to Allison. "Seriously, Al, can I count on you to help me out?"

"I'll have to check with Dad first."

"Swell!" Andrew grabbed his books and slid out of the truck. "See you girls after school," he called as he jogged off to join some of his buddies.

"Heather," said Allison as they walked toward the front door. "Do you think it's okay if I go to the game with Andrew?"

"Of course. Why wouldn't it be?"

"Well, you know—it might seem like a date."

Heather laughed. "A basketball game?"

"Yes, I suppose that's silly. And he really does need help for his story."

"If you're worried about your father, just remind him that Andrew will soon be like a brother to you."

"Yes," said Allison. She knew Heather meant well, but thinking of Andrew as a brother was not helpful. Not in the least.

❦

At lunchtime, Allison invited Caroline and Heather to spend the night at her house on Saturday night. "I can interview Caroline for my article then," explained Allison.

"Good idea," said Heather. "And maybe it would be a good time to teach you both how to knit."

"Yes," agreed Caroline. "You've been promising to show us. I was hoping I'd have time to make something for my mom before Christmas."

"How's your scarf for John coming?" asked Allison.

"Finished." Heather smiled smugly.

"Any letters lately?" asked Caroline.

"Now that you mention it . . ." said Heather mysteriously.

"Come on," urged Allison. "Tell us the latest."

"Well, I finally sent the photos from the Harvest Ball—remember? After John received them, he wrote back a wonderfully sweet letter."

"Now I suppose he's totally smitten," teased Allison.

Heather blushed. "Oh, I doubt that. You know we're just good friends. Besides, he's in college and there are a lot of pretty girls around."

"Not as pretty and sweet as you," proclaimed Caroline with loyalty.

"Thanks," said Heather. "But I would understand. John and I are friends and pen pals. It's probably silly to think there's anything more to it. We live in completely different worlds. But it's fun writing to him."

"I think it'd be romantic to have a sweetheart living far away," said Caroline dreamily.

Heather laughed. "He's not my *sweetheart.*"

"Just the same, it *is* sort of romantic," said Allison as she picked up her tray. "And you might as well enjoy it, Heather."

Heather grinned. "Don't worry, Allison. I do."

After school, James picked up Allison to help out at the airport. She had gladly agreed to work in the office a few hours a week in exchange for flying lessons. During this time she was to learn how to operate the radio as well as some basics of running a small rural airport.

"This place is really coming together," said Allison as she examined the new filing system. "Very organized."

"Compliments of Grace," James said as he wrote in the schedule book. "She's very efficient and orderly. We make a good pair—" he chuckled—"since I'm not."

"Probably comes with her nursing background."

James nodded. "Probably. Say, I tried to reach Marsha today to discuss this Christmas thing, but I had to leave a message with Lola."

"Marsha's not always easy to reach," said Allison as she filed some receipts and bills. "Say, Dad, I forgot to mention that Andrew invited me to the basketball game tonight. He's covering it for the paper, but he really doesn't know much about basketball—and I happen to know a lot."

"You do?" James looked at her in surprise, then grinned. "There's still so much I don't know about you, Allison. How do you know about basketball?"

Allison explained about the team at the academy, and James challenged her to a game of one-on-one sometime. "Maybe I should put a basketball hoop on one of the hangars. We shouldn't let all that fine asphalt go to waste. It would be a fun way to pass the time when there's not much to do around here."

"And when will that be?" asked Allison skeptically. "It seems there's so much to catch up on right now."

James laughed. "Well, at the rate Grace is going, we'll be caught up by the New Year. That woman is indomitable right now." He glanced at the clock. "When is Andrew picking you up?"

Allison blinked. Did that mean it was okay to go to the game? She tried not to register her surprise. "Andrew said the game starts at seven, but he wants to get there a little bit earlier—"

"Good grief, we better get you home so you can get ready and have some dinner. Let me go find Mac and let him know we're going."

The phone was ringing as they walked in the front door, and Allison ran down the hallway to grab it. "Hello?" she said breathlessly, thinking it might be Andrew, but it was the operator announcing a long-distance call.

"Hello, is this Allison?" Marsha's smooth voice sounded small and far away.

"Yes. Is that you, Marsha?" Allison suddenly remembered the Christmas invitation and hoped Dad would hurry along in time to have this conversation with Marsha.

"How *are* you, darling?"

"I'm fine, Marsha. We just got in the door. Dad and I were out at the airport, and I had to hurry home to get ready for the basketball game."

"Goodness, you are a busy girl. I didn't realize there was so much to do in the backwoods of Oregon." Marsha laughed. "But I am glad you're having such a good time, Allison. Did you get my letter?"

"Yes. That's why Dad was trying to reach you." Her father was in the hallway removing his jacket, and Allison mouthed the word *Marsha* to him and pointed to the receiver. "Dad wants to discuss it all with you."

"Is your father around?" Marsha's voice stiffened slightly.

"Why, yes, he's right here. I'll put him on. It was swell talking with you, Marsha."

"Yes, darling. It's so wonderful to hear your voice again. I have missed you."

Allison handed the phone to her father while mouthing, *Be nice*, with raised eyebrows. She wondered how he would deal with her. Marsha was being so incredibly sweet, and Allison didn't want her to feel hurt or rejected right now.

"We're all doing quite well, thank you," said James in a polite but formal voice. "And you?" He listened for a long moment, a slight frown creasing his forehead. "Really?" he finally said with just a tiny smidgen of interest, and then, "You don't say? Jimmy Stewart?" He paused, listening again, and then, to Allison's surprise and pleasure, he actually chuckled. "Well, no one said being a famous film star would be easy, did they, Marsha?"

Allison glanced at her watch. She wanted to change her clothes, and it sounded like he was doing just fine in warming Marsha up before he broke the disappointing news. That was nice. Allison gave him a smile and a little wave, then dashed upstairs.

After trying on her third outfit, Allison finally decided to wear her charcoal tweed circle skirt with her russet mock turtleneck sweater, along with the new clogs she'd gotten on the shopping trip with Grace and Heather. Karen Brown already had a pair and had told Allison where to find them in Portland. After much deliberation, Heather had decided to get a pair, too. So far, they were the only three to have clogs in all of Port View High. Naturally, Shirley had made fun of the thick, wooden soles, calling them little Dutch-girl shoes, but Allison didn't care. She liked to be different and thought the noise the shoes made when walking was fun.

Her dad was still on the phone when Allison got downstairs. She paused to listen, and his voice sounded pleasant—almost as if he were enjoying the conversation. She wondered if he could still be talking to Marsha. Perhaps he was speaking with Grace. When he noticed Allison, he began to wind down the conversation.

"Sure, Marsha," he said. "That would be just fine . . . yes, and you, too. Good-bye."

"Jeepers, Dad, were you talking to Marsha this whole time?"

James rubbed his chin. "She was in a chatty mood, and you told me to be nice to her. Besides," he chuckled, "it was her phone bill."

Allison laughed. "So is it all settled, then?"

He frowned. "Not exactly. Marsha went on and on about

how Stanley wouldn't be there and how lonely she would be and how much she enjoyed your company. . . ."

"So what did you say?"

"Well, I told her about the wedding plans and how this would be our first Christmas, things like that. But I just couldn't bear to tell her absolutely no. I finally said you and I would discuss it some more and I would get back to her."

Allison thought for a moment. "Does that mean you think I should go?"

"Not exactly, Allison. Naturally, I'd rather have you here with me. But maybe that's selfish on my part. I don't want to influence you. You're not a child anymore. I think this should be *your* decision."

Allison sighed loudly. "I think it was easier being a child. You just went wherever people told you without worrying about hurting anyone's feelings."

James cocked his head to one side. "And what about the time they told you to go to camp last summer?"

Allison grinned sheepishly. "Well, that was different."

He put his arm around her shoulders. "You don't have to decide tonight, Allison. Don't worry about it right now. Say, you better grab something to eat before Andrew gets here."

Muriel quickly put a plate of food together for Allison, but she'd barely taken two bites before Andrew knocked at the door.

"Sorry, Muriel," said Allison as she wiped her mouth with a napkin.

"Why don't you let me put that meat loaf into a sandwich for you," offered Muriel.

"No, thanks," said Allison. "Andrew promised to buy me a hot dog if I help him with his sports article."

"That's generous of him," her dad teased as he led Andrew into the kitchen. "Does this mean my daughter works for food?"

Allison pulled on her corduroy car coat. "Just for friends and family."

James nodded, then turned to Andrew. "It's getting foggy out there, Andrew. Maybe you should drive the Buick instead of the jalopy."

"If you think so, sir."

"I think so." James handed him the keys. "Now, drive carefully, young man, and take good care of my little girl."

"You can count on it," said Andrew in a responsible voice. "We better get going so we don't miss the beginning of the game."

"You mean the *tip-off*," corrected Allison.

Andrew rolled his eyes. "See how embarrassing this is? She knows more about the sport than I do."

James laughed. "Don't be too hard on him, Allison."

As they drove, Allison told Andrew how her father had decided that it should be her choice whether or not to go to Marsha's for Christmas.

"Then it's easy," said Andrew. "Just tell her no."

Allison moaned. "It's not that easy, Andrew. I don't want to hurt her feelings."

"Even after all the times she's hurt you?"

"But I've forgiven her, remember?"

"Yes." Andrew nodded. "And I realize that was the right thing to do, Allison. I don't know if I could've done that if I'd been in your shoes. Whenever I think of Marsha Madison, I get a little bit angry."

"That's because you don't really know her; you've only heard lots of bad stories. And the truth is I don't think I could've *not* forgiven her," said Allison. "I was miserable when I was so bitter against her. And now she's being so nice and sweet . . . I'd hate to let her down."

"But what about letting your father down?"

"That's the problem. But at least Dad would understand. Plus he has Grace and the rest of you. Marsha doesn't have anyone right now."

"What about her husband, Stanley?"

"He's going to be in New York."

"Gee, that is tough. Have you prayed about it, Allison?"

"A little. I guess I should pray about it some more, huh?"

"I guess so."

⚜

It was warm and noisy in the gymnasium, but the game hadn't started yet. The gym took on a golden glow, with the overhead lights reflecting off the shiny maple floor. Allison looked around the crowded wooden bleachers and wondered if they'd even find a place to sit. But Andrew led her straight to a bench directly behind where the players sat. It was reserved for reporters. Allison reminded herself that she was a reporter, too, so she flipped open her note pad and hoped to look as official as Andrew.

"You a reporter?" asked a balding man sitting on her right.

"Yes, we represent our school paper," answered Allison in a business voice. "You've heard of the *Pirate Chest*?"

"You bet." The man smiled and held out his hand. "I'm Sam Long from the *Port View Herald*."

"Pleased to meet you, Mr. Long. I'm Allison O'Brian from Tamaqua Point. And this is my friend Andrew Amberwell."

"Since you're a fellow reporter, you better call me Sam." He smiled at Andrew. "And I've already had the pleasure of meeting Andrew, here. You had a great football season, son."

"Thanks. But it's fun being on the sidelines for a change."

"I hear you're being considered for some college scholarships, Andrew. Have you heard anything official yet? Strictly off the record, of course."

Andrew grinned. "Actually, I did hear from a couple of smaller colleges, but I'm hoping to hear from the state schools before long."

"Well, you let me know when you make a decision. I'd like to do a little write-up about you—you know the bit, local sports hero makes good."

"Sure," said Andrew. "I'll let you know."

Soon the basketball game started, and Allison began to discreetly explain to Andrew what was going on. But she could see that it was making him uncomfortable, especially with Sam Long sitting so close by.

"How about if I just take notes?" she whispered. "I can explain it all after the game."

Andrew smiled. "That'd be swell, Al. I'll take notes, too. You can fill me in on the correct terminology later."

At half time, Karen and Beverly came over to chat with Andrew and Allison. Shirley Jenson was right on their heels. Once again, Shirley had on her black-and-gold outfit that looked suspiciously like a cheerleader's. Allison wondered if Shirley had any idea how ridiculous it made her appear.

"How's our new sports reporter doing?" asked Beverly.

"Okay, I guess," said Andrew. "And the team's doing better than I expected."

"Yes," chirped Shirley. "We might even win."

"Hey, there's Howie," said Beverly, waving.

"I just got here," said Howie. He glanced at the scoreboard. "Is that thing right? Are we actually ahead?"

"You bet!" exclaimed Karen, her blue eyes flashing as she shook a pom-pom in the air. "And the Pirates are going to win tonight!"

"I hope so," said Andrew. "It'd be great if my first sports story was about a victory."

Soon, half time was almost over and they returned to their

seats behind the bench. It was no surprise when Shirley followed. "It's okay if I sit in the press seats," she announced as she flopped down on the other side of Andrew. "After all, I *am* on the paper. Besides, I might find something I can use in my column."

Allison's stomach began to rumble. "Hey, Andrew, what about my hot dog?" she asked.

He bit his lip. "Sorry, Al. I totally forgot. Do you think you can wait until after the game? We could go to Wally's then."

Allison nodded. "Sure." Going to Wally's all by herself with Andrew? That was definitely worth the wait!

Howie sat next to Allison in the press area, and when Sam returned with a cup of coffee, Allison introduced the two of them.

"Pleased to meet you," said Sam as he sat next to Howie. "I'd like to have a peek at your paper sometime."

Howie grinned. "You're in luck. I just happen to have a copy on me." He reached into his jacket and pulled out a paper.

"Thanks," said Sam as he scanned the paper.

Allison joined in the shouting as the cheerleaders led a rousing spirit yell. Suddenly, she felt a sharp elbow from Howie. "Sam wants to talk to you," he said urgently.

She looked past Howie and over to Sam. "Yes?"

Sam leaned over and held up the *Pirate Chest*, then pointed to her front-page article about Dad and Andrew's plane going down. "Did you really write this, young lady?" His voice sounded stern—almost accusing.

She nodded with wide eyes. Was something wrong? She noticed Shirley leaning over, listening intently, always a nose for gossip.

"This is something, Allison." He glanced past her to Andrew. "Is this really true, Andrew?"

"Yes, sir," said Andrew. "Every single word."

Sam looked at Allison again. "How old are you, anyway?"

She felt her cheeks growing warm. "Almost fifteen."

"Jumpin' jehosaphat, is that all? I thought you were a senior like Andrew, here. I was half ready to offer you a job with the *Herald* after you graduate next spring."

Allison laughed nervously. "Really?" She wasn't sure which was more flattering, the *almost* job offer or the assumption that she was older.

Sam nodded, then folded the paper and slipped it into the pocket of his sports jacket. Suddenly, it was time for the second half to begin, and their attention returned to the game. Allison could scarcely keep her mind focused after Sam's unexpected praise. Did he really mean it?

The score went back and forth in the second half. Then in the final seconds, the Pirates lost, but only by a single point.

"It still makes a great sports story," said Andrew as he flipped his note pad closed and stepped down from the bleachers.

"You bet," agreed Sam. "No one thought the team would do this well. It's a good start for a season that didn't look too promising."

"Will you be at all the games, Sam?" asked Allison.

"Nope. I'm not really a sportswriter, but I like to fill in when our regular guy can't make it. I like sports."

Howie climbed down and looked at Sam again. "You know, I thought your name was familiar. You're Sam Long, editor of the *Port View Herald*."

Sam nodded. "You got me pegged."

"And what you said about my story—" began Allison. "Was it really true?"

"Sure. I think you've got style, kiddo. In fact, I wouldn't mind running this piece in the *Herald* next week. I think lots of folks would be interested in a local story like this. I can't pay you much—"

"Pay me?" gasped Allison. "You can have it for *free!*"

Sam laughed. "Now, you need to be a better businesswoman than that. But if you ever need a job, just give me a call. I think I can afford you."

"Yeah," chimed in Andrew. "She even works for food."

Allison punched him in the arm. "Yes, and it's time you paid up."

"Right-oh. It's off to Wally's we go."

"Wally's?" echoed Shirley sweetly. "Do you have room for one more?"

Andrew cleared his throat and looked at Allison. "I . . . uh—"

"Oh, please," begged Shirley. "I'm absolutely starved." She glanced at Howie. "How about you, Howie? Do you want to come with us to Wally's?"

Howie looked at Andrew. "Are you offering rides?"

Andrew shrugged, then looked at Allison as if it were up to her. Why was everyone making her decide everything all the time?

"Sure." She hoped her voice didn't sound as deflated as she felt. "The more the merrier." So much for going to Wally's by herself with Andrew. By the time they reached the exit, Beverly and Karen had decided to join them, too.

"This is almost like a staff meeting," joked Howie as they made their way to the green Buick.

"Except for Karen," said Beverly. "But we can let her be an honorary member for the evening."

"Who knows," said Karen. "I might decide to join the paper, too."

Before Allison reached the car, Shirley had already opened the passenger's door in front. She smiled smugly at Allison, but in the same moment Beverly hopped in before Shirley had a chance. Shirley's face looked as if she'd bit into a lemon as she mutely slipped in next to Beverly, and Allison had no choice but to get in the backseat with Howie and Karen. She wondered if Andrew even noticed or cared. Maybe he did only think of her as a kid sister.

They sat together in a booth at Wally's. Andrew with Shirley and Beverly on each side; Howie with Allison and Karen on each side. Very cozy.

"Did you hear what Sam Long said about Allison's story in the paper?" asked Howie after they ordered.

"Yeah, that was something, Allison," said Andrew with what seemed honest admiration. She smiled at him.

"What was it?" asked Beverly. "Tell us all about it."

"Just that he liked Allison's story so well that he practically offered her a job," said Howie proudly. "And Sam Long just happens to be *editor* of the *Port View Herald*."

Allison made a face. "But then he found out how old I am."

"Who'd want to work for some old hick-town paper like *that*?" said Shirley, this aimed in Andrew's direction.

"I wouldn't mind," said Howie. "At least during the summers."

Shirley just shook her head. "Good grief, you people. One would think you've got printer's ink running through your veins."

"Better than ice water," Allison whispered to Howie, and he laughed.

"What's that?" asked Shirley with narrowed eyes.

"I . . . uh . . . I just said I'd like some ice water," said Allison.

"Looked more like you were whispering sweet nothings into Howie's ear," said Shirley. "Didn't it, Andrew?" But Andrew was watching Allison with a slightly creased brow. He just shrugged, then turned to Beverly.

"Wasn't that a great game?" commented Andrew. "I haven't been much of a basketball fan, but I think I could get used to it."

"It's a shame you didn't go out for basketball," said Beverly, her dark eyes sparkling. "With you on the team, I bet they would've won tonight, Andrew."

Andrew's cheeks grew a little ruddier, and a little green monster in Allison wanted to scream. Instead, she turned to Howie and discussed the possibilities of actually working for a paper like the *Port View Herald*.

"I don't know that I'd want to work for a small paper indefinitely," said Howie thoughtfully. "But I'm considering majoring in journalism in college . . . although I'd rather aim for something like magazines, maybe even *National Geographic* . . ." Allison tried to appear fully interested in Howie's plans for the future, but her eyes kept wandering across the table to spy Andrew engaged in a lively conversation with Karen and Beverly.

Finally, it was time to go. They left the booth in pairs: Howie and Allison, Shirley and Karen, Andrew and Beverly trailing behind.

"Don't Howie and Allison make a cute couple?" said Shirley in a voice loud enough for everyone in the soda shop to hear.

Allison couldn't think of any response that wouldn't hurt Howie's feelings. "I wish Shirley Jenson would grow up," she whispered when they reached the door.

"Some people never grow up," said Howie as he held the door open for her.

Andrew became very quiet after they dropped the others off. It was foggy, and he drove carefully along the curving road toward Tamaqua Point. Allison was still angry at Shirley and somewhat irked with Andrew, too, and consequently could think of nothing to say. Finally, Andrew pulled the car into her garage, but she jumped out before he could even come around and open the door for her.

He handed her the keys. "Tell your dad thanks for the car."

"Sure. Thanks for the ride." She started to leave, but he was still talking.

"I confessed to Beverly that I don't know much about basketball, so she and Karen explained some things to me tonight, and I think I'll be okay. Beverly even offered to coach me through my sports story if I need it."

Allison swallowed a hard lump in her throat. "That was nice of her." It was obvious he wouldn't need her help anymore.

"Yeah. Good night, Allison."

"Good night." Allison turned and ran into the house. Why did it hurt so much to care about Andrew? She wanted to tell Dad, but what would he think?

Her father was waiting up for her, but once inside, she shoved the worries of Andrew away. Instead, she told him all about Sam Long and the *Port View Herald*.

"Congratulations, Allison." He patted her on the back. "A news story in the big paper. My little girl is growing up quickly."

Not quickly enough, she thought as she headed up the stairs for bed.

6

The next evening, Allison sat down on her bed, flipped her open note pad, and licked her pencil tip. "Okay, Caroline," she said in a businesslike voice, "how long has it been since you last saw your brother?"

Caroline scratched her head. "Let's see, Kevin joined the army right after he graduated from high school in 1944. I was ten years old then. He went to boot camp in California, then came home for a quick visit before he was shipped off to Europe. August of '44 was the last time I actually saw him. I was just a kid then, and I remember how he suddenly seemed so grown-up in his uniform. But he was really excited about getting to serve our country—he had actually been worried that the war might be finished before he got a chance to go. Can you imagine? My mom kept saying it was all going to end as soon as Kevin got there and that he'd be back in no time."

"And then the war ends, and he still doesn't come back. . . ." Allison shook her head sadly. "Now, tell me about this news that your father recently heard, Caroline."

"Dad has been writing letters for several years now," began Caroline. "When the war ended, we heard that Kevin was in a German prison camp that had been liberated by the Russian army. We were so glad; we thought he'd be home soon. But when he didn't come home, Dad began inquiring. Through various sources, Dad learned that thousands of U.S. soldiers were being held in Siberia—sort of like hostages until all the Russian soldiers were released. It's sort of confusing—"

"Let me get this straight, Caroline," said Allison incredulously. "You mean that our ally, Russia, is in essence holding our soldiers hostage?"

Caroline nodded. "According to the people my dad has spoken with. But the weird thing is that our government keeps saying that it isn't so."

"So how does our government explain all the prisoners that haven't come home?"

"Oh, you know, missing in action, casualties of war. They've sent us nice letters, medals, even a flag. . . ."

"And your parents are sure that Kevin is still alive?"

"Well, they had almost given up hope, but just this year some new information has leaked out. Apparently a few prisoners have escaped and made it home. One soldier even brought photos with him of our soldiers in a prison camp in Siberia."

"Amazing," murmured Allison, her pencil flying across the page.

"Yes," agreed Heather from across the room. "It's incredible!"

"Go on, Caroline," urged Allison. "Tell me more."

"There's really not much more. My dad keeps writing letters to senators and congressmen, even the president. They continue to deny the existence of any Siberian prison camps. They say it's just a way for grieving families to keep their false hopes alive."

"But what about the soldiers who've escaped? And the photos? How do they explain that?"

"I don't know," said Caroline sadly. "But this news *does* give us hope. We certainly don't like the idea of Kevin being in some horrible prison, but we want to continue believing that Kevin is still alive."

"How old is Kevin now?" asked Allison

"He's twenty-two." Caroline frowned. "But I just can't imagine Kevin being that old. I mostly remember him as my goofy big brother, teasing me and pulling my pigtails." She dug into her pocketbook. "I have photos of him—from high school and also in his uniform just before he left."

Allison examined the photos. "Goodness, he's quite good-looking, Caroline." She glanced over to where Heather sat next to the fireplace, listening with a creased brow. Her knitting needles paused for a moment, then continued to click rhythmically as she returned to her work.

"He looks a lot like Caroline," Allison explained to Heather. "Blond wavy hair . . . I'm guessing blue eyes." Caroline nodded. "And he's tall with nice broad shoulders."

"I think Kevin looks like the actor Van Johnson," said Caroline proudly. "He probably would've had a dozen girlfriends, except that he's so shy."

Allison shook her head. Seeing photos of Kevin made him seem even more real. She could almost imagine him shivering with cold in the Siberian snow. "I sure hope he's okay, Caroline," said Allison softly.

"Me too," said Caroline, her voice breaking a little. "Christmas is always the worst. Mom and Dad try to act all cheerful for my sake, but I'd rather they didn't bother with all the presents and trimmings—it only makes me feel worse. And then I feel like I have to put on a big act, too. It's really rather pitiful."

"I have an idea," said Heather as she laid down her knitting. "Why don't we pray for Kevin—right now."

"That would be nice," said Caroline. "Would you?"

And the three of them quietly prayed for her brother, right there in Allison's bedroom.

When they finished, Caroline was actually smiling. "Thanks. You know, I pray for Kevin every single day, but for some reason it felt more effective when you both prayed, too."

"That gives me an idea," said Allison. "How about if I put a suggestion in my article that everyone join together and pray for Kevin this Christmas season."

"Really? You would do that?" asked Caroline.

"Sure. Why not?" Allison continued some wrap-up interview questions with Caroline, and when they were finished, she put a new Doris Day record on her phonograph. She hoped that the happy songs would lighten up the gloom a little. Soon they were singing along with Doris, and Heather began to show them the beginning steps in knitting.

"I just love Doris Day! She's my favorite singer. And June Allyson is my favorite movie star," said Caroline dreamily as she cast clumsy stitches onto her knitting needle. Suddenly, she stopped and looked at Allison in horror. "Not that Marsha Madison isn't—"

"Don't worry," Allison cut her off. "Marsha isn't even *my* favorite actress. Of course, I wouldn't tell *her* that. Actually, I prefer Katharine Hepburn."

"Almost time for dinner, girls," called Muriel from the hallway.

As Allison went down the hall to wash up, she overheard Dad's voice coming from Grandpa's old bedroom. Probably just talking to someone on the phone, but why in there? She paused for a moment. She didn't really mean to eavesdrop, but she was interested.

"I wouldn't exactly say that, Marsha, but yes, things do seem to be picking up for me."

He laughed, and Allison moved quickly past. Why was he talking to Marsha again?

At dinner, Allison eyed her father with curiosity. He was pleasant, as usual, making polite small talk with Heather and Caroline, but Allison couldn't shake the way his voice had sounded when he'd been talking with Marsha earlier. Was it possible that he still had feelings—

"Allison?" said Dad as if trying to pull her back to earth. "You look like you're floating on cloud nine right now."

"Sorry, Dad. Did you say something?"

"I asked how your article with Caroline is coming."

"Oh, it's just fine." Allison looked down at her plate and poked her fork into her mashed potatoes.

"Maybe Sam Long will be interested in it, too," said Heather. "Andrew told me all about what he said last night."

"Oh, I doubt he'd want to use that—"

"But wouldn't it be great?" exclaimed Caroline. "Especially the praying part."

Heather explained to Dad about Allison's idea to ask people to pray, but Allison was too distracted to listen. Instead, she was imagining what it would be like if Dad and Marsha got back together again, living happily with her as their daughter. Of course, she knew it was completely ridiculous. What about Stanley and Grace? And even if some weird miracle made it possible, would she truly want it?

After dinner, her dad went to take Grace for a ride, and the girls settled into the den to continue their knitting lessons. George had made a pleasant fire, and Muriel brought in a plate of homemade doughnuts. While Heather was working with Allison, Caroline sat in the bay window, looking out across the inlet.

"Does someone live in the lighthouse?" asked Caroline suddenly.

"No," said Allison without looking up from her knit-one, pearl-one stitches. "The Coast Guard took it over last fall. They installed an automatic light. Andrew was the last one to work there."

"So no one goes out there anymore?"

"Not really, unless it's just to look around or have a picnic or something."

"Would someone do that at night?"

"I can't imagine why." Allison looked at Caroline. "Why all the questions?"

"I thought I saw a lantern or something moving around over there," said Caroline. "I just wondered what it was."

Allison dropped her knitting and went to the window. Even in the dimly lit bay window, it took a few moments for her eyes to adjust to the darkness out there. All she could see was the lighthouse beam roving across the water. "You probably just saw the lighthouse light," she said, returning to her knitting.

"No, I've been watching the lighthouse light. This looked different."

Allison thought for a moment. "I suppose someone *could* be out there, but I don't know why. And it's awfully cold and windy tonight. I know I wouldn't want to be out there."

"Caroline," said Heather, "have you ever heard the story about when Allison went out there during a storm?"

"I've heard parts of it, but never the whole tale. Please tell me, Allison."

So Allison launched into the story of how she rowed out in the midst of a storm to find her father. She wondered if the story was growing more dramatic with each retelling, or if she had really been so crazy as to risk her life like that. Caroline thought it was a terrific tale, and concerns about the mysterious lantern were temporarily put aside.

Earlier that evening, James had suggested that the girls might be more comfortable sleeping in Grandpa's spacious room, and Allison took him up on the offer. After the three of them were cozily packed into the big bed, they began to chat and giggle.

"Do either of you want to go to the Christmas dance?" asked Allison when the subject finally progressed to boys.

"Not me," said Heather. "I had fun at the Harvest Ball, but I don't mind sitting this one out."

"You'd probably rather be home writing a long letter to John," suggested Allison.

"Maybe," said Heather mysteriously.

"How about you, Allison?" asked Caroline.

"I have to admit it sounds like fun, but I'm certain that I'm not going." Allison tried not to think about her last conversation with Andrew.

"I wish Andrew would take someone," said Heather. "After all, it's his *last* year in high school, and it seems like he should have more fun. I'd even be willing to go with him if it would only get him there."

"If Andrew wanted to go, there are plenty of girls who would jump at the chance," said Caroline. "Not to mention a certain friend—"

"Maybe he'll invite Beverly," said Allison lightly. "They seem to be getting along."

"But what about you?" asked Caroline.

"I don't know . . ." Allison felt a lump grow in her throat. "I think Andrew and Beverly like each other, and she's closer to his age. They were having a swell time together at Wally's last night."

"I suppose that's for the best," said Caroline decisively. "After all, before long you and Andrew will be like brother and sister, with your parents getting married and all."

"Well, at least Beverly is *nice*," said Heather. "She and Karen seem like the most thoughtful of the cheerleaders."

"Yes," agreed Caroline, "they even talk to me now."

"How about you, Caroline?" said Heather. "Would you like to go to the dance?"

"Maybe," said Caroline softly. "Maybe if the *right* person asked. . . ."

"The *right* person?" repeated Allison. "Okay, Caroline, out with it. We want to hear the *whole* story."

Caroline giggled. "It's probably nothing. But there's this boy in orchestra named Tommy Obertti who's been very friendly to me—"

"You mean Tommy who plays cello?" said Heather.

Soon Heather and Caroline were chattering away about Tommy Obertti and several other kids in the orchestra that Allison had never heard of. Allison tuned the girls out and took a trip in her own overly active imagination. She pictured Andrew dressed in a tuxedo with tails, escorting a scarlet-gowned Beverly, who looked suspiciously like Marsha Madison, to the Christmas dance. Oh, why was she being so foolish? And why did it have to hurt so much to think of Andrew with a girlfriend? If this was how it felt to care for a boy, then perhaps she'd be better off without it. If only she could escape her feelings, at least for a while.

Suddenly, she remembered Marsha's invitation. Maybe she *should* accept. If Andrew was going to be dating Beverly, it might help if she could get away during the holidays. Naturally, she would return in time for the wedding, but a little time and distance from Andrew might be a good thing for her right now. She decided to talk to her father about it first thing tomorrow—and while she was at it, maybe she would find out why he was talking so sweetly to Marsha these days.

Allison sighed deeply, then realized that both Heather and

Caroline had drifted off to sleep. Muriel had cracked the window earlier to air out the room, and now Allison got out of bed to close it. She stood in front of the window for a moment, looking over to the lighthouse, when suddenly she saw what looked like a lantern. She blinked her eyes. Perhaps Caroline hadn't imagined it after all. But as quickly as she'd seen it, the lantern disappeared. How strange. Allison sleepily shook her head and returned to the warm bed.

❀

The next day, Allison got up early, slipping out of the room while the other two girls were still sleeping. She dressed for church, then crept downstairs to see if her father was up yet. She found him in the dining room, sipping coffee and reading the paper.

"You're quite the early bird this morning," James said as he laid down his paper.

Allison nodded and sat down. "I wanted to discuss something with you before Heather and Caroline got up."

"Sounds serious." He peered at her curiously.

"Not too serious. Last night, I was thinking about going to Marsha's for Christmas. I think I'd like to go, Dad."

Dad nodded slowly, a slight frown creasing his forehead. "I see. . . ."

Suddenly, Allison knew that he was hurt. She hadn't meant to hurt him. Oh, why hadn't she thought about this more carefully? "It's not that I don't want to be here, Dad. It's just—"

"I understand, Allison. It's okay. Do you want to call Marsha this morning?"

Allison stared at her father. It was as if something in him had shut down. She knew he wasn't going to try to talk her out of this, and suddenly she wasn't so sure she wanted to go. "I don't know, Dad. To tell you the truth, I guess I'm not absolutely sure that I want to go to Marsha's. . . ."

His face brightened a little. "Are you feeling sorry for Marsha? Is that why you want to go?"

"Sort of . . . but not completely."

"Oh." Once again his face clouded over. "Naturally, it must sound very exciting and glamorous to spend the holidays down in movie land. I'm sure any girl your age would leap at the chance—"

"That's not it, Dad. You know me. I don't even like that kind of stuff."

James sighed deeply. "Whatever you decide to do, Allison, you know I'll support you in it. I had just hoped—" He stopped himself, pressing his lips tightly together as if to hold in the words.

"What, Dad? What did you hope?"

"That you'd want to be here."

Allison heard the girls coming down the stairs and knew she'd have to wrap this up fast. "Well, Dad, I guess my mind isn't made up after all. It's not always easy to know what the right thing to do is, especially when you're just a kid."

He nodded and picked up his paper. "That's for sure, Allison. But it doesn't necessarily get any easier when you grow up."

7

"So did you make up your mind about Marsha yet?" asked Andrew as they walked into the journalism room together.

"Not really," said Allison. It was the first private conversation she'd had with Andrew in days, and she wasn't eager for it to end. "But I'm working on it—"

"Hi, you two," said Beverly. "Howie has photos ready from Friday night's game, Andrew. Want to see them?"

"Sure," said Andrew. "That might help me with my opening line."

"They're all developed but still in the darkroom." Beverly opened the door. "Right this way."

Allison watched in dismay as Andrew followed Beverly into the tiny room. What would they do in the privacy of that dimly lit room? They could tell secrets or even hold hands—

"Is your story ready, Allison?" asked Howie with a friendly smile.

"Yes. And I think you're going to be surprised." Allison pulled the three-page story out of her notebook and handed it to him.

"Why's that?" asked Howie, scanning the first page with interest.

"Caroline's story is really pretty amazing."

Howie continued to silently read. Allison stood, waiting apprehensively. What would he think of this Siberian prison camp business?

Howie looked up, adjusted his glasses, then spoke quietly. "Allison, this is almost unbelievable."

Allison frowned. "You mean that you don't believe it?"

"No, I mean this story is incredible—amazing— unfathomable."

"Does that mean you *like* it?"

"Of course I like it. It's great! Front-page stuff. In fact, I'll have to send a copy of the next paper to Sam Long."

Allison beamed. "Really? You think it's that good?"

"You've definitely got a great story, Allison." Then Howie smiled. "However, I'd like to see you do some editing on it."

"Editing?" Allison frowned. "But I thought you liked it."

"I do. But it could be even better with some tightening." He flipped to the next page. "And maybe a little restructuring."

Allison moaned. "That sounds like work, Howie."

"I'll help you. Besides, don't you want to improve your writing?"

"I guess so." Allison wasn't so sure. She had been pleased with the story just the way it was, but she reluctantly followed Howie to his desk and watched as he made ugly red marks across her neatly written pages. When he was finished, she snatched up the article and walked over to a free typewriter.

"What's bugging you?" asked Shirley. Just then Andrew and Beverly emerged from the darkroom, laughing loudly as they closed the door behind them.

"Oh, I think I know," said Shirley, nodding in their direction. She smiled smugly and walked away. Allison rolled her eyes and began to rewrite her story. It seemed she and Howie were the only ones to take this newspaper business seriously. Although she wondered if Howie took it a little too seriously.

She was almost done when Andrew stopped by her desk. "Working hard?" he asked as he leaned over to peer at her paper.

"I suppose," she snapped without even looking up. "*Someone* has to."

Andrew chuckled. "It sounds as if *someone* is having a bad day."

Allison sighed and looked up. She had no reason to be short with him. "Sorry, Andrew. Howie is having me rewrite my article, and I'm not too happy about it."

"Don't feel bad. He's having me do some changes to mine, too. I guess that's why he's the editor. Say, Allison, you were telling me about the deal with Marsha, but you never got to finish. What's going on?"

Allison looked up into his clear green eyes and suddenly wished he didn't have to be so nice all the time. It would be so much easier if he were self-centered or arrogant or just plain mean. But Andrew was Andrew—he couldn't help it.

"I haven't really decided yet. I thought I had made up my mind to go, but I told Dad and he was so hurt that I immediately backtracked. I'm right back where I started." Allison looked down at the typewriter and sighed. She couldn't tell him that the reason she'd wanted to go to Marsha's was to get away from him.

"Of course your dad's going to be hurt. But if that's what you really want to do, he'll understand. I'm sure it would be lots of fun down there in Beverly Hills, lying around a swimming pool in the sunshine, chatting with movie stars—"

"Beverly Hills?" said Shirley with interest. "Chatting with movie stars? We wouldn't be talking about Allison's mother, now, would we?"

Allison suppressed a groan. "Not exactly, Shirley."

Shirley pretended to pout. "Always keeping secrets from me, aren't you, Allison?"

"Allison was just trying to decide where to spend her Christmas holidays," said Andrew. "It's no big deal."

"Are you going to visit your mother?" asked Shirley suspiciously. "You know, Allison, if you need any company, I'd be glad to go, too. In fact, my grandma on my mom's side lives in Los Angeles. I just might decide to go down there."

"Good for you," said Allison curtly. "Right now I want to finish my article." She turned her attention back to her revisions.

"Yes," said Shirley suddenly. "I better go work on my column, too."

"That was too easy," whispered Allison as Shirley hurried to her desk.

"Maybe I shouldn't have mentioned your dilemma to Shirley," said Andrew apologetically. "I thought it might be a way to distract her."

"It's okay, Andrew. She would've found out sooner or later. You know how she has a nose for news."

Andrew chuckled and returned to his typewriter. A little later, Allison observed Beverly hunched over Andrew's desk with him. Allison quickly turned away. What difference did it make to her? Andrew would soon be like a brother to her. The sooner she got over it, the better.

Allison finished her rewriting just before it was time to go. With a sigh of relief, she handed her typed revision to Howie.

"Good for you, Allison." He patted her on the back. "You're a real trooper."

Andrew stepped up and handed Howie his sports story. "How about me, Howie? Am I a trooper, too?"

Howie glanced down at the paper. "You better believe it.

Now everyone has turned in their assignments except for Shirley." He looked over to where Shirley was hunting and pecking on the typewriter.

"Oh, don't worry about me, Howie," chirped Shirley. "Jenson's Jetsam' will be handed in first thing tomorrow. I just need to gather some more facts."

"Facts?" said Beverly with a raised eyebrow. "Now, there's an idea."

"You guys are a great team," said Howie. "I really appreciate your hard work."

❀

The next day, Howie stopped Allison on her way to lunch. "Can I talk to you?" he asked. "Privately?"

She nodded and followed him to an empty stairwell. "What's up, Howie?"

"Shirley handed in her column today," began Howie. He adjusted his glasses and glanced around to see if anyone was listening, then continued with his head close to Allison's. "I thought I should run it past you—" He stopped talking just as Andrew came around the corner. "Oh, hello, Andrew."

"Hi. What's going on?" said Andrew, stopping for a moment.

"Just having a chat with Allison," said Howie in a dismissive tone.

"Oh, sure," said Andrew. He turned and continued toward the cafeteria. Allison noticed him glance back, a curious look on his face, just before he went through the door.

"Sorry to seem so cloak and dagger, Allison. I just don't want Shirley to know. I waited until she was in the cafeteria before I caught you."

"What does Shirley's column have to do with me?" asked Allison.

"Everything." Howie shook his head slowly. "She's written the whole thing about your mother."

"Really? Whatever for?"

"I'm sure because she thinks it's interesting." Howie cleared his throat. "And to be honest, it *is* interesting. But it is also pretty sensational and not very flattering to your mother. I'm not sure that it's even true. I figured you could be the one to make that call." He pulled two pages out of his jacket and handed them discreetly to Allison. "Just don't let Shirley know that you have this."

Allison shoved them into her notebook. "Okay."

"And let me know after school what you think. Whatever you say goes, Allison."

"Thanks," said Allison. "I appreciate that you came to me."

"When you read it, you'll understand why." Howie's face was grave.

Allison had no appetite. Instead, she went into Mrs. Jones' classroom and sat down to read. It required every ounce of Allison's self-control not to rip Shirley's column into shreds. It was too incredible. Shirley even went so far as to suggest that Marsha Madison had a boyfriend for every day of the week. Where had Shirley gathered her information? Probably those trashy movie magazines combined with Shirley's cruel imagination. Not only did Shirley manage to portray Marsha as a demanding, egotistical, over-the-hill, immoral snob, but she had painted Allison in the very same light. And at the end, it came as no surprise when Shirley reported that Allison would spend her Christmas holidays with her movie-star mom, in her den of iniquity, doing who knows what.

Allison leaned her head into the desk and moaned. Why in the world was Shirley Jenson so meanspirited? Was it simply that misery loved company? Or did Shirley just hate Allison through and through? Allison took a deep breath and read the column again, this time more calmly. Perhaps she had imagined it to be worse than it was. But when she finished the second time, she knew it could not go to print. Maybe Allison had overreacted, but the column was inaccurate and unfair.

For the rest of the day, Allison avoided Shirley. Partly because she was hurt, and partly because she didn't want Shirley to know she'd seen the column. To her relief, it seemed as if Shirley was avoiding her, too. Maybe she was having an attack of conscience. Wouldn't that be something! After school, Allison found Howie and thanked him for questioning the column.

"I don't know anything about your mother, Allison," said Howie. "But I couldn't believe half the stuff Shirley had written."

Allison shook her head. "In Shirley's defense, I have to admit that she may have gathered some inaccurate information from those stupid movie-star magazines. They're notorious for not getting their facts straight."

"But Shirley needs to learn that. Even though it's her column, she can't write anything untruthful or hurtful. I was afraid of this in the first place."

"Well, maybe you just need to lay it on the line for her."

"That's exactly what I was thinking." Howie smiled. "Allison, I'm impressed with how well you're handling this. Some girls would have been furious."

Allison laughed. "I guess I'm getting used to Shirley's attacks."

"She does seem to have it out for you." Howie scratched his head. "That's probably because she's jealous."

Allison shrugged. "Who knows? I've learned from experience not to ever assume I have Shirley Jenson figured out. Can you ax her column without letting her know that I saw it?"

"No problem, Allison. Don't worry. I'll handle everything with supreme tact and diplomacy. On your part, it might be helpful if you keep this to yourself."

Just then Andrew and Heather passed by.

"Are you ready to go home?" asked Andrew.

"Sure," said Allison. She turned to Howie. "Thanks again, Howie. I appreciate it."

"By the way, Allison," called Howie as she went to join Andrew and Heather. "Great rewrite on the prisoner of war story."

"Thanks, Howie. You can take half the credit for that."

Suddenly, Allison's worries about Shirley's silly column seemed small and unimportant. She smiled as they walked outside.

"It sounds as if Howie likes your article about Caroline's brother," commented Heather as they climbed into the jalopy.

"Yes," said Allison. "But only after he had me rewrite the whole thing."

Heather laughed. "It's not unlike music, Allison. You know, practice makes perfect."

"I suppose you're right," said Allison. "And I should be thankful. Howie really seems to know a lot about writing."

"Howie seems to know a lot about a lot of things," said Andrew under his breath. He started the engine and shifted into reverse.

"What was that?" asked Allison.

"Oh, nothing," muttered Andrew.

"It sounds like someone is in a grouchy mood," said Heather.

Allison peeked over at Andrew. His face did seem glum as he stared at the road before him. Raindrops began to splatter on the windshield, and he turned on the wipers. Allison wondered if it had anything to do with Beverly. Perhaps he had asked her to the Christmas dance and been turned down. No, that wasn't likely. If Andrew had asked Beverly to the dance, she would have surely accepted.

8

"This should only take a few more minutes, Allison," said Grace as she pinned the bodice darts into place. "James told me that you may be going to Marsha's for Christmas, so I thought I'd better get your dress finished before you're too far away for a fitting."

"I haven't really made up my mind yet," said Allison. She frowned at her reflection in Grace's mirror. Not only was pink not her best color, but the bridesmaid dress looked all lumpy and bumpy, and the sleeves were giant puffballs. She wisely kept these thoughts to herself.

Grace stood up and examined the neckline, taking in another tuck on the shoulders. "Your dad sounded fairly sure that you wanted to go to Marsha's." She paused and looked into Allison's eyes. "Is everything okay, Allison?"

Allison bit her lip. "I guess so."

Grace had Allison slowly turn around, made a few more adjustments, then carefully lifted the gown over her head. "Well, if there's any way I can be of help, Allison, I hope you'll feel free to call."

Allison pulled her skirt and sweater back on, then sat on Grace's bed to tie her shoes. "It's sure not easy being a kid sometimes."

Grace laughed. "Yes, I remember those days. But I'm afraid your life has some additional complications in it, doesn't it?"

Allison nodded. "This whole thing with Dad and Marsha. One moment I've made up my mind to stay home, the next I think I should go."

"Why do you think you should go, Allison?"

Allison sighed. "I don't know. Maybe it just seems easier."

"Easier?"

"To be honest, Grace, it almost seems like a good escape." Now Allison had said more than she intended.

"Why would you need to escape?"

"Oh, I don't know." Allison folded her arms across her chest. "Maybe it just seems like the easy way out. You know how insistent Marsha can be. And Dad seems willing to let me go. . . ."

"Willing, yes. But not eager or happy."

"See how complicated it gets?" Allison stood and reached for her jacket.

Grace nodded. "Perhaps the best thing would be to consider what you want. That, and perhaps it wouldn't hurt to ask God for some direction."

Allison brightened. "You know, that's just what Andrew said a while back. I think that's exactly what I need to do."

Grace hugged Allison. "Good for you. And I meant what I said, Allison. If there's any way I can be of help—an ear to listen, or whatever—promise me you'll call."

Allison smiled. "Thanks, Grace. I promise I will."

❧

Later that evening, Allison made sure that Dad understood that her mind wasn't made up about going to Marsha's yet. He seemed relieved.

"It's not that I have anything against Marsha," he explained as he picked up a chess piece. "In fact, it seems like she's really changed."

Allison studied his face as he decided whether to move his knight to the left or right. She was still interested in the snatches of congenial conversation she had overheard from him and Marsha. "What do you think of her, Dad?"

James plunked down his knight and looked at Allison with a puzzled expression. "Huh? What do you mean?"

"I mean, what do you think of Marsha? I'm just curious. After all, she is my mother, and you are my dad."

"I don't understand, Allison. Do you mean what did I *use* to think of her, back before you were born?"

"Maybe partly, but I mean more of the present."

James scratched his chin. "What do I think of Marsha now?" He paused and looked at the fireplace. "Well, I don't think she's real happy. . . ."

"Why not?"

He shook his head. "It sounds like she and Stanley are having some marital difficulties. Apparently, that's why he's staying in New York over the holidays."

Allison frowned. "That's too bad. I'm not crazy about Stanley, but he seemed to care about Marsha."

"Maybe he still does. It's hard to tell. I must admit that I felt a little sorry for Marsha the last time we spoke. Her life seems rather bleak and meaningless, if you know what I mean."

"But that's the way it's always been. That's the way she likes it."

"I suppose." James leaned back into the chair and sighed. "I just don't understand how she can choose to live that way. I mean, I lived all alone for several years, but it was out of necessity. And in many ways I think I needed the isolation to sort things out. But now that I'm surrounded by family and loved ones, I couldn't imagine wanting to live any other way. I guess I just wonder why Marsha isn't like that."

"Because she doesn't want to be." Then in one swift move, Allison relocated her queen out of harm's way and threatened her opponent's king. "Check."

"Why, you . . ." James leaned forward and pretended to be mad. "Was this some sort of strategy to throw me off course, Allison Mercury?"

"Maybe." Allison smirked. "Or maybe just luck."

He moved his king, but before long Allison gained the advantage and put him into checkmate. He frowned and shook his head. "I think I've been duped."

"Sorry, Dad. I didn't mean to throw your game off with all my questions." Then she grinned mischievously. "But it was a pretty good tactic."

"Off to bed with you," he commanded as he looked at his watch. "And just you wait until next time. I may use your tactics against you."

Allison put a look of mock horror on her face, then kissed him good-night and went upstairs. Her questions about Marsha hadn't revealed much.

❀

Allison's concerns about Dad seemed minor compared to what she read in the school newspaper the next morning. Fortunately, Howie had stopped Shirley's column about Marsha, but in her own way, Shirley got revenge.

"Did you read Shirley's column?" asked Karen in the hallway.

Allison rolled her eyes. "Unfortunately."

"Where does Shirley get these facts?"

"*Facts?*" Allison looked at Karen with raised brows. "Who needs facts?"

Karen laughed. "Well, it says here that Andrew and Beverly are Port View's hottest new romance. But Beverly is one of my best friends, and I didn't even know that. Shirley says, and I quote, 'Andrew Amberwell and Beverly Howard have been observed sharing many intimate moments lately and are rumored to be going to the Christmas dance together.' Now, how does she know that?"

Just then Beverly walked up and grinned saucily. "I guess things are moving a little faster than I'd expected." She winked at Allison. "Sorry to bump you out of the enviable position of being Andrew's sweetheart—"

Allison's eyes flashed. "I am not—"

Beverly laughed. "Don't get in a tizzy, Allison. I don't like Shirley's stupid column any more than you do."

"Besides, Allison," added Karen as she continued to read from the paper, "it says here that 'Allison O'Brian and Howie Ketchum's relationship goes beyond that of editor and reporter, and they are rumored to be going steady—'"

"Spare me!" cried Allison. "As if we don't know who made up all these stupid rumors. Howie better put a stop to her—"

"It's all in good fun, Allison," said Beverly. "No one will take any of that stuff seriously. What good is a society column if she doesn't throw in some juicy tidbits?"

"What about the truth?" asked Allison just as the bell rang.

"The truth is always changing," called Beverly as she dashed to class.

Allison folded her newspaper and hurried into biology. She noticed Shirley already in her seat, head straight forward—the perfect student. Allison stared at the back of Shirley's fluffy pink angora sweater. Oh, how she wanted to give Shirley a piece of her mind! But then that was probably exactly what Shirley wanted. Well, Allison wouldn't give Shirley the satisfaction. She would just pretend she couldn't care less about what

Shirley wrote in her silly column. Suddenly, she remembered how she had stood up for Shirley's column in the first place. She should have known better!

For the rest of the morning, Allison pretended that everything was perfectly fine. She even smiled benignly at Shirley, holding her head high as if nothing whatsoever was troubling her. By lunchtime, she was actually feeling much better.

"Oh, Allison," said Howie as he caught up with her in the lunch line. "I'm sorry about what Shirley said in her column. I . . . I didn't have time to read it too carefully before it went to print. She typeset it herself, and it seemed okay when I glanced at it the first time."

Allison knew that Shirley was only a few feet away and probably listening to every word. "Oh, it's no problem, Howie. I don't think anyone takes these things seriously, do you?"

Howie smiled. "I guess not. Gee, you're being a good sport about everything, Allison. I thought you might be mad."

"I guess as long as she doesn't go *too* far. I wouldn't want to see anyone getting hurt by her words." Allison glanced over her shoulder in time to see Shirley scowl. Shirley quickly turned her head.

"You're absolutely right, Allison. From now on I'll make sure that I read every word that goes into the *Pirate Chest*."

Allison spotted Andrew across the room. He and Bruce Williams were talking with Beverly and Karen. Beverly was waving a copy of the newspaper around, and the four of them were laughing. "It doesn't seem to be bothering Andrew and Beverly, either," said Allison.

Howie followed her gaze. "I didn't think it would since Shirley seemed to hit the nail on the head as far as they were concerned."

"Really?" said Allison. "You thought they were a couple?"

"Sure. I heard that Andrew is taking Beverly to the Christmas dance."

"Oh." Allison stepped forward in line and picked up a tray.

"Maybe after all the hubbub over 'Jenson's Jetsam' settles down, you'll get some feedback on *your* story, Allison. I, for one, happen to think it is superior. I've already sent a copy to Sam Long."

"Really?" Allison set a plate of spaghetti on her tray and looked at him in surprise. "Do you think he'll believe it?"

"Why shouldn't he?"

"Oh, I don't know. Caroline said that the government keeps denying it."

"That's what makes it a great story, Allison."

Caroline waved to her from their regular table, and Allison turned to Howie. "Thanks," she said with a smile. "See you after school." She went over and sat next to Heather and sighed deeply.

"Are you all right, Al?" asked Heather.

"Sure, why do you ask?"

"Caroline just read Shirley's column to me, and I thought you might be feeling a little miffed."

"No more than usual." Allison twisted the long strands of spaghetti around her fork. "Did you read my article yet, Caroline?"

Caroline beamed at Allison. "I sure did. I read it to Heather, too."

"We both think you're terrific, Allison," Heather said proudly. "And when you are some big, famous newspaper reporter, we hope you'll still remember the little people."

Allison laughed. "Fat chance!"

"You mean you *won't* remember us?" Caroline's face looked shocked.

"No, I mean fat chance that I'll ever be a famous reporter."

"Well, I saw Katharine Hepburn play a woman reporter in a movie once." Caroline frowned. "I can't remember the name . . . but if she can do it, so can you!"

"Maybe," said Allison. "Howie is sending a copy of my article to Sam Long."

"Do you think he'll put it in his paper?" asked Heather.

"Oh, I doubt it. He hasn't even put the other story in his paper."

"Not yet, but he will," declared Caroline. "And I hope he runs your story, Allison. Then maybe everyone around here would be praying for Kevin."

"Yes," agreed Heather. "That would be wonderful."

"Do you think the kids at school will really pray?" asked Caroline uncertainly.

"I don't know why not," said Allison. "I know I am."

"Me too," said Heather. "We told people at church, and they've agreed to pray, too."

Caroline's face looked so hopeful. In fact, Caroline actually looked quite pretty today. She had on a new blue sweater that matched her eyes, and her hair was curling nicely around her face.

"Caroline, you look very pretty today," said Allison. "How's your diet coming?"

Caroline smiled. "I've lost thirteen pounds!"

"That's fantastic!" said Heather.

"And I have some news," said Caroline quietly.

"What's that?" asked Allison as she finished her milk.

"Tommy asked me to the Christmas dance, and my parents said I can go!"

"You're joking," said Heather. "And you didn't even tell me!"

"I wanted to tell you both at the same time."

"Congratulations," said Allison. "This time neither of us is going, so make sure your dad takes photographs to show us."

"I will. I'm not sure what I'm going to wear. I don't have a formal dress."

Allison looked at her. She was still too heavy to fit into a Marsha gown. "Maybe your mom can take you to Portland. We saw lots of gowns there when we looked for bridesmaid dresses."

"That might be fun," said Caroline. "I think my mother would like that."

As excited as she was for Caroline, one glance at the newspaper on the table was all it took to destroy Allison's good mood. What was she going to do about Shirley and her column?

9

Everyone seemed to have something to occupy them in the journalism room after school, even Shirley. But Allison just stared at the blank sheet of paper in her typewriter and absently drummed her pencil.

"Does our star reporter have writer's block?" asked Andrew as he stopped by her desk.

She frowned up at him. "I'm just thinking," she replied. They were the first words she'd spoken to him since reading that he and Beverly were an item. Then she forced a smile to her lips, remembering that he was, first of all, her friend. It was silly for her to fret over his relationship with Beverly—whatever it might be.

"So did you decide about going to Marsha's yet?"

"Not really, but I know I have to make up my mind—"

"Did you hear the news yet?" Beverly stepped up, smiling at Andrew brightly. It looked as if she was hiding something behind her back.

Andrew shook his head. "What news?"

"Howie just showed me today's *Port View Herald*. You're on the front page, Andrew!" She pulled out the newspaper and proudly read, "'Port View High Quarterback Survives Emergency Airplane Landing.'" She held the paper before

Andrew. "See, there's your photo and everything. Isn't it great? Don't you feel famous now?"

Andrew studied the paper, then grinned. "Maybe a little."

Just then Howie walked up. "I think Allison deserves some congratulations, too. After all, it was *her* story."

"Yeah, great job, Allison," said Beverly almost as an after-thought, then she turned back to Andrew and continued to bubble about how he should buy a bunch of copies and send them to everyone he knew. Finally, when it seemed the excite-ment had died down, Allison asked if she could see the paper, too. Beverly handed it to her and walked away.

Allison sighed in wonder as she read the by-line—*by Allison O'Brian, Port View High.* How satisfying. She put Beverly and Andrew out of mind. Who cared about romance—*she* was a published writer in a *real* newspaper!

"Pretty nice, eh?" said Howie as he looked over her shoulder.

"It sure is." Allison skimmed the article and found only a few words had been changed. "I can hardly believe it, Howie. This is *so* great!"

Shirley walked up and scowled down at the paper. "Good grief, Allison, don't get all soppy about it. It's only a tiny local newspaper—not the *New York Times.*" She turned and strut-ted away.

Allison was about to spout out a smart answer but then decided not to fall for Shirley's barbed bait. She would only be sorry.

"Hey, look at this," said Howie, pointing to the other front-page news story. "There were two burglaries in Port View this week."

"Better keep your doors locked," said Allison. She watched as Shirley went back to her desk and sat down.

"The reason she's in such a snit," whispered Howie, "is because I told her that next week she doesn't get a column. She has to come up with a news story instead. That way she can practice sticking to the facts. It's sort of like probation."

"That's a good idea," said Allison. She continued skimming her article.

"Well, I'll leave you to bask in your glory," laughed Howie. "Go ahead and keep that copy. It's an extra."

"Thanks, Howie. Maybe I'll send it to my mother."

"Yeah, I bet she'd like that."

Allison finished reading her reprinted story in the newspaper, then looked back at her own blank piece of paper still waiting expectantly in the typewriter. Her story about the emergency plane landing was a hard act to follow, but she'd been lucky to come up with the story about Kevin in prison camp. Now what could she write about? That kind of excitement didn't happen every day. At least not around here.

"Hey, does anybody want to go to the basketball game with me tomorrow night?" asked Andrew. "It's in Shelton, but I've got to cover it, so I'd be glad to have company." He looked at Allison, and she was about to open her mouth to say yes.

"I'd love to ride with you," Beverly said quickly. She stepped up and put a possessive hand on his arm. "After all, didn't I read something in today's paper about you and me? We better give them something *more* to talk about." Beverly glanced at Shirley and laughed loudly.

Allison watched as Andrew's cheeks took on a deeper shade of pink. He seemed slightly embarrassed but not necessarily bothered by Beverly's insinuation. It was probably all true. Now Allison had absolutely no desire to go to the ball game. It was one thing to get over Andrew, but it was another thing to sit in the same car and witness Beverly turning on the charm. To make matters worse, Shirley stepped up and announced that she'd like a ride, too. What an interesting threesome that would be.

"And if you have enough room, Andrew," said Howie, "I'd like to come, too."

"Sure, why not," said Andrew. "How about you, Allison?"

Allison stared at him as he smiled down upon her. A hard lump had begun to grow in her throat. She must get over him, and soon. She knew he was just being polite, or maybe he hoped to use Dad's car if she came along, but it was time for her to take a stand and to be strong. This childish crush on Andrew was not going to rule her life.

"No. Thanks anyway, Andrew. I think I'd rather stay home tomorrow night."

He blinked in surprise. "You're sure?"

She nodded. "Yes. I need to decide what I'm going to do about Marsha. If I go down there, I'll have a lot to get done next week. I haven't even started my story for the paper, and I have a mountain of homework."

"That's right," said Andrew. "There's only one more week of school before Christmas vacation. Fall term has gone by so quickly."

"Yes," agreed Beverly. "I can hardly believe that next Friday is the Christmas dance. Everything just happens so fast."

Allison turned her attention back to the *Port View Herald*, hoping to regain that initial sense of satisfaction when she'd first seen her name in print. Yet it seemed that everything around her was trying to overshadow this accomplishment. Now, if only she could think of a good story. She glanced up at the clock. Less than an hour before Howie would lock up the room, and she still didn't have a single idea. Maybe she could try to make a brainstorm list. Then she could go over it later and see if anything had potential. She had half a page of ideas, mostly silly ones, when it was time to go.

On the way home, Allison told Heather about the local newspaper running her story. Then Heather told them how many kids had come up to Caroline with promises to pray for Kevin.

"That's great," said Allison. "Now maybe Sam will run that story, too, and everyone in Port View will be praying."

Heather chattered for a while about how excited Caroline had been about getting to attend the dance with Tommy and how she and her mom would probably go dress shopping this weekend. But before long Heather grew quiet. Allison wondered if Heather sensed there was a problem between Andrew and Allison. But then again, Andrew didn't really have a problem—it was Allison who was hurting. She glanced at Andrew. As usual he seemed focused on the road. Maybe his brow was slightly creased, but it was foggy and dark out, and Andrew was always a very conscientious driver.

⚜

The next morning passed uneventfully. The main talk around school was tonight's basketball game and the Christmas dance next week. By now, many couples had decided to go to the dance, and the decorating committee was looking for more volunteers. Allison hadn't been eating lunch with Karen's crowd lately. She needed to keep a little distance from Beverly right now, and it was quiet and peaceful to eat with Heather and Caroline. But that was before Shirley arrived.

"Hi, Allison," said Shirley a bit too cheerfully. "How are you doing?"

Allison looked up at Shirley with skeptical caution. "I'm okay."

"Can I join you?"

"It's a free country, Shirley." Allison knew it wasn't a very

300

gracious thing to say, but she wasn't in the mood for any of Shirley's pranks right now.

Shirley frowned but sat down anyway. "You're not being very friendly, Allison. I just wanted to see if you'd made up your mind about going to your mother's."

"Why?" Allison turned and stared at Shirley. "Did you want to write a story about it?"

Shirley laughed. "No, silly. I was just curious. And by the way, Howie told me that I shouldn't have said that you and he were romantically involved in my column. I'm sorry."

Allison blinked in surprise. She almost pinched herself to see if this was real . . . Shirley saying she was sorry? "It's okay, I guess. Just be more careful next time."

"So I assume that means you're *not*."

"Not what?"

"Romantically involved with Howie." Shirley spoke slowly, as if her meaning should've been obvious in the first place.

Allison sighed. "Howie and I are good friends. That's all."

"Good," said Shirley with a sly smile. Then as quickly as she came, she stood and walked away.

❋

Allison was glad when the school day ended. She and Heather rode home with Dad, since Andrew was taking the others to the game. Dad went inside Grace's house to discuss some wedding plans and then decided to stay and visit longer.

"I think I'll walk on home," said Allison. "I haven't been on the beach lately."

"See you at home, then," said Dad.

"Do you want to come, Heather?" asked Allison.

"I'll pass," said Heather. "I think I might be coming down with a cold."

"I'll tell Muriel to make you some of her famous chicken soup," teased Allison as she went outside.

The wind was blowing on the beach, but Allison didn't mind. She breathed deeply of the fresh sea air, willing it to wash away her troubles and worries. They were really so small. Especially compared to things like Caroline's brother locked up in icy Siberia. Once again, Allison prayed for him. She prayed that he was safe and warm and fed, and also that he'd soon be home. Then she sat on a large rock and looked out across the gray-blue sea. It was rougher than usual today, with breakers reaching high, then crumbling into white foam. But it was not as wild as she'd seen the Atlantic in times past.

For a brief moment she experienced a small pang—of what? Homesickness for the East Coast? Of course there were things she missed about the East. Like Nanny Jane, or some of her old friends at Oakmont. But Nanny Jane was long gone, and Allison kept in touch with only a couple of school chums. Allison wondered if she might be missing Marsha.

A sea gull swooped down and screeched, and then its lonely cry was blown away by the wind. Allison felt a rush of guilt—she needed to decide about Marsha, today if possible. It was unfair to keep everyone hanging like this. Only a few minutes ago she had noticed Grace working on Allison's bridesmaid dress, frantically trying to finish it just in case Allison left.

Allison closed her eyes and asked God to show her the right thing to do. Suddenly, she imagined Marsha sad and alone at Christmas with not a single family member around. Dad had mentioned that even Lola would be off to visit a brother in San Jose. Allison knew in her heart she would rather be with Dad in Oregon, experiencing for the first time a big, loving family, celebrating Christmas together. But there would be other times. Allison could afford to give up one. It was really a small sacrifice on her part, and it would mean so much to

Marsha. It was decided. She was going. She took a deep breath and sighed. Now she needed to tell Marsha the good news. She raced up the beach and climbed the steps to the house, dashing straight for the phone in the library. By the time the call finally went through and Marsha answered, Allison was just barely catching her breath again.

"Hello, Marsha," she gasped.

"Hello?" said Marsha on the other end of the line. "Is that you, Allison? Are you okay?"

"Yes, it's me, Marsha." Allison giggled. "Sorry about that. I just came in from the beach—I was running. But I wanted to call you—"

"I'm so glad you did, darling," interrupted Marsha. "I was just about to call your father."

"Dad?"

"Yes, I've just had the most wonderful news, and I wanted to tell him—"

"Hang on, Marsha," said Allison just as her father walked into the library. "He happens to be right here." She motioned him over to the phone. "It's Marsha, Dad, and she wants to talk to you." Allison handed the receiver away and stepped back from the desk. She tried not to show that her feelings were hurt. It seemed Marsha was more eager to talk to her ex-husband than to her daughter.

"Yes, Marsha, I just stepped in this moment." He paused and looked at Allison curiously. "You don't say! Rio de Janeiro— that's in Brazil, right? How exciting for you, Marsha!"

Allison felt like she was eavesdropping and decided to leave until the conversation was done. She could call Marsha later and tell her the good news about coming. In the meantime, she had plenty to do to get ready before her trip. She expected she'd be leaving next weekend. Dad had mentioned flying her over to Portland, and then she could go by train—safer this time of year. But that didn't leave a lot of time for everything she wanted to get done. It was a good thing she had decided not to go to the basketball game tonight. She hurried upstairs and began to get busy. She had several unfinished homemade Christmas presents to complete, a science project, and a writing assignment for English, not to mention her newspaper story. She decided to sit down at her desk and make a list. Just when she finished it, she heard a knock at the door.

"Yoo-hoo?" her dad called. "Anyone home?"

"Come in, Dad."

"Marsha said that you were the one who called, Allison," said James. "She thought maybe you had something to tell her, and she was worried that she had cut you off."

"It's okay. I can call her back. I wanted to let her know that I've decided to go down there after all."

Dad's brows lifted in surprise. "You did?"

Allison nodded. "I prayed about it, and it seemed like the right thing to do."

He frowned. "I see . . ."

"Not that I didn't want to be here with you, Dad. I just felt sorry for Marsha—you know, all alone on Christmas . . ."

"Oh." Dad's face brightened a little. "Well, that was very thoughtful of you, Allison, but it seems that's no longer a problem."

"Is Stanley coming back?"

"No, but Marsha's current film is being moved to location. She said that originally they didn't have the budget for it and were going to just shoot the foreign scenes using sets at the studio lot. But apparently something has changed, and she is going to Rio on the twenty-second."

"Rio?"

"Rio de Janeiro in Brazil. Marsha says that Latin American films are all the rage right now. But the important thing is that means you can stay home with us, and you don't need to feel the least bit guilty!" Dad grinned.

Allison forced a smile. It's not that she wasn't glad to stay home, but it felt like someone had just knocked the wind out of her sails. "That's great, Dad."

"Marsha is just thrilled about the whole thing. She thinks this is the studio's way of saying that they still believe in the old girl."

"That's nice." Allison folded her list in half and stood up. "She has been pretty worried about getting replaced by some of the up-and-coming younger starlets."

"It sounds like she doesn't need to worry, at least for now." James looked at his watch. "I better get cleaned up. I promised to take Grace out for dinner tonight. Do you mind? I arranged it earlier this week when I thought you would be going to the basketball game with Andrew."

"No, I'm fine, Dad. I've got plenty to keep me busy."

"Good girl. And I had told Muriel to take the night off— she had a baby shower to attend—but when she heard you would be home, she left a nice plate of dinner on the back of the stove."

"Sounds good." Allison waved her hand at him. "Now, off with you, Dad. It's not smart to keep a lady waiting."

She closed the door to her bedroom and turned on her radio, and the little orange light on the dial glowed warmly. She tuned in the station, then lay down across her bed and listened as Frank Sinatra crooned a sweet love song that had been popular during the war. It was a pretty song, but it made her feel lonely. She considered asking Dad to drop her at Heather's but remembered that Heather hadn't been feeling so hot. Well, it seemed that she was on her own tonight.

She thought about Marsha going to Rio. Of course, she was

relieved. The idea of spending Christmas in Tinseltown had not been appealing—she had only decided out of pity for Marsha. Now it was no longer necessary. Allison should be happy.

She thought about Andrew and the others on their way to the basketball game right now. Was Beverly sitting next to him, the four of them crammed cozily into the cab of the jalopy? Was the radio on? Were they also listening to Frank Sinatra? Allison sat up and fiercely shook her head. She didn't need to dwell on such things. *The Christmas dance.* Allison wouldn't admit to anyone, hardly even to herself, but she would love to go to that dance. The Harvest Ball had been such great fun . . . but there would be other dances. Suddenly, Allison remembered what Susan Taylor had said in P.E. about the decorating committee. They needed more help, and anyone who volunteered would get to go to the dance—it didn't matter if they had a date or not. Maybe she should look into that. It would be such fun to see Caroline all dressed up! And now that Allison wasn't going to Marsha's, she had more time for things like this. But what if she had to watch Andrew dancing cheek-to-cheek with Beverly? Allison stood up and looked in the mirror, giving herself a little pep talk.

"Get over it! Quit feeling sorry for yourself. Put on a sunny face. There are lots of fish in the sea." That one made her laugh, and she made a fish face in the mirror. "Besides, you dope, you're too young to mope around for some stupid boy." Feeling much better, she ran downstairs to see what Muriel had left for dinner.

❧

Later that evening, Allison snuggled into the window seat in the library and worked on her English paper—a creative writing assignment. Just when she reached a pivotal spot in her story—should the heroine die while saving her true love, or should she just nearly die—Allison thought she saw a glimmer of light out of the corner of her eye. She peered out the window, but there was too much light reflecting off the glass to see much more than the slow-moving beam from the lighthouse. She reached over and turned off her reading lamp, darkening the room so she could see better, then peered out the window again. She watched for nearly an hour but didn't see anything. Perhaps it had been only her imagination. She turned on the reading lamp and finished her story—deciding her heroine could still save her true love without having to die in the process.

10

"Do you want to work at the airport with me this morning?" Dad asked Allison after breakfast.

"Sure," agreed Allison. "But let me run and get my book bag. Then I can do homework if things get slow in the office." She dashed upstairs and quickly returned with her book bag and coat.

Dad smiled. "It's nice to see what a diligent student you are, Allison. Is that something they taught you at that stuffy old boarding school?"

Allison laughed as she pulled on her coat. "Well, there wasn't all that much to do at Oakmont, so there was always plenty of time to study."

Her father frowned as he reached for his jacket. "Sometimes I'm concerned there could be too many distractions for you here, Allison—what with the airport and all your school activities."

"You know how I love being busy, Dad. In fact, I was just thinking last night that I might sign up to be on the Christmas dance decorating committee—if that's okay with you. It means I'll need a ride home after school on Monday and Wednesday next week."

Dad opened the car door for her. "Sure. It sounds like you're keeping up with your schoolwork. I don't mind picking you up. But you are certainly a busy little bee. You remind me of Grace."

Allison smiled. "I shall take that as a supreme compliment."

They drove in silence, and her father seemed preoccupied. Allison didn't really want to interrupt his thoughts, but something was bothering her. She had tried to skirt around the subject once before during their chess game, but it seemed there were still some unanswered questions. The best solution was probably to simply bring it out into the open.

"Did I hear you talking to Marsha this morning?" asked Allison lightly.

He nodded. "Yes. She called again."

"What did she want?"

James sighed. "I'm not sure. Maybe just to chat."

"Do you like chatting with her?" Allison studied his face carefully.

He frowned. "Not exactly."

This surprised Allison. "Then why do you sound so cheerful when you're talking with her, Dad? It sounds like you enjoy it."

Her father glanced at her with a shocked expression. "Really?" Then he began to laugh.

"What's so funny?"

"I'm sorry, Allison. It's just that when I first started talking to Marsha, I was trying to befriend her in an attempt to talk her out of having you go down there at Christmas. I thought you didn't want to go, and I was trying to smooth things over with her. And then she seemed so lonely that I actually felt a little sorry for her."

"Do you feel anything else?"

James chuckled. "Are you asking if I still harbor any romantic feelings for Marsha?"

"Yes, I guess that's what I'm asking." Allison felt her cheeks blushing. She didn't like coming across as a nosy busybody. But she just *had* to know!

James nodded solemnly. "You know, Allison, there was a time when I would have done anything for your mother. Although I had felt somewhat trapped in our marriage to begin with—"

"Trapped?"

"I suppose that's not the right word. But I was down and alone in New York, and Marsha reached out and pulled me into her world—things happened so fast. I must admit that her glamour and wealth fascinated me. I was like a country bumpkin, just ripe for the picking. . . ."

"And Marsha picked you," Allison said quietly.

"I regretted the marriage immediately. I knew in my heart it was a mistake, but after you came along, I decided to do everything within my power to make it work. At that point I felt like I did love Marsha. But things went steadily from bad to worse—it was a marriage that was never meant to be."

Allison nodded. "I know, Dad. Marsha told me her version, too, right before I left from Grandmother Madison's. Marsha blames herself, you know."

"Yes, she just recently said as much to me." Dad sighed. "It was such a relief to hear her say it after all these years. And I suppose when she admitted that and apologized, I began to feel more friendly to her."

"So is it only friendship, then, Dad?" Allison knew her voice sounded hopeful.

"Allison, I can understand how you might wish that your parents could get back together—"

"No, Dad. That's not it. Not really." Allison thought for a moment. "I suppose there were times when I thought it would be easier—on me, anyway. But I'm old enough to understand that it would be a huge mess, unless you really loved each other."

"I don't love Marsha, Allison." James glanced at her. "I would probably actually try to for your sake—if things were different, I mean—if it weren't for Stanley and Grace. But it would be a sacrifice on my part because the fact is, I haven't a glimmer of romantic feelings for Marsha." He turned down the road to the airport. "I hope that doesn't hurt you, Allison, but I have to tell you the honest truth."

Allison smiled. "No, it doesn't hurt me, Dad. I appreciate your telling me the truth. I know it's not easy to talk about Marsha and the past. But I think I needed to know. When I heard you talking to her, I began to imagine things. I worried about you and Grace. I didn't want to see you make a mistake. Marsha is my mother and I do love her, but Grace is very special and I love her, too. Not because she's going to be your wife or because she's going to be my stepmother, but simply because she's Grace."

James parked the car in front of the office, then turned to Allison. There were tears gleaming in his eyes as he spoke. "There's nothing you could have said just now that would've meant more to me, Allison. Thank you."

Allison took a deep breath as she looked up at the overcast sky. It felt as if a huge weight had been lifted.

"I didn't mean to be nosy," she said softly.

James threw back his head and laughed. "Don't ever worry about that, Allison. I promise to never keep secrets from you. I hope you will do the same."

"What about surprises—you know, for birthdays and Christmas?"

He wrapped his arm around her shoulder and gave her a squeeze. "You know what I mean."

"Hey, there," called Mac. "I was starting to get worried. I

need to take off in a few minutes if I'm going to pick up that freight in Portland and make my deliveries before dark."

"Sorry, Mac. It's probably my fault," said Allison with a sheepish smile. "I slowed him down a little. Hey, I was hoping you would be around so I could interview you for an article for my school paper. I figure you must be full of great tales."

Mac winked at her. "I read your bonny story in the *Port View Herald* last week and would be happy to tell you some tales, but it'll have to be another day, lassie. I've got to be on my way now."

"Have a good flight, Mac," James called. He turned to Allison. "Do you think there's any coffee in there?"

Allison grinned. "If not, I know how to make some."

"That's my girl. I'll be out in the hangar."

Allison quickly had a pot of coffee perking on the little stove. It still amazed her to see how neat and efficient the office had become. Such a transformation from earlier days. She answered the phone and wrote a message, then settled down at Mac's desk to do her homework.

"Hi, Allison."

Allison looked up to see Andrew in the doorway. "Hi, Andrew." She smiled up at him. His hair was mussed by the wind, and his cheeks were ruddy. "What are you up to?"

"I was just talking to your dad out there." He nodded over his shoulder. "He asked me to bring him a cup of coffee. Got any?"

She stood and went to the stove. "Do you want a cup, too, Andrew?"

"Sure. But I can get it, Allison. You don't have to wait on me."

"No problem," said Allison, determined to treat Andrew as her good friend, just like he'd always been. "Don't you take cream and sugar?"

"Yeah. That's the only way I can drink it."

"How was the game last night?" asked Allison as she handed him his cup.

"Amazingly, the Pirates won."

"Fantastic. Now you can write a victory story."

Andrew nodded and took a sip. "Your dad said you decided not to go to Marsha's after all."

Allison bit her lip. "Actually, Marsha decided for me."

Andrew's brows raised. "Didn't she want you to come?"

"Her film has been changed to location in Brazil. They leave the week before Christmas."

"Are you disappointed?"

Allison shook her head. "Not really. I was only going because I felt bad that she would be alone. All of you have each other. . . ."

"And now we'll have you, too." Andrew grinned as if he really meant it, and Allison felt warm inside.

"Thanks. It should be a fun Christmas. Probably the best one I've ever had."

"I guess I better get your dad's coffee to him before it gets cold. Thanks, Allison."

Allison returned to her homework, sighing in satisfaction. Being Andrew's friend was really quite nice. It seemed senseless to let silly feelings get in the way. From now on she would try to keep a clear head about things.

⚜

Allison helped the decorating committee after school on Monday. It was fun making foil silver bells and paper poinsettias for the table decorations. She worked with Susan Taylor, who was a sophomore. Susan didn't appear to be involved in any specific group at school, but she did seem sincere and thoughtful, and Allison liked her. She knew that Susan's parents ran a dairy farm just north of Tamaqua Point.

"Are you going to the dance?" asked Allison as she sprinkled glitter along the edges of the red paper poinsettia.

"You mean with a boy?" asked Susan.

"Or on your own?" said Allison. "I heard that dance committee people don't have to come with a date."

"That's right," said Susan. "Actually, I plan to come. How about you?"

"I thought it would be fun—sort of festive, you know—the music and decorations."

Susan nodded. "I don't really care if I don't get to dance."

Allison sighed. "I think it's fun to dance."

"Really?" Susan seemed surprised, then nodded. "Oh, of course, what with your mother and all—"

"Actually, my mother never had much time to teach me to dance. In fact, I'm sure she would think I was greatly in need of some real dancing lessons."

"I didn't mean to sound like because of your mother . . . well, I know you're—" Susan looked embarrassed.

"Don't worry about it, Susan." Allison laughed lightly. "I used to be a lot more sensitive about my mother, but I think I must be getting used to it."

Susan sighed. "Well, I heard that Shirley Jenson had made your life miserable about your mother for a while. I didn't want to come across like *that*. I must admit I find it fascinating that your mother is a movie star, but I liked you before I knew that."

"Thanks, Susan. I'm finding that once people get over it, life pretty much goes back to normal."

"Say, I thought your article on Caroline's brother was very interesting." Susan twisted a green poinsettia leaf around a pipe cleaner. "And I've been praying for him. I think that was a nice idea."

"Thanks. Now, if I could only get an idea for this week's paper."

"Not much going on around here," said Susan. "If the dance were sooner you could write about that."

Allison glanced at her watch and saw it was time for her dad to pick her up. "I've got to go, Susan. I'll see you tomorrow, and I plan to help again on Wednesday."

"Swell. We'll be decorating the big tree then."

"Sounds like fun."

※

By Tuesday, Allison still hadn't come up with a good story for the paper. She had outlined several ideas, but nothing seemed nearly as interesting as her previous feature stories. She knew it was foolish to get too distraught over this, but she wanted to do a good job. Writing for the paper seemed to be the thing she did best—it mattered to her.

In P.E., Allison noticed that Susan Taylor looked about as glum as Allison felt. "What's wrong, Susan?" she asked. "You look down in the dumps."

"I guess I'm feeling a little downhearted." Susan looked at Allison with sad brown eyes. "Our house was burglarized yesterday. My mom and dad were both out in the dairy barn, and the rest of us were at school. Someone came in and took silverware and money, even a sterling tea set that had been in my mom's family for five generations. She's really upset."

"I'm sorry," said Allison. "That must feel horrible."

"It does. We never used to lock our doors. Now my dad says everyone will have to carry their own key. It seems so unfair that perfect strangers could just walk into your house and do that."

"Do you think the police will find them?" asked Allison.

"My dad says it's probably the same thieves who've been breaking in along the coast. You better keep your doors locked."

Allison nodded. "How creepy. I'm so sorry that your family was hit, Susan."

"Thanks. Somehow just talking about it makes me feel a little better. But it does shake your trust in fellow humans. I don't like that."

"I don't like it, either." Allison's eyes lit up. "Say, would you mind if I used this for my newspaper story?"

"I guess not. I'm sure it will be in the *Port View Herald*."

"Right. But it will interest kids in school because it seems more real when someone they know has been hurt. Who knows, maybe someone at school might have some information that could help the police find the thugs."

"That would be nice." Susan attempted a feeble smile. "Thanks, Allison."

Allison tried not to be distracted by her new story idea as she impatiently waited for the afternoon to pass. She couldn't wait to sit down in front of the typewriter. Finally the last bell rang, and she practically ran to the journalism room. On her way she saw Heather and Caroline.

"What's the rush?" asked Caroline.

"I've got a good lead," called Allison over her shoulder.

"Go for it, Allison!" cheered Heather.

Allison had just flopped into a chair and hammered out her opening line when Howie stepped up to her desk.

"Is your story finished yet, Allison?" he asked.

She looked up and smiled beguilingly. "Not yet, Howie. Do you think if I get it to you tomorrow it will be okay? It's going to be a good one, I think."

Howie frowned. "I suppose. It's just that the paper is looking a bit thin right now." He glanced over his shoulder. "Beverly's article is on the short side, and Shirley hasn't turned in anything yet."

"I heard that," said Shirley, rising from her desk dramatically. "It's not *my* fault, Howie. If you'd just let me do my column like I'm supposed to, it wouldn't be a problem. But, no, I've got to come up with a news story."

Howie rolled his eyes, then looked down to Allison's first line. "Susan Taylor's house was burglarized?" he said with concern.

"Yes," said Allison. "She's pretty upset, too. It's too bad creeps like that have to hurt others."

"Doesn't Susan live in Tamaqua Point?" asked Howie.

Allison nodded, eager to return to her story.

"Gosh," said Shirley with wide eyes. "*We* live in Tamaqua Point. I better tell my mom to hide her jewelry."

Howie scratched his head. "From Port View to Tamaqua Point . . . it sounds like the robbers are working a thirty-mile strip of the coast. I'm surprised the police haven't caught up with them yet. It couldn't be that hard to patrol Highway 101. That's the only way to get up and down the coast."

"Unless you had an airplane," said Allison impatiently. "But we've got the only airstrip in the area, and I hardly think that Mac and Dad are burglars."

"There're also boats," said Howie thoughtfully. "But that's pretty farfetched."

A wild thought struck Allison. "But what if . . ."

"What if—what?" asked Howie with curiosity.

"Oh, it's probably nothing. But you never know. And if I was right, it could make a great story." Allison looked at her watch. "I wish I could get out there right now."

"What is it, Allison?" demanded Howie.

"Just a crazy hunch," said Allison. "A couple of times we thought we saw strange lanterns moving around at the lighthouse. It's probably nothing, but what if the thieves were using boats, like you just suggested, and using the lighthouse island to stash their loot?"

Howie laughed. "I'm sure it *could* happen, Allison. But I must admit it sounds a bit fanciful. If it was true, it would make a great story. Maybe you should call the police and tell them your hunch. And now I better get to work thinking of some way to fill this paper in case my reporters don't come through." He looked directly at Shirley, then returned to his desk.

Allison frowned. If she called the police, they would get there before her and she might lose the story. She wished that Andrew didn't have to wait to take Heather home. Where was Andrew? And where was Beverly, for that matter?

Shirley leaned over with interest. "What are you going to do, Allison?"

"I don't know. It's probably nothing. Like Howie said, just my fanciful imagination."

"But maybe not," said Shirley.

"It doesn't really matter, since it's impossible. I'd have to leave right now to get to the island before dark."

"So what's stopping us?" Shirley smiled down at Allison.

"Us?" Allison eyed Shirley with suspicion.

"Sure. I can take you."

"You?" Allison blinked in surprise. "How?"

"Silly girl. Don't you remember that I turned sixteen a couple weeks ago? I got my driver's license last week. And you're in luck, since Mom let me drive her car to school today."

Allison had almost forgotten that Shirley was a year older. But still, to ride in the car with Shirley Jenson at the wheel? It seemed crazy. "I . . . uh . . . I think I better pass, Shirley. But thanks just the same."

"Fine," said Shirley. "I'll go by myself, then. I need the story."

"But you can't—"

"It's a free country, Allison. And if you'll try to remember—that lighthouse happens to be named after *me*."

"After your grandfather!" snapped Allison. She grabbed up her books and followed Shirley. "Wait. I'm coming, too."

"Where you going?" asked Howie.

"To the lighthouse," called Allison. "Tell Andrew that I don't need a ride today."

11

Allison wondered if she'd lost her mind. She gulped and clutched the door handle as Shirley swerved around another steep curve.

"This isn't a chase, Shirley," said Allison, trying to appear calm. "You don't need to drive so fast."

Shirley laughed. "Am I frightening you, Allison?"

"A little." Allison watched nervously as Marge Jenson's red Pontiac's tires crossed the center line. "How long have you been driving, Shirley?"

"Long enough," snapped Shirley. "Don't be such a baby, Allison!"

Allison decided it might be wiser and safer to keep quiet. Shirley didn't need any distractions right now. In the meantime, Allison silently prayed for safety and vowed *never* to ride with Shirley again!

Shirley parked on the dock road, and with great relief Allison escaped from the car.

"I should go tell my dad what we're up to," said Allison.

"We only have about an hour before the sun goes down, Allison. I say we go right now." Shirley began to march down to the dock. Allison dashed after her, certain that Shirley would leave in the boat without her. And Allison was not about to get scooped on her own story. She suspected that Shirley was hoping to get a story out of this, too, but Allison felt fairly certain that Howie, forced to choose between her story or Shirley's, would probably pick hers.

It was obvious that Shirley's narrow pencil skirt and heeled shoes weren't designed for outdoor explorations as she climbed into the boat with great difficulty. Allison waited as Shirley gingerly sat down, then hopped in. She was thankful for her own full woolen skirt and sturdy saddle shoes, but she noted with dismay that Shirley had left the rowing seat for Allison.

"I suppose *I* get to row," grumbled Allison as she reached for the oars.

Shirley laughed. "Well, *you're* the athletic one, Allison. Besides, you've had more experience with boats and things."

"So what if I hadn't come?" questioned Allison. "Would you have rowed out by yourself?"

"I knew you would come," retorted Shirley.

Allison narrowed her eyes and began to row. Fortunately, the tide was in and not moving.

"Can't you row any faster?" Shirley complained.

Allison scowled. "Do you want to give it a try?"

"No. But do hurry. I'm getting cold."

Allison continued to row steadily. At least the movement warmed her, and her clothing was probably heavier than Shirley's. Allison looked up to see Shirley frowning at her. "What is it now?"

"I thought you said that there wasn't anything between you and Howie," said Shirley unexpectedly.

Allison stopped rowing for a moment and stared at Shirley with disbelief. *"What?"*

"You told me that you and Howie were just friends."

Allison shook her head in wonder. "That's right. We are just friends. Why are you bringing this up *now*?"

"Because on Friday night I thought that Howie and I were becoming something—like a couple. And then he kept talking about you! It was infuriating. You tricked me, Allison O'Brian."

Allison laughed and pulled the oars again. Honestly, she sometimes wondered if Shirley was mentally unstable. "Shirley," began Allison, trying to remain patient, "I didn't trick you. I do think of Howie as just a friend. I can't help it if he's not interested in you. You can't blame me for that, can you?"

Shirley folded her arms across her chest and turned her face toward the island.

Despite Shirley's complaints, Allison made good time to the lighthouse dock. But as she tied off the boat, the reality of what they were doing hit her with fresh impact.

"What if we actually found the thieves?" she whispered to Shirley as she glanced nervously around the island.

Shirley's eyes widened. "They wouldn't be here in the daytime, would they? Didn't you say you only saw the lanterns at *night*?"

Allison rolled her eyes. "But they wouldn't need lanterns in the *day*, Shirley."

"We'll only stay a few minutes," ordered Shirley. "If we see anything out of the ordinary, we'll leave immediately."

"Now who's frightened?" asked Allison as she led the way up to the lighthouse.

They walked the perimeter of the lighthouse but didn't see anything unusual. Although it was a small island, they wouldn't have time to search everywhere.

"I think your hunch was stupid," snarled Shirley when her heel got stuck in a rock crevice.

"No one made you come."

"I'm ready to go." Shirley pulled her foot out of her shoe and bent down to extract the heel.

"Not yet." Allison looked over to a slight rise in the island. "I'm going to check that out first."

"I'm leaving," proclaimed Shirley.

"Wait for me at the boat," instructed Allison. "This will only take a few minutes." Allison heard Shirley grumble something, but she paid no mind as she climbed up the rocks and over to the rise. Maybe it was a wild-goose chase, but there was no sense in giving up without a good look.

As Allison rounded the corner, she realized that the rise was actually the backside of a small cave—a perfect place to stash stolen property. Allison considered yelling for Shirley to come but didn't want to risk her wrath without some actual proof. Instead, Allison proceeded into the mouth of the cave. It was a small opening about six feet in diameter, dark and damp inside. Allison wished she had thought to bring a flashlight. She paused for a moment, waiting for her eyes to adjust to the darkness, then continued. After just a few feet, the walls of the cave narrowed a little. She continued a few more steps but still didn't see signs of anything out of the ordinary. Now it was only about five feet wide, and she had to stoop to continue, peering through the shadowy darkness.

Something seemed to glint from the back of the cave. It was reflecting light. She stepped closer and made out the shape of a large candelabra amidst a pile of other shiny objects. As her eyes adjusted to the dimly lit area, she began to discern jewelry, silver, various pieces of china, and even a large oil painting with an ornately gilded frame. Suddenly, her heart caught in her throat. *This is it! I found it!*

She crawled deeper into the cave, just far enough to make absolute certain that it wasn't just her imagination. But it was real. She reached out her hand and touched the cold metal of the candelabra. With a feeling of victory, she turned and practically stumbled out of the cave toward the light of the western horizon. She was about to cry her discovery out to Shirley when she heard the low rumble of a boat engine trawling in the distance. She paused, hunching down behind the rise, and waited to see if the boat was coming this way or just passing by. It seemed very close to the shore for a fishing boat. What if it was the thieves who were stashing their loot there? She knew if she tried to make her way to the dock right now she would be highly visible from sea. But if she didn't go, Shirley would be a sitting duck, waiting in the rowboat at the dock.

Allison listened hard. The boat seemed to be north of the island. The dock was on the south side. For Shirley's sake, she would have to make a run for it. Holding her gray tweed jacket over her head as camouflage against the leaden sky, Allison scuttled over the rocks like a crab. She tripped once, catching her knee on a sharp rock, but continued scurrying as fast as she could go. Finally she reached the lighthouse. She was so glad to see the round white building that she almost hugged it, but instead she ran around to the other side and looked anxiously down toward the dock.

Shirley and the boat were gone!

Allison shook her head and looked again, but no one was there. She ran down to the abandoned dock and looked out across the inlet. There, almost at the other dock, Allison spotted the little rowboat. She wanted to scream, but she could hear the motorboat steadily churning around the backside of the island—near enough to hear her. It might not be the thieves, but just in case, she needed to hide. And she needed a place away from the dock and away from the cave.

Allison ran around to the east side of the island, the side that faced the shoreline, and quickly hunted until she found a large rock that she could slip behind. From her hiding place she could peek out and barely see the dock—that way if the boat turned out to be the Coast Guard, she would know. Hunched behind the rock, she prayed.

Her heart pounded so hard it sounded like thunder in her ears, and it was difficult to hear the boat's motor. She peeked out, but it hadn't come to the dock yet. Perhaps it was only passing by. It was getting darker now, and the wind was picking up. Allison pulled her jacket tighter and tucked her skirt down around her ankles like a blanket. She tried to think. If only the mystery boat would come to the dock and reveal its identity. She hated to think it might be a Coast Guard boat that she was hiding from, but did she dare take the chance of leaving her hiding spot to see? Tears burned in her eyes, a mixture of fear and anger. Why had she ever trusted Shirley?

Allison shivered and waited. How long would it take for Dad to figure out where she was? Would she have to spend the night out here? Then a hopeful thought crossed her mind; perhaps Shirley had heard the approaching boat, gotten scared, and gone for help. *That must be it!* Everyone knew that Shirley Jenson had her problems, but she wouldn't abandon Allison out on this island with a bunch of criminals. *Would she?*

The sun went down and darkness enfolded her, but not in a frightening way. It felt more like a protective blanket. Now they wouldn't be able to spot her—at least not without a light. The sound of the boat engine had dissolved. Perhaps it had only been a fishing boat that had simply passed on by. Or else it had stopped on the island. She waited, listening intensely, but all she heard was wind and lapping waves. She sighed and leaned her head back against the rock. What should she do?

Suddenly, she caught the sound of male voices as snatches of hurried conversation were caught and tossed by the wind.

Perhaps someone was here to help her. Allison sat up and cupped her hand to her ear, hoping to recognize a voice.

"Grab that rope, Roy. . . ."

"Gimme the lantern. . . . Hey, watch out, Fred!"

Allison held her breath. It didn't sound like anyone she knew. It must be the thieves! She hunkered down behind the rock, her heart pounding with fresh fear. *Please, God*, she prayed silently, *send help for me—fast!*

12

After what seemed like hours, the sound of the boat's engine started up again, then steadily churned away. Allison was cold and stiff. Her back ached from being wedged against the hard rock, but she was still too frightened to move. Her mind told her that she was safe now, that the thieves would be long gone, but she couldn't make her legs move. Besides, what could she do? Without a boat, she was stranded. Who knew for how long?

Then it began to rain. Not just a sprinkle but big, hard drops—the kind that promised to go on for hours. Allison knew she couldn't last long in this weather. She was already chilled to the bone. The lighthouse would be locked, but perhaps she could break in somehow. She stood up stiffly and looked around, not completely convinced that all the robbers had left. But by now her coat was soaking wet and she was shivering so badly that she realized her greater fear would be to die from exposure. She made her way to the lighthouse, praying as she went. She remembered another time she had been cold and desperate, trying to get inside the lighthouse, but that time her dad had been inside. Tonight there was no one.

She tried the door, hoping against hope that it might be

327

unlocked. But it wasn't. She picked up a large stone and used it to beat on the doorknob. She knew she was making a lot of noise, but she was too cold to care. Over and over again, she threw the heavy stone against the latch, but the stubborn lock wouldn't give. With the last of her strength, she raised the rock high over her head, then dashed it down on the knob with a loud bang. The knob fell off and the door cracked open.

"Thank you, God," whispered Allison as she pushed open the door and went inside. It was no warmer inside, but at least it wasn't raining. She could barely see in the darkness but felt her way over to where she knew the old wood stove was. She reached to the wooden mantel above and carefully felt along the surface until she found a kerosene lamp and a box of matches. She moved the lantern down to the floor and away from the view of a window and lit it, turning it down low. It gave her enough light to see around the interior of the lighthouse and decide what must be done next. She closed the door and scooted a heavy dresser in front of it, then located an old coat that she hung over the thick glass window. Hopefully that would keep anyone from noticing the light inside.

She looked over to the firebox, which was equipped with kindling and firewood. Did she dare start a fire and risk attracting attention from the smoke? Did she dare not? Besides, it was so rainy and cloudy, maybe no one would notice. She quickly stacked the wood like a tepee over a crumpled piece of brown paper—Grandpa O'Brian had taught her how to make a good fire—then lit it. Soon it was crackling. She then peeled off her soggy coat and hung it by the fire to dry. Her clothes were damp, too, but as she hovered over the snapping flames, she slowly grew warmer. She noticed the old patchwork quilt on the little bed and wrapped it around her like a cape, continuing to rub her hands over the fire until the feeling returned to her fingers. She sighed. This wasn't so bad.

After a while she searched the cupboard in the kitchen area to uncover some tea, dried beans, flour, sugar, and a tin of sardines. She ate the sardines as she waited for the water to boil on top of the wood stove. Then she made herself a big mug of tea with a couple spoonfuls of lumpy sugar thrown in. It was delicious. She pulled a chair up to the fire and sat down.

She would probably be just fine for the night. That is, as long as the thieves didn't return and find her! Now that her fear of freezing was gone, the threat from the thieves became terrifyingly real again. What if they returned and noticed smoke or her lantern in the lighthouse? She looked around the room for another piece of furniture that she could wedge against the door. She moved the heavy wooden table against the dresser, then shoved a wardrobe up against that. It would take a strong man to push through all those pieces. Just to be safe, she turned off the lantern.

She sat back down in front of the fire, thankful for the warm glow that kept the room from being completely dark. She leaned back in the rocker and for the first time in hours relaxed. She had done everything she could do. She would trust God for everything else. She dozed off for a while, then awoke with a start in the darkness. *Where am I?*

Then it all came back to her, and she noticed that her fire was almost out. She threw on a couple more pieces of wood and looked at her watch in the dim light of the fire. It was nine o'clock, but it felt more like midnight. By now she felt fairly certain that Shirley had purposely abandoned her. What would people think of her when they heard about this little episode? Would anyone ever trust Shirley Jenson again?

Allison made another cup of tea and wondered how long it would take for someone to come. Would she have to spend the night here, then perhaps make a signal fire in the morning for Dad or George to spot? She looked at a small desk that sat under the window. Perhaps she could find paper and pencil and begin to write the news story that had been forming itself in her head. "Thieves' Lair Uncovered at Jenson Light" . . .

She found an old, weathered school tablet and began to furiously write her story. It sounded like something from another century, with pirates and booty, yet it was a modern-day tale with an interesting twist. It was even more unique that she was writing it from the lighthouse while awaiting her own rescue. For a moment, but only a moment, she was almost thankful to Shirley for her deviousness. Naturally, Allison didn't have all the facts yet, but that would be easy to fill in once the police picked up the thieves. She hoped that would be soon.

Just as she finished her story, she heard a sound outside. Something beyond the steady rhythm of wind and rain. She quickly blew out the lantern and held her breath as she listened. Her heart was beating furiously again, and thoughts of the robbers lurking outside the door filled her with panic. What if they could get it open? There was no place to hide in the tiny lighthouse. If she went up the stairs to the light, she would be trapped for sure. Perhaps she could hide behind the door, then make a break for it when they weren't looking. She could try to hide outside—

Someone was pounding on the door. *Dear God, help!* she prayed as she tried to put on her shoes and find her jacket. The pounding increased.

"Allison!"

Allison leaped from the chair. It was Dad! She knew it. She ran to the door.

"Dad?" she cried, but her voice came out in a trembling whisper.

"Allison? Are you in there?"

"Yes!" she screamed this time, and her voice cooperated. "Dad, I'm in here! Just a minute and I'll open the door." She pushed the wardrobe aside and then the table. Finally, she shoved the dresser back just as James forced the door open.

"Allison!" he cried as she tumbled into his arms. "Thank God, you're okay!" He looked over his shoulder, then shouted, "She's in the lighthouse, Andrew. Safe and sound."

"Oh, Dad, I'm so glad you came," sobbed Allison. She clung to him tightly, unwilling to let go. "I thought I'd have to spend the night. I was so scared."

"How in the world did you get here?" asked Dad.

"You mean you don't know?" Allison stepped back and looked at him in wonder. Just as she was about to answer, Andrew came inside the lighthouse.

"Are you all right, Allison?" His face looked pale with concern as he closed the door behind him.

"I'm fine now," said Allison. She turned to her father, who was busy lighting the lantern and throwing more wood on the fire. "You really don't know how I got out here?"

He shook his head as he dusted off his hands. "When you didn't come home after school, I assumed you were at Grace's. But when dinnertime came and you still weren't home, I decided to call and check. Andrew said that Shirley had given you a ride home—"

"That's what Howie said," agreed Andrew.

"So," James continued, "I tried calling the Jensons, but no one was home. I know this is their bridge night, but I figured I might get ahold of Shirley. I tried several times with no luck. I was starting to feel frantic—almost ready to call the police. But then I thought perhaps I could track down Shirley's parents. With Muriel's help I managed to call all their bridge friends until we finally found them at the Hatfields'. But they said Shirley was at home. I explained that you were missing, and they said they hadn't seen you but to try calling their house again. So I tried and tried. . . ."

"But how did you know I was here?" asked Allison again.

"Well, I got worried about tying up the phone in case you were trying to call me. So I hung up the phone and sat down and prayed. In just a few minutes the phone rang. And it was the strangest thing. A muffled voice said that I would find you on the island."

"By then I had come over," added Andrew. "When James told me what the mysterious caller said, we told George to phone the police, just in case, and then we ran to see if the rowboat was gone."

"And it wasn't?" Allison knew that Shirley had returned it but wasn't certain that she knew how to tie it properly. It could have floated out into the ocean.

"The boat was there, but it did appear that someone had used it," James said. "The oars were sticking out, and it had a pretty loose knot."

"So we hopped in and came over," said Andrew. "No easy trip, since the tide's going out right now."

"I'm so sorry," said Allison again. Suddenly, she realized what a foolhardy expedition this had been—even if her hunch *had* been right. "Let me explain everything."

Dad nodded. "We deserve some explanations."

"Let's see . . ." Allison sighed deeply. "When I heard my friend Susan's house had been burglarized, Howie and I were trying to imagine how the burglars were moving up and down the coast without getting caught. We thought of them using a boat, then I remembered that Caroline saw a lantern moving around the lighthouse last week. I wondered if they might be stashing their loot here. It seemed like a wild hunch at the time—"

"Pretty crazy," agreed Andrew.

"But when Shirley heard me talking about it, she said she

was going to come investigate. She said that she had a right to, since the lighthouse has her name."

James chuckled. "It figures. But what happened then?"

"Well, I didn't want her to steal my hunch and come make some big discovery without me." Allison looked down at her feet. "And so I came with her. I wanted to run up to the house to let someone know, but Shirley wouldn't wait. I'm sorry. It was stupid."

"But where's Shirley?" James asked, looking around the lighthouse with alarm. "Is she okay?"

Allison laughed. "I'm sure she's just fine." She held her hands over the fire and continued. "Shirley was ready to leave, but I wanted to have a look beyond that little rise on the north side—"

"You mean where the cave is?"

"That's right. Only I didn't realize there was a cave there."

"I almost forgot about that cave," said Andrew thoughtfully. "That would be a good place to hide something."

"Exactly," said Allison. "So when I found the cave, I took a closer look. Do you know what I found?" She stared at them both with wide eyes. "A bunch of silver stuff and what looked like stolen goods."

Her father's face looked worried. "You were right? The thieves are using the island?"

Allison nodded with satisfaction. "Yep."

James looked at the pile of furniture near the door. "So you had good reason to barricade that door like that."

"Do you think they'll come while we're here?" asked Andrew.

"They already have," said Allison. "I was afraid they might come back, though. That's why I put that stuff there."

"Maybe we should put it back," suggested Andrew. "At least until the police or Coast Guard get here."

"Not a bad idea, Andrew." James stood, and they quickly shoved the pieces back into place. "Now, tell us, Allison. What became of Shirley?"

"Well, just when I discovered the cave, I heard the sound of a boat and got scared that it might be the thieves. I climbed over the rocks and began to run for the dock. But the boat was gone. I spotted Shirley on the other side of the inlet. She had left without me."

"You're kidding!" Andrew looked at her in shocked disbelief.

"I couldn't believe it, either," said Allison. "I told myself that she was going for help. But I doubt if she even realized that the thieves were coming. I hadn't had a chance to tell her about the cave yet."

"So what did you do?" Andrew asked with wide eyes.

"I hid behind a rock on the west side. I could hear their voices—it was pretty scary. I just prayed and waited until I was sure they had gone." Allison sighed. "It seemed like hours, but it was really only about forty minutes. Then it began to rain, and I was freezing cold. So I broke into the lighthouse. Sorry about that, Dad. You'll have to fix the knob."

"Don't you worry about that." He put his arm around her. "I'm so glad that my little girl is a survivor, but I don't know if I can take any more of these hair-raising adventures."

"I'm really sorry, Dad. I never dreamed it would turn into something like this. When we left it was daylight, the tide was out, and it seemed safe. But I should have let you know."

"Yes," James agreed. "You should've let me know." He shook his head. "I still cannot believe that Shirley would do such a thing. I know she's pulled some crazy stunts, but I never would've imagined this—"

"Do you think she's the one who called you, Dad?"

He nodded. "I'm sure of it now. It was a female voice."

334

"Maybe she felt a twinge of guilt," said Andrew. "Or maybe she was afraid she was going to get into trouble."

"I'll see that she gets into plenty of trouble," James said. He looked at his watch. "I wonder if George got anyone to come out here. I thought we could wait until the tide shifted, but that won't be for a while. Still, I don't like the idea of us rowing out there when there could be a boatload of crooks nearby."

"I could fix you both a cup of tea," suggested Allison. "And maybe the Coast Guard will come."

"Sounds like a good plan." He glanced at the empty sardine tin. "That your dinner, Allison?"

She nodded as she poured steaming water into the cups. "I thought it would take too long to cook the beans."

"Now I wished I'd waited a minute for Muriel. She was running around like a wild woman trying to throw some food together for you."

"Don't talk about food," warned Allison as she handed Andrew a cup of tea.

"Thanks, Al," Andrew said with a warming smile. He pointed at her tablet now splayed across the floor. "Were you working on something?"

"Yes. I decided to write my story about finding the thieves for the paper. I promised Howie that I would have something for him by tomorrow."

Her father laughed. "You're supposed to report the news, Allison, not make it!"

"I couldn't help it—" Allison stopped in midsentence. She heard something outside. They all stood silently listening. Had the thieves returned?

13

The sound of a horn blasted outside, and Allison nearly jumped out of her skin.

"It's the Coast Guard!" James exclaimed. He and Andrew began to remove the furniture barricade so they could get out the door. Allison grabbed her tablet and picked up the lantern; following them out, she waved the light for a signal. Before long the cutter was docked at the lighthouse. It seemed that George had called the police and the Coast Guard to check on them. James quickly explained all that had transpired in the past several hours to the worried captain.

"You'll have to talk to my daughter, Allison, about all the details," said James as he proudly presented her to the captain.

"Pleasure to meet you, miss. Now, tell me, can you describe their craft?"

Allison frowned. "I didn't actually *see* their boat because I was hiding, but I heard the motor—it didn't sound like it was a real big boat, though. And I did hear a couple of names—"

"What were the names?" asked the captain.

"Roy and Fred," said Allison. "I wrote them down."

"When do you think the men were last on the island?"

"I'd guess it was about four-thirty when they arrived," said

Allison. "And I'd say they left after about an hour, but it was too dark outside to read my watch by then."

"Have they been back?"

"Not to my knowledge. But I've been inside the lighthouse; I might not have heard them."

"Thanks for all your help," said the captain. "We better check this out right away."

Flashlights were quickly found, and the captain organized a small search crew to explore the cave and other parts of the island. He told Allison, Andrew, and James to stay with the remaining crew—in case the thieves were anywhere nearby.

"I hope the stash is still there," said Allison as they sat in the cozy cabin of the cutter. "It sounded like they were carrying boxes and stuff. It could be that they moved it all away. . . ."

"Well, if that's the case, maybe they can still have a stakeout here," suggested Andrew. "If the thieves think this is a good hideout, they might come back."

A Coast Guardsman brought the three of them paper cups of hot chocolate. "You folks look like you could use a pick-me-up," he said. "Have you been stuck out here for long?"

"Allison's been out here since around four," said James. He pushed a curl out of her eyes. "I think she's pretty worn out." He turned to Andrew. "This is making an awfully late night for you, too, Andrew. I figure Allison should stay home tomorrow, but I hope we're not messing up your week."

"No problem," said Andrew. "You think I'd rather be home missing out on all this excitement?"

"Probably not," James grinned.

"Thanks for coming with Dad, Andrew," Allison said quietly.

"Well, I was worried about you, too."

"I feel bad worrying people so much," said Allison. "It seems I'm good at it."

"Hey," Andrew called to the guardsman, "can you let the folks on the mainland know that Allison is okay?"

"Sure, we can radio the police, and if you give us a phone number, they can call and let someone know."

"Good thinking, Andrew," James said after he told the guardsman the number.

Allison reached up and rubbed a sore spot on her neck. "My locket!"

"What's wrong?" asked Andrew.

"I must've lost my locket when I was running around on the rocks." Allison frowned sadly. "I guess things could be worse, but I'll miss my locket." She finished her cocoa and leaned into her Dad's shoulder, then closed her eyes and sighed. Safe. She breathed a prayer of thanks, then allowed the quiet rumbling of the boat's engine to lull her into a half sleep.

Before long the captain's search party returned.

"We found the loot," announced the captain as Allison jolted awake.

"That's great," said James. He looked around. "But where is it?"

The captain chuckled. "Well, we were about to haul it out when we realized that we would only recover the goods, but not the thieves. So we collected a few bits of evidence and left everything as it was. We'll leave a couple guardsmen, a short-wave radio, and some provisions to wait it out at the lighthouse. And hopefully, we'll catch some thieves."

Two volunteers were chosen, and the rest of the crew quickly gathered the necessary items and helped take them to the lighthouse. Allison didn't envy the two fellows who were staying behind, but they seemed to think it was a great adventure. And she noticed that they each had a gun.

"I'll be happy to keep an eye on things, too," James offered.

"We have a pretty good view of the lighthouse from a couple of windows."

"That would be helpful," said the captain. "And now, I think we should get you good people home. I tied your rowboat to the cutter, and we'll take you across to your dock."

"We'd appreciate the lift," said James.

"Not nearly as much as we appreciate this young lady's help in solving this crime spree," said the captain.

When they reached the dock, the captain helped them all off, tipping his hat to Allison. "Oh, one more thing," said the captain. "I'll have to request that you all keep this business quiet until the crooks are caught. You can imagine how it would mess things up if word got out."

Allison groaned. "Does that mean I can't run my story in the school paper?"

The captain frowned. "Sorry, but until the thieves are caught—mum's the word. Otherwise you would be risking the lives of my men out there."

"Of course," said Allison. "I understand. But do you think you could let us know when the thieves are caught? I'd like to run my story then."

He winked at her. "You'll be the first to know, Allison O'Brian. And thanks again for your help."

Allison sighed as they walked up the road toward home. "Looks like I still don't have a story for the school paper."

Her dad laughed. "Don't tell me that after all that has happened, you're still worried about that. Besides, I think you better stay home tomorrow. You could wind up sick as a dog after all you've been through. And I'm pretty sure that Muriel will be having a stakeout right next to your bedroom door tomorrow morning."

"Oh, Dad," said Allison in mock exasperation.

"And as for you, Andrew," James added, "maybe you should

339

just spend the night here. I know that Muriel has already gotten my old room cleaned out for you."

"Thanks," said Andrew, "and I would, but I'm worried about Grace and the kids being alone when there are still burglars around. I think I'll head for home, sir."

James threw an arm around Andrew's shoulder. "You're more on the ball tonight than I am, Andrew. Of course that's the right thing to do."

They told Andrew good-night at the jalopy, then went inside the house. Allison was greeted by a warm hug from Muriel and then whooshed up the stairs and into a hot bathtub before she could even protest. "It's the only way to take the chill out of your bones," said Muriel. "Now, don't fall asleep in the tub, and I'll be right back with a snack and a flannel nightie."

Muriel had been right about the tub. For the first time in eight hours, Allison finally felt thoroughly warmed. After her bath, she sat in bed and ate toast and peaches and a cup of warm milk.

"You look like you're being well taken care of," said James as he peeked in her door. "I just got off the phone with Hal Jenson. I decided not to wait until morning to give him a piece of my mind. Besides, I didn't want to take the chance of having Shirley getting off to school without knowing that her 'best friend' was okay."

Allison laughed. "As if she'd care."

"Hal couldn't believe that Shirley would do such a dreadful thing—he was actually offended that I would even suggest it. I told him it was easily proved."

James shook his fist dramatically. "Who knows what she'll do next. I know that I don't want you ever getting in a car with her again, Allison. Not unless some serious changes take place."

Allison nodded soberly. "I won't, Dad. To tell you the truth, I had reservations at the time—"

"You've got to learn to listen to that still, small voice, Allison," he instructed gently. "Remember what the pastor said last Sunday?"

"I know, Dad. But sometimes it's not real clear. Because I know I'm supposed to love Shirley—even if she's my enemy."

"That's right, Allison. But loving her doesn't mean that you have to trust her. Or to put your life in her hands."

"I think I understand. And you know, it's funny, Dad, I don't even feel horribly angry at her anymore. I actually feel sorry for her. I think she has some serious problems inside her." Allison leaned back and yawned.

"I think you are exactly right." James leaned over and removed the empty tray, then kissed her good-night. "Time for someone to get some rest. Don't worry about school in the morning."

"I won't," said Allison sleepily. "I just wish I could have turned in my story. . . ."

"All in good time, Allison. Sweet dreams."

❦

The next morning, Allison awoke to the jarring sound of a telephone ringing. She looked at her bedside clock. *Half past nine!* She was just about to leap out of bed when she remembered her late night and misadventures of the previous day. No school for her this morning. And it was a good thing because her entire body felt as if she'd been used as a punching bag. Probably a result of getting chilled and scrambling around on the rocks. She sighed and leaned back into her pillow. Her only regret was that she had no story for Howie. The *Pirate Chest* would look awfully barren this week. Maybe it didn't matter, since it was almost Christmas vacation. Still, she felt badly for Howie—she had seen the concern on his face yesterday.

"Are you awake?" her father knocked lightly on her door.

"Yes, just barely. Come in."

"I've got some good news," he said with a wide grin.

"Tell me—what is it?" She sat up in bed eagerly.

"They caught your pirates red-handed."

"Are you serious? When? How? Where—"

"Slow down, reporter girl." James held up both hands and laughed. "One question at a time. Maybe you'd like to take notes."

"Actually, I would." Allison jumped out of bed.

"Okay, then, I've got an idea. Why don't you get yourself dressed, and I'll fill you in on the details while you eat breakfast."

"I'll be down in a snap."

Allison decided to dress for school. She wanted to finish her story and then hand deliver it to Howie in time to make the paper. She wished she could send it into the *Port View Herald*, too, but Sam Long had probably already assigned it to a reporter by now. She knew that newspapers kept close contact with the police on stories like this.

Her father was already seated at the table reading the *Herald* when she came downstairs. "That was record time," he said as he laid down his paper. "There's a story about the most recent robberies, including your friend Susan's home. But nothing about the lighthouse yet."

Allison sat down at the table. "I was hoping I could finish my story and take it in to Howie today."

"You kids these days!" he said in mock concern. "Grace told me that Andrew got up and went to school this morning, too. Now, when I was a kid I'd do anything to get a day off from school. But you kids won't even let us keep you home."

"You should be happy, Dad. That means we like school."

James grinned. "Well, I'm not surprised. I figured that's what you would do. And I have an idea, Allison."

"What's that?"

"How about if you type it at home and use carbon paper. That way you can give a copy to the *Port View Herald*."

"Really? You think they'd want my story? I thought they'd probably already have a reporter on it."

"Maybe . . ." Dad's eyes twinkled with mystery.

"Have you been talking to someone?"

"Actually, the phone's been ringing all morning. But Sam Long did get wind of yesterday's events and would like to interview you today. I mentioned that you were writing your own story for the school paper, and he sounded very interested. He did mention that a reporter is already covering the main story, but that yours would make a very interesting sidebar."

Allison beamed at him as she set down her empty orange juice glass. "Sounds like this is going to be a fun day!"

Muriel stepped in and placed a plate of ham and eggs in front of Allison. "Just don't you be overdoing it," she warned. "If I had my way, we'd keep you in bed all day—what with getting soaked to the skin and sitting in a drafty lighthouse all night."

Allison smiled up at her. "Don't worry, Muriel. I feel just swell. If it makes you feel any better, I'll go to bed extra early tonight."

"That makes me feel a little better."

Allison turned back to James. "Now, tell me how they caught the burglars." She picked up her pencil, ready to write.

"Okay, but don't let your breakfast get cold." He took a sip of coffee and slowly began. "Early this morning, the crooks decided to pick up their ill-gotten gain. Maybe they suspected that someone was on to them—"

"Or maybe they saw smoke from my fire last night."

"Could be. Anyway, the guardsmen in the lighthouse heard their boat and slipped out and caught them loading the stolen property into their fishing boat. There were three of them. I've got their names written down at my desk, the number of houses they broke into, and a partial list of stolen goods. The police think almost everything will be recovered."

"That's great, Dad. Susan will be so pleased." Allison took a big bite of eggs, then furiously wrote some notes.

"The Coast Guard cutter came by and picked them up, then towed their boat out around eight this morning. I wanted to wake you up, but Muriel said absolutely not. George and I went out on the dock to watch, and I took quite a few photographs for you."

"Thanks, Dad. Hey, maybe I could give them to Howie to develop in time for the paper."

"Sure. Maybe Sam Long would like some, too. I didn't see any newspaper people around."

Allison finished her last bite, then hastily wiped her mouth with her napkin. "Thanks, Dad. If you'll excuse me, I'd like to go finish my story."

"Off you go," he said. "I'll be in the basement. Let me know when you need a ride to school."

14

Allison took her Dad's advice and used a piece of carbon paper in the typewriter to make a carbon copy of her article. It was tricky work and somewhat messy, but by noon, she had corrected her last mistake and carefully rolled the two pages out of the upright Underwood typewriter. What a story! She almost didn't believe it herself when she skimmed it for the final time. Howie would be so pleased, and maybe Sam would like it, too.

She ran down the basement stairs to let her dad know she was finished, but when she saw what he was working on, she stopped in her steps and just stared.

"Wow, Dad," she breathed. "That is absolutely gorgeous."

He turned and smiled. "You like it?"

"Yes. And I think Grace is going to like it, too." Allison stepped closer and studied the painting. As usual, it was a somewhat impressionist style, only softer somehow. It almost seemed as if Grace were draped in a soft white cloud, but upon closer look, Allison could see it was a dress, perhaps even a wedding gown. She put her hand on his arm. "I think it's beautiful, Dad. Does Grace know about it?"

"No, and I don't want you to spill the beans. It's a Christmas-wedding present. And if she doesn't mind, I'd like to hang it over the fireplace in Father's old bedroom. I think Grace and I will take that room, since it's the largest."

"I won't say a word." Allison looked at the portrait again. Somehow seeing Grace in this light erased any lingering doubt that Allison might have had about Dad still caring for Marsha. There's no way he could paint a picture like this without being totally in love with Grace.

"Well, I'm sure you didn't come down here to ogle my work," he said as he wiped off his brush. "And I'm ready when you are."

"Swell. I finished my story—complete with a carbon copy for Sam."

"Good girl. Let me clean my hands, and we can be on our way."

James decided it would save time to swing by the newspaper office first. He led Allison to the reception desk and proudly introduced her to a sweet-faced, gray-haired woman.

"I'm so happy to meet you, Allison," said the woman. "I'm Clara Long. Sam is my boy, and he gets me to come fill in for the receptionist sometimes." She winked at Allison. "I've heard a lot about you, Allison O'Brian. I'll let Sam know you're here."

After a short wait, Sam came out and shook hands with both of them. "Good to see you, James," he said as he led them to his office. "You must be awfully proud of your daughter."

James nodded. "You better believe it. And I think you're going to like what she's brought you."

Allison produced the carbon copy. "I'm giving the original to Howie for the *Pirate Chest*," she said apologetically. "But Dad thought you might like to see a copy, too."

"That's for sure." Sam took a few minutes to scan the story. "This looks intriguing, Allison. Do you mind if I edit it and run it in tomorrow's paper? Of course, it might end up scooping your own school paper."

Allison laughed. "It'll only scoop us by a couple of hours. Our paper comes out on Thursday morning."

"Great. Then we'll both be happy. I have a reporter, Henry Biggs, working on the whole story. He would like to ask you a few questions if you have time."

"Sure," agreed Allison. "Lead me to him."

Henry wrapped up his questions within twenty minutes, and Allison and her father got a burger at Wally's, then headed over to school.

"I wonder if I should have tried to call Howie," fretted Allison. "He may have already put the paper to bed by now."

"Just tell him to stop the presses," teased James.

Suddenly, Allison remembered Shirley. Would she see Shirley at school today? And if she did, what would she say to her?

James glanced her way. "Are you all right? You look like you're not feeling too well. Maybe Muriel was right about resting today."

"I'm okay, Dad." She spoke slowly. "I was just thinking of Shirley."

"Oh." Her father shook his head as he turned into the school parking lot. "I never heard back from Hal. I was planning on following up with him this afternoon. At the time, I didn't think you'd be going to school today. You know, Allison, you don't have to go to class if you'd rather not. I already called the office and excused you. I could drop the story in the office—"

"No, Dad. I am not going to let Shirley ruin my life."

James smiled. "That's the O'Brian spirit. And remember, like you said last night, it's Shirley who has the problem. As long as you keep a safe distance, you should be just fine."

"Right." Allison hoped that was true.

"Do you want me to wait for you? Or do you want to catch a ride with Heather and Andrew?"

"I'll ride with them." Allison blew him a kiss. "Thanks for everything, Dad. Tell Muriel not to worry—I'm fine."

"Have a good afternoon. And if you see Shirley Jenson, don't let her get to you."

Allison gave him the thumbs-up sign, then dashed up the steps and into the front door. Students were already in sixth-period class, and Allison hurried down the deserted hallway toward the art room. She wondered if Shirley would be there. Allison explained to her teacher that she had been excused for the day but then decided to come for her last two classes. Mr. Roper just smiled and waved her to her seat. She glanced around the room, but Shirley was not there. Allison sighed and pulled out her pen-and-ink drawing of a clipper ship. She wanted to finish it in time to have it framed for Dad for a Christmas present, but there were only three days to fill in a whole lot of details. So she got right to work, and when the bell rang, she realized she had accomplished quite a bit.

She knew that she probably wouldn't be able to locate Howie until after school, and besides, she had an assignment due in algebra, so she hurried to her last class of the day. She tried to keep her eyes off the clock, but it seemed like the math class would never end. Finally the bell rang, and she sprang from her seat and practically ran for the journalism room.

"Hey, you're here!" exclaimed Andrew when she nearly tackled him coming around a corner.

"Yes," said Allison breathlessly, "and I've got to find Howie."

Andrew frowned slightly. "Howie?"

"To give him my story," said Allison. "For the paper."

"Oh yes, of course." Andrew jogged to keep up with her on her way to the journalism room. "I'm heading that way, too. So what kind of a story did you manage to put—"

"Oh, that's right," said Allison. "You don't know yet!"

"Don't know what?"

"They caught the robbers this morning! So I finished my story."

"They *caught* them?" Andrew looked at her incredulously as he opened the journalism room door. "Tell me all about—"

"Hey, Allison!" called Howie. "I was about to give up on you."

"Then stop the presses!" she cried for pure dramatic pleasure. "Because have I got a story for you!"

"What a relief! I was saving a spot for you, but when I heard you weren't at school today, I thought I'd have to use some filler that Beverly had pulled together yesterday. Not only that, but Shirley hasn't turned in anything, either. This was going to be a pretty sorry edition to wrap up the year."

"Have you seen Shirley today?" asked Allison as she handed over her story.

"Nope." Howie adjusted his glasses, then skimmed the article. "You're kidding, Allison!" He looked up at her in amazement. "You mean your hunch was right? This is incredible." He turned to Andrew. "Do you know about this?"

Andrew nodded. "Mostly. I helped rescue her last night. Well, not exactly rescue—"

Allison stopped him. "I'd call it a rescue. I was scared out of my wits before you and Dad got there."

"You seemed in control to me," said Andrew. "You should have seen her, Howie. She was holed up in the lighthouse with a barricade blocking the door—"

"Wow!" interrupted Howie. "This is terrific, Allison. And they already caught the criminals and everything. What a story."

"Yes," agreed Allison. Then she reached into her pocket for the undeveloped film. "And I almost forgot. My dad got pictures of the Coast Guard hauling away the pirate boat." She handed it to Howie. "I hope you have time to develop these. I told Sam I was handing it over to you. He may give you a call."

Howie held on to the film as if it were a precious diamond. "This is absolutely great, Allison. You must feel rather proud of yourself."

"I hoped it would make the last newspaper of the year a paper to remember. And I'm sure I'll never find a story half this exciting again. In fact, I don't even want to. It's not something I'd care to repeat."

"So what happened to Shirley, then?" Howie looked from Allison to Andrew with mild curiosity. "Did you leave her out there on the island?" he teased.

"Actually, you've got the right story," said Andrew. "Now you just switch characters."

Howie's eyes widened. "You mean Shirley left Allison out there?"

"Not only did she leave her," declared Andrew, "but she didn't even tell anyone until after nine o'clock at night."

Howie shook his head. "No kidding?"

Allison was uncomfortable with them both staring at her as if she were worthy of great pity. "Well, at least I got a good story out of it," she quipped lightly.

"But don't you just want to strangle her?" asked Howie.

Allison shrugged. "I don't know. I'm still sort of mad, but I feel sorry for her."

"Sorry for *her*?" exclaimed Howie. "Whatever for?"

Allison sighed. "I just think she must be awfully unhappy inside. . . ."

"Or just mean," said Howie. "Well, if this is going in the paper, I better get a move on."

"Oh, another thing," said Allison.

Howie looked up hopefully. "Yes?"

"The *Port View Herald* is using the story, too. It will come out tomorrow just like our paper. I hope you don't mind."

"Not at all. Thanks again, Allison. This is really swell!"

As Andrew and Allison walked slowly through the nearly deserted hallways, she recapped the story that Dad had told her that morning about how the Coast Guard caught the crooks. He listened with genuine interest, asking good questions in appropriate places. Suddenly, it seemed as if nothing had ever come between them. Allison thought about all she'd been through recently—how during that time she had completely forgotten the heartache she had been suffering because of him. Now it all seemed so trivial and childish.

"Andrew," said Allison as they reached the door, "thanks for being such a good friend."

He smiled down on her. "I wouldn't have it any other way."

Part of her wondered what that really meant, but the rest of her said to just let it go and simply enjoy the friendship. That was the best part of their relationship anyway. Why spoil it?

15

It was foggy and gray out, but Allison's heart felt light. She spotted Heather already waiting by the jalopy. Allison ran up and gave Heather a big hug.

"I've missed you," cried Allison.

Heather smiled. "That's nice, but it's only been a day."

"But it was a *very long* day," said Allison, then she laughed. "Didn't Andrew tell you what happened?"

A look of realization crossed Heather's face. "Oh, you mean about the Christmas dance—"

"No," interrupted Andrew. "I didn't tell anyone yet, Allison. Remember what the Coast Guard captain said?"

"Coast Guard?" repeated Heather.

"Christmas dance?" questioned Allison.

"Would someone please tell me what we are all talking about?"

Heather looked thoroughly confused, and Allison knew how she felt. She wondered if Heather knew something about Andrew and the Christmas dance. Perhaps that he had invited Beverly. Well, it didn't matter. The important thing was that she and Andrew were friends once again.

"Let me explain," began Allison, and she launched into the colorful drama of all that had happened yesterday, and then how the thieves were caught just this morning, and finally about how her news story would be in both papers tomorrow. She paused to catch her breath.

"I had no idea you were in such danger," said Heather. "Andrew was very clandestine about the whole thing last night. In fact, I thought he'd gone over to talk to your dad about the dance—"

"It's starting to drizzle, Heather," interrupted Andrew as he opened the passenger's door. "How about if we finish Allison's story on our way home."

"But, Allison," continued Heather as Andrew began to drive. "How did you get stuck on the island without a boat?"

"Oh, I guess I left out one little detail," chuckled Allison.

"A rather big detail, don't you think?" said Andrew.

"Actually, about a five-foot-five detail."

"What?" said Heather. "You two are driving me mad with suspense. Have you ever considered starting your own mystery hour on the radio?"

Allison explained the role that Shirley had played in yesterday's adventure episode.

"Oh my," said Heather. "I'm so sorry, Allison."

"*You're* sorry. Whatever for?"

"I'm always telling you not to be so suspicious of Shirley— that she really isn't all that bad."

Allison laughed. "Oh, that's okay. I know that you like to think of people in a positive way, Heather. I like that. And most of the time you're right."

"But not about Shirley," said Heather glumly.

"Not about Shirley," agreed Andrew.

Heather sighed. "Well, now that we've wrapped that up. Did Andrew tell you?"

"Tell me what?" asked Allison.

"Not now, Heather," urged Andrew.

"But why put it off? It's only two days away!"

"Heather!" hissed Andrew.

Allison just knew that Andrew had asked Beverly to the Christmas dance. And while she wasn't thrilled with the idea, at least she wasn't upset. Perhaps the best way to smooth things over would be to seem excited about the whole thing.

"I think I know what you're talking about," said Allison.

"You do?" Andrew glanced quickly at her, then focused his attention back on the road.

"Yes," said Allison. "I think it has to do with the Christmas dance."

"That's right," said Heather triumphantly.

"Let's see," said Allison. "I'll bet that Andrew is planning to go."

"You're good, Allison," said Heather.

"And I'll bet that he is taking Beverly Howard!" She forced a smile to her lips.

"Beverly Howard?" cried Heather. "Andrew, you didn't invite Beverly, did you?"

Andrew cleared his throat. "Actually, Beverly asked me."

"Beverly asked you?" Heather sounded horrified. "I didn't think Beverly was like *that*. That's more a Shirley Jenson sort of thing."

Andrew laughed. "Actually, I think it's okay for a girl to invite a guy. It takes a lot of nerve, if you ask me."

Allison was listening silently, desperately trying to think of something light and witty to say, but no words came. Instead, she simply said, "Well, that's nice that you're taking Beverly to the dance, Andrew. You should both have a very nice time."

"I'm not taking her—"

"But I thought you said—"

"I said *she asked me*. I didn't say that I accepted."

"Poor Beverly," said Heather.

"Oh," said Allison.

"But don't worry about Beverly," said Andrew. "She *is* going to the dance."

"But not with you?" asked Heather.

"Not with me. She's going with Howie."

"Howie?" Allison repeated incredulously.

"Yes," said Andrew. "Does that surprise you?"

"Well, a little, I suppose . . ."

"But Beverly and Howie are good friends."

"Yes, I suppose . . ."

Andrew groaned.

"What is it, Andrew?" asked Heather.

"Maybe I just ruined everything."

"What do you mean?" asked Allison. She felt as confused as Heather had seemed earlier.

"Let me tell you the whole story," said Andrew. "Yesterday, while we were working on the paper, Beverly asked me if I wanted to go to the Christmas dance with her. I thanked her for asking me but said that I had been thinking of asking someone else. She asked who, and I said I was thinking of asking Allison if her father would give me permission—"

Allison gasped, afraid to raise her hopes too soon. "Really?"

"Of course," said Andrew. "Why not?"

"I just thought that you and Beverly . . ."

"Beverly's nice and all, but she's a little too serious about this dating stuff for me. I wanted to take someone to the dance who is a good friend—someone I can have fun with. A pal."

Allison smiled. That's what she wanted, too.

"So after Beverly realized that I wasn't game, she headed over for Howie and asked him." Andrew glanced nervously at Allison. "This is where I might have blown it, Allison. You see, when Beverly asked Howie, he mentioned that he had been thinking of asking you but hadn't had the opportunity. Well,

Beverly got a little nutty then—going on about how it seemed everyone wanted to take Allison O'Brian to the dance. It's probably a good thing you weren't there, Allison. And she told Howie that I was already taking you. So Howie agreed to go with Beverly, and then Beverly was back in good spirits again and actually suggested that the four of us might go together. You know, just four friends out having a good time." Andrew paused and took a breath. "So did I mess everything up, Al? Did you want to go to the dance with Howie?"

"No, not at all."

"So," Andrew took a breath, "do you think you'd like to go to the dance with me?"

"Sure. It sounds like fun. But I don't know what Dad—"

"I mentioned it to him last night when I stopped by your house. He didn't seem to think it was a problem."

"There," said Heather triumphantly. "I thought we'd never get that worked out. Andrew told me on Sunday that he was thinking of asking you. Talk about a bad case of procrastination."

Allison laughed. "Actually, I think Andrew's timing is perfect."

"You do?" said Andrew.

Allison grinned. "Yep. I needed a couple of days to work some things out."

"Like what?" asked Heather.

"Oh, just things like who your friends are, what's really important, you know . . ."

Heather laughed. "You're lucky that you're asking a girl to a formal dance who happens to have a closet full of beautiful gowns to choose from."

"Not a whole closet, Heather," argued Allison good-naturedly. "But my movie-star mother has been more than generous with her hand-me-down gowns."

"So you think my last-minute timing won't be a problem?" said Andrew.

"Not at all, Andrew. I'm already looking forward to Friday. And I think it will be great fun to go with Howie and Beverly. Like you said, four friends out having a good time—it sounds great to me."

Andrew sighed loudly. "Phew, I'm glad that's done. I don't know how Beverly got up the nerve to ask not only me, but then Howie, too."

"Beverly is a gutsy gal," said Allison. "I don't think I could do that."

Andrew laughed. "And Howie confessed to me later that it was his *second* invitation to the dance!"

"Who was the other?" asked Allison.

"Shirley Jenson."

Allison nodded. "Of course, that would explain something."

"Explain what?" asked Heather.

"Yesterday, when we were rowing—rather, *I* was rowing—out to the island, Shirley was getting all worked up about Howie. She insinuated that I had something going on with Howie that was keeping him from being interested in her."

"I don't know who would be interested in Shirley," said Andrew. "Especially once the word gets around about what she did to you."

"Maybe we should keep it quiet," said Allison.

"But what about your news story, Allison? Won't people find out when they read that?" said Heather.

"I didn't mention what Shirley did in my article."

"Then I guess it all depends on how Shirley handles it," suggested Andrew.

"Maybe," said Allison. "And you can never tell with Shirley."

"Do you think she'll apologize to you, Allison?" asked Heather.

"I don't know. Dad's determined to make Hal understand the seriousness of what she did. But I have to admit, I almost wish we could just forget the whole thing."

"That probably wouldn't do Shirley any good," said Andrew.

"That's true," said Heather. "She needs to realize the danger she placed you in and be sorry about it."

"Well," said Allison, "as Muriel would say, you can lead a horse to water, but you cannot make it drink."

"And Shirley Jenson is as stubborn as an old mule," laughed Andrew.

16

"It's a beautiful gown, Allison," Muriel said through the stick-pins in her mouth. "And this gorgeous green is perfect for Christmas. It reminds me of glossy holly leaves. Give another little turn, dear."

Allison carefully pivoted a few degrees on the footstool. "Thanks for hemming it up, Muriel. I hated to bother Grace right now; she's so busy getting things ready for the wedding."

"It's so nice that Andrew decided to go to the dance," said Muriel. "Although it would've been nice if he'd given us a little more notice! Another turn, dear."

Just as Allison began to turn, a quiet knock sounded on her bedroom door. "Come in," she called out cheerfully.

Allison cranked her head to see who it was without messing up Muriel's hemming, but she nearly fell off the stool when she saw Shirley Jenson step into her room.

"What are you doing here?" asked Allison with wide eyes.

Muriel turned to see. "My word!" she exclaimed, rising to her full height.

"Your dad told me I could come up to talk to you," said Shirley sullenly. "My dad is down there talking to him right now."

"Oh." Allison looked down at Muriel, then back to Shirley. "You'll have to wait until Muriel is finished here."

"It's okay," said Shirley. She stood next to the door and waited.

"You can sit down if you want," offered Allison stiffly as she got back into position for Muriel. Why had Shirley come? Had Shirley's dad forced her to come up here to apologize? It wouldn't be pleasant. Perhaps the best thing would be to just get it over with.

"Another turn, dear," mumbled Muriel.

"What did you want, Shirley?" asked Allison with her back to her.

"Well," began Shirley slowly. "I wanted to tell you that I'm sorry I left you out on the island yesterday."

"I see," said Allison.

"Another turn, please," said Muriel quietly.

Allison turned again. "Why did you do it, Shirley?"

Shirley took a deep breath, then exhaled slowly. "I don't know," she said. "I was getting cold, and I called for you, but you didn't come. . . ."

"Did it ever occur to you that I might get cold, too," asked Allison, "after you left me there with no way to get home?"

"Not really."

"Another turn, dear," said Muriel.

Allison turned again. Now she could see Shirley sitting on her bed. Her head was down, and she was fidgeting with her hands. "I did get cold, Shirley," continued Allison. "It began to rain, the wind was blowing, and soon it was dark. Not only that, the thieves were on the island. Did you know that?"

Shirley shook her head without looking up. "I didn't know it at the time."

"I actually thought that you might have gone to get help," said Allison. "I thought perhaps you were calling the police and getting my dad."

"I said that I didn't know about the thieves, Allison."

"Right. You just left because you were cold. And you didn't care that you abandoned me out on the island, in the dark, to freeze to death." Allison wanted to get through to Shirley—to somehow make her understand the seriousness of her actions.

"I tried to call your dad later on," said Shirley without looking up, "but the line was busy."

"He tried to call your house, but no one answered," said Allison.

"I might've been in the tub."

"Yes, I'm sure a hot bath would've felt nice. While you were in your warm tub, I was probably sitting on the rocks getting soaked and cold, worrying that the robbers might find me."

"I really am sorry, Allison," said Shirley, looking up. There were streams of tears coming down her cheeks. "It was a stupid thing to do. Okay? Probably the stupidest thing I've ever done in my life, and I've certainly done plenty!"

Allison had never seen Shirley cry before. She didn't think the girl was capable of tears and even wondered now if they were genuine.

"Turn again, please, Allison."

Allison turned. Now she was facing Shirley head on and didn't know what to say. For a long, silent moment she studied Shirley, sitting on the bed. Shirley's face was red and blotchy and streaked with tears. Perhaps this wasn't an act after all.

"Are you *really* sorry, Shirley?" asked Allison quietly.

Shirley nodded, then looked up. "You probably think I'm only sorry because I got in trouble, but the truth is I *am* sorry that I left you out there all by yourself. It was the meanest thing I've ever done, and I'm not very proud of it. I wouldn't blame you if you never forgave me."

Allison sighed. She knew what she needed to say, but why was it so difficult? Finally, she spoke. "I *will* forgive you, Shirley. Jesus says we're supposed to forgive those who hurt us *and* to love our enemies. It's not always the easy way, but it's always the best way."

"And I'm sure you think that I'm your enemy."

"What do you think, Shirley?"

Shirley didn't answer, and Muriel slowly stood. "That's the last of it, Allison. I'll come back up later to get the dress. Watch out for the pins when you take it off."

Allison took Muriel's extended hand as she stepped down from the stool. Her back to Shirley, Muriel was smiling at Allison with moist eyes.

"Thanks, Muriel," said Allison. "I really appreciate it."

Muriel left, and Allison stood looking at Shirley, wondering what more needed to be said. Shirley had wiped her tears, but her eyes and nose were still red.

"I don't think I could forgive anyone if they did what I did *to me*," Shirley said quietly.

"I couldn't, either," said Allison, "not without God's help."

"Oh," said Shirley. "I doubt that God would help me."

"You've done some pretty rotten things, Shirley. But that doesn't mean that God would give up on you. In fact, the reason that Jesus died on the cross was to forgive all the people who were bad—which includes everyone."

Shirley looked skeptical. "I don't think so, Allison. All that religious stuff is just for good people—people like you."

Allison laughed. "I'm not so good, Shirley. I've lied and cheated. I've even stolen."

Shirley's eyes popped open wide. "I don't believe it, Allison. Not you."

"Sure. And it wasn't that long ago. Last summer I lied about going to summer camp, I stole money from my mother, and then I ran away."

"No kidding?"

"I'm not saying it to impress you, Shirley," said Allison. "It's just to show you that I'm not perfect—not even close."

"And I always thought you were such a goody-two-shoes."

Allison laughed. "That shows how little you know me. Even after I wanted to change, I went through some really hard times. But I finally realized that I needed God—I couldn't turn my life around by myself. That's when I invited Jesus into my heart, and since then it's been a whole lot easier."

"It sounds too simple, Allison. Is that really all you did?"

Allison nodded. "The changes didn't happen overnight, and I still make mistakes all the time. Like if I could've put my hands on you when I was angry out on the island—I don't know what I might've done."

Shirley nodded. "I can understand that."

"But that would've only made me more miserable," said Allison. "That's why it's better to just forgive you."

Shirley clenched her fists and frowned. "I can't understand that, Allison. I don't think I could forgive anyone like that. The reason it was so easy to leave you out there was because I was mad at you. I felt like I hated you at the time."

"Why?"

Shirley held up her hands and shrugged. "Why not? You have it all, Allison. It's just not fair. *It makes me really hate you.*"

"I don't 'have it all,' Shirley."

"Your mom's a famous movie star."

"Don't you realize how awful that's made my life? I would've traded places with anyone hundreds of times."

"And then there was the thing with Howie. . . ."

"Howie is just a friend."

"But he likes you better than me." Shirley's eyes filled with fresh tears.

"I can't help that."

"And I hate how your newspaper stories are always getting all the attention—"

"I put a lot of work into them."

"And then you make friends so easily—*everyone* seems to hate me."

"That's just it, Shirley. If you could quit worrying about your life and just hand it over to Jesus, He'd do a much better job with it. Believe me! You've managed to make a pretty bad mess of it so far."

Tears began to pour down Shirley's cheeks again, and Allison wondered if she'd said too much. "I don't mean to hurt your feelings, Shirley. But you must know it's true. Your life looks pretty messed up from where I'm standing."

"I know it is." Shirley nodded and blew her nose. "I just don't know how to fix it."

"*You* don't have to fix it, Shirley. You just have to let God. He'll do all the fixing."

"I don't know how to let Him."

"You just *ask*, Shirley."

"You mean like praying?"

Allison nodded.

"I don't know how to. . . ."

"Do you want me to pray with you?"

"I guess so, but I'm kind of scared." She looked up at Allison with the most sincere expression that Allison had ever seen on her face.

Allison sat on the bed next to Shirley, and the green taffeta made a soft rustling sound. She reached over and took Shirley's cold hand. Shirley bowed her head, and Allison could hear her crying softly.

"Dear God," began Allison. "I'm here with Shirley because she needs your help, and you said all we need to do is to ask. So we're asking." Allison paused. She had heard others lead people in a repentance prayer, but she had never done it herself. She hoped God would help her. She turned to Shirley and spoke quietly. "Now, Shirley, if you are really serious about this, you have to invite Jesus into your heart, *yourself*. You can repeat the words after me, if you want." Shirley nodded solemnly and Allison continued to pray.

"Dear God, I know that I've done lots of things wrong. . . ." She paused and waited for Shirley to repeat her words, then continued. "But I know that you promised to forgive me if I believe in your Son, Jesus Christ. . . ." Again she paused. "So I confess that I believe in Jesus, and I invite Him into my heart right now. . . ." Allison sneaked a peek at Shirley as she echoed the words. "Please help me to live my life the way you want me to, God, not the way I want to." Allison waited for Shirley, then said, "Amen."

Now Allison was crying, too. She turned to face Shirley and was surprised to see her actually smiling through her tears now. Shirley hugged Allison.

"Thank you so much, Allison. I feel different already. Do you think that's possible?"

Allison nodded. "I know it is."

"It's amazing," said Shirley as she stood. "I feel like I've been given a brand-new start."

"You have."

Shirley's eyes grew wide. "But what if I blow it?"

"You will."

Shirley frowned. "I will?"

"Of course. We all do. But then we have to tell God we're sorry and ask Him to forgive us again—and again and again."

"Oh."

"Not only that," continued Allison as she stood, "but we have to forgive others, too. The Bible says to be forgiven we must forgive. See, that's why it was important for me to forgive you."

"Oh. Is there a whole lot that I need to know?"

"Not really. But you'll want to start reading the Bible and praying every day. And it helps to go to church."

"I go to church sometimes."

"But now when you go, you'll have to listen, too."

"How did you know I wasn't listening?"

Allison laughed. "Just a lucky guess. Now, could you help me get this dress off?" She waited while Shirley unfastened the back, then lifted it carefully over her head.

"This is absolutely beautiful, Allison. Is it for your dad's wedding?"

"No. It was my mom's. I'm wearing it to the Christmas dance."

Shirley's face fell. "You're going to the dance?"

Allison nodded, then pulled her sweater over her head. "Does that make you hate me, Shirley?"

Shirley frowned slightly, then shook her head. "Not exactly. Who are you going with? Howie, I suppose."

"Nope. I'm going with Andrew."

"Andrew?"

"Sure. We're good friends, you know. We just want to have fun."

"Oh." Shirley fingered the dark green taffeta as Allison hung it on a hanger. "Did your mother actually *wear* this gown, Allison?"

"I think so. Probably a few years ago."

Shirley pinched her own arm, then laughed. "I was just checking to see if this is real. Here I am in Allison O'Brian's room, and we're having a real conversation, and I don't feel like I want to kill you."

"Did you really want to kill me?"

"Sometimes. Like I said, you just seemed to have everything I wanted."

"Maybe all you wanted was to know that God loves you."

Shirley smiled. "Maybe that was it."

17

The next day, Allison told Andrew and Heather all about Shirley's amazing conversion as they rode to school.

"It's incredible, Allison," said Andrew when she finally finished.

"It's wonderful," breathed Heather. "I can't wait to talk to her and tell her how happy I am for her."

"I know it happened, and I believe Shirley was sincere . . ." Allison paused. "But after all we've been through, I still find myself having doubts. I almost expect to get to school and have her laugh right in my face about the fast one she pulled on me last night."

"Oh, ye of little faith," teased Heather.

"I don't know," said Andrew skeptically. "I can understand how Allison feels. You probably don't know Shirley as well as we do, Heather."

"You two!" Heather scolded. "Well, there's no point in arguing. Time will tell."

To Allison's delighted surprise, Shirley *did* seem like a changed person. She was quieter than usual and actually polite. She seemed to be genuinely trying. At lunch she sat with Allison, Heather, and Caroline.

"I hear you're going to the dance, Caroline," said Shirley.

"Yes," said Caroline carefully, as if waiting for the barb that might be attached.

"I wish I were going," sighed Shirley.

"Maybe you'll go next year," suggested Heather hopefully. "I'm not going, either, but I don't mind."

"Yes, I suppose there will be lots more dances." Shirley turned back to Caroline. "What's your dress like, Caroline? I saw Allison's last night and it was gorgeous."

Caroline blinked and adjusted her glasses. "My dress? Uh, it's gold."

"Gold like our school color, or like the metal?" asked Shirley with real interest.

"Actually, it's like the metal, and it sort of shimmers." Caroline's eyes lit up as she continued to describe it. "The style is kind of sophisticated. I couldn't believe my mom really let me get it. It has a fitted bodice, and the skirt's sort of smooth and then flares out at the bottom. It has padded shoulders with short sleeves, and the neck comes down in a V."

"That sounds nice," said Shirley. "I wish I could see it."

"I'll bring a photograph if you like," offered the stunned Caroline.

"That'd be swell."

※

"Hey, wait up," Shirley called to Allison as they headed for the journalism room after school.

Allison stopped and waited. "How's it going, Shirley?"

Shirley smiled. "Pretty good. It's really weird, Allison. Everyone is being so nice to me. Did you tell them to do it?"

Allison laughed. "No. It's probably just that you are being nice to them for a change."

"Well, I like it," said Shirley. "I just hope I don't blow it.

Sometimes I start to say something mean and I try to catch myself. You know, it's not that easy being good."

"I know," agreed Allison. "But it has its rewards. I wonder what we'll do on the paper this afternoon, since we don't have school for two weeks."

"Yeah, I was wondering, too." Shirley opened the door and actually let Allison walk in ahead of her. When they got inside, they saw a plateful of Christmas cookies and a punch bowl. Howie, Beverly, and Andrew were already there.

"Greetings," said Howie. "I thought I would reward my fine newspaper staff with a little Christmas party."

"Thanks, Howie," said Allison as he handed her a cup of punch. "This is great."

They all chatted congenially. It was fun to see Shirley actually participate in the conversation without taking over or offending anyone. Allison could see that Howie and Beverly were noticing it, too.

"Great story today, Allison," said Howie. "Did you see the *Port View Herald* yet?" He ran over to his desk and grabbed a copy, then held it for all to see. There on the front page was a photo of Allison and the headline "Local Girl Uncovers Thieves' Hideout."

"This is great," said Andrew as he patted her on the back. "And there's your story on the side, Allison. How does it feel to be so famous?"

"Oh, I'm not famous. . . ." But Allison smiled as she read the first few lines. "Although, it is fun to see this in the paper. That was a grueling night. It's nice that some good came out of it."

"You must've been so scared," said Beverly as she read over Allison's shoulder.

"I was there, too," said Shirley suddenly.

Everyone turned and looked at Shirley. Allison bit her lip. How was Shirley going to explain *that*?

"*You* were?" said Beverly in disbelief.

"Yes. I went out there with Allison."

"Well, why doesn't Allison mention you in her story, then?"

The way Beverly spoke had an accusatory tone. Allison hoped that Shirley wouldn't get mad and say something stupid. She had been doing so well up until now.

"Because I left her out on the island," confessed Shirley quietly, her eyes on the paper cup in her hands.

Now everyone was staring at Shirley.

"You *what*?" exclaimed Beverly.

Shirley nodded and looked down at the paper again. "I know it was wrong. And I've apologized to Allison. . . ."

Allison stepped up and put an arm around Shirley's shoulders. "And I have forgiven her, so let's all just forget about it. All's well that ends well."

Andrew grinned and held up a cup of punch. "Here's to good endings."

Everyone else lifted their cups. "And here's to a great newspaper team," said Howie. "A big thanks and merry Christmas to you all."

❄

On the night of the Christmas dance, Allison began to feel nervous. She suddenly wished that Heather was going, too. She remembered what fun it had been getting ready for the Harvest Ball and how Grace had helped them with their hair. Allison had tried to fix her hair the way Grace had, but she wasn't too pleased with the results. She wished Muriel were around to help, but she and George had gone to see a movie. It would be nice when Dad and Grace were finally married. Allison was looking forward to having a stepmom around. She studied her reflection in the mirror as she fastened Grandmother Mercury's pearls around her neck. The dark green taffeta dress seemed to bring out the green in her eyes. It was an exquisite gown, possibly something that Marsha had salvaged from a movie set. The long-waisted bodice was perfectly fitted, with hundreds of tiny tucks running down to a very full skirt. A delicate ruffle framed the scooped neckline, and the sleeves were puffy and trimmed with ruffles, as well.

"Are you ready?" James called from the hallway. "I'd like to get some pictures before Andrew gets here."

"Sure, come on in, Dad."

James whistled. "I don't know, Allison," he said in a worried voice. "I'm not sure I should let you go out looking so glamorous and sophisticated. Don't you go off forgetting that you're still my little girl."

She turned and smiled at him. "Don't worry. If anything, I feel like I'm a five-year-old playing dress-up."

He began to adjust his camera lens. "Hold that happy look for a second." He snapped a few pictures. "Now let's get one of you coming down the stairs." He went on ahead of her, taking pictures as she walked slowly and gracefully down the steps, pretending that she was a Southern belle on her way to the ball.

"Wow!" said Andrew. And they both turned to see him standing at the foot of the stairs holding a small white corsage. "Sorry to bust in on you, but when I knocked and no one answered, I just let myself in. Hope it's okay."

"Perfectly fine," called James. "Just let me get one more shot. Then one of the two of you." He posed them at the foot of the stairs and took several more photos.

"I thought you said just one more," teased Allison.

"Okay, okay," he surrendered. "You can go now." He handed Andrew the keys to the Buick. "I'll spare you my speech tonight, Andrew. You know how I feel."

Andrew saluted and grinned. "Yes, sir. Have her home by midnight, sir."

They picked up Howie and Beverly, and the four of them laughed and joked all the way to the dance. They sat with Karen and the rest that had been at the Harvest Ball. Only this time Caroline and Tommy were at their table, too. Caroline had never looked so gorgeous in her life. Everyone commented on it.

"Allison," said Janet as she stood, "stand up and let me get a closer look at that gown. It's beautiful."

Allison stood and gave a little turn for her to see. "Thanks, it's from my mom."

Janet reached out and touched the fabric as if touching the pope's ring. "I thought I recognized it."

Allison looked puzzled. "What do you mean?"

"Don't you know this is exactly like the gown Marsha Madison wore in *Southern Belle*?"

Karen jumped up and looked more closely at the dress. "I think you're right, Janet. Remember that scene where she is coming down that beautiful staircase—"

"Right," exclaimed Janet. Now all the girls at the table were gathered around Allison reminiscing over a film that Allison had never seen. In the old days Allison might have been irritated, but tonight she just laughed.

"Why, I feel like such an ignorant little fool," said Allison in a pretty good Southern drawl.

The girls looked at her in surprise, then Beverly asked, "Why is that?"

"Oh, fiddle-dee-dee," drawled Allison, "I just never had the pleasure of seeing that little ol' film y'all are talking about. But I'm just certain y'all are right about my mama wearing this little ol' dress in that movie. Why, it just seems like I'm always traipsing around in Mama's hand-me-down gowns."

By now all the girls were laughing hysterically.

"Oh, Allison," gasped Karen. "You should go out for drama this spring."

The boys returned, and soon all the couples were out on the dance floor.

"I saw you making all the girls laugh," said Andrew as they danced. "What was that all about?"

Allison grinned. "I was just giving them my rendition of *Southern Belle*—apparently it's a movie that Marsha made wearing this very dress, but I never saw it."

Andrew chuckled. "That must've been quite entertaining."

"Now Janet and Karen think I should go out for drama."

"And why not? You'd be great."

"You really think so?"

"Sure. I think you're great at everything you do, Allison."

"Even for a kid?" she asked.

"Especially for a kid."

Allison didn't say anything. She still didn't like Andrew thinking of her as a kid, but his friendship was too important to worry about something like that.

"If it makes you feel any better, Allison," said Andrew, "I think of myself as a kid, too."

"You do?" said Allison as she looked up into his eyes.

He nodded. "Yep."

18

The week before Christmas, Allison and her father flew to Portland to go Christmas shopping. Allison was happy to use her own money—some of it was from Marsha and some of it was from selling her stories to the *Port View Herald*. But it made her feel grown-up not to need to ask her dad for any help. She remembered a year ago when Stanley had taken her Christmas shopping for Marsha on Fifth Avenue in New York City. He had treated her as if she were a child, practically holding her hand while crossing the street. He had let her pick out some things for Marsha, then paid for them himself. It was all done quickly and efficiently and not with much fun. It hadn't been much of a Christmas, either. Stanley and Marsha had gone to a big party on Christmas Eve and then slept in very late on Christmas morning. So much had changed since then. All for the better, as far as she was concerned.

Allison had already sent Marsha a Christmas gift—something she had made herself last summer before Grandpa died. She had taken a small wooden box and glued sea shells she had collected along the beach all over it. She didn't know if Marsha would like it or not, but she wanted to give it to her just the same. Inside the box she had placed a short poem she had written. She hoped Marsha had gotten it before her trip to Brazil.

Allison had made a few other gifts at home, too, like the ink drawing for her dad and a knitted scarf for Andrew, but she wanted to buy some things, as well. By noon she had found something for everyone on her list except for her father. She had gotten a red sweater set for Grace, an ant farm kit for Winston, a Braille book and a Doris Day record for Heather, pigskin gloves for Muriel, and a new pair of pruning sheers for George. After lunch she told her dad she wanted to go into a shop across the street by herself and she would meet him outside in about twenty minutes. The Curio Shop had all sorts of weird things in the window and had caught her eye while they were eating. Surely she could find something for him in there. After a long hunt she finally found it. It was a small brass statue of a lighthouse, with a compass set into the base. It looked like something that might have gone in a boat, but she thought it would make a handsome paperweight on his desk.

❧

Christmas was all that Allison had hoped for and more. In the few days before Christmas, Allison joined Muriel in the kitchen making cookies and fruit cake and all sorts of wonderful things that, until now, Allison had only seen after they were already made and beautifully arranged on trays. Now she got to learn how to make them herself.

"I haven't had so much fun in years," said Muriel. "Christmas just feels more jolly when there are lots of loved ones around to share it. This old house is going to be in its prime with all you kids living here."

"It might mean more work for you, Muriel," said Allison. "But we'll all pitch in and help."

"Don't you worry about old Muriel," she laughed. "I like to stay busy, and I'm not afraid to ask for a hand when I need it."

On Christmas Eve they all went to a candlelight service. Allison was pleased to see all three Jensons present, along with Shirley's grandmother, Bea. Shirley's face looked bright and cheerful as she heartily sang along with the others. And there was Caroline sitting between her parents, right in the front row. The old stone church seemed cozy and sweet with the candles glowing as they sang carols and hymns. Then, just after the pastor wished them all a merry Christmas, Caroline's dad got up from his seat and asked if he could make an announcement. The pastor smiled and nodded as if it had all been prearranged, and everyone listened quietly as Caroline's father began to speak.

"I want to thank you all and everyone else who has been praying for my son, Kevin. As you may know, it's been hard going on us, not knowing where our boy was or what condition he was in. But now we've learned by way of another soldier who escaped last fall that our Kevin is alive—"

Everyone in church began to clap, but Caroline's dad waved his hands for them to stop. "And that's not all," he continued with excitement. "This soldier who escaped said that some others were trying to do the same thing, and Kevin was among them. We don't know anything more than that, but I can tell you, this makes us feel very, very hopeful this Christmas season. And we would appreciate your continued prayers."

Now everyone clapped again. Long and loud this time. The pastor came back up and led them in one last victorious Christmas carol, and Allison was sure there wasn't a dry eye in the house—not even Marge Jenson's! It was an evening Allison would remember always.

On Christmas morning Grace and the kids came over, and

they all ate a big breakfast, then unwrapped presents around the Christmas tree.

"Thank you, Allison," cried Heather when she opened the book and ran her fingers over the title page. "*Emma*, by Jane Austen. Oh, Allison, this is swell."

Allison grinned, then held up her mittened hands. "Hey, thanks, Muriel. I sure could've used these when I was stuck out on the island."

"This is great, Allison," said Andrew as he unwrapped the blue woolen scarf to find an aviation book within. "Did you make the scarf?"

Allison nodded as she opened the small box from him. "My locket," she cried. "How did you ever find it?" She gently pulled it out of the box.

"I spent half a day searching the island," said Andrew. "The chain was broken in several spots, so I got a new one. It's real gold."

Allison opened the locket and to her surprise saw a picture of Andrew in it. She quickly closed it without saying anything and looked over at him. His cheeks looked slightly pink. "Thanks, Andrew. I hope I never lose it again."

"Thank you, Allison," James said as he held up the pen-and-ink drawing of the clipper ship for everyone to see. "I think we've got another artist in the family. This is very good. I think I'll hang it in the library." He handed her a big box, and she quickly opened it to pull out an authentic leather bomber jacket and aviator's hat, complete with goggles.

"Oh, Dad," she cried, "this is great!" She pulled on the jacket and hat and strutted around the room. "Now I'm ready to go up into the wild blue yonder." She stopped by Dad's chair and waited as he opened the other present from her. He carefully unwrapped the lighthouse and studied it without saying anything.

"I hope you like it, Dad," said Allison quickly. "I know it's sort of strange, and it probably really belongs on a ship, but it reminded me of us. You know how a compass helps you find your way, and then I found you in the lighthouse, and finally I found a home—"

"It's perfect, Allison," he said with misty eyes. "Everything is just perfect."

"And my lovely turkey will be perfectly ruined if I don't go check on it," announced Muriel. "Dinner is at two. And I could use a couple of kitchen helpers in another hour or so."

❀

They all sat around the big dining room table. James insisted that even George and Muriel join them, and there were no protests. They said a special Christmas blessing, thanking God for all the amazing miracles that had allowed them to gather at the table together for their very first Christmas ever.

"Wonderful ham, Muriel," said Grace.

"Yes, and the turkey is so moist and tender," said Allison. "I used to hate turkey at Grandmother Madison's because it was always so dry and tasteless."

"I like the mashed potatoes the best," commented Winston. "What's so funny?" he asked defensively as everyone laughed.

"It's just that we *always* have mashed potatoes," explained Andrew gently.

"I don't care," said Winston. "I like 'em."

Just then the phone rang.

"Who would call at this time on Christmas?" asked Dad as he rose from the table. "Excuse me, I'll try to keep it short."

Everyone continued to visit and eat while Dad was gone.

Winston told everyone how he planned to start his ant farm right away. "First you have to send for the ants," he explained. "Isn't that weird? I could go out and dig up my own ants."

"But maybe the ones you send for are special," suggested Allison.

"Like smarter, you mean?" asked Winston.

Just then Dad returned. "Allison," he said. "Telephone for you."

Allison went into the hallway to answer the phone. "Hello?"

"Hello, darling" came her mother's voice over a crackling line. "I just wanted to wish you a very merry Chrismas, Allison, dear."

"Thank you, Marsha. Merry Christmas to you, too. How is the movie project going?"

"Just fine, dear. Although it's hard being away from home and family during the holidays. And I wanted to say that I'm sorry that you couldn't come to visit me for Christmas. I never dreamed that they'd change the location for this film. But I must admit it's grand being in Rio—so festive! I wish you were here to see it."

"It sounds like fun."

"Yes, I think you'd enjoy it. And I know I'd enjoy having you here. In fact, I was missing you today, Allison."

"Really?"

"Of course, dear." Then Marsha's voice grew hushed. "After all, Allison, I *am* your mother."

Allison smiled. "That's right. You *are*. Maybe I could come visit you for Easter—if you don't already have plans—"

"Oh, do you think so?" Marsha's voice sounded hopeful. "I'd love to see you then, darling!"

"I'd love to see you, too, Marsha. And—" Allison paused to gather her nerve. *"I love you, Marsha."*

Marsha made a slight choking sound, then said, "I love you, too, darling. But I've got to go now."

"Have a happy New Year, Marsha!"called Allison as she heard the line disconnect between them. She hung the phone back on the wall and sighed. *Yes*, Allison thought happily, *1949 has all the makings of a very good year indeed!*

Melody Carlson is the award-winning author of more than 200 books, including *Just Another Girl* and *Anything but Normal*. She recently was nominated for a Romantic Times Career Achievement Award in the inspirational market for her many books, including the Diary of a Teenage Girl series and *Finding Alice*. Visit her website at www.melodycarlson.com